Dark Guardian

Christine Feehan

piatkus

PIATKUS

First published in the US in 2002 by Dorchester Publishing Co., Inc.
First published in Great Britain in 2007 by Piatkus
This paperback edition published in 2007 by Piatkus

11 13 15 14 12 10

A CIP catalogue record for this book
is available from the British Library.

ISBN 978-0-7499-3811-6

Printed and bound by Clays Ltd, Elcograf S.p.A.

Papers used by Piatkus are from well-managed forests
and other responsible sources.

MIX
Paper from
responsible sources
FSC® C104740
www.fsc.org

Piatkus
An imprint of
Little, Brown Book Group
Carmelite House
50 Victoria Embankment
London EC4Y 0DZ

An Hachette UK Company
www.hachette.co.uk

www.piatkus.co.uk

This book was written for
Jonathan Woods, Jr.

We could never have asked
for a more wonderful son-in-law.

Husband to our daughter Manda,
Father to our granddaughter Skyler,
Guardian and Protector of those we love,
You're everything a man should be.
Everything a hero is.
You will always be in our hearts.

Dark Guardian

Prologue

Lucian
Walachia, 1400

The village was far too small to stand against the army advancing so quickly toward them. Nothing had slowed the Ottoman Turks. Everything in their path had been destroyed, everyone murdered, cruelly murdered. Bodies were impaled on crude stakes and left for the scavengers to finish off. Blood ran in rivers. No one was spared, not even the youngest child or the oldest elder. The invaders burned and tortured and mutilated, leaving behind only rats and fire and death.

The village was eerily silent; not even a child dared to cry. The people could only look at one another in despair and hopelessness. There would be no help, no way to stop the massacre. They would fall as had all the villages before them in the wake of that terrible enemy. They were too few and had only their peasant weapons to fight off the advancing hordes. They were helpless.

1

Christine Feehan

And then the two warriors came striding out of the fog-filled night. They moved as one unit, in perfect accord, in perfect step. They moved with a peculiar animal grace, fluid and supple and totally silent. They were both tall and broad-shouldered with long, flowing hair and eyes of death. Some said they could see the red flames of hell burning in the depths of those icy black eyes.

Grown men moved out of their way; women shrank into the shadows. The two warriors looked neither left nor right yet saw everything. Power clung to them like a second skin. They ceased to move, became as still as the surrounding mountains as the village elder joined them just above the scattered huts, where they could stare out at the empty meadow separating them from the forest.

"What news?" the elder asked. "We heard of the slaughters in every direction. Now it is our turn. And nothing can stop this storm of death. We have nowhere to go, Lucian, nowhere to hide our families. We will fight, but like all the others, we will be defeated."

"We are traveling fast this night, Old One, as we are needed elsewhere. It is said our Prince has been slain. We must return to our people. You have always been a good and kind man. Gabriel and I will go out this night and do what we can to help you before we move on. The enemy can be very a superstitious people."

His tone was pure and beautiful, like velvet. Anyone listening to that voice could do no other than what Lucian commanded. All who heard it wanted only to hear it again and again. The voice alone could enthrall, could seduce, could kill.

"Go with God," the village elder whispered in thanks.

The two men moved on. In perfect rhythm, fluid, silent. Once out of sight of the village, without speaking a word aloud, they shape-shifted at exactly the same moment, taking the form of owls. Wings beat strongly in the night

2

as they circled high above the timberline, searching out the sleeping army. Several miles from the village the earth below was strewn with hundreds of men.

Fog moved in, thick and white and low to the ground. The wind ceased, so that the mist lay dense and stationary. Without warning, owls dropped silently out of the sky, razor-sharp talons directed straight at the eyes of the sentries. The owls seemed to be everywhere, working in precise synchronization so that they were in and out before anyone could come to the guards' assistance. Screams of pain and terror filled the void of silence, and the army rose up, grabbing weapons and searching for an enemy in the thick white fog. They saw only their own sentries, empty sockets for eyes, blood running down their faces as they ran sightlessly in any direction.

In the center of the mass of warriors a *crack* was heard, then another. Crack after crack, and two lines of men dropped to the ground with broken necks. It was as if hidden within the thick fog were invisible enemies moving quickly from man to man, breaking necks with their bare hands. Chaos erupted. Men ran screaming into the surrounding forest. But wolves boiled out of nowhere, snapping with powerful jaws at the fleeing army. Men fell on their own spears as if directed to do so. Others rammed their spears into comrades-at-arms, unable to stop themselves no matter how hard they fought the compulsion. Blood and death and terror reigned. Voices whispered in the soldiers' heads, in the very air, whispered of defeat and death. Blood soaked the ground. The night went on and on until there was no place to hide from the unseen terror, from the specter of death, from the wild beasts that came to defeat the army.

In the morning the Walachian villagers went forth to fight—and found only the dead.

Christine Feehan

Lucian
Carpathian Mountains, 1400

The air reeked of death of destruction. All around were the smoking ruins of the human villages. The Carpathian ancients had tried in vain to save their neighbors, but the enemy had struck as the sun reached its peak. The hour rendered the ancients helpless, as their powers were weakest at that time. So many Carpathians, as well as humans, had been destroyed—men, women, and children alike. Only those of their people who had been far away had escaped the crushing blow.

Julian, young and strong yet a mere boy, surveyed the sight with sad eyes. So few of his kind remained. And their Prince, Vladimir Dubrinsky, was dead along with his lifemate, Sarantha. It was a catastrophe, a blow from which their species might never recover. Julian stood tall and straight, his long blond hair flowing well past his shoulders.

Dimitri came up behind him. "What are you doing here? You know it is dangerous to be out in the open like this. There are so many who would destroy us. We were told to stay close to the others." Despite his youth, he moved protectively closer to the younger boy.

"I can take care of myself," Julian declared staunchly. "And what are you doing out here?" The young boy gripped the arm of the older boy beside him. "I saw them. I am certain it was they. Lucian and Gabriel. It was they." Awe filled his voice.

"It cannot be," Dimitri whispered, looking in all directions. He was excited and scared at the same time. No one, not even the adults, named the twin hunters aloud. Lucian and Gabriel. They were legend, myth, not reality.

"But, I am certain. I knew they would come when they heard the Prince was dead. What else could they do? I am sure they have gone to see Mikhail and Gregori."

Dark Guardian

The older boy gasped. "Gregori is here also?" He followed the smaller boy through the thick forest. "He will catch us spying, Julian. He knows everything."

The blond boy shrugged, a mischievous grin curving his mouth. "I am going to see them up close, Dimitri. I am not afraid of Gregori."

"You should be. And I have heard that Lucian and Gabriel are really the undead."

Julian burst out laughing. "Who told you that?"

"I heard two of the males talking about it. They said no one could survive as long as they have, hunting and killing, and not turn."

"The humans have been at war, and our people have been destroyed in the process. Even our Prince is dead. Vampires are everywhere. Everyone is killing everyone else. I do not think we have to worry about Gabriel and Lucian. If they were really vampires, we would all be dead. No one, not even Gregori, could defeat them in battle," Julian defended. "They are so powerful, no one would be able to destroy them. They have always been loyal to the Prince. Always."

"Our Prince is dead. They are not necessarily loyal to Mikhail as the heir." Dimitri was obviously quoting adults.

Julian shook his head in exasperation and continued forward, this time making certain to be silent. He inched his way through the thick vegetation until the house was in sight. Far off, a wolf howled, the note high and lonely sounding. A second wolf answered, then a third, both much closer. Julian and Dimitri shape-shifted. They were not going to miss seeing the legendary figures. Lucian and Gabriel were the greatest vampire hunters in the history of their people. It was well known that no one could defeat them. The news that they had singlehandly destroyed an entire invading army during the night had preceded their arrival. No one knew their exact body count over the last few centuries, but it was extremely high.

Julian assumed the shape of a small marmot, moving in close to the house. He kept a watchful eye out for owls as he approached the front porch. He heard them then. Four voices murmuring softly from within the house. Although he was young, Julian had the incredible hearing of the Carpathian people. He used that acute hearing, determined to get every word. The four greatest Carpathians alive were in that house, and he would not miss the event. He was barely aware of Dimitri joining him.

"You have no choice, Mikhail," a soft voice said. The voice was incredible, pure velvet, commanding yet gentle. "You must assume the mantle of authority. The bloodline dictates it. Your father had a foreshadowing of his own death, and his instructions were clear. You must assume leadership. Gregori will help you in this time of great need, and we will do the job your father asked of us. But the mantle of authority does not belong to our bloodline. It is yours."

"You are an ancient, Lucian. One of you should rule our people. We are so few, our women lost to us, our children gone. Without women, what are our males to do?" Julian recognized Mikhail's voice. "They have no choice but to seek the dawn or become the undead. God knows, we already have enough of them doing that. I have not yet acquired the wisdom to lead our people in a time of such great need."

"You have the blood and the power, and, most of all, our people believe in you. They fear us, our power and knowledge and all that we stand for." Lucian's voice was beautiful, compelling. Julian loved the sound of that voice, could listen to it for all time. It was no wonder the adults were afraid of his power. Even at Julian's young age he recognized the voice as a weapon. And Lucian was simply talking normally. What would it be like if he wished to take command of those around him? Who would be able to resist such a voice?

"We give you our allegiance, Mikhail, as we did your father, and we will provide you with whatever knowledge we can to aid you in your difficult task. Gregori, we know you as a great hunter already. Is your tie to Mikhail strong enough to see you through the dark days to come?" Lucian's voice, although as soft as ever, demanded truth.

Julian held his breath. Gregori was blood kin to Gabriel and Lucian. *The Dark Ones*. Those of that bloodline were always the defenders of their race, the ones who brought the undead to justice. Gregori was already powerful in his own right. It didn't seem possible that he could be compelled to answer, yet he did.

"As long as Mikhail lives, so do I, that I may provide for his safety and that of his line."

"You will serve our people, Mikhail, and our brother will serve you as we did your father. It is right. Gabriel and I will continue the fight to defeat the stranglehold the undead have on the humans and our own race."

"There are so many," Mikhail observed.

"There is, indeed, much death, much fighting, and our women have been all but stamped out. The males need hope for a future, Mikhail. You must find a way to provide them with one, or they will have no reason to hold out when the darkness stretches on. We must have females to provide our males with lifemates. Our women are the light to our darkness. Our males are predatory, dark, dangerous hunters, growing more deadly as the centuries pass. Eventually, if we cannot find lifemates, all will turn from Carpathian to vampire, and our race will become extinct as the males give up their souls. There will be devastation such as we cannot imagine. Preventing that is your task, Mikhail, and it is a monumental one."

"As is yours," Mikhail said softly. "To take so many

lives and stay as one of us is no small thing. Our people have much to thank you for."

Julian, within the body of the marmot, scampered back into the bushes, not wanting to be caught by the ancients. There was a rustle in the bushes behind him, and he turned. Two tall men were standing there in complete silence. Their eyes were dark and empty, their faces as still as if carved in stone. Around him a mist seemed to fall from the sky, leaving him and Dimitri in a stunned heap. Julian caught his breath and stared in astonishment. Gregori materialized just slightly in front of the two boys, almost protectively. When Julian moved his head to look around him, the mythical hunters were gone as if they'd never been, and the boys were left to face Gregori.

Lucian
France, 1500

The sun faded from the sky, leaving behind brilliant colors. Those colors slowly yielded to the charcoal of the night. Beneath the earth a single heart began to beat. Lucian lay in the rich, healing soil. His wounds from the last terrible battle were healed. He mentally scanned the area around his resting place, noting only the movement of animals. Dirt spewed upward as he burst from the earth into the sky, drawing in air to breathe. His world would be changed this night for all time. Gabriel and Lucian were identical twins. They looked alike, thought alike, fought alike. Over the centuries they had acquired knowledge in all areas and subjects and shared that knowledge with each other.

All Carpathian males as they grew older lost their emotions and the ability to see colors, leaving them in a dark, bleak world where only their sense of loyalty and honor kept them from turning vampire while they waited for a lifemate. Gabriel and Lucian had made a pact with each other. If one were to turn vampire, the other would hunt and destroy his twin before facing the dawn—and his own destruction. Lucian had known for some time that Gabriel was wrestling his inner demon, consumed by the darkness spreading within him. The constant battles had taken their toll. Gabriel was far too close to turning.

Lucian inhaled deeply, taking in the clear night air. He was determined to keep Gabriel alive, to keep his soul safe. There was one way to do so. If he could convince Gabriel that *he* had joined the ranks of the undead, Gabriel could do no other than hunt him. That would prevent Gabriel from battling any other than Lucian. By being unable to kill, due to their equal powers, and by having a purpose, Gabriel would be able to hold on. Lucian took to the air, searching for his first victim.

Lucian
London, 1600

The young woman stood on the street corner, her smile painted on. The night was cold and dark. She was shivering. Somewhere in the darkness was a killer. He had already murdered two of the women she knew. She had begged Thomas not to send her out tonight, but he had slapped her several times before pushing her out the door. She crossed her arms over her chest and tried desperately to look as if she enjoyed what she was doing.

A man was coming up the street. Her breath caught in her throat, and her heart began to pound. He wore a dark coat and top hat and carried a cane. He looked to be from the upper class, slumming in her part of town. She struck a pose and waited. He walked right past her. She knew Thomas would beat her if she didn't call out, try to entice this stranger to her, but she couldn't make herself do it.

The man paused and turned. He circled her slowly, looking her up and down as if she were a piece of meat.

She tried to smile at him, but something about him frightened her. He pulled out a handful of money and waved it at her. His smile was taunting. He knew she was frightened. He pointed with his cane toward the alley.

She went. She knew better, but she was just as afraid of going home to Thomas without money as she was of going into the alley with the stranger.

He was ruthless, forcing her to perform all kinds of acts right there in the alley. He hurt her deliberately, and she endured it because she had no other choice. When he was finished, he shoved her to the ground and kicked her with one elegant shoe. She looked up to see the straight razor in his hand and knew he was the killer. There was no time to scream. She was about to die.

Then another man loomed up behind her killer. He was physically the most beautiful male she had ever seen. Tall and broad-shouldered with long, flowing dark hair and icy black eyes. He materialized out of nowhere so close to her attacker that she had no idea how he could have gotten there unseen by either of them. The man simply reached out with his hands, caught the murderer's neck, and wrenched hard.

Run. Run now. She heard the words clearly in her head and could not even wait to thank her rescuer. She ran away as fast as she could.

Lucian waited until he was certain she had obeyed his order before he bent his head to the neck of the murderer. It was imperative that he drain the blood from his victim and leave the evidence for Gabriel to find.

"I find you here as I expected, Lucian. You cannot hide from me." Gabriel's soft voice came from behind him.

Lucian allowed the body to fall to the ground. Over the long years it had become a game of cat-and-mouse no other could play. They knew each other so well, they had choreographed their battles together for so many years, that each knew what the other was thinking almost before he thought it. They knew each other's strengths and weaknesses. Over the last years they had scored many near-mortal wounds on each other, only to break apart and go to ground to heal. Lucian turned toward his twin brother, a slow, humorless smile softening the hard edges of his mouth. "You look tired."

"You were too greedy this time, Lucian, killing your prey before you fed."

"Perhaps it was a mistake," Lucian agreed softly, "but do not worry about me. I am more than capable of finding myself warm bodies. None can defeat me, not even my brother, who gave me his word to do this one small thing."

Gabriel struck hard and fast, as Lucian knew he would. And they came together in a deadly battle they had been practicing for centuries.

Lucian
Paris, Present Day

Gabriel crouched low, his stance that of a fighter. Behind him, his lifemate watched with sorrow-filled eyes as the tall, elegant man approached. He looked what he was: a dark, dangerous predator. His black eyes glittered dangerously, graveyard eyes. Eyes of death. He moved with an animal grace, a ripple of power.

"Stay back, Lucian," Gabriel warned softly. "You will not endanger my lifemate."

"Then you will do as you vowed so many centuries ago. You must destroy me." The voice was a whisper of velvet, a soft command.

Gabriel recognized the hidden compulsion even as he leaped forward to strike. At the last possible second, with his lifemate's denial loud in his mind, he whipped his clawed hand at his twin brother's throat and realized Lucian had opened his arms wide in acceptance of the kill.

11

No vampire would do such a thing. Never. The undead fought with their dying breath to kill everyone and everything around them. To sacrifice one's life was not the act of a vampire.

The knowledge came too late. Crimson droplets sprayed, arced. Gabriel tried to go back, to reach his brother, but Lucian's power was far too great. Gabriel was unable to move, stopped in his tracks by Lucian's will alone. His eyes widened in surprise. Lucian had so much power. Gabriel was an ancient, more powerful than most on earth—Lucian's equal, he would have said until that moment.

"You must let us aid you," Francesca, Gabriel's lifemate, said softly. Her voice was crystal clear, soothing. She was a great healer. If anyone could prevent Lucian's death, she could. "I know what you are attempting to do here. You think to end it now."

Lucian's white teeth gleamed. "Gabriel has you to keep him safe. That had been my task, and it is ended now. I seek rest."

Blood was soaking his clothes, running down his arms. He made no attempt to stop it. He simply stood there, tall and straight. No accusation lit his eyes or voice or his expression.

Gabriel shook his head. "You did this for me. For four hundred years you have deceived me. You prevented me from the kills, from turning. Why? Why would you risk your soul this way?"

"I knew you had a lifemate waiting for you. Someone who would know told me many years ago, and I knew he would not tell an untruth. You did not lose your feelings and emotions quickly, as I did. It took centuries for it to happen to you. I was a mere fledgling when they ceased for me. But you merged your mind with mine, and I could share your joy in life, see through your eyes. You

12

made me remember what I could never have for myself."
Lucian staggered.

Gabriel had been waiting for the moment when Lucian
would weaken, and he took advantage, leaping to his
brother's side, sweeping his tongue across the gaping
wound he had created to close it.

His lifemate was at his side. Very gently she took Lucian's hand in hers. "You think there is no more purpose
to your existence."

Lucian closed his eyes tiredly. "I have hunted and killed
for two thousand years, sister. My soul has so many
pieces missing that it is like a sieve. If I do not go now, I
may not go later, and my beloved brother would be
forced to attempt to destroy me. It would be no easy task.
He must remain safe. I have done my duty. Let me rest."

"There is another," Francesca told him softly. "She is
not like us. She is mortal. At this moment she is young
and in terrible pain. I can only say to you, if you do not
find her, she will live a life of such agony and despair, we
cannot imagine it, even with all our great gifts. You must
live for her. You must endure for her."

"You are telling me I have a lifemate?"

"And that her need of you is great."

"I am no gentle man. I have killed for so long, I know
of no other existence. Tying a mortal woman to me would
be sentencing her to live with a monster." Even as he
made the denial, Lucian was not resisting as Gabriel's lifemate began to work on his savage wound. Gabriel filled
the room with beneficial herbs and began the ancient healing chant as old as time itself.

"I will heal you now, my brother," she said softly. "A
monster such as you think you have become will be able
to protect the woman from the monsters who would otherwise destroy one such as she."

Gabriel cut his wrist and pressed the wound to his
twin's mouth. "I offer my life freely for yours. Take what

you need to heal. We will put you deep within the soil and guard you until you are at full strength."

"Your first duty is to your lifemate, Lucian," Francesca reminded him softly. "You can do no other than find her and remove her from danger."

Jaxon, Five years old
Florida, USA

"Look at me, Uncle Tyler," Jaxon Montgomery called proudly, waving from the top of the high wooden tower she had just climbed.

"You're crazy, Matt." Russell Andrews shook his head, shading his eyes against the sun as he stared up at the replica of the high platform used for training Navy SEALS recruits. "Jaxx could break her neck if she fell." He glanced away toward the fragile woman lying on the chaise longue, cuddling her newborn son. "What about it, Rebecca? Jaxx isn't even five yet, and Matt has her training for Special Forces," Russell said.

Rebecca Montgomery smiled absently and looked up at her husband as if asking his opinion.

"Jaxon's great," Matt said immediately, reaching to capture his wife's hand and bringing her knuckles to his lips. "She loves this stuff. She was doing it practically before she could walk."

Tyler Drake waved to the tiny girl calling to him. "I don't know, Matt. Maybe Russell's right. She's so small. She takes after Rebecca in looks and build." He grinned. "Of course, we were lucky in that department. The rest of her is all you. She's a daredevil, a little fighter, just like her daddy."

"I'm not so certain that's a good thing," Russell said, frowning. He couldn't take his eyes off the child. His heart was in his throat. His own little girl was seven years old, and he would never allow her near the tower his compatriots, Matt Montgomery and Tyler Drake, had constructed in Matt's backyard. "You know, Matt, it's possible to force a child to grow up too fast. Jaxon is still a baby."

Matt laughed. "That 'baby' can cook breakfast for her mother and serve it to her in bed *and* change diapers for the little one. She's been reading since she was three. I mean, really reading. She loves physical challenges. There's not much on the training course she can't do. I've been teaching her martial arts, and Tyler has been working on survival training with her. She loves it."

Russell scowled. "I can't believe you're encouraging Matt, Tyler. He never listens to anyone but you. That child adores both of you, and neither of you has any sense where she's concerned." He manfully refrained from adding that Rebecca was a washout as a mother. "I hope to hell you don't have her swimming in the ocean."

"Maybe Russell's right, Matt." Tyler sounded a bit worried. "Jaxon's a little trouper with the heart of a lion, but maybe we push her too much. And I had no idea you were allowing her to cook for Rebecca. That could be dangerous."

"Someone has to do it." Matt shrugged his wide shoulders. "Jaxon knows what she's doing. When I'm not home, she knows very well she's responsible for Rebecca's care. And now we have little Mathew Jr. And just for your information, Jaxx is a good swimmer already."

"Are you listening to yourself, Matt?" Russell demanded. "Jaxon is a child, a five-year-old—a baby. Rebecca! For God's sake, you're her mother." As usual, neither parent responded to anything they didn't want to hear. Matt treated Rebecca like a porcelain doll. Neither paid much attention to their daughter. Exasperated, Russell appealed to Matt's best friend. "Tyler, tell them."

Tyler nodded slowly in agreement. "You shouldn't put so much pressure on her, Matt. Jaxon is an exceptional child, but she's still a child." His eyes were on the small girl waving and smiling. Without another word he got up and began striding toward the tower where the little girl was calling to him persistently.

Jaxon, Seven years old
Florida, USA

The screams coming from her mother's room were horrible to hear. Rebecca was inconsolable. Bernice, Russell Andrews's wife, had called the doctor to administer tranquilizers. Jaxx put her hands over her ears to try to muffle the terrible sounds of grief. Mathew Jr. had been crying for some time in his room, and it was obvious her mother was not going to go to her son. Jaxon wiped at the steady stream of tears falling from her own eyes, lifted her chin, and went across the hall to her brother's room.

"Don't cry, Mattie," she crooned softly, lovingly. "Don't worry about a thing. I'm here now. Mommy is very upset about Daddy, but we can get through this if we stick together. You and me. We'll get Mommy through it, too."

Uncle Tyler had come to their house with two other officers and informed Rebecca that her husband would never be coming home again. Something had gone terribly wrong on their last mission. Rebecca had not stopped screaming since.

Jaxon, Eight years old

"How is she today, honey?" Tyler asked softly, stooping to kiss Jaxon on the cheek. He laid a bouquet of flowers down on the table and turned his attention to the little girl he had loved since the day she was born.

"She isn't having a very good day," Jaxon admitted reluctantly. She always told "Uncle Tyler" the truth about her mother, but no one else, not even "Uncle Russell." "I think she took too many of those pills again. She won't get out of bed, and when I try to tell her things about Mathew, she just stares at me. He's finally stopped needing diapers, and I'm so proud of him, but she won't say anything at all to him. If she does pick him up, she squeezes him so hard, he cries."

"I have something to ask you, Jaxx," Uncle Tyler said. "It's important you tell me the truth. Your mom is sick most of the time, and you have to take care of Mathew, manage the house, and go to school. I was thinking maybe I should move in and help out a little."

Jaxon's eyes lit up. "Move in with us? How?"

"I could marry your mother and be your father. Not like Matt, of course, but as your stepfather. I think it would help your mother, and I'd sure like to be here for you and little Mathew. But only if you want me, honey. Otherwise, I won't even talk to Rebecca about it."

Jaxon smiled at him. "That's why you brought the flowers, isn't it? Do you think she'll really do it? Is there a chance?"

"I think I can persuade her. The only time you get a break around here is when I have you on our training course. You're getting to be quite a marksman, too."

"Marks*person*, Uncle Tyler," Jaxon corrected with a sudden teasing grin. "And the other night in karate class I kicked Don Jacobson's butt." The only time she found herself laughing anymore was when Uncle Tyler took her off to the Special Forces training area and they played soldier. Female or not, Jaxon was becoming someone to contend with, and it made her proud.

Jaxon, Thirteen years old

The book was a mystery and well suited to the stormy night. Tree branches were scratching the window, and rain drummed heavily on the roof. The first time she heard the noise, Jaxon thought it was her imagination, just because the book was so scary. Then she stiffened, and her heart began to pound. He was doing it again. She knew it. As quietly as possible, she crept out of bed and opened her door.

The sounds coming from her mother's bedroom were muffled, but she heard them all the same. Her mother was weeping, pleading. And there was the distinctive sound Jaxon knew so well. She had been in karate classes as long as she could remember. She knew what it sounded like when someone got punched. She ran along the hall to her brother's room to check on him first. She was thankful he was sound asleep. When Tyler was like this, she hid Mathew from him. He seemed to hate Mathew at times. His eyes grew cold and ugly when they rested on the little boy, especially if Mathew happened to be crying. Tyler didn't like it when anyone cried, and Mathew was little enough to cry over almost every tiny scratch or imagined hurt. Or every time Tyler glared at him.

Taking a deep breath, Jaxon went to stand just outside her mother's bedroom. She found it so hard to believe that Tyler could be the way he was with her mother and Mathew. She loved Tyler. She had always loved him. He spent hours training Jaxon like a soldier, and everything in her responded to the physical training. She loved the courses he set up to challenge her. She could climb nearly impassable cliffs and slither through minuscule tunnels in record time. She was in her element out on the range, firing weapons and fighting hand to hand. Jaxon could even track Tyler now, a feat most of those in his unit were unable to perform. She was especially proud of that. Tyler always seemed pleased with her and very warm and loving toward her. She had believed Tyler loved her family with the same fierce, protective loyalty she did. Now she was confused, wishing her mother was someone she could talk with, reason things out with. Jaxon was coming to realize that her stepfather's easy charm hid his constant need to control his world and those in it. Rebecca and

Mathew didn't meet his standards of what they should be, and he made them pay dearly for it.

Jaxon took a deep breath and quietly pushed the door open a crack. She stood perfectly still as Tyler had taught her to do in times of danger. Tyler had her mother pressed against a wall, one hand squeezing her throat. Rebecca's eyes were bulging and wide with terror. "It was so easy to do, Rebecca. He always thought he was so good, no one could ever do him, but I did. And now I have you and his kids, just like I told him I would. I stood over him and watched the life go out of him, and I laughed. He knew what I would do to you—I made certain of that. You've always been so useless. I told him I would give you a chance, but you just couldn't manage it, could you? He spoiled you just like your daddy did. Rebecca, the little princess. You always looked down on us. You always thought you were so much better than us just because you had all that money." He leaned close so that his forehead was bumping Rebecca's, and sprays of spit washed over her as he enunciated each word. "All your precious money would go to me now if anything happened to you, wouldn't it?" He shook her like a rag doll, an easy thing to do, since Rebecca was such a small woman.

At that moment, Jaxon knew that Tyler was going to kill Rebecca. He hated her, and he hated Mathew. Jaxon was bright enough to realize, even hearing something out of context, that Tyler had very likely murdered her father. Both of them were Navy SEALs and not easy to kill, but her father wouldn't have been expecting his best friend to betray him.

She could see her mother's eyes trying desperately to warn her away. Rebecca was afraid for Jaxon, afraid if she interfered, Tyler would turn on her.

"Daddy?" Deliberately Jaxon said the word softly into the menace-filled night. "Something woke me up. I had a bad dream. Will you sit up with me? You don't mind, do you, Mommy?"

It took a few moments before the tension seeped out of Tyler's ramrod-stiff shoulders. His fingers slowly loosened from around Rebecca's throat. Air rushed back into her lungs, yet she remained cowering against the wall, frozen with terror, trying to suppress the cough welling in her raw throat. Her gaze was still on Jaxon's face, desperately, silently, trying to warn her daughter of the danger. Tyler was completely mad, a killer, and there was no escape from him. He had warned her what would happen if she tried to leave him, and Rebecca knew she didn't have the strength to save them. Not even Mathew Jr.

Jaxon smiled up at Tyler with childlike trust. "I'm sorry I disturbed you, but I really did hear something, and the dream was so real. When you're with me, I always feel safe." Her stomach was cramping, protesting the terrible lie; her palms were sweaty, yet she managed perfect, wide-eyed innocence.

Tyler sent Rebecca a hard stare over his shoulder as he took Jaxon's hand. "Go to bed, Rebecca. I'll sit up with Jaxon. God knows *you've* never done it, not even when she was sick." His hand was strong, and she could still feel the tension in him, yet Jaxon could also feel the warmth he always exuded whenever they were together. Whatever had possessed her stepfather in those earlier moments seemed gone once was he was physically linked to Jaxon.

In the two years that followed, Jaxon and Rebecca tried to hide their growing concern about Tyler's mental state from Mathew Jr. They kept the child as far from Tyler as possible. The boy seemed to be some kind of catalyst, changing what once had been a loving man. Tyler often complained that Mathew was staring at him. Mathew learned to avert his gaze when Tyler was in the room.

Tyler looked at the boy coldly, unemotionally, or with absolute hatred. He looked at Rebecca with a stranger's eyes. Only Jaxon seemed able to connect to him, to keep him centered. It frightened her, that terrible responsibility. She could see the evil within "Uncle" Tyler growing ever stronger, and after a time her mother relied completely on Jaxon to cope with it. She stayed in her room, taking the pills Tyler supplied, ignoring her two children. When Jaxon tried to tell her that she was afraid Tyler would harm Mathew, Rebecca pulled the covers over her head and rocked back and forth, making a keening sound.

Desperate, Jaxon tried to tell "Uncle Russell" and other members of Tyler's team that something might be wrong with him. The men merely laughed and passed on what she had said to Tyler. He was so furious, Jaxon was certain he would kill the entire family. Although she was the one who had told, he placed the blame on Rebecca, repeating over and over that she had forced Jaxon to lie about him. He beat Rebecca so badly, Jaxon wanted to take her to the hospital, but Tyler refused. Rebecca remained in her bed for weeks and was confined to the house after that. Jaxon spent a great deal of her time creating a fantasy world for Tyler, pretending to believe that all was well in their home. She kept her brother far away from him and deflected his anger from her mother as much as possible. More and more she spent time with Tyler on the range, learning as much as she could about self-defense, weapons, hiding, and tracking. It was the only time she knew her mother and brother were truly safe. The other SEALs contributed readily to her training, and Tyler seemed normal at those times. Rebecca had retreated so far from the real world, Jaxon dared not take Mathew and run, as she would have had to leave her mother behind, and she was certain Tyler would kill Rebecca. Little Mathew and Jaxon had their own secret world they dared not share with anyone; they lived in constant fear.

Jaxon, her fifteenth birthday

Sitting in science class, she suddenly knew. She felt it, an overwhelming premonition of danger. She remembered gasping for breath, her lungs refusing to work. Jaxon ran from the classroom, knocking her books and papers from her desk so that they scattered on the floor behind her. The teacher called to her, but Jaxon ignored him and continued running. The wind seemed to rush past her as she sped down the streets, taking every shortcut she knew.

As she neared the house, Jaxon slowed abruptly, her heart pounding. The front door was gaping open, an invitation to enter. At once darkness took hold of her mind. She felt a sharp demand to stop, to turn back, the premonition so strong it held her frozen for a moment. Mathew had stayed home sick from school. Little Mathew, who looked so like her father, who could send Tyler into a killing fury so easily. Her Mathew.

Her mouth was dry, and the taste of fear was so strong she was afraid she was going to be sick. Her stomach clenched, and the pounding in her head increased until it nearly drowned out the overwhelming urge for self-preservation. Jaxon forced her right foot forward. One step. It was difficult, like walking through quicksand. She had to look inside the house. She had to do it. The pull to do so was stronger than the instinct for survival. A smell was flowing out to her, an odor foreign to her, yet every instinct she possessed told her what it was. "Mom?" She whispered the word aloud, a talisman to make her world right again, to drive away the truth and knowledge that was pounding in her head.

The only way she could force her body to move was to hold the side of the house and inch her way painfully forward. She was fighting her own instincts, fighting the reluctance to face what was in there. Keeping one hand pressed firmly against her mouth to keep from screaming, she turned her head slowly to allow her eyes to see into the house.

The living room looked the same as ever. Familiar. Comforting. But that did nothing to stop the fear. Instead, she felt terrified. Jaxon forced herself forward to the hallway. She saw a smear of bright red blood on the doorjamb to Mathew's room. Her heart began to beat so hard she was afraid it might pound right through her chest. Jaxon edged her way along the wall until she was right outside Mathew's room. She prayed fervently as with one finger she slowly pushed open his door.

The horror of that sight would be imprinted on her brain for all time. The walls were sprayed with blood, the covers soaked with it. Mathew lay sprawled sideways on the bed, his head hanging off the mattress at a right angle. His eye sockets were empty, his once laughing eyes gone forever. She couldn't count the stab wounds on his body. Jaxon did not go into the room. She couldn't. Something far more powerful than her will was stopping her. For a moment she couldn't stand, sliding unexpectedly to the floor in a huddled heap, a silent scream tearing through her body in absolute denial.

She hadn't been there to defend him. To save him. It was her responsibility. She was the strong one, yet she had failed, and Mathew, with his shining curls and his love of life, had paid the ultimate price. Jaxon didn't want to move, didn't think she could. But then her mind seemed to go mercifully blank, and she was able to drag herself back up the wall and proceed down the hall to her mother's bedroom. She already knew what she would find. She told herself she was prepared.

This time the door was wide open. Jaxon forced herself to look in. Rebecca lay crumpled on the floor. She knew it was her mother by the mop of blond hair that spilled out like a halo around the crushed head. The rest of her was too mangled and bloody for recognition. Jaxon couldn't pull her gaze away. Her throat was closing, strangling her. She couldn't breathe.

She heard a sound. The hint of a sound really, but it was enough to trigger her years of training. She leaped to one side, whirling to face her stepfather. His hands and arms were wet with blood, his shirt splattered and stained. He was smiling, his face serene, his eyes warm with welcome.

"They're gone now, honey. We won't ever have to listen to their whining again." Tyler held out a hand to her, clearly expecting her to take it.

Jaxon backed a cautious step down the hall. She didn't want to alarm Tyler. He didn't seem to notice he had blood all over him. "I'm supposed to be in school, Uncle Tyler." Her voice didn't sound natural even to her own ears.

A sudden scowl crossed his face. "You haven't called me Uncle Tyler since you were eight years old. What happened to Daddy? Your mother turned you against me, didn't she?" He was moving toward her.

Jaxon stayed very quiet, very still, a look of innocence on her face. "No one could ever turn me against you. That would be impossible. And you know Mom doesn't want to have anything to do with me."

Tyler relaxed visibly. He was close enough to touch her. Jaxon couldn't allow that; her tremendous self-discipline would not extend far enough to let him touch her with the blood of her family on his hands. She struck without warning, jabbing a fist straight into his throat, kicking his kneecap hard. The moment she connected, Jaxon turned and ran. She didn't look back once. She didn't dare. Tyler was trained to respond despite being injured. In any case, she was very small compared to her stepfather. Her blows might stun him but would never incapacitate him completely. With luck her kick might have broken his knee, but she doubted it. Jaxon ran through the house and straight out the door. Rebecca had always liked the protection of living on the naval base, and Jaxon was grateful now. She screamed at the top of her lungs, running straight across the street to Russell Andrews's house.

Russell's wife, Bernice, rushed out to meet her, distress on her face. "What is it, dear? Are you hurt?"

Russell joined them, circling Jaxon's slender shoulders with one arm. "Is your mother ill?" He knew better; he knew Jaxon. She was always a child in complete control, calm under fire, always thinking. If Rebecca were ill, Jaxon would have called for medical aid. Right now her face was so pale, she looked like a ghost. There was horror in her eyes, terror in her expression. Russell glanced across the street at the silent house with its door wide open. The wind was blowing, the air crisp and cold. For some unknown reason, the house gave him the creeps.

Russell started across the street. Jaxon caught his arm. "No, Uncle Russell, not by yourself. You can't save them. They're already dead. Call the MPs."

"Who's dead, Jaxon?" Russell asked quietly, knowing Jaxon wouldn't lie.

"Mathew and my mother. Tyler killed them. He told Mom he killed my father, too. He's been so strange and violent lately. He hated Mother and Mathew. I tried to tell you, but none of you would believe me." Jaxon was sobbing, her hands over her face. "You wouldn't listen to me. None of you would listen." She felt so sick, her stomach rebelling, her mind replaying the scenes she'd just seen until she thought she might go insane. "There was so much blood. He gouged out Mathew's eyes. Why would he do that? Mathew was only a little boy."

Russell pushed her toward Bernice. "See to her, honey. She's going into shock."

"He killed everyone, my entire family. He took every-

25

one away from me. I didn't save them," Jaxon said softly.

Bernice hugged her tightly. "Don't worry, Jaxon, you're with us."

Jaxon, Seventeen years old

"Hey, beautiful." Don Jacobson leaned down to ruffle Jaxon's mop of wild blond hair. He tried not to act too possessive. Jaxon always shot down anyone who tried to get close to her. She had a wall erected so high around her, no one seemed to be able to break into her world. Since the death of her family, Don had seen her laugh only with Bernice and Russell Andrews and their daughter, Sabrina. Sabrina was two years older than Jaxon and home for spring break. "Where you off to in such a hurry? Master-Chief told me your times were better than his new recruits.' "

Jaxon smiled rather absently. "My times are always better than his new recruits' every time he gets a new group. I've been in training my entire life. I'd better be good, or Master-Chief would have thrown me out a long time ago. Too bad women can't serve in the SEAL. It's the only thing I'm suited for. I graduated early with so many college credits, and now I have no idea what I want to do." She shoved a hand carelessly through her hair, tousling it even more. "I'm younger than most of the other students, but, to tell you the truth, I feel so much older than most of them, sometimes I want to scream."

Don had a burning desire to hold her close, to comfort her. "You've always been smart, Jaxx. Don't let anyone get to you." He knew her distress was really because she couldn't get over the trauma of what had happened to her family. How could she? He doubted if anyone could. "So, where are you running off to?"

"Sabrina is home, and we're going to the movies tonight. I promised I wouldn't be late this time." Jaxon made a face. "I'm always late when I come to the training center. I never seem to get out of here on time." The training course was the one place her mind was so occupied with other things that she couldn't think, couldn't remember anything else. She worked herself hard physically, keeping the demons at bay for just a little while.

Jaxon hadn't felt safe in so long, she couldn't remember what it was like to get a good night's sleep. Tyler Drake was still out there somewhere, hiding. She knew he was close by; she felt him watching sometimes. Only Russell believed her when she told him. Russell knew her now. Jaxon didn't give in to her imagination. She wasn't prone to hysterics. She had some kind of very strong sixth sense that warned her when danger was close. She had trained beside Tyler for years. If she identified a sign as his, Russell believed her absolutely.

"What show?" Don asked. "I haven't been to a good film in a long time." He was blatantly fishing for an invitation to go along.

Jaxon didn't seem to notice. She shrugged, suddenly distracted. "I'm not sure. Sabrina was going to choose it." Her heart was beginning to pound. It was crazy. She was standing out in the open with a boy she had known all her life, yet she felt detached, far away, and peculiarly alone. Darkness was spreading within her, and with it a terrible dread.

Don did touch her then. She had gone so still and pale, he was afraid for her. "Jaxon? Are you sick? What is it?"

"Something's wrong." She whispered the words so softly, he nearly missed them.

Jaxon sprang past Don, brushing him aside. He raced beside her, reluctant to leave her in such a state. Jaxon was so cool and withdrawn all the time, Don couldn't believe he was seeing her like this. She didn't glance his way, instead running flat out toward her foster home. After her mother's and brother's deaths and her stepfather's mysterious disappearance, Russell and Bernice Andrews had taken Jaxx in and given her a loving home. Russell and the other members of his SEALs team had continued her training, recognizing she needed the physical action to alleviate the memories of her traumatic past. Don's father was part of that team and often talked to his son of the tragedy. No one was absolutely certain whether Tyler Drake had really killed Mathew Montgomery as he had bragged to Rebecca, but there was little doubt he had killed Rebecca and Mathew Jr.

Don had a bad feeling as he sprinted alongside Jaxon. It wasn't all that hard to keep up; he was in good shape and far taller than she, yet he was sweating. Jaxon had a look on her face that made him certain she knew something he didn't. Something terrible. He wished he had a cell phone. As he rounded a corner, he spotted an MP.

"Hey, follow us! Come on, something's wrong!" He yelled it with conviction, not even afraid of making a complete fool of himself. He knew it this time; he knew it the same way Jaxon knew it as they raced up the street toward her foster home.

Jaxon stopped abruptly in the driveway, staring up at the door. It was partially open as if in invitation. Don started past her, but she caught his arm. She was shaking. "Don't go in. He might still be there."

Don tried to put an arm around her. He had never seen Jaxon so shaken up. She looked fragile and grief stricken. She pulled away from him, her gaze darting around the yard, searching the terrain. "Don't touch me, Don. Don't come anywhere near me. If he even thinks I care about you, he'll find a way to kill you."

"You don't know what's in that house, Jaxx," he protested. But a part of him didn't want to go see if she was right. Evil seemed to permeate the house.

The MPs swaggered their way up the driveway. "You kids better not be wasting our time. What's going on here? You know whose house this is?"

Jaxon nodded. "Mine. The Andrews'. Be careful. I think Tyler Drake has been here. I think he's killed again." She sat down abruptly on the lawn, her legs giving out.

The two MPs looked at each other. "Is this for real?" Everyone had heard about Tyler Drake, a former SEAL operative who had allegedly murdered his family, eluded capture, and was still hiding out somewhere. "Why would he come back here?"

Jaxon didn't respond. The darkness in her was her answer. Tyler had killed the Andrews family because they had taken her in. She was his, and in his twisted mind they had usurped his position. It should have occurred to her that he would do such a thing. He had murdered her father, thinking her father had no right to her. The same with her mother and brother. Of course he would murder the Andrews. It would make perfect sense to him. She drew up her legs and began to rock herself back and forth. She only glanced up when the two MPs rushed from the house and began to vomit on the immaculate lawn.

Chapter One

Jaxon Montgomery snapped the clip into her handgun and glared at her partner. "This is a setup, Barry. I can smell it. It's amazing to me that you don't have a clue. Where's your sixth sense? I thought men were supposed to have some kind of built-in survival instinct."

Barry Radcliff snorted derisively. "You're the one leading the party, honey, and we're all following you."

"My point, partner. You have no sense of self-preservation." Jaxx threw him a teasing grin over her shoulder. "The entire lot of you are worthless."

"True, but we have good taste. You look great from behind. We're men, honey—we can't help the hormones."

"Is that your excuse? Hormones running amok? I thought you liked living on the edge, you gung-ho kamikaze type daredevils."

"That's you. We just go along to pull your cute little butt out of all the trouble you get into," Barry returned. He glanced at his watch. "You've got to decide, Jaxx. Do we try it or call it off?"

Jaxx closed off her mind to everything—the darkness of the night, the biting cold, the adrenaline surging in her blood, needing action. The warehouse was too easily accessible; no way could they search the upper lofts without exposing themselves. She had never been all that happy with the informant. Everything in her screamed it was a setup and she and her fellow police officers were walking into an ambush.

Without hesitation she moved her mouth over the tiny radio. "Abort, guys. I want all of you to pull back and out. Signal when clear. Barry and I will cover until we hear from you. Go now."

"That strong?" She could hear the grin in Barry's voice. "Wonder woman."

"Oh, shut up," she replied rudely, her voice mild but edged with worry. Her eyes were restless, constantly moving, sweeping the entire area around them. The feeling of danger was intensifying.

The tiny receiver in her ear crackled. "Are we going to let a woman losing her nerve cost us the biggest bust in history?" That was the new guy. The one who had been placed on her team against her will. The one who had some kind of political pull in the department and was on his way up. Benton. Craig Benton.

"Stand down, Benton. That's an order. We can argue over it later," Jaxx commanded, but she knew, with a sinking heart, that he was the cause of the inner warnings shrieking at her. Benton wanted to be a hero. But there was no room for heroes in her line of work.

Barry was swearing beside her, his body already rigid. He knew it as well as she did. Barry had been her partner long enough to know that when Jaxx said there was trouble, there was hell out there. "He's going in. He's going in. I see him at the side door."

"Fall back, Barry," Jaxx snapped, already moving forward. "I'll try to pull him out. You get the rest of the world down here, because there's going to be a war. Keep our guys out of there until we have help. It's an ambush."

She was so small and slender, dressed in her dark clothes and cap, Barry could barely make her out in the darkness of the night. She never made a sound when she moved. It was eerie. He found himself continually glancing at her to assure himself she was with him. Now he moved, too. No way was his partner going into that building without him. He issued the orders, called in the backup, but he followed her. He told himself it had nothing to do with Jaxx Montgomery and everything to do with partnership. It had nothing to do with love and everything to do with the job.

"You should see this place," the radio crackled in their ears. "Get in here. It's loaded with enough chemicals to blow up half the city."

"You idiot, it's loaded with enough chemicals to blow up the building with you in it. Now get the hell out of there." It was Jaxx at her best. Her voice was soft and cutting, a whip of pure contempt. Anyone hearing that voice became a believer.

Craig Benton glanced uneasily to his right and then his left. The place suddenly gave him the creeps. He began a slow retreat, backing toward the door. At once something bit at his leg, high and ugly, knocking him backward and down. He found himself on the cold cement floor, staring up at the loft. The place remained silent. He put his hand down to touch his leg and found a mush of raw hamburger. He screamed. "I'm hit, I'm hit! Oh, God, I'm hit!"

Jaxon would have gone through the door first, but Barry slammed his shoulder into her, knocking her slight figure to the side. He dove into the warehouse, rolling to his right, looking for cover of any kind. He heard the whine of bullets as they zipped past him and embedded themselves in the crate behind him. He thought he got off a warning to Jaxx, but he couldn't be sure as he crawled toward Benton. Things were happening too fast, and his vision had narrowed toward his purpose—pulling out the stupid kid and getting the hell out of there.

He made it to Benton. "Shut up," he snapped. Did the rookie have to be as big as a linebacker? Dragging him out of there was going to be difficult, and if Craig kept screaming, he was going to shoot the rookie himself. "Let's go." He caught Benton under the arms, tried to stay low and behind cover, and began to make his way back toward the door. It was a long way. They were spraying the area with bullets now and deliberately sweeping the chemicals, so explosions were going off all over the place. Fires broke out. He felt the sting of the first hit on his scalp. The second was well placed. His left arm went numb, and he dropped Benton and found himself on the floor.

Then Jaxx was there. Jaxon Montgomery, his partner. Jaxon never stopped until it was over, and she never left her partner in trouble. Jaxon was going to die in that warehouse right beside him. She was providing covering fire, running toward them. "Get up, you lazy ass. You're not that hurt. Haul your butt out of here."

Yeah, that was his Jaxx, always sympathetic to his problems. Benton, damn him, was dragging his body toward the door, trying to save himself. Barry tried. He was very disoriented, and the smoke and heat didn't help. Something was wrong with his head; it pounded and throbbed, and everything seemed hazy and far away. Jaxx's small frame landed beside him, her beautiful eyes enormous with worry. "You landed us in a hell of a mess, my friend," she said softly. "Get moving." She gave him a quick once-over, assessing the damage and dismissing it for more important things. "I mean it, Barry. Move your butt out of here now!" It was a clear command.

Jaxx slammed another clip into her gun and rolled across the floor to draw fire away from her partner, coming up on her knees, firing up toward the loft. As he dragged his leaden body toward the entrance, Radcliff caught a glimpse of a man falling. Satisfaction was instant. Jaxx was an expert marksperson. What she shot at went down. Even if they died here, they took at least one of the enemy with them. Something made him turn his head just as the bullets struck Jaxx, taking her small body and flinging it backward several feet across the warehouse. She fell like a rag doll onto the floor, a dark stain spreading out around her.

Furious, enraged, Barry tried to bring his gun up, but his arm refused to respond. The only thing he could do was crawl forward or crawl back. He crawled back, dragging his body across the distance to hers. She was just lying there. She turned her head slightly to look at him.

"Don't, Jaxx. Don't you do this to me."

"Get out of here."

"I mean it, damn it. Don't you do this." He was desperate to reach her, motivate her to move. She had to move. Had to get out with him.

"I'm tired, Barry. I've been tired for a very long time. Someone else can save everybody now." She murmured the words so softly, he almost didn't hear them.

"Jaxx!" Barry tried to gather her in his arms, but his arms wouldn't work.

To his left, the small door suddenly slammed shut, trapping them inside. And Benton was right; there were enough chemicals in there to blow them all over the city. He waited, expecting death at any moment.

He heard screams then, horrible, gut-wrenching screams of fear. He saw bodies falling through the smoke and the glow of flames. He saw things that couldn't be. A wolf, huge and savage, leaping at a fleeing man, powerful jaws boring through the chest to get at the heart. The wolf seemed to be everywhere, bringing down man after man, ripping through tissue and flesh, cracking bones with its jaws. Barry saw that same wolf contort, shift shape so that it was a huge owl with talons and a beak that dove at another man, plucking the eyes right out of the head. It was an unbelievable nightmare of blood and death and retribution.

Barry had no idea he had such violence inside him to envision such terrible images. He knew that at least two bullets had hit him; he could feel the blood trickling down his face as well as his arm. Obviously he was hallucinating. That was why he didn't attempt to shoot when the wolf finally made its way to their corner of the warehouse. He watched it approach, admiring the way it moved, its muscles rippling, the way it leaped so easily over anything in its path. It came straight to him, drawn no doubt by the smell of blood, or, Barry thought, his own vivid imagination running wild.

The wolf looked at him a long time, looked into his eyes. The eyes of the wolf were very strange, almost completely black. Intelligent eyes but empty of any emotion. Barry felt no threat but more as if the wolf were staring into his very soul, perhaps judging him. He lay still, feeling only a willingness to do whatever the creature wanted him to do. He felt sleepy, his eyelids far too heavy to keep up. As he was drifting off, he could have sworn the wolf contorted once more and began to take the shape of a man.

Jaxon Montgomery woke to the sound of a heart beating. It was beating fast and hard, frightened and loud. She felt automatically for her gun. She was never without a weapon, yet she found nothing under her pillow or beside her body. The heart pounded even harder, and she tasted the coppery flavor of fear in her mouth. Dragging in a lungful of air, she forced herself to open her eyes. She could only stare in astonishment at the room she was in. It was no hospital, and certainly not the bedroom in her tiny apartment. This room was beautiful. The walls were a soft mauve, so light it was impossible to tell if the color was really there or merely her imagination. The carpet was thick and a deeper mauve, picking up the colors in the stained glass high up on three walls. The pattern was soothing and intricate. It gave Jaxx the illusion of being safe, something she knew was impossible. Just to make certain she was really awake, she dug her fingernails into her palms.

She turned her head to examine the other contents of the room. The furniture was antique and heavy, the bed a four-poster that was more comfortable than anything she had ever slept on in her life. The dresser was large and held a few feminine articles on it—a brush, a small music box, and a candle. They were beautiful and looked antique. There were several candles in the room, all lit so that the room itself seemed to bask in the soft light. She had often dreamed of a room like this, so beautiful and elegant, with stained-glass windows. It occurred to her again that she might not be awake.

The sound of the heart pounding so loudly convinced her she was wide awake and others must be taking care of her. Others who had no way of knowing the danger she brought with her. She would have to find a way to protect them. Jaxx looked around frantically for her gun. She had definitely suffered an injury; she couldn't move very well. She took an inventory, carefully trying to shift her arms and then her legs. Her body did not want to respond. She could move if she concentrated every bit of her determination, but it hardly seemed worth the effort. She was very tired, and her head was aching. The relentless beating of that heart was driving her crazy.

A shadow fell across the bed, and her own heart slammed hard enough to cause her pain. She realized then that the sound had come from her own chest. Jaxon slowly turned her head. A man was standing over her. Very tall, powerful. A predator. She saw that instantly.

She had seen many predators, but this one was the ultimate. It was evident in his complete stillness. A waiting. A confidence. A power. A danger. He was dangerous. More dangerous than any criminal she had encountered so far. She didn't know how she knew these things, but she did. He believed himself invincible, and she had a sneaking suspicion that he just might be. He was neither old nor young. It was impossible to tell his age. His eyes were black and emotionless. Empty eyes. His mouth was sensual, erotic, really, his teeth very white. His shoulders were wide. He was handsome and sexy. More than sexy. Completely hot.

Jaxx sighed and tried not to panic. Tried not to allow her thoughts to show on her face. He definitely didn't look like a doctor. He did not look like someone she could take down easily in hand-to-hand combat. He smiled then, amusement touching his eyes for just one moment. It made him look completely different. Warm. Even sexier. She had a feeling he was reading her thoughts and laughing at her. Her hand was moving restlessly beneath the covers, forever seeking the gun.

"You are in distress." He made it a statement. His voice was beautiful. Smooth like velvet, alluring, almost seductive. He had a strange accent she couldn't place and a way of turning his words that sounded very Old World.

Jaxon blinked rapidly in an attempt to cover her confusion, surprised by the direction her thoughts were taking. She never thought about sex. She had no idea why she was equating this stranger with eroticism. To her shock, she had to search for her voice. "I need my gun." It was a dare of sorts, a test of his reaction.

Those black eyes studied her face intently. His scrutiny made her uncomfortable. Those eyes saw too much, and Jaxon had a great deal to hide. His face was expressionless, giving absolutely nothing away, and Jaxx was very good at reading people.

"Are you planning on shooting me?" He asked it with that same gentle voice, only this time it held a hint of amusement.

She was very tired. It was becoming a struggle to keep her eyelashes from drifting down. She noticed a peculiar phenomenon. Her heart had slowed to match the rhythm of his. Exactly. Their two hearts were beating simultaneously. She could hear them. His voice was familiar to her, yet he was a total stranger. No one could ever meet such a man and forget him. She could not possibly know him.

She moistened her lips. She was incredibly thirsty. "I need my gun."

He moved to the dresser. Not walked. Glided. She could watch him move like that for all time. His body was like that of an animal, a wolf or a leopard, something catlike and powerful. Fluid. Totally silent. He flowed, yet when movement ceased, he was completely still again. He handed her her gun.

It felt familiar in her hand, an extension of herself. Almost at once some of her fear faded away. "What happened to me?" Automatically she tried to check the clip, but her arms felt like lead, and she couldn't raise the gun enough to do the job.

He took the gun back, his fingers brushing her skin. The flood of warmth was so unexpected, she jerked away from him. He didn't react but gently pried her fingers loose and showed her the full clip with a round in the chamber before returning the gun to her palm. "You were shot several times, Jaxon. You are still very ill."

"This isn't a hospital." She was always suspicious; it was what kept her alive. But she wasn't supposed to be alive anymore. "You're in great danger here with me," she tried to warn the man, but her words were too low, her voice fading.

"Sleep, honey. Just go back to sleep." He said it softly,

yet his velvet tone seeped into her body and mind, as powerful as any drug.

He touched her then, stroking her hair. His touch felt familiar and slightly possessive. He touched her as if he had a right to touch her. It was like a caress. Jaxon was confused. She knew him. He was a part of her. She knew him intimately, yet he was a total stranger. She sighed, unable to prevent her lashes from drifting down and giving in to the powerful demand that she sleep.

Lucian sat on the edge of the bed and simply watched her sleep. She was the most unexpected thing he had experienced in all his centuries of living. He had waited for this being nearly two thousand years, and she was not at all what he had envisioned. The women of his race were tall and elegant, dark-eyed, with an abundance of dark hair. They were creatures of power and skill. He was well aware that his species was on the edge of extinction and that their women were guarded as the treasures they were, but still, they were powerful, not fragile and vulnerable like this young woman.

He touched her pale skin. Sleeping, she looked almost like a pixie, a fairy out of the legends. She was so small and slight, she seemed all eyes. Beautiful eyes. The kind of eyes a man could drown in. Her hair was several shades of blond, thick and soft but short and shaggy, as if she carelessly took scissors to it whenever it got in her way. He had assumed she would have long hair, not this mop. He found himself constantly touching her hair. Soft, like strands of silk. It was untamed and went in whatever direction it chose, but he found himself partial to her wild hair.

She lived in fear. It was her world. It had been her world from the time she was a small child. Lucian had no idea he had such a protective streak in him. For so many centuries he had had no feelings. Now, in the presence of this human woman, he had far too many. Those who had tried to harm her had paid dearly for their crimes in the warehouse. Lucian had sent her into a deep sleep, slowing her heart and lungs while he carried her away from that place of death and destruction. He had saved her partner, too, implanting in the man's mind the memory of an ambulance carrying her off. Lucian managed to save her, giving her his ancient, powerful blood. He had transformed himself into light and entered her battered body in the way of his people, to begin the healing from the inside out. Her wounds were great, her blood loss massive. Using his blood was the only way to save her life, but it was dangerous to both of them. Discovery of the existence of his species by any of her kind would be a death sentence for his people. His first priority was her protection, the second was to ensure the continuation of his race. His job had always been the protection of both species.

He had bought himself time by covering his tracks at the hospital where she would have been taken. He implanted memories of calling in Lifeflight, sending her to a trauma unit. The paperwork seemed to be lost, and the computers went down. No one had figured out exactly what happened.

Lucian found himself tangling his fingers in her hair once more. She didn't even have a decent name. What kind of a name was Jaxon for a woman? He shook his head. He had been watching her for some time, figuring the best way to approach her. If she had been a woman of his race, he simply would have claimed her as his own, bound them together, and allowed nature to take its course. This woman was human and so fragile. He had touched her mind many times over the last few weeks while he had established his home. He found she had many secrets. Gabriel's lifemate had told him he would find this woman somewhere in the world and in great need. Francesca had been right. Jaxon's life had not been an easy one. She had had no childhood to speak of, only memories of struggle and death and violence. Jaxon believed she was responsible for keeping those around her safe. She had lived her entire young life that way. Taking responsibility for others. No one had ever really taken care of her. He intended to remedy that situation. He had a feeling she would have no idea how to respond to his interference.

Her first thought upon awakening had been the protection of others. Of him. That intrigued him. It warmed him that she had tried to warn him of the possible danger to him. She had known he was a predator, that he could be dangerous, yet it still mattered to her to protect him. She fascinated him. Something about her turned his heart over and made him want to smile at the mere sight of her. That was all it took. Looking at her, and he was happy. He had never experienced these emotions, and he took them out to examine them.

With the first sound of her voice, he had seen colors. Vivid, brilliant colors. Having lived in his black-and-white world for so many centuries as did the Carpathian males who had lost emotions, Lucian was almost blinded by the hues. Blues and reds, oranges and greens—every shade of color everywhere he looked. He rubbed strands of her blond hair between his thumb and forefinger, unknowingly tender. The feelings he was experiencing were intense.

Hunger was slowly creeping into his thoughts. He had expended tremendous energy healing her, and his blood needed to be replenished. He sent another strong push to her mind to ensure she remained asleep while he hunted. The city was filled with prey just waiting for him. He went to the balcony, then shape-shifted, choosing the form of an owl. Powerful wings swept him over the city. The sharp eyes were made for seeing in the dark, his acute hearing picking up every sound beneath him. He could hear hearts beating, the murmur of voices, the sound of life being lived. Traffic and city noises were beckoning, the sound of blood pumping through veins bursting with life.

He found his way to the park, a perfect hunting ground. The owl landed in the top of a tree and folded its wings carefully. It inspected the surrounding area. Off to his right he could hear the voices of two men. At once he shape-shifted into his normal form, floating to the ground as he did so. He sent out a silent mental call, demanding that his prey come to him. He had spent so many centuries delivering murderers into the hands of death, it had taken a great deal of discipline to retrain himself simply to feed.

The two men answered his call, both healthy and stocky, runners stretching their legs after a late-night meeting. Neither smelled of alcohol or drugs. He fed quickly, needing to return to Jaxon. She had been unconscious for longer than he would have liked. But now that she was sleeping, Lucian realized she never really allowed herself to enter into the normal human slumber pattern that was so necessary to their bodies. When she went to sleep without the aid of his command, she was restless and in distress. Lucian was well aware that Jaxon spent the majority of nights working at her job, physically driving herself to the point of exhaustion. But her dreams were merciless. Lucian had shared a few of them with her, merging his mind with hers so that he might know her demons intimately. She had far too many demons, and he intended to exorcise every one of them.

Mostly, Lucian didn't want to be separated from her for any longer than was strictly necessary. He couldn't be separated from her. He found he needed to be with her. He, who had never needed anyone. He needed to touch her, to know she was all right. Now that she was in his care, he intended to bind her to him so that neither humans nor other Carpathians could possibly take her from him. Jaxon would not escape him. He had given her his blood and had taken a minute amount of hers, just enough to be able to merge their minds at will.

He returned to her, once again at full strength. And his strength was enormous. He would have to be gentle with her. If there was any gentleness left in him, if there had ever been any gentleness in him, he intended to utilize it for Jaxon. If anyone deserved it, she did.

He sat down on the edge of her bed, removed the command to stay asleep, and gathered her into his arms. "I am your lifemate, young one. You have no idea what that means, and you are not Carpathian, so I expect a certain amount of resistance from you." Lucian rubbed his chin over the top of her head. "I promise you I will be as gentle and as patient as I can, but I cannot wait long for you. The emotions I am feeling do not tame the wild beast within me."

Jaxon's eyelashes fluttered open. She felt confused, hazy, as if she were in a dream. The soothing voice she heard was so beautiful and familiar. It kept the demons at bay and allowed her to feel a measure of safety. "Who are you? How do I know you?"

"Your mind knows me. Your heart and soul recognize me." His thumb caressed the perfect line of her cheekbone tenderly just because he loved the feel of her skin beneath his. "I must bind us together, Jaxon, I have no other choice. It would be dangerous to wait. I am sorry that I cannot give you more time."

"I don't understand." She looked up into his black eyes and should have felt fear at what she saw there. He was looking at her possessively, something no man had ever dared to do. Jaxon didn't encourage such feelings in men. Yet for some strange reason, this dangerous stranger made her feel cared for. Wanted.

"I know you do not understand at this moment, Jaxon,

but you will in time." Lucian caught her chin in firm fingers so that his dark eyes captured her gaze.

It was like falling into a black, bottomless pool. Endless. Timeless.

Lucian murmured her name softly and bent his head to the softness of her throat. He inhaled her scent. There was nowhere she could go that he could not find her. His arms tightened possessively until he reminded himself that she was very fragile. She felt incredibly small and light in his arms but also warm and enticing. She was stirring things in him best left alone. The sudden, urgent demands were shocking to him. She was young and vulnerable, and at that moment he should want only to protect her.

His mouth touched her skin gently, tenderly, a small caress. At once need slammed into him, hard and imperative. He could hear her heart beating to the rhythm of his. He could hear her blood run in her veins, an enticing heat that beckoned to him, that triggered a tremendous physical hunger for her body. Closing his eyes, he savored his ability to feel, no matter that it was terribly uncomfortable and his body was screaming for relief. His tongue found her pulse, bathed the area once, twice. His teeth scraped gently over the vein, then sank deeply into it.

At once she moved restlessly in his arms and moaned, a soft whisper of intimacy that tightened his body even more. She was sweet and spicy, a taste indescribable and one he had never before encountered. She was addicting, as if she had been designed precisely to please his every need. He would never get enough of her. Discipline overcame his hunger for the ecstasy her body promised. With a sweep of his tongue, he closed the tiny pinpricks his teeth had made, leaving no signs for a doctor to discover.

Careful to keep her deep within his enthrallment, Lucian opened his shirt and shifted her in his arms so that he could palm the back of her head. His body was raging with need, and her natural sensuality was emerging under his sorcerery. One of his fingernails lengthened into a razor-sharp talon. He sliced a line over his heart and pressed her mouth to his chest that he might continue the ritual of binding her to him.

At the first touch of her lips, fire raged through him, a need so intense, so deep, Lucian, who was noted for his rigid control, nearly gave in to the temptation to take what was rightfully his. He found he was trembling, his body covered with a fine sheen of sweat. Bending close to her ear, he breathed the words into the night, into her mind, that no one could ever separate them again, that she could not be apart from him for more than a few scant hours. "I claim you as my lifemate. I belong to you. I offer my life for you. I give you my protection, my allegiance, my heart, my soul, and my body. I take into my keeping the same that is yours. Your life, happiness, and welfare will be cherished and placed above my own for all time. You are my lifemate, bound to me for all eternity and always in my care."

The relief he experienced was tremendous and occurred despite the fact that his body had not merged with hers. His heart and hers were one, bound together, two halves of the same whole. Their souls merged so that her feminine light shone brightly within him, alleviating the terrible darkness that had threatened him for centuries. At that moment he realized that when one had lived in darkness nearly all of his life, in a bleak, ugly hell of an existence, finding a lifemate was beyond any dream he could imagine.

Jaxon Montgomery was literally his heart and soul. Without her there was no reason to continue existing. He could never go back to the emptiness and darkness he had lived in for so long. The ritual words bound them together so that neither could ever escape the other.

Lucian didn't fool himself. He needed her far more than she could ever need him, though, from his point of view, she needed him a great deal. He had to stop and think before he pushed his claim any further. Very gently he stopped her feeding, closing the wound himself. His blood would both tie them together and aid her healing. It would also work on her human body to convert her to his race. Conversion was risky, hard on the body and mind. And once done, there was no going back. Jaxon would be as he was, needing blood to survive, seeking relief from the sun in the welcoming arms of the earth. If she was not a true psychic—the only kind of human female to successfully convert to Carpathian—the experiment would push her over the edge into madness, and Jaxon would have to be destroyed. Lucian sat back, releasing her from his dark spell.

Her eyelashes fluttered as he slipped her back onto the pillows. Lucian knew that very few humans could be converted successfully. But he also believed she must belong within those ranks, as she was his true lifemate. Her heart matched his. He knew that. When he uttered the ritual words, he felt the threads binding them together. Even so, knowing something intellectually didn't make his heart believe it. He wanted to take no chances with her safety. Three exchanges of blood were necessary for complete conversion. Already her hearing and eyesight were more acute, more like those of Carpathians. She would soon have trouble consuming meat products and most other foods. She would need him near. He had changed her life as much as he dared to at this time.

"I still don't know who you are." Beneath the covers of the bed, Jaxon's fingers wrapped securely around the butt of her gun. She was very drowsy, and this stranger was far too familiar. She didn't like puzzles. She had no idea where she was, only that she was ill and had strange dreams of a dark prince taking her blood and tying her to him for all time. There was something exotic and different about the stranger she found hovering over her bed.

Something elegant and courtly yet wild and untamed. Jaxon found the dangerous combination sensual and difficult to resist.

Lucian smiled at her, a flash of even white teeth that softened the hard lines of his shadowed features. "I am Lucian Daratrazanoff. A very old and respected name but difficult in this country to pronounce correctly. Lucian is fine."

"*Do* I know you?" Jaxon wished she wasn't so weak. She wished she hadn't had such erotic and peculiar dreams about this man. It made her feel strange to be in his presence, especially when nothing was making sense to her. "Why am I here instead of a hospital?"

"You needed extraordinary care," he answered truthfully. "You came very close to dying, Jaxon, and I could not afford to take any chances with your life."

"My partner, Barry Radcliff, was shot. I remember, he came back for me." Everything else was a blur to her. She had no idea how she had gotten out of the warehouse, since Barry had not been in any shape to carry her.

"He is in the hospital and doing better than expected. He is a tough man and very courageous." Lucian gave her partner his just due, although he didn't add that the man was in love with her.

"I thought I was going to die. I should have died." She murmured the words softly almost to herself.

She had wanted to die. The terrible responsibility that weighed on her slender shoulders was far more of a burden than she wanted to carry for all time. She forced her lashes open so that she could look at him. "You're in terrible danger. You can't be with me. Wherever we are, it isn't safe. You're not safe."

Lucian smiled and reached down to brush at the hair tumbling down around her face. His touch was incredibly tender and gave her that strange sense of security. His voice was so beautiful and pure, she wanted him to go on talking forever. His accent was sexy, sending a wave of longing through her she hardly recognized for what it was.

"Do not worry about me, young one. I am able to protect both of us. I know of the man you fear, and as long as you are in this house, you are safe. He is well trained, but it would be impossible for him to enter these grounds undetected."

"You don't know him. He will kill anyone without remorse or thought. Even though you're only helping me, he'll interpret it as a threat to him." She was becoming agitated, her eyes enormous with concern for him.

"If you believe nothing else of me, Jaxon, believe this. There is no other in this world as dangerous as the man in this room with you. Tyler Drake cannot reach you. He can no longer dictate your life, as you are under my protection now." He sounded matter-of-fact, not arrogant, not a braggart.

She was falling into his dark eyes again. His beautiful, very unusual eyes. Jaxon felt a little lost, and she blinked rapidly to break away from his mesmerizing spell. "I know you think that. My father was a Navy SEAL, and so was my foster father, Russell Andrews. Tyler Drake managed to murder both of them. You can't think you're safe as long as you're with me." Her lashes were far too heavy to keep up. They drifted down in spite of her intention to convince him. She didn't have the strength to guard him. That frightened her, and her heart slammed painfully against her chest.

"Be calm, Jaxon. Take a breath and relax. I am the one taking care of you, not the other way around, although I greatly appreciate that you would want to protect me. In any case, no one knows where you are. I have kept you entirely secure. Just sleep, honey, and heal."

His voice was so soothing and persuasive, she soon found her breathing regulating itself exactly to his. Why she wanted to do as he commanded, she didn't know, but the urge to obey was far too strong to ignore. She allowed her eyes to close. "I hope you're as good as you think you are. It would be safer for you if you called my boss and had him station a couple of the guys to watch over you." Her voice was trailing off to a soft slur. "Better yet, it would be safer if you just walked away from me and never looked back."

Once more Lucian's fingers tangled in her soft hair. "You think I would be safer, do you?"

There was a tinge of amusement in his voice. For some reason it made Jaxon's heart turn over. He was so familiar, as if she knew him intimately, when she didn't recognize him at all. Except his touch. She knew his touch. And the sound of his voice. She knew his voice. The accent, the velvet seduction of it, the way he turned his phrases. The way it seemed to belong in her mind. The really crazy part was, Jaxon was beginning to believe in him.

Lucian watched her go under without so much as a fight. She hadn't wanted her life to be saved, but she had picked up the torch of being his guardian, worried for his safety. She was ready to protect him without even knowing who he was. He had spent a good deal of time now with his mind merged firmly with hers. It had been necessary at first just to keep her alive. Later, he did it because he wanted to know her, her memories, how she thought, what she dreamed of, the things that were important to her. She had far more compassion in her than was good for her. She needed him to balance her out.

He was amazed at how powerful the sexual urges he was experiencing for her were. That it had never happened to him before. He had seldom looked at a woman for other than satisfying hunger. Now his hunger was different and far stronger than anything he had ever imagined. For the sake of knowledge Lucian had sometimes shared the minds of humans to see what sex felt like. This urgent demand raging throughout his body was completely different from even that. It seemed to take over his mind, driving out every sane thought.

Protective. Lucian knew every Carpathian male was born with the tremendous duty of protecting the women and children of their race. This protectiveness he felt toward Jaxon was also different. Lucian had dedicated his life to guarding humans and Carpathians alike, yet again, the intensity of his emotions toward Jaxon was so much stronger. He was unprepared for how powerful his attachment to her would really be. He had lived nearly all his life in darkness and shadow, was comfortable and familiar with violence. He was wholly dark and dangerous. Now he wanted to know tenderness, gentleness. He knew himself as most men never did. He knew he was powerful and dangerous, and he accepted it in himself. Now, however, with Jaxon lying so vulnerable and fragile in his bed, he was even more so.

With a sigh he sank down on the bed beside her. While she remained human and needed to stay above ground to survive, he would be unable to fully protect her during the day, when sunlight diminished Carpathian powers. Normally he would take to the earth until nightfall. Which posed a problem for both of them. She could not be separated from him for that many hours without suffering tremendously. He stretched out on the bed beside her. He would command her to to sleep until the next sunset. Meanwhile, the safeguards he would weave around them and the wolves he would release would keep them safe from any creature, human or otherwise, that might seek to harm them. He gathered her small body into the shelter of his larger frame and buried his face in the silky fragrance of her hair.

Chapter Two

Jaxon smelled him first. Clean. Fresh. Sexy. She inwardly shook her head at herself in reprimand. She knew him now. Knew his touch, his voice, his scent. Even in sleep her hand had been curled around the familiar butt of her gun. Now she relaxed her hold on it and actually allowed it to drop to the sheet beside her. She felt safe. She lay with her eyes closed, contemplating that. The feeling of safety. She didn't remember ever having experienced such a thing before. It interested her that, although she was weak and injured, alone with a complete stranger and with no idea of where she was, she felt safe.

She opened her eyes and found him looming above her, exactly where she knew he would be. She felt him inside her mind, knew she could find him in a crowd without looking. The very sight of him stole her breath. He was so tall, and he wore power like a second skin No. That wasn't exactly right. He was power personified. She waited for him to speak, needing to hear his voice. She loved the sound of his voice. It frightened her, her tremendous reaction to him. She had trained herself not to feel anything for anyone, particularly a man. She was convinced Tyler Drake would resurface if she were to show interest in a man.

"Are you feeling any better this evening?" Lucian's hand brushed her forehead.

Jaxon felt the warmth of his touch like a rush of lava through her body. "You look tired." She frowned. "Have you been taking care of me nonstop without sleeping?" The thought of having a stranger tend to her while she slept should be disconcerting, yet she didn't really mind it so much with him. Jaxon studied him. Physically he was beautiful, much like the mythical Greek gods. But his weary eyes had seen far too much, and she was definitely worried that he wasn't getting enough sleep. She had an unexpected urge to reach up and touch his beard-shadowed jaw.

"I am the one taking care of *you*, honey." A faint smile curved his perfectly sculpted mouth. "You do not need to think of anyone else but yourself. Your wounds are healing nicely. Another day and we can return you to the hospital, so your friends can see for themselves that you are alive and recovering. I have reassured them, but they need to see you with their own eyes."

Lucian controlled human minds easily without giving it much thought. He had done so for many centuries. But this was a little more wearing, controlling so many different humans and at such a distance. He was not ready to relinquish his care of Jaxon to hospital workers until he was certain they would immediately release her to come home. He wanted no blood tests performed on her, and he knew she would be very vulnerable in a hospital should Tyler Drake or any of the enemies she had acquired through her work decide to finish the job someone had clearly started.

"I want to sit up." She attempted to do so, surprised she still felt so weak.

At once Lucian caught her slight body in his hands and easily lifted her into a sitting position. He carefully tucked the pillows behind her and the blankets around her. She was even paler than usual. "Breathe deeply, and you will not faint." He made it a decree.

She found herself smiling. "Do you have any idea how bizarre this is? I know this is no hospital. It isn't even some kind of sanitarium, is it? And you're no doctor."

He moved across the room with swift, fluid, totally silent steps. She couldn't help comparing the way he moved to that of a large jungle cat. There was something menacing about him, yet at the same time something quite sensual. He made her feel secure and safe, yet threatened in a way she had never been before. Which was it? Safe or in danger? If he was such a predator, why wasn't her inner warning system shrieking at her? She let her breath out slowly, carefully. She felt threatened as a woman, not as a law enforcement officer, she realized.

Lucian turned to face her, the window behind him. Outside, the night was dark and a bit stormy. She could hear rain falling in a steady pattern and wind blowing through the trees, making their branches rake the walls. "I may not be a doctor in the usual sense of the word, but I do heal people. I healed you."

Again, Jaxon knew it was true. She knew all kinds of things about him. Things she shouldn't have known. Intimate things. She knew he had traveled the world, every continent, several times. He spoke countless languages. He was wealthy, yet money meant nothing to him except as a means to an end. She knew he had been searching for her for a long, long time.

As she assessed the situation, Lucian's black eyes watched her carefully, unblinking, the eyes of a predator watching its prey. His mind was a shadow in hers, observing her thoughts, the way her mind worked, the way she was analyzing her own feelings.

Jaxon was aware of that strange phenomenon, the way her heart beat matched the rhythm of his, the way her breathing seemed to slow to the pace of his. How did she know so much about Lucian when he was a complete stranger to her? She knew he loved art and antiquities. He had extensive knowledge of both and of the artists and artisans who had created them, yet only recently had he found joy and beauty in paintings and sculptures, antiques and music. He had healed countless people, healed them in some strange and unique way. That part was hazy to her, locked away somewhere in her brain for further study. He had healed her in the same way he had those others.

"You talked to me while I was asleep," she murmured, trying to come up with a reasonable explanation for why she knew so much about him. "Is that how I know so many things about you?"

Lucian shrugged carelessly, the movement fluid and flawlessly casual. "Does it really matter?" Simply looking at her made him want to smile. It was amazing how her mere existence had already changed his life. He wanted to look at her for all time. The shape of her face, the curve of her cheek, her long lashes, everything. After all the dark ugliness, the truly evil things he had seen over the centuries, Jaxon was a miracle to him.

Everything about Lucian was mesmerizing to Jaxx. She never wanted to leave him. She wanted to remain here, locked away in their own world, far from what she knew was reality. She felt safe and warm. She loved the way he looked at her. Occasionally she saw in his eyes unexpected flashes—flashes of desire, of possessiveness, of warmth and tenderness. She very much wanted to savor those things. To hold them to her.

"I guess it doesn't matter," she found herself replying.

His voice was so soft. Hearing it was like being wrapped in velvet. But Jaxon was not about to fool herself. As sexy and exciting as Lucian was, she had the feeling that if she was stupid enough to give him a free hand, he could easily take on the male, domineering arrogance that set her teeth on edge.

He burst out laughing, the sound drifting over her skin like the touch of fingers. A shaft of desire hit her, then blossomed into full-blown need. That terrified her. She was unprepared for such intense feelings. Did her reaction to him show? She actually looked around guiltily, afraid someone else might observe her looking at Lucian.

"You have to take me home," she said. Her voice was husky. She could feel tears clogging her throat. This was all a fantasy. Reality was stark and ugly. Her presence here would get this beautiful man killed. He would pay the ultimate price because she had looked upon him with longing. Because he had been kind enough to help her.

Lucian glided across the room so swiftly, she actually didn't see him move. He was a tall, muscular man, elegant in every way, silent when he walked, but she still should have seen him. All she had done was blink, and he was standing over her, reaching for her chin with two fingers. He tilted her head up, forcing her to look into his black eyes. At once she felt herself falling forward, into him, a part of him, warm and safe.

"There is no need for your distress, honey. I cannot have it. You actually make my heart ache." His thumb was feathering back and forth across her skin, sending waves of heat racing through her bloodstream. "No one can harm you."

"I'm not worried about me, you idiot." Jaxon was provoked. He didn't seem to understand the danger he was in. He really was arrogant.

Suddenly his demeanor changed completely. His smile faded, and his eyes became as cold as ice. He turned his head toward the window. She clearly saw the predator in him then. The hunter. There was no gentleness, no softness; he was a warrior without any conscience to hinder him.

"Stay here, Jaxon," he murmured almost absently, clearly expecting obedience. "I will be back soon."

And just like that, he was gone. Another blink, and he was no longer in the room. She sat there, unerringly finding her gun beneath the covers. Her hand wrapped around it—an extension of her arm, it was so familiar. She felt now what Lucian had felt, the darkness stealing into their world. It crept in slowly, seeping into her mind so insidiously that, at first, she hadn't recognized it. Danger had found them in this place of safety.

The feeling was overwhelming, so much so that Jaxon almost couldn't breathe. Whoever was stalking them was wholly evil. She was certain Tyler Drake had found her once again. He was relentless in his pursuit. Invincible. No one had so much as come near enough to him to even wound him. He killed at will.

Once, since he had murdered her family and then her foster family, it had been a neighbor of hers, one Jaxon enjoyed having coffee with—a young woman in a wheelchair with a zest for life and a ready smile. Jaxon had never allowed herself to have a real friend since. Even on the job she made certain it appeared as if she changed partners often. In public she never smiled at them or socialized with them, not wanting to trigger Tyler's killing rage. This situation—Jaxon alone in a man's house—was the perfect scenario to provoke Tyler once more, a vengeful maniac determined to murder Lucian.

Lucian clearly didn't appreciate the extent of Tyler's Navy SEALs training. He was a chameleon, blending into any landscape. He was a superb sniper, capable of taking out a target from an extraordinary distance. Jaxon recognized Lucian as a dangerous man. It was in his eyes, in the set of shoulders, the confidence in his walk, the way he moved. But that didn't mean Tyler Drake couldn't get to him just as he had gotten to her equally well-trained father and foster father, Russell Andrews.

Jaxon tossed back the covers. She was wearing only a man's silk shirt. As she was short, the shirt fell well past her knees, and, in any case, modesty was the last thing she was worried about. The feeling of danger was now stronger than ever. Lucian was in trouble, and she needed to go to him. He didn't know her that well, didn't realize the extent of her training and what an asset she could be.

Standing was more difficult than she'd thought it would be. She hadn't been in an upright position for days. Her legs felt rubbery, and she was terribly weak. Ignoring the way her body protested, she moved toward the door, careful not to make a sound She didn't know the layout of the house, and, judging by the size of her room, the building was huge, but she was confident she could find Lucian. She felt connected to him. She wouldn't allow anything to happen to him. To Jaxon, it was that simple. She would not let him be hurt for any reason, least of all on her account.

Her bedroom opened out into a long, wide landing with a sweeping staircase on either end. The carpets were thick and looked brand new. Every detail about the house looked ideal. Jaxon noticed it all because it was so perfect, as if Lucian had lovingly brought in every item personally. Each painting, each sculpture, the wall paper and carpets and stained glass—it was everything she had ever dreamed of, right down to her preference in antique furniture.

Jaxon went by it all silently, her bare feet making no sound as she began her descent down the stairs. Halfway down, she spotted an alcove cut into the wall, an ornate glass door leading to a small balcony. She opened the door, taking great care to do so in complete silence. At once the rain drenched her, the wind so cold she began to tremble. She barely noticed. Her eyes were adjusting to the darkness, seeking her target.

At first she could see nothing. A jagged bolt of lightning arced across the sky, lighting the courtyard below. She could see Lucian standing completely motionless in the very center of the immense patio. Several yards away from him a second figure cloaked in along black cape stood in deeper shadows. She found that her eyes seemed to adjust quickly to the lack of light, giving her excellent night vision, and her acute hearing, new and odd to her, picked up the strange conversation between the two men.

Lucian's voice was even more beautiful than usual, pitched low and with a velvet purity that crept beneath the skin and seeped into the mind. "I can do no other than oblige you, Henrique," he said, "when you have come so far to call on me with so blatant a challenge."

"I did not know it was you, Lucian." The second voice was a horrible, scratchy noise that grated like fingernails on a chalkboard. "You have been thought dead these last five centuries. Indeed, it was believed you had joined our ranks."

The figure turned, and Jaxon could see him perfectly. The sight was horrifying. His head was a mere gray, pitted, bullet-shaped skull, with a few strands of long hair straggling across the top. His eyes glowed crimson, and his nose was no more than a gaping hole. His gums were receded, his teeth jagged and stained. When the creature lifted a hand, his long nails were like talons. He looked hideous.

Jaxon wanted to cry out a warning to Lucian. The stranger tried to sound ingratiating, but she could feel the strong waves of hatred radiating from him. Deep inside where she knew things others didn't, she knew the monster facing Lucian had every intention of attacking him at the first opportunity.

"The trouble with listening to gossip, Henrique, is that it can be so completely wrong. I am the dispenser of justice for our people. I have always been loyal to our Prince and always will be. You have chosen to break our Carpathian laws and those of all mankind."

Lucian's voice was so beautiful, Jaxon felt completely caught up in it. She had to shake her head several times to keep her mind on what was important. The biting cold helped considerably, as did the driving rain. She sighted down the barrel of her gun, the weapon rock steady in her hands. She was going for a head shot, taking no chance that the stranger might be concealing a weapon of his own.

Henrique began to move slowly, his feet weaving a strange pattern on the cobblestones in the courtyard. He looked like a stick figure, ugly and evil, something out of a horror film. Lucian seemed not to turn, yet he remained facing Henrique at all times. Jaxon found the movement of the stranger's feet fascinating. She leaned farther out over the wrought-iron railing in order to see better. The rain plastered her shaggy mop of hair to her head. Raindrops hung on her long eyelashes, and the wind blew water into her eyes. But once more the weather served to help Jaxon free herself from the strange enthrallment the stranger's movements produced in her. The gun was once more aimed steadily on the stranger's head. Should he make a move, he would not have the time to hurt Lucian.

Without warning the stranger's tall, thin frame contorted. Jaxon fought back a scream as the man became an animal, a wild wolf, patched and maned, sharp fangs filling the jaw thrusting straight at Lucian. Powerful hind legs dug into the stones, allowing the animal to leap at Lucian in an attempt to tear at flesh and arteries.

Lucian burst into the air so swiftly he was a mere blur. Jaxon tried to compose herself despite the bizarre phenomenon, sighting on the terrible beast. Its fangs were

Christine Feehan

dripping saliva, and the eyes were glowing red with hatred. Thunder was cracking so loudly it was hurting her
ears as bolt after bolt of lightning lit the sky. Even as she
thought Lucian would come crashing down to the hard
stones and the wolf would tear him apart, he landed easily, almost casually, on top of the beast, his hands twisting
the head savagely. The crack of its neck was loud in the
night air. Then Lucian leaped away from the animal.

It bellowed loudly, shape-shifting again so that it was
once more a man, its head flopping hideously to one side,
its discolored teeth snapping and gnashing at Lucian.
Jaxon could see that Lucian's powerful hands had broken
its neck, yet the creature was somehow still extremely
dangerous. She squeezed the trigger and saw the hole
blossom in the center of the repulsive forehead even as
Lucian seemed to disappear for a moment.

Jaxon nearly fainted when she saw Lucian appear right
beside the creature. She wanted to scream at him to get
away from the awful thing, but her throat was closed with
terror, and no sound emerged. To her horror, the beast
was still ripping at Lucian with the grotesque talons he
had for fingernails. Lucian thrust one arm forward, a
powerful blur that buried his fist deeply in the creature's
chest cavity. Jaxon heard a terrible sucking sound, and
when Lucian withdrew his hand, in his palm was the creature's pulsating heart. Lucian leaped back as the body
flopped to the ground with a high-pitched scream. Impossibly, the creature wriggled around, the hands stretching greedily toward Lucian. It began to pull itself
relentlessly across the cobblestones.

Intellectually Jaxon knew none of this could be happening—all of it was beyond the scope of reality—but she
aimed her gun squarely on the repulsive creature dragging
itself toward Lucian. She could see its dark blood spreading like a stain across the cobblestones. Without warning
a fiery ball slammed from the sky onto the ghastly, night-

marish figure flopping about in the courtyard, incinerating it. It completely consumed all evidence of the creature and the blood that had been spilled. She watched as Lucian casually tossed the heart into the flames and then held his hands over the fire. The blood staining his skin was gone as if it had never been, yet, miraculously, he was not burned. Jaxon stared down at the scene below. The storm was passing, the wind carrying the ashes off to the south. And then there was only Lucian standing alone in the courtyard. He turned and looked straight up at Jaxon.

She couldn't breathe. She could only stand there staring at him with her mouth open. She realized she was still aiming her gun. The thought entered her head to shoot him. Had she gone crazy, or had he done impossible things? She was already backing into the house. It would take him only a few minutes to make his way from the courtyard back into the house, and he knew the grounds and the layout of the building, while she did not. Jaxon ran lightly down the stairs and turned in the opposite direction from the courtyard. Almost immediately she spotted a door. Jerking it open, she ran out into the darkness of the night. She sought high ground, somewhere she could conceal herself but observe if he was moving toward her. But she ran straight into what appeared to be a solid wall.

Instantly she was steadied by two strong hands. Lucian was standing in front of her—another impossibility. No way could he have gotten from the courtyard to where she was that fast. The whole house had been between them.

Jaxon attempted to bring the gun around to point at him. She heard his soft laughter very close to her ear.

"I do not think that is a very good idea for either of us, honey." He swept the gun from her hand, taking possession easily, and swung her into his arms, cradling her against his chest, his upper body leaning forward to shelter her from the rain. "You do not obey very well, do you?" He asked it with that same note of mild amusement that always did something peculiar to her heart.

"I want to leave." She was trembling so hard her teeth chattered, uncertain whether it was from the cold and rain or her fear of Lucian and of what he was. Because, clearly, he was no ordinary man. No matter that he was handsome and sexy and had a beautiful voice.

He moved rapidly into the house. Behind them the door closed firmly. "I told you to stay in bed."

"I wanted to help." She buried her face against his shoulder because there was nowhere else to go, and she was freezing and scared and exhausted. He was warm and strong and gave her the impression that he could manage anything easily. He gave her the feeling that she was safe with him. "I couldn't let you face whatever was out there by yourself." To her horror, it came out as an apology.

"You managed to scare yourself to death," he observed without inflection.

She raised her head and glared at him accusingly. "*I* didn't do it. What *was* that thing? I shot it straight through the head. You broke its neck. Even after you ripped out its heart—and don't even tell me how you managed that—the thing kept coming for you."

"It was a vampire." He said it softly, as he said everything, calmly, matter-of-factly.

Everything in Jaxon went still. Even her breath seemed to cease. She wanted to believe there was no such thing, but what she had witnessed was undeniable. Her breath came out in a long hiss as she held up a hand. "Don't tell me any more. Nothing. I don't want to hear another word."

"Your heart is beating too fast, Jaxon," Lucian pointed out gently. He pushed open the door to the large bathroom with one elegantly shod foot.

"Answer me this one thing. Am I in a sanitarium? If

I've lost my mind, it's okay to tell me. I think I want to know at least that much."

"You are being silly," he said softly in his black-velvet voice.

She closed her eyes to get away from him, from the tremendous power he seemed to wield over her. Due to the fact that she was freezing and weak and he had her gun, the only real attack that might work long enough to free her would be to go for his eyes. But he had extraordinarily beautiful eyes. It would be such a shame to ruin them. She didn't know if she could force herself to do such a thing.

She heard his laugh then, low and intimate. *Thank God for the gift of my beautiful eyes. I would not want you to attempt to do something so terrible to me.*

Her long lashes flew open, and she stared up at him more in accusation than astonishment. "You can read my thoughts! That's how you knew which door I chose to run out of. You read my thoughts!"

"I must confess, that is the truth." He sounded very amused now. He cradled her in his lap, next to the heat of his body, while he ran steamy water into the huge sunken tub. He added some bath salts from a beautifully shaped bottle. A wave of his hand lit several aromatic candles.

"I *didn't* see you do that," Jaxon denied, turning her head away from him. "But I've caught the fact that you don't necessarily always speak out loud to me. You laugh and talk to me, but in my head, in my thoughts." She pushed her forehead into her hands. "I'm in real trouble this time, aren't I?" She was trembling hard, and this time she was certain she was more afraid than cold. At least she still had enough of her faculties left to know she should be afraid of him.

"You are just as capable of speaking to me in the same way, honey," he replied, his voice soothing. "Jaxon, look

Christine Feehan

at me. Do not hide from this. What would be the point?" Lucian found she was turning him inside out. She brought such joy into his formerly bleak, violent world.

She raised her head so that her large chocolate-brown eyes could meet his black ones.

"You are not afraid of me," he insisted. "Search inside yourself. The knowledge that there are things in your world you knew nothing about is understandably frightening, but you do not fear me."

"And how do you know that?" She would not fall into his eyes and allow him to mesmerize her. That was it, right? He had some kind of black magic spell thing he did with his eyes. She just wouldn't look into them again.

His perfect mouth curved into a smile. "I have shared your mind. I know all kinds of things about you. Just as you know all manner of things about me."

"Well, I don't want to know them," she snapped. "I don't want any part of any of this. I shot that thing right in the middle of his forehead, dead center, and he didn't die."

"There is only one way to kill a vampire and ensure that he does not rise again. You must extract his heart and incinerate it. His blood acts like tainted acid on the skin or poison if ingested into the bloodstream. It must also be destroyed. Even after death a vampire can cause tremendous damage if not disposed of properly."

She glared at him. "I told you I didn't want to know any more."

He began to undo the buttons of her shirt, slipping each one carefully from the buttonhole. His fingers brushed warmth over her soft skin, leaving behind tiny dancing flames. She caught at his hands, stilling their actions. "Just what do you think you're doing?" She tried to look outraged instead of shocked and horrified by her own body's reaction to him.

"I am removing your wet clothes. They are not doing

64

you much good, honey, if your intention is to hide your body from me. The rain-soaked shirt is now completely transparent." He pointed out the obvious without any inflection in his velvet-soft voice. "You are very cold, and you need to warm up. I thought this was the best way. But I would be most happy to choose another, if you wish."

She pushed at the wall of his chest, turning bright red at his implication. He was right; the wet silk shirt revealed everything. "Go away. I am absolutely not taking a bath with you in the room."

He studied her face. She was very pale. All eyes. In her mind was confusion and fear but no real resistance. She was not the type to throw herself out a window. "I would not like it if you slipped and fell, young one."

"It's insulting to have you refer to me as 'young one,' as if I were a child. I'm a grown woman," she informed him haughtily.

His smile nearly took her breath away.

"That is what I am afraid of," he said.

"What does that mean?"

"It means, Jaxon, that I am much too old for you." Lucian's black eyes moved over her face with that possessive glint very much in evidence. "And yet there is no other for me, for either of us. We are stuck with each other."

"Go away." She pushed impotently at his broad chest again. "I'm going to soak in the bathtub for a very long time and convince myself none of this happened. I must be on drugs or something. Or the blow to my head has left me very confused."

"You never received a blow to the head." Amusement turned the warm velvet of his voice to pure seduction. "That was your partner."

"Go!" This time she pointed to the door.

He gently allowed her feet to touch the tiles. Shaking

his head at her silliness, he glided casually out of the room.

Jaxon took a deep, calming breath and let it out slowly. There simply were no such things as vampires in the world. It just wasn't so. She tossed the wet shirt aside and slipped thankfully down into the hot water.

Yes, there are. You just saw one. His name was Henrique, and he was not very skilled. There are many more. Do not worry, Jaxon. I am a hunter of the undead, and I will protect you.

He was in her mind again. She shook her head as if that would remove him. "I don't want to know anything about vampires. I could go my entire life without that information and be perfectly happy. I don't want to know." What if Lucian was a vampire himself? He had gotten from the courtyard to the door she was fleeing out of, and the entire huge house had been between them. How had he managed it? "And what about all my dreams of dark princes and blood and icky things like that?" she murmured aloud to herself.

Icky things? He was definitely laughing at her. *I am no vampire, although I pretended to be for a few centuries to help out my brother. I am a Carpathian, a hunter of vampires, those of my kind who have surrendered their souls to the darkness that exists within all Carpathian males.*

"A few *centuries*? Just how old are you, anyway? Wait! Don't answer that. I don't want to know. Just stop talking to me. This is crazy. I must be on very powerful drugs, and soon I'll wake up in the hospital, and everything will be back to normal. I made you up. What I'm going to do is ignore you and take a bath. Vampires and you are gone forever from my mind. So don't talk to me."

Lucian found himself laughing aloud. The sound startled him. He couldn't remember laughter. It felt good. He placed a palm on the bathroom door. He had endured nearly two thousand years of emptiness, of darkness and violence. No emotions. Nothing. His own people, those he had protected, had been so afraid of his power and skill that they whispered his name and hid when he passed through the land. Yet one small human woman had worked a miracle and brought laughter into his life.

He had no qualms about what he was. A killing machine designed to protect Carpathians and humans alike from evil. He was more than good at his role. He destroyed easily without anger or remorse.

But Jaxon Montgomery was the most beautiful thing he had ever encountered. She was his, and he would never give her up. But was she changing him? His palm caressed the door behind which she bathed, his heart turning over strangely, unexpectedly.

The hot water warmed Jaxon's insides but stung her healing wounds. She frowned down at the evidence of the recent shoot-out at the warehouse. She should have died from those grave wounds. And all her misery finally would have been over. She drew up her knees and rested her head on top of them. Now her burden of responsibility was worse than ever. She would have to protect the world not only from human criminals but from the things of nightmares. She couldn't do it. Not anymore. She just couldn't be in this world anymore and be so completely alone. The mere thought of it left her raw and aching.

You will never be alone again, honey. The voice, so soft and beautiful, was filled with compassion.

Jaxon made every effort to rally. "I told you not to talk to me."

I am thinking, not talking. The tenderness mixed with amusement in his voice made her heart turn over, made her feel all the more vulnerable.

"Well, don't think either." She ran a hand through her wet hair. This kind of thing just didn't happen to normal people. Why did she attract such weird things?

I am not a thing.

"I can't hear you." She was smiling in spite of herself. There was something almost endearing about him, if such a frightening creature could be called endearing. Her eyes suddenly widened. He had known she was out there. The entire time. He had known she was on that balcony.

"You did, didn't you?" She whispered it, but she knew he would hear her. If she could hear him in her head, he could hear her whisper.

Yes.

"And you can erase all this from my mind." It made sense. How else could someone like Lucian remain hidden from the world? "Why did you let me see that hideous thing? I'll never get that image out of my head."

You would not want me to erase your knowledge. Not of anything. I know you would not. The temptation is there, naturally, but you would not wish such a thing, and I have too much respect for you to make the decision for you.

She rubbed her aching forehead. He was right. It was a temptation to forget the horrors she had seen. She wanted to scream at him that no one could assimilate such knowledge. But he was right. She would hate for him to make such a decision for her, and she would never choose ignorance. But what did this new knowledge mean to her future? What could it mean?

For no apparent reason, Jaxon started to cry. Once the tears started, she could not control them. Great sobs welled up, shaking her with their intensity. She never cried. Never! Jaxon deliberately went under the water, hoping to wash away the tears. It would be humiliating to have Lucian catch her crying. At once came the knowledge that he had to be aware; he was there in her mind, a shadow monitoring her most private thoughts and memories. She came up so fast, she hit her head on a faucet. Yelping, Jaxon stood up in the enormous tub, water running off her body.

Lucian materialized directly in front of her, his black eyes anxious as he reached for a large bath towel. Jaxon gasped audibly. "My God, you just appeared out of nowhere! You didn't even come through the door!"

He enveloped her in the towel. She was far too much of a temptation standing there naked, confused, her eyes enormous and water running off her slim body. Pulling her into the shelter of his large frame, he began to dry her. "Doors really are not all that necessary, honey."

"Evidently locking them wouldn't do much good," she pointed out. She tilted her head to study his handsome face. "I'm tired, Lucian. I need to lie down."

He swept her into his arms. She looked so fragile. One good, strong wind might blow her over. "If you cry anymore, honey, my heart is going to break." He meant it, too. His heart actually ached for her. There were dark circles under her eyes. Cradling her close to his chest, against the steady beat of his heart, he glided through the house, up the stairs, and back to her bedroom. Very gently he placed her back in bed.

"You will sleep now, Jaxon," he commanded.

His voice made her want to do whatever it was he asked of her. No, commanded of her. That was what it was—a command—and she was so mesmerized by the beauty and purity of his voice, she succumbed to his power.

"Am I right? Is that what you do?" She allowed him to help her into another shirt His fingers once again spread flames everywhere they brushed her skin as he buttoned it for her. Resolutely, he pulled the covers up to her chin.

"Yes, with my voice and my eyes I can easily control others." He admitted it shamelessly, the same way he did everything else, matter-of-factly, in his soft, gentle tone.

A faint smile lit her large eyes for a moment "You admit it so easily. How many others like you exist out there?"

"Not many anymore. We Carpathians are dying out. Very few of our males can find their lifemates."

She closed her eyes. "I know I shouldn't ask. I know I shouldn't, but I can't help myself. What is a lifemate?" Her long lashes lifted, and laughter danced warily in the depths of her eyes, despite their shimmer of teardrops.

He ruffled her hair, his fingers combing it into some semblance of control. "You are a lifemate, honey. My lifemate. It has taken nearly two thousand years to find you, and I never dared to believe in such a miracle in all that time."

She held up a hand, palm out. "I knew better. I knew I wouldn't want to hear this. Nearly two thousand years, you say? That would make you *way* old. You're right— you're far too old for me."

His strong white teeth flashed. They were perfectly straight, his mouth sensuous. Everything about him was perfect. She glared at him. "Couldn't you at least look wrinkled and dusty, with most of your teeth missing?"

Lucian laughed, the sound so beautiful she could feel the whisper of butterfly wings in her stomach. He was incredibly charismatic. She knew she had fallen under his spell. Were her emotions real, or was he suggesting them to her? She had never had these feelings for anyone. It was frightening how strong the emotions he evoked in her were.

"Neither have I felt such before." He said it starkly. Honestly. The purity of his voice made it impossible for him to be lying. "I have never wanted another woman this way, Jaxon. For me, there is only you."

"You can't have me. I live in a world that doesn't include love. There's no room for you. Tyler Drake may not be a vampire, but he's very dangerous. I will not be

70

Dark Guardian

responsible for any other deaths. I have enough blood on my hands for an entire army." She wasn't going to believe in this vampire nonsense, she decided. That was all there was to it. Otherwise, she would have to be committed. God in heaven, maybe she *wanted* to be committed.

He took her hands in his, turned them this way and that to inspect them carefully. He brought her palms to the warmth of his mouth, then pressed a kiss into the exact center of each hand. "I do not see one drop of blood, honey. You have never been responsible for what Tyler Drake has chosen to do."

"You aren't listening to me." She sounded sad, snuggling more deeply into the pillows. Once again she felt safe, when she knew that couldn't possibly be true. "I will not take chances with your life."

Lucian laughed again. Jaxon could hear the genuine amusement in his voice.

"You still do not understand me, young one, but you will soon enough."

71

Chapter Three

The sounds and smells told Jaxon she was in a hospital. She opened her eyes warily. She was lying in a bed, but she could still feel her gun in her hand. A nurse was hovering nearby.

The woman smiled at Jaxon. "You're awake. Good. The doctor is planning to release you this evening. He was worried about your going home alone, but your fiancé assured him you would be well taken care of."

Jaxon's heart sank. She was hoping she had merely dreamed about vampires and dark, sexy, "Carpathian" strangers, but she was more than certain she had had no fiancé prior to being shot. She stayed very still. She had no idea what to say, how to respond. She didn't know even know how she had come to be in a hospital. The nurse was bustling around, opening the curtains, and allowing Jaxon to see that the sun was already down.

Jaxon realized she no longer felt safe. She was in an environment where she had little or no control. If Tyler wanted to get to her, it would be easy. He could disguise himself as an orderly and waltz right into her room. And she was alone again. For a few precious moments of her life she had really shared with someone—Lucian—however bizarre that event had been. Now she was alone and once more responsible for the safety of those around her.

You do not listen very well, Jaxon. There was that soft, soothing voice. *Either that, or I have completely misread your intelligence and need to explain things much more clearly and carefully to you.* She heard a tinge of masculine amusement.

Jaxon looked around her quickly. No one else was in the room with her but the nurse. The nurse appeared not to have noticed any disembodied voice. *Now you've got me hearing voices. I'm going to the nearest mental institution and insisting on immediate help.* She chose her thoughts carefully, willing him to hear her response.

He laughed. She could hear his genuine amusement, that velvet-soft and beautiful, perfectly pitched voice that seemed to caress her whether he was touching her or not. It was so very familiar now, a part of her she never wanted to lose.

But you have to go away. She was taking a firm stand on this. Either she was completely crazy and he was a figment of her imagination because she needed someone so desperately, or he was very real—and more trouble than she could handle.

I doubt if you would make up someone as domineering as I. You would want some fop to order about so you could continue believing you have to protect everyone.

That isn't funny, Lucian. You have no idea what Tyler Drake is like. Some of the best people in this country have tried to catch him and failed. You're so arrogant, you're going to get yourself killed. I hate that trait in men. It isn't bravery; it's sheer stupidity. I know Drake is dangerous, and I'm always prepared, because I don't imagine myself so much more skilled than he is. There was an edge

73

to her voice. She was becoming irritated with Lucian's arrogance.

His voice never changed, remaining as gentle and soothing as ever. *It is not arrogance, Jaxon, when one knows one's own abilities. I have confidence because I know who I am, what I am. I am a hunter. It is what I do.*

He's a killer. It's what he does.

You are becoming distressed. I will be with you soon to take you home with me. We will have plenty of time to discuss this. In the meantime do whatever the doctor says to get you released.

Jaxon became aware that the nurse was staring at her. She blinked rapidly to focus her attention on what the woman was saying. "I'm sorry, I was off in my own little world. What were you saying?" She forced a small smile.

"I think anyone with a fiancé like yours *would* be off in her own little world. Is he really a billionaire? What would that be like? I can't conceive of a billion dollars. He met last night with the hospital board and is giving a huge donation in thanks for taking such good care of you. He had this room guarded day and night." Her voice turned dreamy. "He said you were his world and he couldn't breathe without you. Imagine a man saying that right out loud to a roomful of other men. I'd give anything to have my husband feel that way about me."

"He probably does," Jaxon murmured, afraid of saying anything else. She was not engaged to Lucian. "Did he call himself my fiancé?"

What else could I do, honey? Refer to you as my lifemate? They understand that being your fiancé gives me certain rights to direct your life while you are ill. They would never understand that as my lifemate you are the other half of my soul. Do not panic yet. I am merely ensuring your safety.

I don't understand what being a lifemate means.

I could explain it to you. . . . he offered solemnly.

No! I don't think I want to hear another word about it! Not one word, Lucian. She knew darn well that he wasn't in the least bit serious, and his annoying habit of laughing at her was going to get him into major trouble. He had the idea that because she was so small, she was not a force to reckoned with. She intended to change that impression soon if he kept it up. *A billionaire? Isn't that just a bit dramatic? What if someone asks you to prove it? I thought the idea was to keep a low profile.* She was deliberately impudent, trying to hide the fact that she was happy he was so very real.

Hiding out in the open is always the best way. And living for centuries gives one the ability to amass a fortune. It is relatively easy. The more money one has, the more one has the ability to hide his true identity. People expect a certain amount of eccentricity in those with money. Thus, it is merely another tool I use.

You cannot be a billionaire on top of everything else. You're making me completely crazy. You know that, don't you?

"Jaxx!" Barry Radcliff was in her doorway, his large frame leaning against the jamb, a huge grin of relief spreading across his face. "Thank God. They kept telling me you were getting better, but for some reason or other, I could never actually lay eyes on you. They've been feeding me all kinds of crap about some fiancé. I keep telling them you don't have one, but no one listens to me, not even the captain. He claims he met the guy, some foreign billionaire, and that the rumors are true. I thought maybe that bullet in the head put me in another world."

The nurse left to give them privacy.

"At least you have an excuse." Jaxon was so relieved to see someone normal, she felt like crying again. "And why didn't you keep your butt out of that warehouse, like I told you? Do you have a hero complex, too, Barry?"

He walked slowly, carefully, across the room as if his legs were shaky and managed an awkward, one-armed hug.

I forgot to mention I am a very jealous man, honey. Do not go too far with being happy to see this male. The texture of Lucian's voice in her head was the same, yet not. It was softer than ever, velvet over iron. A subtle warning.

Get over it. He's my partner. Deliberately Jaxon hugged Barry back when normally she never would have done so.

You hide your own feelings from yourself. You regard this one with great affection.

If that's so, it was pretty dumb of you to clue me in on my true feelings, now, wasn't it? she asked sweetly, allowing Barry to retain possession of her hand as he sat at the end of her bed. "Do you remember what happened, Barry? Because I don't remember anything but getting shot." She was curious. She didn't have a clue how either of them had gotten out of the warehouse when they were both seriously wounded.

Confusion clouded Barry's gray eyes. "You know, I have nightmares about it. I don't know either. In my nightmare a huge wolf kills all the bad guys like some avenging angel, then turns into a man, drags my butt out of there, and then carries you off. Don't tell the boss, though—he's already got some psychiatrist hanging around my door." Barry rubbed a hand over his face. "I can't remember the man, only the wolf, the eyes. The way it looked at me. But I'd swear a man appeared out of nowhere to rescue us."

It was you. You saved us. I should have known. She had known. Deep down inside was a memory—Lucian's or her own, she wasn't certain—but she had touched upon it and rejected it. There was blood and death and something so erotic and altogether wrong—some kind of bizarre healing ritual perhaps?—that Jaxon never wanted to touch on it again.

I was not about to allow you to escape me even through death, Jaxon. I enjoy your sense of humor so much. There was that gentleness that turned her heart over, that told her he knew she was frightened and alone and utterly confused.

Jaxon had the feeling that he was much closer this time, his presence stronger in her mind, not a mere shadow. Involuntarily she glanced nervously at the door. "Don't worry, Barry, I think both of us need to stay as far from a psychiatrist as possible. They'd probably commit me. I'm having a few nightmares of my own."

Barry shifted toward her, leaning close. He lowered his voice. "Since we're alone here, I might as well tell you this isn't the first weird experience I've had. Do you remember that serial killer who was terrorizing the city a few months back? Of course you do. I was first on the scene after the third murder. I was off duty and in the area. I swear I saw a wolf there. He turned his head and looked at me, and I saw intelligence in his eyes. Real intelligence. It was eerie. He looked at me as if he was measuring my worth or something, deciding whether or not to kill me. Just like in the warehouse. But then it wasn't a wolf anymore; it was a man, and for the life of me, I can't remember what he looked like. Not even his build. You know me, Jaxx. I remember the smallest detail, yet twice now I've seen a wolf where there couldn't have been one, and I can't describe a man I saw, not the one at a murder scene and not the one who saved our lives."

"What are you saying, Barry?" Jaxon's heart was beginning to pound in alarm again. Had it been Lucian? What was Lucian? Could he have projected the image of a wolf?

Barry shrugged. "I don't know what I'm saying. I only know I saw the damn thing. It was real. And it looked

like the one in the warehouse. It was massive, well-fed.
Not some stray dog, like the captain suggested. It had
peculiar eyes. Very black, different than an animal's. They
burned with menace, and I mean burned. And they held
an almost . . . human intelligence." He shoved a hand
through his hair. "I checked to see if a wolf could have
escaped from a zoo or wildlife preserve, but no go, and
no one else saw the thing. There couldn't have been a
wolf, but . . . I don't know where I'm going with this, but
you're the only person I would admit this to."

*I was there hunting the vampire, Jaxon. Stop trying to
scare yourself.*

"I didn't see a wolf, Barry, but I've had some strange
nightmares myself. Maybe we're both crazy." She managed a faint smile. The sound of her heart pounding was
so loud she thought she might go mad.

"Maybe it goes with the territory, Jaxx. By the way,
are the rumors I'm hearing about you true, or another
nightmare? I'm your partner. Wouldn't I know something
like whether you had a fiancé? Especially if he was some
hotshot billionaire?"

Jaxx heard the hurt in his voice, could feel his pain cut
through her like a knife.

Lucian could feel her answering pain. *That is the problem, honey. You have way too much compassion in you.
You are not responsible for his feelings.*

*He's my partner, and I owe him my loyalty. Our little
charade will hurt him. I'm telling him it isn't really true,*
she said defiantly.

"Jaxx?" Barry prompted, his eyes steady on her face.

"You know how difficult my life has been, Barry," she
began reluctantly, not sure just what to say.

Lucian's wide shoulders filled the doorway. He was
dressed impeccably in a tailored suit, his long hair, as
shiny black as a raven's wing, pulled back and secured
with a leather thong at the nape of his neck. He took her

breath away. His very presence filled the room. He moved easily, fluidly, power clinging to him as he flowed across the floor to bend down and brush the top of her head with a kiss. The touch of his lips made her feel slightly faint. Then her heart found the slow, calming rhythm of his.

"Good evening, angel. I see you are allowed to visit with your partner. Barry, I am Lucian Daratrazanoff, Jaxon's fiancé. Please allow me to thank you for saving her life."

Barry turned his steady gray eyes back to Jaxon's face accusingly

Lucian sat on the edge of the bed, his large body crowding protectively close to hers. "Jaxon wanted to tell you about me; she agonized over it all the time. But she was afraid that somehow Tyler Drake would find out about me or that you were her confidant and he would harm you." He curved an arm around Jaxon's shoulders. "It is a difficult life she leads, and those of us who love her know she tries to protect us even when we would prefer she didn't. I know you understand why she kept silent."

Barry couldn't help listening to the cadence of the man's incredible voice. He looked away from Jaxon to Lucian, and it was like falling into a deep, bottomless sea of tranquility. Of course he understood. Jaxon always protected those around her. How could she have done anything else? And he liked Lucian; he could see that Lucian was good for Jaxon, would be able to take care of her. They would end up being great friends.

Don't you dare plant something in his head! Outraged, Jaxon tried to get around Lucian to shake Barry out of his trance. He was staring with what appeared to be rapture into Lucian's eyes.

Lucian did not take his gaze from Barry's. He merely restrained Jaxon with one hand. *Is this man important in your life?* he silently asked her.

You know he is. Don't you mess with his head!

If he is important to you, then it is imperative that he accept me. Hear me well, Jaxon. I cannot allow any other to know that my species exists. Do you understand what I am saying? I am willing for this man to come under my protection because of your affection for him. That is no small thing. But he must accept our relationship.

I don't accept our relationship. We don't have a relationship. For God's sake, I'm talking to you with my thoughts, not out loud like a normal human. I hear and see far better than I should, and you and I both know I should be dead. I wasn't, was I? You did some weird thing to me to bring me back, and now I'm a zombie or something. She ended on a note of near hysteria.

Lucian laughed softly and leaned to brush the corner of her mouth with his. "You are so beautiful, honey."

He didn't have to have that mouth. It had to be a sin to have a mouth like his. And his voice should be banned, too. "I am not, but I appreciate that you would say so." No one had ever described her as beautiful.

"There was no one to do so. Now you have me." He looked once more at Jaxon's partner.

Barry found himself smiling at the man. "I wish she had told me sooner, but of course I understand. Drake's a threat we haven't been able to keep out of her life. I hope you realize you will have to be on guard at all times. If you come down to the station, I'll show you everything we have on him. It's important you recognize him. There's a good chance he'll try to kill you."

Jaxon pulled her hand from Barry's and shifted away from Lucian, withdrawing into herself. "I think both of you should leave. This is too public a place. There's a good chance he's watching us right now."

Lucian again cradled Jaxon's small body, protectively sweeping her close beneath his shoulder as if he hadn't noticed that she was trying to keep away from him. *You worry altogether too much about Tyler Drake, honey. He is not invincible.*

Neither are you. Her wide dark eyes moved over his face almost lovingly, although she didn't know it. She decided she liked having someone to argue with. To worry about. To tease and laugh with.

I knew I would grow on you. There was his laughter again, velvet soft, seductive.

I'm just lonely. She tilted her chin at him defiantly. *A troglodyte would have done just as well, so don't start puffing up your chest.* He had a darn nice chest, truth be told.

His laughter set her pulse rate soaring, and the warmth of his breath on the back of her neck sent shivers of longing throughout her body. She turned to her partner, determined to ignore Lucian and his effect on her. "When do you get out of here, Barry? They're letting me out today."

"You nearly died. What are they thinking?" The shock was clear on Barry's face. "Are the doctors idiots?"

"I have connections," Lucian intervened softly, smoothly, once again his voice and eyes holding Barry spellbound. "I'm taking her to my home. The security there is very tight. No one gets in without my knowing about it. And I'll see to medical care for her. We won't have to worry so much about her. Here, let me give you my private number and address. You can reach us anytime in the evenings. I work almost exclusively in the evening and night, as I deal with so many different countries and time zones. Just make certain you leave your name, and either Jaxon or I will get back to you as soon as possible. When are you to be released?"

"They said maybe three days. Then I'm off work, on disability, for another three months at least. Then a desk job for a while. What about you, partner? You coming back soon?"

Lucian's fingers tangled in hers. Deliberately he brought her knuckles to the warmth of his lips. "I would rather she not answer that or even think about it at this time. You know how stubborn she is."

"There's no question that I'll be going back to work. It's what I do to make a living," she said indignantly.

Barry threw back his head and began to laugh. "You happen to be engaged to one of the wealthiest men on the face of the earth. I don't think making a living is going to be much of a problem for you."

She glared at him. "For your information, Lucian isn't nearly as rich as everyone keeps saying. And in any case, I like to work. We're not married yet, and anything could go wrong. Maybe it will never even happen. Did you think about that? And what if we did get married and it didn't work out? Do you have any idea how many marriages fail?"

"That is so like you, Jaxx. She already has her marriage failing," Barry pointed out, "and hasn't even tied the knot yet. Little Miss Pessimist."

"I'm a realist, Barry," she answered quietly.

Lucian's arms tightened around her, almost as if he was protecting her from Barry's teasing. He could feel the hurt in her mind. She was laughing, but her mind was filled with sorrow. Barry had no idea, though he was her partner and had been for some time. Lucian was certain none of those who thought they really knew her could read her at all. There had been no real laughter in her life; she tried to find moments to enjoy where she could, but always she was aware of the threat to those she became too friendly with. It never left her mind, that terrible burden. The idea of sharing her life with someone was nothing more than a beautiful fantasy to her. An impossible dream.

Lucian's fingers found the nape of her neck and began a slow, soothing massage. He was asking quite a bit of Jaxon to accept the things she had seen, the things he had told her. She hadn't closed her mind to the possibility of another humanlike species. She also hadn't closed her mind completely to the possibility that she might be going crazy or that he might be an enemy.

"I'm glad your wounds weren't as bad as I thought they might be, Barry," Jaxon said softly, meaning it.

"You told me in the warehouse to quit being such a wimp," Barry contradicted.

"I was only trying to get you moving, to get you out of there," she pointed out.

"Oh, sure," her partner said, winking at Lucian over her head. "Of course, the docs thought they were going to have to take my arm off," Barry informed her. "The first X-rays showed such shattered bones, the doctors said the inside of my arm was just mush and they couldn't possibly save it. But I was lucky. I woke up a few hours later, before they were taking me to the operating room, and they said some mix-up must have occurred. My shoulder was broken, but otherwise the bullet just passed through without doing much damage. No one could explain it, but I didn't mind. I figured it was a miracle, and I was willing to accept it."

Jaxon went still inside. She knew what had happened. Lucian had happened. He had healed Barry because Barry mattered to her. She knew it instinctively; she knew it without asking. And she didn't want to know, because it meant Lucian really could do the things he said he could. Deliberately, she didn't look at him. How much had Barry actually seen that night in the warehouse? Was there anything in his memories that might in some way harm Lucian? Or, worse, would Lucian decide there was something that could condemn him? She rubbed at her suddenly pounding temples.

"Barry," Lucian said softly, "Jaxon is becoming tired, and I still have to get her home tonight. I know the two of you want to catch up, but it is too early for her to wear herself out." He added a subtle mental "push" to his voice, creating a gentle command but one impossible to disobey.

Barry nodded immediately, leaning over to brush a kiss on top of her head. Jaxon actually felt the sudden stillness in Lucian. He was like a great jungle cat coiled and ready to strike, yet as motionless as a mountain. She found herself holding her breath for no reason at all.

Lucian was smiling with what appeared to be genuine warmth, shaking Barry's hand and walking with him to the door. Then, when Barry was gone, he turned to look at her. "You do not trust me."

"You sound as if that amuses you." Jaxon was tired of pretending. "I don't know you, Lucian, not at all. The truth is, I haven't spent a whole lot of time with other people. I've made it a habit to be alone. I'm not sure I'm comfortable being around a stranger who knows so much about me, when I know nothing about him."

"You are quite capable of reading my mind, angel. Merge your thoughts with mine. You will find out anything you might want to know."

She shook her head, determined not to get caught by the magic of his voice. "I want to go home to my own apartment and think about everything for a while."

The telephone chimed before he could respond. Jaxon was oddly grateful. She was uncertain if she wanted him to agree with her or protest. The thought of being separated from him brought a great heaviness to her heart. She picked up the phone, expecting her captain's voice.

"Jaxx, sweetheart? This is Daddy."

Tyler. His voice made her instantly sick inside. It brought back every detail of her life with this man. The terrible responsibility of her childhood, shielding her mother and brother, only to fail in the end. The guilt over the Andrews family losing their lives simply for giving her a home. And over Carol Taylor, whose only sin was that she liked to share a cup of coffee in the morning with Jaxon. Drake had called Jaxon one long-ago morning, telling her Carol was weak and useless, like Rebecca, playing on Jaxon's sense of compassion, the woman was nothing but a leech, a burden. Jaxon had known she would find Carol dead that morning, but she had dropped the phone and run to her apartment anyway.

Now she remained silent, her stomach churning, her hand automatically finding her gun while her eyes began to move restlessly, searching the windows. Could Drake see into the room? Did he have an angle? Drake was an expert marksman. Without thought she slid out of bed and placed herself between the window and Lucian. Lucian, without a word, simply swept her behind him, pinning her there with one strong arm.

"This man is trying to destroy our family, Jaxx," Drake's voice barked into the phone. "You can't allow him to do it. Tell him to go away. You don't know what men are like or what they want. You can't trust him." The voice was steely with authority.

Lucian took the phone out of her hand—an easy enough task, although she tried to hang on to it. "Come and get me, Drake." As always, his tone was soft, almost gentle. "I have no intention of giving her up. You have no hold over her anymore. Jaxon is under my protection, and your reign of terror is over. Turn yourself in. It is what you wish to do. You've wanted to do it for a long while."

Lucian heard Drake replace the phone in its cradle, cutting off their conversation.

Lucian turned to regard Jaxon with his black, steady gaze. There was no remorse, no fear, nothing at all but the burning blackness of his eyes and the hard, slightly cruel edge to his mouth. Jaxon felt pale and fragile. He looked solid, calm, an anchor, invincible. Very gently he reached out and touched her face. "Jaxon?"

"Why did you do that? Why did you challenge him that way?" Her voice was barely a whisper "You don't understand. I can't protect you from him. He will wait. A month, a year—it means nothing to him. Even if I never see you again, he'll come after you now. You don't know what you've done."

Jaxon was trembling visibly. She looked so lost, so forlorn, so young and vulnerable, Lucian felt his own heart twist with pain. He reached down, gathered her unresisting body into his arms, and sheltered her close to his heart. Lucian simply held her until the warmth of his body seeped into hers. Until her frantic heartbeat matched the calm, steady rhythm of his. Until the terrible churning in her stomach subsided.

How did he do it? Jaxon lay against his large, heavily muscled frame and allowed herself to rely on him for just a few more minutes. He made her feel as if everything would be all right as long as she was close to him. Lucian seemed to have the ability to project his complete confidence in himself to her.

Finally Jaxon pushed away from him, and he set her on her feet. "You've been setting yourself up as a target from the very first, haven't you? You claim you're my fiancé and you've got all this money, so it makes you newsworthy. It's plastered all over the newspapers, isn't it? The handsome billionaire with the cop. I bet it's been quite a story. You knew Drake would read it and come after you."

He shrugged, completely unconcerned, those black eyes steady on her face. The movement of his broad shoulders was fluid and masculine, a ripple of casual strength that admitted she spoke the truth. "I have not had a way to track him until I knew more about him. With your memories, I had a place to start. Now he will make it much easier. If he does not turn himself in, he will be mad enough to make mistakes. He will show himself. He will not have his usual patience. He has lost control of you. Always, from the time you were a mere baby, Tyler Drake believed himself in control of your life. This has never happened to him before."

"He won't turn himself in," Jaxon said with complete conviction.

"Probably not," he agreed complacently. "Drake is unbalanced, and I was not able to connect with him."

"Why me? What was there about me that he fixated on?" Her enormous dark eyes moved over Lucian's face. "Why did *you* find me? Why did that . . . that *thing* come to your house when he so obviously wanted no part of you?" With sudden insight she backed a step away from him. "It was me, wasn't it? I drew him there somehow."

His smile held little humor, more an appreciation of her ability to reason things out. "You are far more adept than you realize, honey. Merging my mind with yours gave you more information than I had planned."

"Just tell me." She was almost holding her breath for his answer, but, just as she always knew when there was danger, she knew the truth.

Lucian sighed. "I know what you are thinking, Jaxon, but it is more complex than that. You are unique among your kind, a true psychic. Our species can convert only a true psychic from the human race; all others become deranged if conversion is tried. It is necessary for our males to find their lifemates. I have explained that to you. Vampires—those Carpathians who have chosen to lose their souls and cannot be redeemed—still seek to try. Still seek a lifemate, though it is too late for them. Your presence would draw them."

She closed her eyes. "The serial killer. That was a vampire?"

He nodded. "I found his kill just as your partner arrived. I was not certain who the killer was at the time. Vampires often use evil men in a variety of ways. Like

Carpathians, the vampire cannot stand the light of day. Humans can accomplish certain tasks that vampires cannot, so they use them as puppets."

"They can force people to kill others? Is that what you mean?"

He nodded slowly, watching her carefully. She looked as if she might bolt at any moment. "Among other things, yes, they can program one of their puppets to kill." If it was possible for her to become any paler, she managed it.

Jaxon shook her head. "This is insanity. You know that, don't you? I can't believe I'm buying into all this. I don't even want to know any of it."

"You are doing fine, angel. I do not expect you to handle every detail at once. I have the permission of your doctors to take you home with me. I do not want to raise suspicion by waiting too long."

"I want to go to my home," she said stubbornly.

"You want to protect me."

"I want to get away from you." She avoided his eyes. She desperately needed to think. She needed to be away from him, away from the lure of his presence.

Lucian moved without seeming to do so, covering the distance between them in the blink of an eye. "No, you do not, Jaxon. I can read your mind. It is too late. He is going to come after me. And you still want to protect me."

"Yes, he is coming after you," she burst out, "and I'm not going to walk into a room and find you dead on the floor, your body mangled and bloodied. I can't go through that again. I won't. I mean it, Lucian."

His arms snaked around her easily, drawing her back into his embrace, calming her with a touch. "You are so beautiful, Jaxon. You amaze me the way you are so determined to give up your life for others. Come home with me where you will be safe and where we can get to know each other. Look at it this way: If Drake comes after me, at least you will be there to warn me."

She was falling under the enchantment of his sorcerer's black-velvet voice. Drowning in the depths of black sexy eyes. Mesmerized by the curve of his sensual mouth. "I have things at my apartment that really matter to me."

"Your mother's things." He said it softly. "I had them moved from your apartment. They are safe in your room in my home."

Her eyes flashed fire at him. "You had no right."

"I had every right. You are my lifemate, always in my care. I can do no other than see to your happiness. You are under my protection at all times. The things that are important to you are important to me."

"If that's true, why in the world did you provoke Drake?" Her fingers were twisting the material of his immaculate shirt nervously.

His hand covered hers, holding her palm flat against his heart. "I cannot leave such a man out there threatening your life. You would not leave such a threat to my life."

Jaxon sighed, a heavy weight pressing on her chest. "You're right, Lucian, I wouldn't. I have no choice now. I have to try to find him."

Lucian actually found himself smiling. He couldn't help himself. She was so determined that she was the one who had to take care of him. He shook his head, then bent to touch her hair with his lips.

Jaxon's heart skipped a beat. What was the use of arguing with him? She couldn't stay in the hospital. Every doctor and nurse she smiled at would be at risk. Who knew what went on in Drake's twisted mind? What did she have to lose? Besides, someone needed to find out who Lucian really was and what he wanted. And he wasn't going to die. She owed him—for saving Barry, if for nothing else. Neither she nor Barry ever would have made it out of the warehouse alive. She had to stay with Lucian as his bodyguard at least until Drake was found.

Lucian's hand cupped the back of her head, his fingers tangling in her thick mop of blond hair. The strands were like silk. "You are worried for your partner's safety."

"Drake may strike at him. I've always worried about that. I used to change partners constantly until Barry came along. He refused to switch, and the captain listened to him, despite what a risk it was. Drake might be angry enough to hurt me through him."

"He has never tried to hurt you, angel," he said softly. "His motive has nothing to do with harming or punishing you. In his mind he is your savior—in a sense, your protector. You are his beloved daughter. That is how he thinks. All the rest of us are merely trying to separate the two of you."

"Even now, after all this time? How could he think that?"

His hand could not stay still, his fingers continually caressing her hair. Why he was so partial to that short, untamed mop was beyond him, but he decided it was something he didn't want to live without. She was essential to him. It amused him that she couldn't comprehend what he was: a Carpathian hunter with tremendous powers and knowledge. His skills went far beyond those of any human male. He could become a shadow, the mist itself. He was far stronger than any mortal, could read the wind, command the heavens. He could run like the wolf and fly like the birds of prey. He could control the thoughts of the humans around him, draw them to him with his voice, and entice their compliance in anything he might choose. He could destroy from a distance, even command his prey to destroy itself. He could track anyone or anything once set on the correct path Nothing could escape him—not the undead and certainly not human prey.

To Lucian, Tyler Drake was as good as dead. The man

had murdered everyone who ever meant anything to Jaxon. There was no rage in Lucian, only that quiet stillness that was forever a part of him. He was justice for his people, the executor of their law. Yet even before his Prince, before his own life, before that of his twin brother and his people, he held dear the life and happiness of Jaxon Montgomery. Tyler Drake was condemned and had little time left to live.

"It is time to go home, Jaxon," he murmured softly, aware of the evening giving way to night. He had fed well. He would eventually have to reveal much to her that she would find hard to accept. She was courageous and accepting, her mind open to the possibilities of other life forms. But she was not ready to accept them in proximity to her own life.

He could read in her mind how torn she was. He could read the sorrow in her, the guilt. He could read determination that she guard not only him, but Barry Radcliff as well. With a little sigh, he gathered her up.

Getting through the red tape of leaving the hospital should have been one of those nightmares Jaxon couldn't stand—she had little patience with paperwork—yet somehow Lucian managed it all smoothly. The entourage of hospital personnel and reporters seemed to grow as she was taken down to the hospital entrance. She glared at Lucian a few times, but he pretended not to notice. He seemed very much in his element, old friends with various reporters; even her captain joined the crowd, wanting to shake his hand. She noticed the captain hadn't rushed to *her* side; likely he was too busy looking at a possible campaign donation when he decided to run for mayor.

That is not very nice. There was that laughter again, the one that sent flames dancing over her skin and started a fire in the middle of her stomach. She glanced around to make certain no one was watching her too closely as a faint blush crept up into her face.

I can't believe these people are falling all over you. It's disgusting, she told him silently. It was probably his voice. Or his eyes. Or maybe his looks that drew them. And then there was his perfect mouth.

He leaned down to place that perfect mouth against her ear, deliberately, in front of all the cameras, his hand cupping the nape of her neck possessively. "It is all the money, honey. No other reason, simply money. Only you see me as sexy and handsome."

"I never said *sexy*. And I know I didn't say *handsome*," she hissed in return. She wasn't adding to his oversized ego by pointing out all the women who were talking about him. He had to have heard them. She could hear them. She ducked her head. Lucian really didn't seem to be aware of his looks as anything special. He wore his attractiveness the way he wore his air of confidence, of authority, as if it were merely a part of him and always had been.

A huge white limousine was parked in front of the hospital. A chauffeur stood at the door waiting. Jaxon closed her eyes. This was so absurd, such nonsense. She did not belong in a limousine. Whatever kind of life Lucian had, Jaxon could not possibly fit in.

Knowledge hit her without warning as she was reluctantly walking beneath Lucian's shoulder toward the chauffeur. The feeling came out of nowhere. Dark. Ugly. Intense. It was dark now, the light leeched from the sky to be replaced by night. Clouds covered the moon, and a slight drizzle was misting the streets. There was laughter all around, talk, hundreds of voices, yet all at once she was alone again in the middle of a war zone.

Automatically she darted out from beneath Lucian's arm, shoving his large frame away from her to put more distance between them. She already had her gun drawn, and her eyes were tracking, moving, looking for a target. It was there. It was close. This was the nightmare of every cop. A large crowd and an assassin.

Chapter Four

Where was Barry? Was he the target? Jaxon didn't dare stop looking for the source of the alarm, not even long enough to assure herself Barry had remained inside the hospital and out of harm's way. Her sharp gaze checked the surrounding rooftops, moved restlessly over the crowd itself. She was very still inside. This was what she knew. This was her way of life.

Lucian had not moved from her side despite her attempt to put him in the clear. He caught the warning signal from her and knew the threat was a human one, not from the undead. He would have felt the presence of the undead far before she would. He swore softly to himself in the ancient language. He should have been scanning the crowds instead of enjoying her reaction to him. It was the first mistake he could ever recall making in his lifetime, and he wasn't very happy with himself. One muscular arm simply swept her behind him where she would be completely protected. His larger frame easily shielded her smaller one, forcing her toward the limousine with its bulletproof, tinted glass.

She struggled, trying to warn him of danger, but he was too preoccupied to take much notice. His mind was probing the crowd for signs of hostility. Her alarm system was working perfectly. Three individuals were attempting to position themselves to catch her in their crossfire. Their instructions were to make certain she was dead this time. Their boss had ordered them to finish the job or to start running. Jaxon Montgomery had made far too big a dent in their boss's business to be tolerated any longer. Barry Radcliff was their secondary target. Lucian read their intent quite easily.

He focused his attack the way he always did, calmly and without rage or anger. First he extracted the information he needed to ensure he could stop any further attempts on Jaxon's life. With that done, he carefully orchestrated the scenario differently than what the assassins' boss had in mind. The three men found themselves drawing their weapons right in plain sight. Screams came from all around them. None of them had a clear sight of their primary target, yet their guns seemed to take on lives of their own, turning toward each other. One man tried to open his hand and drop his weapon, but his hand remained locked around it, his finger slowly tightening so that he felt his gun discharge. The sound of the guns firing simultaneously was loud in the night. Chaos broke out, pandemonium, people racing for cover in all directions.

Lucian remained standing, one hand easily pinning Jaxon in the car where no one could see her around his larger frame. He watched dispassionately as the three men dropped to the street, the water from the darkened skies carrying their blood in tiny streams away from them. For just one moment lightning arced from cloud to cloud, throwing the ground below into stark relief, etching the sight of Lucian standing still and calm in the midst of chaos into Jaxon's mind for all time. The captain and several police and security men were crouched low, looking for any other attackers.

"I think you should put some extra guards on Radcliff," Lucian advised the police captain softly, using that same "push" in his voice that ensured obedience. "Get him out of this hospital, and take him somewhere no one knows. Jaxon and Radcliff made enemies, and the warehouse was an ambush set to get rid of them. These men were here to finish that work and kill the two of them." He spoke so low that only Jaxon and the captain heard. The captain was already nodding in agreement as Lucian turned back to her.

She was still trying to get around his body to see what was happening, but he simply reached into the car and swept her over so that he could slide in beside her. At once the chauffeur closed the door, and they were alone and racing away from the scene.

Jaxon shoved a trembling hand through her short blond hair, a habit when she was agitated. It left the soft, silky strands falling in all directions, wild, the way Lucian liked it. "I can't believe you did that. Lucian, you have to let me protect you. I had the gun. You just stood there, not moving. You're a huge target—did you ever think of that? A sniper on a roof could have had you before you blinked."

She was really afraid for him. He could feel it in her like a living, breathing entity. It was nearly suffocating her. Lucian automatically became aware of his own breathing, deliberately tuning his to hers so that his heart raced and his lungs ached. Just as deliberately he began to slow both of their hearts, breathing calmly for both of them.

"You don't seem to have any instincts for self-preservation at all," she accused. "Have you hunted those horrible creatures for so long, protecting other people, that you no longer give a thought for your own life?" Her eyes actually burned with tears. Fear formed a hard knot in her throat. She had seen little glimpses of his life, and it distressed her. He had trained himself to be disposable, to place himself in harm's way to protect others. He had stood tall and straight, his shoulders square, his expression never changing. It frightened her to think of him like that. He had been far more alone in that moment than she had been her entire life.

Lucian pulled her stiff, resisting body into the curve of his arm and held her to him. His miracle. The light in his unrelenting dark world. Her show of fear for him melted his heart as nothing else could. She thought she didn't know who he was, but she knew him better than he knew himself. Lucian dropped his head protectively over hers, his arms wrapped securely around her so that they clung to each other. How could he have managed to exist in such a bleak void for all those long centuries without her? He knew he could never go back. The will and determination, the remembered love and loyalty, the vow to protect or destroy he had made and kept all those centuries would never be enough now to keep him going should he lose her. If she were taken from him, he would dispense only death and retribution for the rest of his endless days. He would never go quietly into the dawn. His arms tightened, and a smile touched the dark bleakness of his eyes. Joy spread a warmth through his entire body. Yes, he would. He would go wherever she went. If Jaxon moved on to another life, he would follow her there without hesitation.

Jaxon realized her heart had slowed and was matching the rhythm of Lucian's. She was once more able to breathe more easily. The warmth of his body had seeped into hers, and she felt incredibly safe. She closed her eyes and didn't fight the emotions he brought out in her. She liked being in his arms. She liked feeling safe and not so alone. Most of all, Jaxon was determined that Lucian would never feel such stark loneliness again. She knew about being lonely, but the few times she had touched on his mind, his solitary existence had been utterly cold and bleak. It didn't matter that she couldn't examine the why of it very closely; she knew only that nothing else mattered to her quite so much as his safety.

"I am well aware you did something back there to those men," she murmured against his chest, a note of drowsiness creeping into her voice. "Is this chauffeur yours?"

"He is on loan."

"I noticed he didn't hit the ground for cover. He dropped into a crouch and was fishing in his jacket for something. What do you think it was?" Jaxon opened her eyes and studied Lucian's shadowed jaw. Without conscious thought her fingers crept up to touch his chin.

"I have no idea what most chauffeurs do in such circumstances," Lucian replied innocently. "Perhaps he had a cell phone and was going to call for help."

"Half the police force was already there." She snuggled closer to him. She liked the feel of Lucian's hand in her hair, the way he caressed the silky strands, the touch of his fingertips against her neck. "Who lent him to you?"

"He is the son of a friend's housekeeper"

"A friend's housekeeper?" she echoed, the suspicion in her voice increasing.

He sighed. "This is beginning to sound like an interrogation. Are you a police officer by any chance?"

"Absolutely. Tell me the whole story. I like tall tales."

His hands crept around her neck in a mock threat. "You are going to give me no end of trouble, I can tell."

"No one else does. It isn't good for you to have all that deference paid to you all the time. You get so you believe you deserve it." She was laughing, her body relaxed and pliant against his.

She belonged there. He felt it. Knew it in his deepest

soul. There was no doubt in his mind that Jaxon was his other half. Created for him. Destined for him. Each time he looked at her, he found he wanted to smile. Each time he looked at her, his insides turned to molten lava.

Wrought-iron gates loomed up before the limousine, tall and intricate and as beautiful as the estate itself. The chauffeur drove the limousine smoothly through the opening and up the long drive to the house. Tall shrubbery on either side lent the grounds a wild, forestlike appearance. Everywhere she glanced were trees and ferns and bushes of some kind. Looking up at the house, she could see it had several stories, with turrets and balconies in unexpected places. Stained glass was woven throughout the walls in all shapes and sizes. It was beautiful and old-fashioned.

"The lifemate of my twin brother, Gabriel, sent me most of the stained glass. She does incredible work. She is a great healer, and it shows in her work. Many of the pieces were wrought by Francesca and their young ward, Skyler. The patterns offer much protection for those inside the house." He said it quietly, matter-of-factly, as if offering up mundane conversation.

Jaxon realized that what he was telling her was far more important than it appeared on the surface. She took the hand he extended to her as she slipped out of the huge car. "I want you to know I'm not riding in that thing again. It's so wasteful, it's a sin. And if you don't know how to drive, I'm excellent at it."

The chauffeur cleared his throat, trying valiantly to hide his smile. "Excuse me, miss, you wouldn't be trying to cut into my livelihood, would you?"

She tilted her head to one side and studied the man with shrewd, assessing eyes. He moved like a boxer, his gait perfect. There were heavy muscles under his absurd uniform. Whatever this man was, he was no chauffeur.

"What's your name?" With that information, it should be easy enough to find out more about him.

He grinned at her, tipped his hat, and slid back into the car.

"Chicken," she whispered into the night. She looked up at Lucian standing as still as a statue. "And you. What am I going to do about you?"

"I was not the one in danger, angel. That was you" His hand crept around the nape of her neck, urging her up the stairs to the front entrance.

"It doesn't matter which one of us they were after, Lucian," she explained patiently. "You would have been the one they hit. I tried to move you out of the way, but you're immovable when you go all stubborn."

"There was no danger, Jaxon. They had abominable aim. It was rather desperate of their boss to send out three such incompetent hit men, don't you think?" He was standing close enough to her that she could feel the warmth of his skin, yet only his hand rested on the nape of her neck.

Jaxon heard herself laugh. The sound surprised her. He was acting, oh, so innocent. Nothing ruffled him, nothing disturbed him. His voice was unchanged, soft and beautiful, not responsible for any mischief-making or wrongdoing. He reached around her to pull open the heavy front door. Very briefly his hand rested on her shoulder; then he dropped it and moved away from her. "You are not ill this time. Do you enter my home of your own free will?" He asked the question seriously, his seductive voice melting her heart.

For some reason she hesitated, standing just outside. She could see the foyer, the marble entrance. It beckoned, drew her, a sanctuary. Why had he asked her so formally? Why didn't he just stay quiet and allow her to enter? Jaxon turned over his words in her mind. There was a formality, almost a ritual feeling, to them. Lucian remained silent, adding to her apprehension that there was something she wasn't comprehending.

Jaxon turned to face him, tilting her head to look up into his black eyes. Soulless. Lost. Alone. He stood tall and straight in complete stillness, his face in the shadows. "If I enter of my own free will, does that give you some kind of power over me?" She couldn't help sounding nervous.

He didn't laugh at her as she feared he might. He simply watched, unblinking, steady. Jaxon moistened her suddenly dry lips. "Answer me truthfully. Does it somehow bind us together or make it so I'm a prisoner here?"

"If you fear me so much, why would you think I would reveal the truth simply because you ask it of me?"

"I just know you would." She shrugged delicately. "I know things, and you don't lie to me. So tell me."

"I have already bound us together with the ritual words. You cannot leave me any more than I could leave you."

She blinked. "Ritual words?" Before he could reply, she shook her head. "Don't go there. I'm not going to get distracted. Will I be a prisoner?"

"As for being my prisoner here in this house, you are able to come and go as you please." She remained looking up at him. Lucian slowly smiled, his mischievous little-boy smile that would likely get him out of lots of trouble. "Unless, of course, there is danger to you."

"I can't wait to hear who determines what constitutes danger. You aren't making this easy for me. I have no idea why I'm allowing you to walk into my life and take it over. And, Lucian"—she smiled sweetly up at him—"I am not the same as you. Whatever you are, and I'm not ready to find out yet, your ritual words can't bind us. I make my own decisions in matters of relationships. Yes, I will enter your home of my own free will."

She stepped across the threshold and nearly panicked.

Something deep within her shifted and came alive. It was so strong, she almost turned around to run back outside, unable to identify what it was but certain her body, her heart, and her soul recognized this place, this man. Lucian's larger frame blocked the doorway. He caught at her small waist and simply held her, the strength in his arms enormous, yet he was so gentle he never could have hurt her. "What is it?"

"I don't know. I feel as if I'm not me anymore. As if somehow you're slowly taking me over. Are you doing that?" She didn't try to get free. She wasn't even certain she really wanted to be free Her large eyes searched his expression seriously.

"I would never want to take you over. You are exactly who you are supposed to be. We have spent so much time, each of us alone, it is strange, perhaps, to share so much together so soon. But we are lifemates, and we will adjust."

She leaned into him even as she turned to face the huge room. "I feel as if I belong here, as if I know this place."

"You do belong here. Go explore. If there is anything you wish to change, feel free to do so." He opened his arms, allowing her to step away from him.

The house was even more beautiful than Jaxon had remembered. She tried not to stare around her in complete awe. In her job as a police officer, she had certainly been in more than one mansion, but this was extraordinary. In a way it evoked an Old-World elegance, a forgotten time. There was even a ballroom with a parquet dance floor. Her favorite room was a massive library made cozy by a large fireplace with two comfortable chairs placed in front of it, an antique reading table between them. On three walls were floor-to-ceiling bookcases, a ladder on rails the only way to ascend to the top shelves. She saw every kind of book imaginable, from fiction to science, old to new. She noted that the books, some of them ancient, were in several languages. It was a virtual treasure trove. Jaxon felt she could spend a good portion of her life right in that room and be happy.

The house was far larger than she had imagined, even larger than it appeared from the outside. The kitchen alone was bigger than her entire apartment. Lucian glided up behind her so silently, she nearly jumped out of her skin. "It is not your apartment any longer. I told your landlady she could rent it out." He said it softly, proving he was still a silent shadow in her mind.

"You did not." Jaxon swung around, her hands on her hips, daring him to be telling her the truth.

"Of course I did. You do not belong there. You never belonged there," he answered complacently.

"I know you wouldn't dare give away my apartment. They're not exactly easy to come by, especially on my salary." Jaxon stared up at him, trying to read his expression. "You couldn't have, Lucian." She was trying to convince herself as well as him. "Surely my landlady would have insisted on the lease being fulfilled."

He shrugged, not in the least perturbed. "She was willing to accept cash. I find in most cases it works quite well. Have you not had similar findings?"

"You really did it, didn't you? Oh, my God, I've got to call her. Where the heck are the telephones in this place? You can't just do that. You can't." She glared at him. "You don't even feel remorse. I'm looking at you, and I don't see one speck of remorse in you at all. You don't even feel it, do you?"

"I see no reason to experience such an emotion. You are in our home, where you belong. The elderly woman was more than satisfied with the cash for the lease and will be able to find a new renter immediately. It worked out quite well for everyone."

"Not for me. I need my own space, Lucian. I really do." Exasperated, she shook her head. What was the use? He didn't seem to understand what he had done.

"There is more than enough space here, is there not?" He looked puzzled, his black eyes seeking out every corner of the room. "There is much you have not even seen yet. The grounds are immense, and in many of the walls are secret passageways and other rooms. I am certain there is enough space for you right here." Just in case Jaxon should touch his mind, Lucian made certain his amusement was buried deeply. He continued to look innocent and straight-faced.

Jaxon shook her head and gave up. He was exasperating, and she was too tired to deal with him. She would work it out another day—phone her landlady and get her place back. Right now she was too tired and confused. Maybe she was hungry. She should be hungry, but every time she actually thought of food, she felt slightly sick. The refrigerator was intimidating. She stood in front of it. "When I was shot, was my stomach affected?"

For the first time she was aware of his hesitation. Jaxon felt her breath catch in her throat.

"Why do you ask? Are you hurting?" His voice, strictly neutral, gave nothing away.

"I'm hungry, but the thought of food makes me feel nauseated. In fact, I can't remember eating or drinking anything since I woke up. Is something wrong with me, or am I being paranoid?"

"I can hear that fear in your voice again. The unknown. It is the worst fear of all, is it not?" He said it so softly, she shivered. Whatever he was about to reveal, she did not want to know.

Jaxon held up a hand and shook her head without looking at him. "I think I'll walk around outside. The grounds look beautiful. In any case, I need to know my way around." She went to move past him, attempting to duck under his arm.

Lucian's arm dropped down like a gate. He curved it

around her and swept her up against him. "Do not fear the truth. It is different, but it is not evil."

She squared her shoulders. "Then tell me. Get it over with. Whatever needs to be said, just come out with it. I'm an adult, not the child you think me."

Lucian's body urged hers out of the kitchen and into his den. A wave of his hand produced dancing flames in the stone fireplace. She gasped aloud, enthralled by his magic yet frightened by it all the same. Jaxon broke away from him to stand in front of the flickering tongues of heat, needing the distance from him to think clearly. He was so tremendously powerful.

"I am a Carpathian male, as I have explained to you. We are a species that has existed from the beginning of time. I am not evil, angel face, but the darkness, the loss of color and emotion, that slowly overtakes our males who lack the light of their lifemates has grown strong in me for many centuries, making it a struggle to tame the predator inside us all. We are like the human race, yet not. We are blessed and cursed with enormous longevity, often called immortals. If and when we find a lifemate, the emotion is intense and grows steadily over the centuries. If we do not . . . we may become complete predators, the undead. The night is ours, and the sunlight is difficult to endure. But we have enormous powers, as you are beginning to understand. My blood now flows in your veins, angel. It has already affected your tolerance to sunlight, not to the extent of mine, yet it will be impossible for you to endure daylight without special sunglasses."

A heartbeat went by. One. Two. Jaxon took a deep breath, then let it out slowly. "I can accept that." *My blood flows in your veins.* A transfusion? She wouldn't challenge that; she wouldn't ask. She didn't want to know how his blood had gotten into her veins.

"The sun will burn your skin. Sunblock will help, but not very much. You will have to learn to stay indoors during certain hours of the day, but your body will be sleepy during those hours anyway."

She heard the distinct thud of her own heart. Her fingers twisted nervously in the material of the cotton shirt she was wearing. "What are you saying? Do you think I've never read *Dracula* before? You're describing a vampire, aren't you?" Her chin was up defiantly; she was challenging him openly.

Lucian could see her courage in her battle with her fear. She was fragile, so vulnerable, with much to admire in her. And he wanted her. He was acutely aware they were alone. He watched the struggle within her, the way her instincts worked, trying to war with the ties with which he had bound them together.

"I have said I am not a vampire, and I am not. If the males of our species grow weary of the darkness that descend upon them after their youth and choose to lose or defile their souls, they become the undead. They are then wholly evil, killing their prey for the momentary rush of pleasure and power it brings, rather than feeding from them and leaving them unharmed. I lived as one, mimicking the ways of the undead, but I never killed for blood nor took the blood of a necessary kill. It would be impossible for you to become vampire from my blood. You of all people are wholly in the light."

Jaxon rubbed her aching temples. There was something wrong in the things he was saying. "Why can't I stand the thought of food, Lucian?"

"You are able to tolerate water and some natural vegetable and fruit juices. You must begin with vegetable broth and build your tolerance slowly. Do not try to eat meat products; they will not agree with you."

"Is that what you live on? Juices and broth?"

"Do not ask what you cannot yet face, my love," he said softly, his black gaze resting on the pulse beating so frantically in her throat.

She knew then. She didn't faint, although her entire body went weak, her legs rubbery. She would not faint. "Lucian, please move away from the door."

His mesmerizing gaze moved over her face like a caress. "Do you think to run away from me?" His voice was so soft and sensuous, it was all she could do not to run *to* him for comfort.

"That's exactly what I think. You told me I'm not a prisoner, and I've decided I want to leave." She tried not to sound defiant. She noticed his large frame still filled the doorway, and his body was as still as a mountain, his face expressionless. If only he didn't have that voice.

"Where would you go, Jaxon?"

She tilted her chin. "Where I go is none of your business." There was a long silence while he waited, unmoving, those black eyes watching her. Jaxon counted her own heartbeats. Sighing softly, she capitulated. "Barry's apartment. He won't be there, remember? The captain was moving him to a safe house."

"I think not. It would not be safe."

There was a double meaning behind those softly spoken words. Jaxon shivered, chilled despite the heat of the fire dancing behind her. "You said I could leave."

"I did not say run away. There will be truth between us, little one, whether it is difficult or not. You are a strong woman. I will not hide things from you."

"Am I supposed to thank you for that?" She raked a trembling hand through her hair, creating a windblown effect. "I don't want this."

"Yes, you do," Lucian replied as gently as ever.

Where his eyes had been black and impossible to fathom, she now glimpsed hunger, a stark possessiveness. Her hand moved to find the comforting butt of her gun. How could she ever resist those hungry eyes? "Why are you doing this? I have enough trouble in my life without

106

your expecting me to accept vampires and God knows what else. I can't do it, Lucian."

"Yes, you can." He said it quietly. "Take a deep breath and relax. Sit down before you fall down."

Her dark eyes flashed at him. "Do you really think I'm so needy that I'd sell what little self-respect I have left just to be with someone? I feel the difference in my body. The way I can hear, the way I'm able to control the volume. I can see in the dark better than if it was daylight. I feel you all the time. With me. Needing me. Calling to me." She rubbed her temples again. "How can you talk to me without speaking? More importantly, how can I talk to you that way?"

"My blood flows in your veins, as yours flows in mine. We share the same heart and soul. Our minds seek to merge, just as our bodies cry out for each other."

"My body does not cry out for yours," she denied, more frightened than angry.

"Little liar."

"Go back to the blood in the veins thing. Exactly how did your blood get into my veins and mine into yours? Did you give me a transfusion or something like . . . ?" She trailed off, images of a dark, erotic dream intruding. Her hand went protectively to her throat. "You didn't drink my blood. God, tell me you didn't drink my blood. No, first tell me I didn't drink your blood." Now her legs were threatening to fail her. She actually looked at the floor, prepared to fall. Only the thought of being more vulnerable than she already was stopped her from collapsing.

He moved swiftly toward her to help, but Jaxon was so alarmed that she brought the gun up. She used a two-armed stance to try to steady her badly shaking hands. This was a nightmare, insanity. She didn't have enough imagination to make all this up. The gun pointed directly at his heart.

"Please move away from the door, Lucian. I don't want to hurt you. I really don't. I just want to get out of here so I can breathe again." She was pleading with him, not taking her usual command of a situation. She wanted so much to be with him. So much. He was tall and sexy and terribly alone, just as she was. She understood that in him. She wanted to make everything all right for him, to rid him of that terrible hunger. But to have a man like Lucian look at her for all time with heat and hunger, with need and possessiveness, was a dream she could never accept. Lucian was not really a man. He was something else. Something she didn't ever want to identify.

"Jaxon, put down the gun before you accidentally shoot someone." There was no inflection whatsoever in his voice.

"It wouldn't be an accident, Lucian. Please, I'm going to ask you one more time. Just step aside, and let me go."

"My people regard the human eating of flesh with the same repugnance as you regard our taking of blood for nourishment."

She took a tentative step, trying to shut out his words and the importance of what he was revealing. She circled to his right, hoping he would abandon his position. Lucian remained as still as the mountains. "Just imagining what you're trying to tell me makes me feel sick. I don't think we're compatible." She was in earnest now. If he didn't step aside, she was going to have to find a way around him. She wasn't going to shoot him. The thought of him hurt in any way was too much to bear.

Lucian moved so fast that he was a blur. Not even a blur. One moment he was standing in the doorway; the next moment he had the gun in his possession and his arms around her. "You only think it is repulsive, angel, because you do not yet know anything other than evil."

Being so close to him was dangerous. His body was

hard and hot and needy. She felt an answering response right down to her toes. Her breathing betrayed her, her racing heart, her own body. She felt tears burning behind her eyes.

"Tell me you're controlling my reactions to you," she whispered, lifting her face so that she could examine his expressionless mask.

At once his harsh features softened, his steely strong arms locking her to him as gently as possible. "You know I am not. I have forced your compliance only on the occasions when I was healing you, binding you to me, and when you needed sleep. You are the other half of my soul. I cannot be apart from you, Jaxon. I am not making it up." His hand moved over her face with great tenderness. "Do you think I wish to cause you such distress? Look into my mind and see the truth. I want only your happiness. In truth, honey, I would gladly lay down my life if I knew you wished such a thing and would be happy without me, but it is not so." His mouth touched her forehead, her eyelids. "It is not so, little love. It is not so."

"You can't ask me to accept such a thing."

"I have no other choice. It is my way of life, Jaxon. I am Carpathian. I cannot change that. I would not want to change it." His mouth found hers, gently, his lips barely brushing the corner of hers. It started a tremor deep within her. "I survive on blood, my love, but I do not kill. I have dedicated my life to the preservation of both of our species."

"But, Lucian," she tried to protest.

"It is different, that is all. It is something unknown to you."

She buried her face against his chest. "You don't sleep in a coffin, do you?" It was meant as a joke but came out far more soberly than she'd intended.

Lucian chose his answer carefully. "In all the centuries of my existence, all the vampires I hunted and destroyed,

I never actually found one who slept in a coffin. If anyone was going to try such an idea, I imagine the undead would do so first."

"That's one good thing." Jaxon was already pulling away from him, moving gingerly, as if by touching him she might become more infected with some strange disease. "I don't think I could ever get used to the coffin thing. Can you undo what you've done?" She tried to keep her voice neutral. She was very tired and wanted only to lie down somewhere and not think anymore about anything. "You can't, can you?"

"I would not want to if I could. I do not want to give you up." His hands fell to his side. "That is selfish of me, I know, but I cannot. It is not only for my own sake, Jaxon, but for yours—and for others."

She held up a hand and gave a faint smile "Overload, Lucian. I can't take in any more. Let's do something normal." Jaxon bit her lower lip, a small frown flitting across her face. "I don't know what normal people do, do you?"

His hands framed her face, his thumbs feathering over her satin-soft skin in a small caress. He had to touch her. He couldn't seem to stop himself. "You look tired, Jaxon. You should be resting."

"I was thinking we could go for a walk on your grounds. I'd like to look around outside."

"Scouting. Of course you would want to do that. It is so *normal*."

She found herself smiling. "Maybe you're right. After all, neither one of us knows what to do when we're not tracking some killer."

His smile was slow and sexy. "I did not say I did not have other, much more interesting things in mind to do."

Her breath caught in her throat. He could so easily get around her. It wasn't natural. He whispered to her in her mind, shared erotic images, and made her think things she never would have on her own. Jaxon shook her head.

"You are bad, Lucian. What am I going to do about you?"

"Be with me. Live with me. Learn to love me. Accept me as I am," his black-velvet voice whispered, and his words touched her in her deepest soul.

She reached out to take his hand, weaving her smaller fingers through his. "I think you should be outlawed. That voice of yours can get you almost anything." She had no real way to resist him. Not when he could say such things to her in his beautiful voice with such stark truth in his gaze.

He turned her hand over, bringing her palm to his lips. His black eyes were burning with possessiveness. "Does that include you?"

Jaxon found herself smiling. "I'm considering it. Walk with me."

"You wish to go outside?"

She shook her head. "There's a reason you're not so certain you want me to go outside. What's out there? I know it's not a coffin. I think we've pretty much covered that issue, and we're clear on it."

"No coffin," he acknowledged.

"So, what is it?" she demanded. "Out with it."

"Wolves." He said it straight-faced.

Jaxon snatched back her hand. "Give me back my gun. Wolves? I should have known. Of course you have wolves. Doesn't everybody?" She snapped her fingers. "The gun, Lucian. Hand it over. I've decided I have to shoot you after all. It's the only way to preserve my sanity."

His hands curved around her neck in mock threat. "I do not think I will ever give back that weapon of yours. It gives you hostile ideas."

She was very much aware of him as they moved together toward the back of the house. Why did his home have to be so perfect? Everything she had ever wanted?

Why did it make her feel so safe when she should have felt threatened by such a powerful and dangerous being as she knew Lucian to be? How could she simply accept his differences so calmly? Well, maybe not calmly, but she was accepting them.

Lucian enjoyed the way her mind worked. Jaxon was sometimes overwhelmed by the enormity of the information he had given her, but she didn't allow herself to panic. She took her time assimilating what she could and then gave her mind a small break before processing the next influx of information. She used humor to get herself through frightening situations. She never once condemned him out of hand.

Jaxon didn't know him. She did not understand what he really was. She had no real concept of what it had done to him to destroy others for centuries. That his bleak, dark world was so cold and shadowed, he would do anything to keep from going back there. He was a predator, had terrible darkness in him, and she was too much of the light to understand that each kill had taken a piece of his soul. Only Jaxon could make him whole.

Chapter Five

The moment Jaxon stepped out onto the grounds and inhaled the fresh air, the terrible weight threatening to crush her dissipated. The air was cold and crisp, the rain having ceased for a short time. Clouds swirled overhead, dark and ominous, blocking out any moonlight, yet it was a beautiful sight. She loved storms and the sound of rain. She loved the cloud formations and the scent of the air after a downpour.

She was aware of Lucian's powerful body moving close to hers as they emerged from the house. Jaxon raked carelessly at her hair with one hand, sending it into further disarray as she surveyed the acres of forest that lay behind the mansion. "This is a bodyguard's worst nightmare, Lucian. Drake would love this. He could be here right now, up in the trees somewhere. This is his element."

"You worry too much about my safety, honey." His fingers tangled in her hair on the pretext of taming it into some semblance of order. "I would know if a human approached my property. It is well protected, not by a se-

113

curity system such as humans use but by ancient safeguards, powerful and dangerous. Tyler Drake cannot get
through them. As long as you are on this property, you
are perfectly safe from him."

"What about from a sniper's bullet? He doesn't have
to be on the property to shoot you, Lucian. All he has to
do is perch on a hilltop somewhere and get you in his
sights."

"I am not so easy to kill, angel. You only pretend not to
know what I am because you do not want to think too
closely about it." He was in her mind. She was avoiding the
idea of their sharing blood, mainly because it brought up
dark, erotic memories she didn't want to touch. And she
was definitely having trouble with the idea that she had
taken his blood. It bothered her far more than she wanted
to admit, yet she was turning it over and over in her mind.

Lucian looked down at her. Jaxon had tipped her head
back to look up at him, her large eyes dark with such
mixed emotions it turned his insides to molten heat. More
than anything he wanted to taste her soft lips. The need
was fierce and urgent and this time he gave in to the demand without a fight. He simply wrapped his arms
around her small waist and pulled her to him, his head
descending to take possession of her mouth.

Time stopped. Beneath their feet the earth itself shifted
and rolled. Burning heat erupted everywhere, electricity
arcing between them. Still, his mouth was slow and gentle, coaxing her response rather than commanding it. His
hands moved to cup the back of her head, holding her so
that he could explore, lose himself in the silken heat of
her mouth. She was everything to him. A secret world of
light and heat and color and emotion and magic. He never
wanted to be anywhere else. He wanted this perfect moment to go on for all time.

Lucian lifted his head slowly, almost afraid to stop,
afraid the moment couldn't be real, it was such perfection,

afraid she would vanish and leave him alone once more. His hands tangled in her hair. "I thought there were few secrets left in this world for me to discover, angel, but the mystery of how I came to deserve one such as you, I will spend eternity unraveling."

Her fingertips touched his perfect mouth. The truth was, Jaxon was in awe of him. She had known if he touched her that way, if his mouth found hers, she could never be truly free of him. She would crave him for all time. His taste, his power, his scent. Everything. "I shouldn't have let you do that, Lucian," she whispered. "Now what are we going to do?" He had said she could leave anytime, she wasn't a prisoner, but she knew it wasn't the truth. She was locked to him in some way, bound by something far more powerful than she had ever imagined. Her eyelashes lifted, and she looked up at him with tremendous sorrow. "What are we going to do?"

Lucian caught the nape of her neck in the palm of his hand and drew her against him so he could hold her. "When you look at me with such sadness, Jaxon, you break my heart." The wind provided a soft music, and he moved in perfect rhythm to it, moving her with him so that they were one. She rested her head against his chest and seemed to melt into him, pliant and soft when she should have been protesting.

"Our fate is sealed, honey," he said as gently as he could. "There is no Lucian without Jaxon, and there is no Jaxon without Lucian. We must find a way to merge our two worlds together. We have no choice. It was written long before either of us was sent to this earth. We are fortunate that we were able to find each other, when there are so many who have been unable to remain hopeful."

"You think that, Lucian? You really think that we're lucky? I've brought you into a sick world where someone is stalking me and killing anyone who matters to me. You're bringing me into a nightmare world where creatures out of horror stories exist." Jaxon sounded very sad, her voice muffled by his white silk shirt. "I don't even know if I want to be with you. I don't know if you've got me under some black-magic spell or not." Their bodies were swaying together, as close as they could get, with only thin layers of clothes between them.

He found himself smiling again. He was more than likely the most powerful creature on the face of the earth. He could command the heavens. She was not much more than five-foot-one, probably didn't weigh in at a hundred pounds, yet she didn't think anything of standing up to him.

The truth was, Lucian was used to complete awe and respect. Even among the more powerful males of his race, he had always been treated with deference. No one had defied him in centuries. He mused over that. No one other than enemies he had to destroy had *ever* defied him. Not once in all those centuries did anyone ever disobey his will. Lucian was used to having his way in all things. In his arms Jaxon felt so small and fragile. He was suddenly aware of his strength, of his power, something he had always taken for granted. He inhaled her scent; she was already the very air he breathed. The bond between them was growing stronger with every moment that passed.

A sound intruded, a soft cry, music on the wind. The wolves knew he was out on the grounds and had come close to visit him. Seeing he was not alone, they were in the woods, dark shadows watching him, waiting for a signal. Attack or stay back? He touched their minds, sending images to them. Jaxon was a part of their clan, their pack, his female, a leader right alongside him. She was under his protection. Under their protection. They must at all times look out for her first.

Jaxon raised her head. "They're out there now, watching us, aren't they? Where did you get them? You have to secure all sorts of special licenses to have a wild animal.

I would have thought, even for you, it would be difficult to attain the permits when you live so close to the city. How did you manage it?"

He shrugged his wide shoulders carelessly. "I simply told the gentleman he was going to give me the permits, and he did so."

Jaxon sighed and stopped dancing with him. "I need to get away from you. I really do. I can't believe someone so perfectly logical and down-to-earth as I am is falling for this fantasy world you've created. Lucian, you can't just go around getting your way by crawling into people's minds and hypnotizing them into doing whatever you want."

His black eyes glittered with what could have been amusement. "Jaxon, I have been doing just that since the beginning of existence."

"What does that mean?"

"Centuries. I have been doing it for centuries."

Jaxon held up her hand. "Just stop saying *centuries*. Don't use that word anymore. Something about it makes me crazy." She pressed a hand to her stomach. "Give me back my gun before you call those animals to you." She could see the wolves, their eyes reflecting in the dark. Without realizing it, she moved back beneath the shelter of Lucian's wide shoulder for protection. "I'd just feel better, you know?"

"The wolves are my brothers. They would never seek to harm me or mine," he said quietly. "They are noble creatures, Jaxon, with a strict code. They would give their lives for us. Do not fear them."

Her heart was beginning to pound. Right away she noticed his heartbeat match hers, and then both hearts slowed to normal. She glanced up at him. "What *are* you?"

"Not vampire, little love. Never that." His every instinct was to scoop her up and run off with her, claim her body and tie her to him irrevocably. Lucian's mind was

117

a shadow in hers; he knew she would be unable to resist him, but it was not what she wanted. She was still struggling to accept his existence and their strange bond. With a sigh he circled her slight body with his arms and dropped to one knee. *Come to me, brothers and sisters. Come and meet my lifemate.*

The wolves raced from the woods, eager to welcome her into the pack. Lucian held her tightly, reassuring her physically as well as mentally. In her head his voice was soft and soothing; his heart and lungs directed hers so that she could remain calm in the midst of the large pack. The animals pushed against her legs, rubbed along her thigh, sought to have her hands in their fur. When she was reluctant to do so on her own, Lucian's hand guided hers, so that her palm was immersed in the thick dark coat of one of the larger wolves.

Jaxon found a smile curving her mouth, joy in her heart. She almost felt as if she could see into the minds of the animals. Images of what they were thinking and feeling. Their fur was incredibly soft and thick. It was amazing to be so close to a wild animal, to be touching one, having it accept her. She turned her head to look up at Lucian. "This is so wonderful. Have you been doing this all your life?"

"I would say for *centuries,* but I know how much you dislike that particular word," he teased her.

She made a face at him. "You are so bad."

He ruffled her hair, trying to treat her like a child instead of the woman he knew her to be. She was tired. He could sense her exhaustion. Her wounds were not completely healed. She needed nourishment, though her mind shied away from that particular need. Lucian sent the wolves back into the woods, scooped Jaxon into his arms, and glided back into the house, cradling her against his chest.

"I'm quite capable of walking," she pointed out.

"It is faster this way. Your legs are short."

"They are not!" She was seriously offended. "I can't believe you even said that."

He laughed and tossed her into the deep cushions of the sofa in his den, where it was warm. "I have to go out for a short time this evening. You will, of course, remain indoors and out of harm's way."

She looked up at him with wide-eyed innocence. "Where exactly did you think I was planning on going at this time of night? Out dancing? I can wait a few days."

"Promise me you will try to eat something."

"Absolutely." She nodded solemnly.

Lucian regarded her through half-closed eyes. "Why is it I am not certain I can trust you?"

"You have the longest, darkest eyelashes I've ever seen," she replied, trying not to stare at his eyes. "You should be locked up. It's not safe to have you around women."

"I have not noticed *you* falling all over me, angel."

"Thank God for that." Jaxon snuggled deeper into the cushions and smiled up at him. "Notice I'm not even asking you where you're going. I'm just happy to be rid of you for a while."

"That is not nice."

"Keep it in mind when you're thinking about this lifemate stuff. I'm not a nice person," she said smugly.

He laughed softly. "I do not have to reinforce my request that you remain indoors with a little help, do I?"

Her dark eyes flashed fire. "You wouldn't dare!"

"Try me." His voice was as soft as ever.

Jaxon did her best to look demure. "Do I look in any shape to go running around like an idiot? But you need a couple of bodyguards. Take the chauffeur. He looks as if he can handle himself in a crisis. Not that I have any intention of worrying about you."

His white teeth flashed at that blatant lie. "If you need

me, honey, just reach for me with your mind. We can talk to each other anytime."

She held up a hand. "Go away. It's the only safe thing for you to do. And leave my gun while you're at it. I don't want to be here alone unarmed."

"You have a complete arsenal upstairs in your bedroom. I never saw so many weapons. It made me wonder just what type of woman I was getting myself involved with. There will be no shooting me when I come home this night, no unfortunate accidents, I trust," he teased as he put her gun on the table beside her chair. He bent to brush her temple with his warm mouth before he walked away from her, laughing softly.

Lucian made certain he had stepped out into the darkness before his tall frame shimmered into transparency, slowly dissolved into millions of tiny droplets, and streamed out into the mist rising from the ground. He moved fast, traveling at preternatural speed, moving straight toward the city.

The three men sent to murder Jaxon had all worked for the same person. Samuel T. Barnes. The man was a banker, wealthy and very social. He was seen at all the prominent parties, supported the local mayor, the congressman, and the senator. He did not appear to have any drug connections, yet he had ordered all three assassins to get rid of Jaxon. She had been far too successful in slowing the drug traffic in her city. Her team had virtually put a stranglehold on the incoming routes. She found and took away shipment after shipment.

Lucian found Barnes's condominium in an exclusive neighborhood. The stream of mist circled the house, testing the defenses. Each window was sealed, every door bolted. Lucian returned to the front door, shimmering once more into solid flesh and blood. He stood tall and straight, a faint smile touching his mouth, although his eyes were completely expressionless. He listened for a moment, noting the position of all people in the house and what they were doing. His knock was sharp and authoritative and brought an instant response.

A young man in a suit, the poorly concealed bulge beneath his jacket indicating he was armed, opened the door. Lucian nodded politely. "I am Lucian Daratrazanoff, here to see Mr. Barnes. I do not have an appointment, but I was in the area and thought I would take a chance."

The man blinked several times in surprise. He obviously recognized the name. "Please come in, sir. I'll tell him you're here."

Lucian didn't move. "I would not want to disturb him if he has settled in for the evening. After all, it is quite late. I will wait out here."

"Mr. Barnes wouldn't like that, sir," the man insisted. "I've heard him speak of you often. Please come in."

"You are certain you have the authority to invite me into his home?" Lucian's voice was soft, his accent very much in evidence.

The man nodded. "Yes, sir. Please come in. Mr. Barnes would have my job if I kept you waiting on the doorstep."

Lucian graciously allowed the man to talk him into entering the foyer. He stood quietly while the man hurried off to get Samuel Barnes. He could clearly hear the whisper of conversation in the room above him.

"Are you certain it's Lucian Daratrazanoff? My God, where's my jacket? Quick, Bruce, mix a couple of drinks, and bring them into the library. No, wait. Escort Daratrazanoff into the main sitting room. I'll make the drinks myself."

Lucian remained quite still, waiting while Bruce hurried back to him. "Mr. Barnes said to bring you right up," he announced, indicating the staircase.

Lucian moved up the stairs without hesitation. He had not used his voice to persuade or enthrall. He had not needed to do so. His name, that of the elusive foreign billionaire, was enough. To a man like Barnes, he would have celebrity status. He moved silently, remaining aware of the location of all those in the house. There were four men, including Barnes. Bruce was right behind him, and two others were playing pool in a recreation room on the first floor toward the back of the house.

Samuel Barnes met him halfway across the room, his right hand outstretched. He was a slim man with a quick, practiced smile and thinning hair. "Lucian Daratrazanoff, this is quite a surprise. What can I do for you?"

Lucian's black eyes were hard and uncompromising. "I believe we have some private business to discuss."

Barnes indicated the door with a nod to Bruce. The man immediately went out, closing the heavy oak door behind him. Barnes crossed to his leather bar. "What can I get for you?" He poured himself a scotch and water.

"Nothing for me, thank you," Lucian replied softly. He waited until Barnes was seated comfortably across from him before leaning toward the man and fixing his black eyes on the other man's gaze. "We have a small problem, Mr. Barnes," Lucian said very gently. "I know you will be more than pleased to help me with it."

"Of course, Mr. Daratrazanoff. Anything at all."

"I would like you to tell me quite frankly why it is you wish Miss Jaxon Montgomery and her partner, Barry Radcliff, dead." Lucian's voice had dropped an octave, so that the tone wrapped around the other man, every bit as mesmerizing as those empty black eyes.

"My partners and I have made several attempts to pay off her or some of those in her unit, but they're all very loyal to her. She seems to know where every shipment is before it even arrives. She's putting a stranglehold on our cash flow. I told my partners that we couldn't hit a couple of cops, but they said we had to or they would find a more agreeable partner. I had no choice."

Lucian nodded seriously, as if they were simply discussing the weather. "And who are these people who are insisting upon her death? Because, you know, you do not really want such a thing."

"Dennis Putnam and Roger Altman. They have big connections in Colombia and Mexico."

"And where would I find these two men?"

"It's hard to get to them. Bodyguards surround them all the time. I think they've got one of their men planted here, but I can't figure out who it is. They always know what I'm doing. They have a base of operation in Miami."

"Write down the address for me."

Barnes complied immediately. Lucian rose with his casual, fluid grace. "The men in this house—how many of them are aware of the fact that your partners want Miss Montgomery dead?"

"All of them."

"Thank you. I appreciate your help. I want you to wait until I have left this room, and then you will suddenly cease to be able to breathe. Do you understand?"

"Yes, Mr. Daratrazanoff."

Barnes walked him to the door and held out his hand. "It's been a pleasure doing business with you."

Lucian took the hand offered to him and stared directly into Barnes's eyes, ensuring his instructions would be carried out swiftly. "I cannot say the same for you, but, then, you are a deceiver and a murderer, are you not?"

Barnes frowned and rubbed his temples.

Lucian's white teeth flashed. "Good-bye, Mr. Barnes."

Bruce was waiting just outside the door. "Please follow me, Mr. Daratrazanoff. I'll show you out. I trust everything went well."

Lucian put a friendly hand on the man's shoulder. "Please show me to the pool room. That would make me very happy."

Bruce blinked rapidly several times. "Of course, sir. This way."

As they descended the long stairs, they heard a faint noise from the upstairs sitting room. A strangling, a gasping, and then a thud, as if someone had fallen to the floor. Bruce turned quickly. Lucian merely smiled. "You will not go to his aid, because I do not wish it. Take me to the pool room."

Bruce nodded and led the way down the hall to a set of double doors.

Lucian waved a hand, and the doors opened wide. The two men looked up from their game, both putting their hands on the weapons in their shoulder holsters. They relaxed visibly when they saw Bruce.

Lucian walked directly up to the first man. "I want you to get into your car and drive very carefully, obeying all traffic rules, until you come to the entrance to the cliff road. You will go up that road and drive straight off it. Do you understand me?"

"Yes, sir."

"You will do so immediately."

Without replying, the man picked up his jacket and car keys and left the room.

Lucian turned to the second man. "You have killed many times."

"Yes, sir."

"You feel bad about that, do you not? It is a very difficult thing to live with, the taking of innocent lives. I have never done so in all the long centuries of my existence. Those I have condemned to death have always been murderers such as yourself. You are evil. You know that you are, and you no longer wish to continue your pitiful existence. Go to your residence, and end the misery you bring to others. Do you understand?"

"Yes, sir." The second man picked up his jacket and left the room without a backward glance.

Lucian studied Bruce. "You have not killed."

"No, sir."

"Why would you work for such a man as Barnes?"

"When I was fifteen I got involved in a car-theft ring. I served time, and once I was out, no one but Mr. Barnes would give me a job."

"You do not like Barnes or the things he does."

Bruce couldn't look away from those mesmerizing eyes. In any case, the sound of that voice demanded the truth. "He disgusts me. He'd murder his own mother for money. I have a wife to support. We're expecting twins any day now. I have to make enough money for them to live, and no one is going to hire a felon."

"You will go home and stay there for a few days thinking about your future. You will get rid of the gun, tell your wife you are getting a legitimate job, and you will call this number. The man there will interview you and give you honest work. Do you understand me? You will remember nothing of my presence in this house, and you will not remember that Miss Montgomery and her partner were ever on a hit list."

Bruce took the small piece of paper, folded it carefully, and slipped it into his jacket pocket. When he looked up, he was alone in the pool room, and he couldn't remember why he had gone there. He was sick of his job, sick of Barnes. Mary was due any day now. She hated his working for Barnes and begged him all the time to quit. Maybe now was the time. Maybe he should just quit and think things over while they waited for the babies to be born. There had to be something better out there for him. Something legitimate. Bruce went upstairs to tell Barnes he was finished. He found him on the floor, his features gray, tinged with blue. Immediately he called 911 and started CPR. All the time he worked, he knew it was too late for Barnes, and he couldn't find it in his heart to be all that sorry.

Jaxon waited until she was certain Lucian had left his house and was off his property. At once she sought a telephone to call Don Jacobson, her childhood friend.

"Don, I want you to do some looking for me. Drake called me."

"Good God, Jaxx, what did you expect? It's all over the news that you got yourself engaged to some big-shot moneybags. That would be like a slap in the face to Drake. What were you thinking? If you were going to run off and get engaged, you could have stayed here and married me."

"You would have divorced me inside of a week." Jaxon laughed. "I can still kick your butt, and your macho ego would have a hard time with that."

"What about moneybags? Can you kick his butt?"

"I wish. Anyway, I need information. Put an ear to the ground, ask some of the guys to look around, and see if there's any sign that Drake has been out on the range somewhere. You know how he is—he haunts those hills. Maybe you'll get lucky."

"Be careful, Jaxx. Drake's insane. He's just as likely to turn on you."

"I'm always careful. Unfortunately, I don't think Lucian comprehends the extent of Drake's training. He won't take me seriously when I tell him how dangerous it is to deliberately draw Drake out."

"Trust you to find an adrenaline junkie worse than you."

Jaxon made a rude sound and gave him her number. "Call me if anyone so much as finds a sign they *think* might be his."

"Sure thing, Jaxx. But you promise me you won't do anything dangerous."

"Careful is my middle name," she said softly and hung up the telephone. In the upstairs bedroom she found her things. Jaxon dressed carefully, pulling on dark clothes and a dark hood to cover her blond hair.

She was grateful Lucian had brought her weapons, including her sniper's rifle with the night vision scope. She scooped it up to put it over her shoulder and filled her pockets with shells. She added a couple of knives, her handgun with extra clips, and a rope. Lucian didn't believe Drake was a real threat to him, but she intended to scout the entire neighborhood around his property to find every spot where a sniper might lie in wait.

Jaxon was suddenly aware just how fatigued she was. Her wounds were mostly healed, but she was not as strong as she would have liked. The rifle seemed much heavier than she remembered. She stood just inside the front door, staring at the intricate pattern in the stained glass. It was not only beautiful, but there was something else, something she couldn't quite put her finger on. The pattern seemed to beckon, to soothe, to draw her in. She could have stayed there forever and simply stared at it.

Shaking her head to clear her mind, Jaxon opened the door and went out into the night. It was drizzling again. No hefty storm, but the fog was thick, and mist was rising like steam from the ground. The wolves were confined to the woods behind the house, so the courtyard and the front were free of wild animals. She had felt safe with Lucian holding her, commanding the wolves, but on her own, she feared she might have to destroy the beautiful creatures.

Jaxon continued down the front drive. She found she was having difficulty walking. The air felt heavy and oppressive. Each step she took seemed to be through quicksand. She was breathing hard, the weight in her chest giving her the illusion she couldn't breathe. *Illusion*. This was some sort of illusion. Or maybe it was part of some security system Lucian had that worked on the human nervous system. Whatever it was, Jaxon had no intention of allowing it to defeat her. She had to secure the area for her own peace of mind.

Jaxon treated her distress as she would any other discomfort she might experience in the midst of a mission.

She pushed it out of her head and moved forward, one step at a time. There was no question she would make it out; there could be no other outcome. Jaxon had been trained to overcome all obstacles. Sweat broke out on her forehead, but it didn't matter. She made her way to the gates and pushed them open.

Once out on the street she could breathe more easily, and the heavy weight in her chest lifted. *A bodyguard's nightmare.* She had named Lucian's home such, and it was true. In this exclusive neighborhood each estate had several acres; thus, few houses were near by. Most of the surrounding area was covered in trees and heavy brush. Tyler Drake would love that. And the high bluffs a mile or so down from the house worried her. What a perfect place from which to observe Lucian's house and grounds.

Jaxon sighed as she moved swiftly along the road, keeping in the shadows of the trees. A moving target was easier to spot than a stationary one, so Drake had all the advantages if he had already started scouting the area. She didn't want to think about Lucian and what he had revealed to her. Vampires. There was no such thing. There just couldn't be. Maybe what she had witnessed was some weird trick. But she was the one who had shot the thing. And she never missed. Never. She saw the bullet hit him squarely in the center of his forehead. It hadn't even slowed the creature down.

Jaxon inched her way as she approached high ground. She didn't want to skyline herself. If she was hunting this night, Drake could be, also. She began a meticulous study of the ground, quartering each approach for a sign that Drake had passed this way. She would recognize his work. The cold air was getting through her clothes. Jaxon found herself shivering despite the fact that her movements should have kept her warm. Still, her night vision was so improved, she now had a wonderful asset. She tried to concentrate on that thought to block out the numbing cold.

She was scanning the ground, her eyes searching restlessly, back and forth, for one thing out of place. Only one. That was all she would need to know that Drake was in the area. The first few years Jaxon had tried to hide from him, until she realized it was impossible. Now, she stayed out in the open, where he could come after her if he desired. But he never tried to harm her, only those around her. Only those he perceived as a threat to him. Lucian had set himself up as a target. Where he lived was common knowledge now, with the press following the story of their engagement.

She dropped to her stomach and slithered through the wet grass to the top of a knoll. There, she used her rifle scope and surveyed the property. From this angle one had no real shot. Thick foliage and trees protected the entire side of the house. Even the balconies there were completely hidden from view. She studied her surroundings carefully, picking out the next high point where Drake might go.

She was halfway up the bluff when she began to get that peculiar feeling she always did when she knew trouble lay ahead. It was more than instinct. A gift. A curse. Whatever it was, Jaxon knew Drake had been here before her. She slowed her pace and was careful to keep utterly silent. Not even her clothes could whisper of her presence. She took particular care to study the rocks as she climbed. She found a scuff mark, faint but there. Farther up, near the top, was a distinct rope scrape deep in the dirt, the impression of a thumb near by. She had seen that mark before. She had spent her childhood training with Drake. She knew the way he moved, the way he went up a rope, and the way he tied off. The knuckle of his thumb always brushed the dirt when he tied off.

Her heart was pounding now. He could easily be at the

top, making her position extremely vulnerable. She hesitated long enough to drag a knife from her boot and clamp it between her teeth before making the last effort to mount the top of the bluff. She lay quietly, waiting to catch her breath, listening to the sounds of the night. She could hear insects singing, suggesting to her that she was alone up there. She didn't move, wasn't fooled. Drake would never stir up the insects enough to silence them. He was a professional; he knew exactly what he was doing. He would never give away his position by making careless movements.

When Jaxon moved, she did so inch by inch, on her belly, keeping low to the ground, using her elbows to propel her forward. She covered the open ground and found relative shelter in some heavy bushes. Very carefully she slipped the rifle from her shoulder. It felt solid and safe in her hand, but it was meant for distance shooting, not hand-to-hand combat. This might her one chance to rid the world of Tyler Drake. If he was up there, she was determined that only one of them would go back down. And Drake would never submit to arrest.

She covered every inch of the cliffs. Tyler had spent time here; she knew he had. She could smell him everywhere. Actually smell him. It brought back so many nightmares, that smell. The signs were fresh enough that she knew Tyler must have been scouting the estate while Lucian was at the hospital with her. He hadn't shot at them, and she'd had no premonition of danger, so he must have left before they arrived. When she was satisfied Drake was no longer on the cliff, she allowed herself a moment to rest. With so many unwanted memories crowding in, her stomach was in hard knots. Just being this close to Drake made her sick. Taking a deep breath to settle her nerves, Jaxon scooted across open rock to the edge of the bluff so she could once more scope out the house. Here she had a better view.

Dragging her scope out, she took aim. Dense foliage mostly obscured the front of the house, but the upper stories rose above the trees. She could partially see into two windows despite the stained glass. She wasn't familiar enough with the layout of the house to know which rooms she was seeing, but neither appeared to be her bedroom. Drake could conceivably get a shot off from here and score a hit if Lucian entered either of the two rooms. Rolling over, she pulled out a small notebook and meticulously entered each calculation.

It took longer to make her way back down the cliff and around to the far side of the house. The forest was thick, and bushes grew everywhere. Her rifle was becoming more and more cumbersome. Jaxon realized she was far weaker than she had thought. The wounds she had been certain were healed were now throbbing. Her breath was coming in gasps. As a child, training on the base, she had been drilled to overcome all obstacles, including pain or discomfort of any kind. She took inventory quickly, assessed the damage to her body, and dismissed it. Protecting Lucian was all-important. He refused to believe her when she said Drake was dangerous to him, a pro, a chameleon when he needed to be.

The estate was immense. Lucian had been right in that, even from high ground, Drake would not find a decent shot. But there were other ways. She began to walk along the massive stone wall around the grounds. It was very high, very thick. On the other side, the wolves paced. She couldn't see them, but she sensed they were there. It was odd, but in her mind she thought she could hear them calling to her. Drake had come this way. She put a hand on the wall. Would he poison the wolves? That wouldn't pose much of a problem to him. Was that the security Lucian was counting on so heavily? Wolves wouldn't even slow Drake down.

Chapter Six

Jaxon tilted her head to assess exactly what it would take to climb the wall. Not much. She sighed. What would she be able to see of the house from the top of the wall? She was studying the best way up, seeking finger and footholds, when a cold wind whirled leaves and twigs around her legs. In the midst of the wild blast Lucian loomed up directly behind her, his large frame so close, Jaxon was trapped between his body and the high wall.

She swung around with a low cry of alarm, trying to bring up her hand with the knife in it. Lucian's fingers curled around her fragile wrist, easily holding her still. He leaned into her, pressing her small frame right into the wall. His mouth touched her ear. "You are not waiting at home for me."

Her heart was pounding. She wasn't certain if it was from the proximity of his body or the suddenness of his appearance. "Technically, I think I could get away with saying I'm on the property. Sort of. Just checking things out a bit." She made an attempt to face up to him, feeling very vulnerable locked between the wall and his muscular frame. He had removed the knife from her hand, but she was still shackled to him, his fingers tight around her wrist.

"You are definitely not on the property where I left you, honey," Lucian whispered into her ear, his warm breath stirring tendrils of hair at her neck, stirring unwanted excitement in her body. He pulled the hood from her head to reveal the silky blond hair spilling wildly in all directions.

She wasn't cold anymore. He had managed to heat her up with a few simple words. "Things didn't go well on your little to-do list?" she asked sweetly.

His hand slipped around her throat so that her pulse was beating into his palm. His thumb stroked a caress along the delicate line of her jaw. "He has been here before you, angel. You have needlessly placed yourself in danger." Lucian spoke in his most gentle voice, yet she recognized a note of reprimand. More than that. A warning, perhaps.

"It isn't needless. You just aren't getting it. He's probably watching us right now." Realizing it might be so, she made every attempt to swing them around, to somehow cover his big body with her own.

Lucian could easily pick her intentions out of her mind. She was frantic to protect him from Drake. "Be still, Jaxon," he breathed, his voice a soothing balm, filling her mind with warmth. He held her close to his body with his enormous strength. Sheltering her. Savoring her. "He is not close at this time. I have scanned the area. Had he been near, I would not be so gentle with you. There is no need for you to protect me. Tyler Drake cannot harm me."

His hand on her throat was warm and possessive, his thumb inducing molten heat in her veins where once there had been only blood. "I don't know what you mean by 'scanned the area,' but I scouted it. I found evidence of him at two sites. We can protect ourselves from one of them easily enough, but this is impossible."

Lucian bent his head to hers. "You do not listen well." He appeared not to be paying much attention to the conversation, distracted by other things. "Hold still, Jaxon," he murmured.

She went perfectly still. Jaxon didn't know how, but she felt heat inside her where her wounds were throbbing. His fingers splayed wide across her abdomen. He did nothing else, simply laid his palm over her, but she felt him inside her. At once the pain disappeared. Lucian turned her into his arms. "Do not do this again. You are needlessly tired and cold." He was framing her face between his palms.

Jaxon watched his eyes go from black ice to burning possessiveness as he lowered his head to hers. Mesmerized, she stood waiting for the touch of his mouth. She felt his breath, the heat, the beckoning. She felt him touch her mind, gentle and warm. His mouth moved over hers, coaxing, tasting. The world fell away from her. There was only silken heat, molten fire. She closed her eyes, willing to give herself up to pure feeling. Sensation. Dark fires.

He gathered her close, lifted her slight body into the hard strength of his arms, and whispered to her. She didn't hear, couldn't hear. His mouth was perfect. He drove out every sane thought, every responsibility, and replaced it with a burning magic. The earth dropped away, and the wind rushed past. She felt it in her hair, on her face. The dizzy sensation of a roller coaster. But his mouth was all that really mattered.

When Lucian lifted his head, Jaxon felt dazzled and had to blink several times to focus on her surroundings. At once she gasped and pushed him away. He set her down on legs that were rubbery, but sheer shock held her up. They were at the house, right at the kitchen door. Her teeth bit deep into her lower lip, drawing a tiny dot of blood. She could taste the bead welling up.

"How did we get here?" She was holding one hand up to ward him off.

Lucian ignored her hand to step close so that he could lean down and once more find her mouth, his tongue lingering along her lips, caressing, healing, savoring the taste of her. Jaxon pushed at the wall of his chest, not wanting to get caught up in his black magic.

"Answer me. How did we get here?"

He looked amused. "It is not that hard to move through—"

"Stop!" Jaxon put both hands over her ears. "Don't say anything until I think about this. Every time you say anything, you make me more nuts."

His black eyes were shamelessly laughing at her. He reached out a lazy hand to remove the rifle from her shoulder. She was wildly beautiful and incredibly appealing to him, standing there with her huge chocolate eyes and untamed hair. But her mind was struggling to find answers, and she had a penchant for violence, so the rifle had to go.

A wolf cry sounded, the note joyful in the night. "There." She waved toward the forest. "Your little friends are calling you. Go run and play with them for a while. You overwhelm me at the moment. I could use a break."

He put an arm out toward her. "Running with the wolves is truly a great joy, angel." His arm rippled with fur. Black glossy fur. His hand contorted, shifted shape.

Jaxon heard herself scream. She couldn't believe the strangled sound came from her own throat. She whirled around, jerked open the door to the kitchen, slipped inside, and slammed it shut. She locked every single dead bolt on the door before sliding to the floor. She drew her knees up and rocked herself for comfort.

This wasn't happening. It couldn't be happening. *What*

are you? She cried it in her mind. What was he? What should she do? If she called the police, no one would believe her. And the alternative would be that they did believe her, and the government would put Lucian in a laboratory and dissect him. Jaxon buried her face in her hands. What was she going to do? Maybe it was another trick. Another illusion. Just because he had named that hideous creature vampire didn't mean it was true. It was an illusion. It had to be. He was a master magician. That was how he made all his money, right? Weren't all magicians billionaires? Please let them all be billionaires.

Something made her lift her head. She was very careful to keep her hands over her face and only peek out between her fingers. Through the open door leading into the hall, she saw what looked like a low bank of fog. It just seemed to hang there for a moment silently. She bit at her knuckles with her teeth. Fog. In the house. Of course there was fog in Lucian's house. Wasn't fog in everyone's house?

Then Lucian's tall elegance filled the doorway, blocking her view of the hall. His black gaze moved slowly over her face. She saw stark possessiveness in his eyes. She recognized it, when all she wanted to do was run. But she could no more have gotten to her feet than fly. "Go away, Lucian."

"I have frightened you, honey. I am sorry. I was only teasing you."

Her long eyelashes fluttered for a moment before she actually found the courage to look up at him again. Why did he have to have such presence? He exuded power. "Everyone I know can turn into a wolf. That's what you were doing, wasn't it? Turning into a wolf?" Her teeth bit down hard on her knuckles.

He crossed the room with his silent, easy stride. Her heart slammed painfully. She tried to make herself smaller. Lucian simply sank to the floor beside her, his back to the door, his body close to hers. He drew his knees up, every movement slow and deliberate so as not to frighten her any further. "I was showing off." His hand touched her hair. "Nothing else, nothing sinister, just showing off."

Jaxon winced. "Well, don't do it again. People just can't do those things, Lucian. They can't, okay? You really aren't able to do them, so stop thinking you can. It isn't possible."

His hand found her silky hair again, his fingers gently rubbing the strands together before his palm curved around the nape of her neck. He began a slow, soothing massage to ease some of the tension out of her. "Angel, we talked about this when you spoke with Barry about the wolf. You knew it was me."

She shook her head adamantly. "I didn't think you meant it literally. I thought perhaps that you had a wolf or a dog with you. You can make people think things with optical illusions. I thought you might have made Barry see an illusion, not that you were actually a wolf. That never occurred to me. You can't turn into a wolf. No one can do that."

"I am Carpathian, not human, though you persist in thinking me so. I have many abilities, and I have told you that." His voice was deliberately soft and soothing.

"Well, you're just crazy, that's all. People like you don't exist in the world, Lucian, so get over it already." She rubbed her forehead. "You just can't do things like that anymore."

"You are not breathing, honey. Take a minute and listen to your body," he advised. He kept his voice soft and persuasive.

At once she was aware of her heart beating too rapidly, her lungs gasping for air. Immediately she became aware of his heartbeat, slow and steady, the air pushing easily through his lungs. Immediately her body began to tune itself to the rhythm of his. Jaxon flung up her arms to knock his hand from her neck. "See? Right there! You can't do things like this. No one can synchronize heartbeats exactly the way we do. Stop whatever you're doing right this minute. You're making me crazy."

His hand had not moved from the nape of her neck, a curiously intimate position she found rather soothing in spite of everything. Jaxon sighed and rested her head against his arm. "You're making me crazy," she murmured again tiredly.

"You think you cannot accept the things I tell you, but eventually your mind will overcome its human limitations." He said it so gently that her heart turned over.

The moment she gave in to the inevitable and relaxed against him, her heart and lungs immediately took on the slower, calming rhythm of his. Lucian pulled her into his arms and cradled her like a child so that she felt protected and safe. Jaxon stared up at his face, so still it could have been carved from stone, so beautiful he could have posed for the statues of the Greek gods.

"I don't want to feel anything for you." She traced his perfect mouth with one fingertip. "It would hurt too much to do that."

He became shadow in her mind, carefully, so she wouldn't recognize his touch, stilling the chaos of her thinking. He easily read her terrible fear for him. *For* him. Not really so much *of* him. "Listen to me, Jaxon, and this time hear what it is I am saying to you. Tyler Drake is human. He is not a vampire. He does not have supernatural powers. Drake has no chance against one such as myself. I have been in your mind, was with you as you examined the sites he chose to spy on this house. Did you think I really left you alone and unprotected? Did you really believe I would not know the moment you chose to leave this house? I will recognize his presence the moment he comes close to our property again. Tyler Drake cannot harm me in any way."

"If you knew I was out of the house and looking for Drake, didn't it worry you that I might run into him?" she challenged. A man like Lucian would have secured her protection, had he really known.

A faint smile took the edge of cruelty from his mouth. "I would have destroyed him from a distance. I am in your mind, honey. I can 'see' through your eyes. Anything I can see, I can destroy. If I connect with a person, and he hears my voice, I can destroy him. As I've said, I have certain abilities."

She lay in his arms quietly, trying to take in what he was telling her. "Lucian, how can any of this be? How can someone like you exist all this time and not one single person know about you?"

"There are some who have found us out. We originated in the Carpathian Mountains, and we refer to ourselves as Carpathian. There are humans who hunt us, who seek to murder us, There are scientists who would take us apart in a laboratory. They fear we are vampire, and, although we are few, they fear our powers."

"You scare me to death."

"No, I do not. The differences are difficult for your mind to accept. Do not confuse that with fear of me. You know I would never harm you. I am incapable of harming you. You are my heart and soul. The air I breathe. You bring light to the terrible darkness in my soul." He captured her hand and brought it to the warmth of his mouth. "There are moments when I feel you can collect all the missing pieces of my soul and put them back into place and make me whole once again."

"Is that how you really see me, Lucian?" Jaxon's large eyes looked into the dark, empty depths of his.

"It is who you are, Jaxon," he said softly. "I need you. The rest of the world does not need you the way I do. To

139

live. To breathe. You are my laughter and, I suspect, my tears. You are my very life."

"You can't feel that way about me when you've just met me. You don't know me at all."

"I have been in your mind many times, Jaxon. How could I not know you? You have already captured my heart. I am the one who must find a way to make you love me in spite of all my sins."

"Do you have so very many?" she asked softly. He was turning her inside out with what he was admitting. He seemed so self-sufficient, how could he ever need anyone, least of all someone with all her problems?

"My soul is stained so black, my love, there is no real way to ever redeem it. I am a dark angel of death. I have carried out my duties for centuries and know no other way of life."

"There's that word again. *Centuries.*" A faint smile chased the shadows from her face. "If you're such a dark, terrible person, why don't I sense evil when I'm around you? I know I don't have your"—she floundered for a moment, unable to think of the right word—"gifts, but I have a built-in radar system for anything evil. I feel the presence of it immediately. You can't possibly have a black soul, Lucian."

He moved then, a mere casual ripple of muscles, but he was standing without any effort, Jaxon in his arms. "You must eat, little one. You are wasting away right in front of me."

"You pick me up so much, I thought you'd appreciate the fact that I'm not carrying extra pounds."

Lucian plopped her down on the counter. "You are not going to try to tell me you do not eat because you worry I will not be able to pick you up."

She crossed her legs and arched one eyebrow. "I was more worried you'd strain your back." She tried not to

140

watch the way the muscles rippled suggestively beneath the thin white silk of his shirt.

He laughed softly at her outrageous suggestion as he began to put together a base for a soup. "You will not disobey me again, Jaxon, not when it comes to matters of safety."

" 'Disobey'? Interesting word. I don't think I really fully understand the meaning of the word, being a grown woman and all."

"Grown woman. Is that what you call it? You think you are as grown as you are going to get? A frightening thought."

"I hope you don't really think I'm going to obey you," Jaxon said softly, meaning it. She leaned over to get his attention. "You don't, do you?"

He shrugged with that casual grace, the movement that always took her breath away. "I have never had to ask more than once."

She sat back with a quick frown. "What does that mean? You wouldn't dare to use that threatening voice of yours on me."

He looked up from his task, his black gaze holding hers. "You would never know if I were, would you?" His voice was very, very soft.

Jaxon jumped to the floor, barely restraining herself from kicking him in the shins. "I've had enough of this. You know, it isn't as if you're asking me to accept some weird aunt in your family or something. You're not exactly the everyday, average fiancé. I'm not changing who I am for you. I worked my way up in the department because I'm good at what I do. I'm very good. Have a little respect."

He stirred the soup without changing expression. "You think I have no respect for you and the things you have had to cope with in your life? You cannot possibly think that. You are angry for no reason, Jaxon. I cannot change

141

who I am either. It is my sworn duty to care for you. It was imprinted on me before my birth. Do you think that changes because you are mortal?"

"Oh, God, the mortal thing again. At least someone actually gave birth to you. That's a relief." She pushed a hand through her hair. "Look at me, Lucian."

At her command, he turned obediently. She examined his face intently, a slow sweep of his sensual features before her gaze rested thoughtfully on his black eyes. "I would know. You would never even attempt to hide such a thing from me. You'd feel guilty."

"I would never feel guilty for forcing you to care for your health, angel. Do not make the mistake of giving me too much credit. I would feel guilty for concealing things from you, true. It is not right between lifemates. In any case, you have only to examine my mind."

Jaxon found herself laughing at the thought. "I can barely comprehend the things you tell me. I'm certainly not going to go trotting around in a brain that's several centuries old. That's just asking for trouble. How is it you can sound modern—sort of—if you're really so darned ancient?"

Lucian turned back to his soup. "It is not hard. I study and adapt quickly to new environments. It is necessary when one wishes to fit in. Sit at the table."

She tapped her foot. "The smell is not making me sick. That's you, isn't it? You're doing something so I can smell food without feeling sick."

"Yes." He saw no reason to deny it. "It is necessary that you eat. I do not want to make the decision to bring you over because you are unable to take sustenance. That would not be right."

Bring you over. Jaxon found a chair and sat down in it rather abruptly. Why did that sound like something straight out of a vampire novel? She waved a hand dismayingly in the air at him. "No more of that. Don't think it, and don't ever say it again. I'm getting used to the 'centuries' thing, but the 'bring you over' thing is too much."

Lucian placed a bowl of soup in front of her. His mind, connected as it was with hers, assumed the lead. He built the feeling of hunger in her. The idea that the broth smelled delicious and she wanted to eat it. He commanded her body not to reject it and reinforced the order with a "push" so there would be no mistakes. Very gently he rested a hand on her shoulder, needing the physical contact with her.

Never once had he allowed himself to express what he had felt when he realized she was leaving the house. He examined it now, there in the kitchen, turning the unfamiliar emotion over and over in his mind. *Fear.* He had been afraid for her. Not that Drake would find her, but of having to use her to destroy Drake. He would not want her to have to face such a thing. *Fear.* Fear that a vampire would discover her away from the protection he had woven for her within the grounds and the house. *Fear.* He had never experienced such an emotion. It had been gut-wrenching.

Lucian tangled his fingers in the wealth of her blond hair. She tipped her head back to look up at him, surprised by the way his fist was clenched in her hair. "What is it? What are you thinking about?" There was no expression on his face, nothing in his eyes to give him away, but Jaxon was beginning to know him. That small telltale sign of tension revealed that his thoughts had not been pleasant. "Tell me."

"I feared for you. Earlier, when you were away from the safety of the house." Lucian did not think to avoid the truth.

Jaxon responded immediately, wrapping her fingers around the thickness of his wrist. "You said yourself that I was perfectly safe."

"From Drake, you were safe," he admitted, staring down at her hand in wonder. Her fingers didn't even curl halfway around his wrist, yet she wielded so much power over him. "Drake cannot harm you."

"He has power, Lucian. He could get to Barry. I know you think you're invincible, but a sniper's bullet can kill from a great distance, and Drake is an excellent marksman. He doesn't have to face you." She ducked her head. "That's how Drake can harm me. That's how he's always done it—through someone else, someone who matters to me. That's why I don't want to be with you."

Above her head he found himself smiling. "You are beginning to have feelings for me."

"Keep telling yourself that," she told him. "This soup is good. I'm surprised you know how to cook." She didn't want to examine too closely or allude in any real way to what he did or didn't eat. Now wasn't the time to scare herself to death. She stood up carefully, moving away from him in a feminine little retreat he found secretly amusing.

Everything she did was like that. It lit him up inside. Filled him with warmth. Made him want to smile. More than that, he *had* to smile. He watched as she very carefully, very domestically, washed out the bowl and spoon.

Jaxon caught him watching her. "What?" She sounded defensive.

"I like watching you," he admitted easily. "I like having you in my house."

She tried not to let him see how much his words pleased her. Maybe she was just lonely. Maybe she was entirely too susceptible to his beautiful eyes. His voice. Or maybe his mouth. Or maybe it was because he was drop-dead gorgeous. She sighed aloud. "I'm going upstairs to rest for a while. Life with you is way too much excitement for me."

Lucian followed her up the stairs, carrying her sniper's

rifle. "This thing weighs almost as much as you do, Jaxon."

"You said you knew I was out of the house," she suddenly mused aloud, completely ignoring his teasing. "Why didn't I know what you were doing?"

"You didn't look."

She glanced at him over her shoulder, her large eyes eloquent with censure. "Look? Look at what?"

"My mind." He spoke in an even voice without any inflection at all. "I stay a shadow in your mind. Aside from the fact that it is much safer for me to know what you are doing at every moment, it is necessary for us to touch each other to be comfortable."

"You know, Lucian, if I had any brains at all, I wouldn't let you suck me in this way. You throw out these casual statements, and my curiosity always gets the better of me." She flung her knives and guns onto the dresser, pulled her cap from her pocket, and added that to the growing pile.

Lucian was watching her through half-closed eyes, a small smile curving his mouth. "Look at you, a walking arsenal."

"Well, at least I know how to protect myself. You think you're so powerful, not even a sniper's bullet can get you."

"We are back to that. Honey, I can command the heavens, move the earth, move my body through time and space. I am much more armed at all times than you will ever be. Do not look at me with your big brown eyes and that little frown on your face. You are in grave danger, for I have a desire to kiss that look right off your face."

Jaxon backed away from him so quickly, she fell backward onto the bed, alarm on her face. "Stay across the room, you fiend." She held up one hand to ward him off. "No talking, and no looking at me either. You use unfair tactics to get your way."

He stalked her right across the room, looming over her small figure like a conqueror of old. "You deserve some kind of punishment for leaving this house after you so sincerely promised me you would stay put."

"I assured you I had no intention of going out dancing," she pointed out virtuously. "I can't think where you ever got the idea that I intended to sit around waiting for you. I have things to do. Modern-day women do not sit at home while their men go out and play."

He touched her face with one fingertip, tracing her soft skin, the delicate line of her high cheekbone. "I told you to stay here."

"I was merely out walking. Fresh air is good for a person—didn't you know that? And walking is the greatest exercise of all. It can be done anywhere, anytime." She looked absolutely convinced of it. "Walking doesn't count as going out."

Lucian sat on the bed, crowding her. "Walking." He murmured the word absently, his fingers tangling in her hair. The feel of it against his skin distracted him. "Do not place yourself at risk again, angel. I will take action next time."

She shoved at the wall of his chest, more to get some breathing room than for any other reason. He seemed capable of robbing her of her very air. "I hope you don't think you're threatening me with something. I'm a police officer, Lucian. Threats are not a great way to win favors."

"I do not need favors, and I do not much care for your rather strange choice of occupations. This may not be a good time to bring it up, but you do not seem to understand. I have never had anyone question my decisions. You will not place yourself at risk again." He never raised his voice; if anything, it was softer, gentler than ever before. He sounded mild, almost absently giving his order to her.

Jaxon frowned at him. "You don't improve much as one gets more acquainted with you. I don't like bossy men."

His hand slipped to the nape of her neck, his fingers caressing her soft, scented skin. He didn't seem to notice, and she sat very still, not wanting to draw attention to the fact that he was scattering her senses in every direction.

"I do not consider myself bossy. There is a vast difference between being bossy and being in command."

"Go command something else then, Lucian, because I am in charge of my own life. Total charge. If I decide to leave the house, I'll do so anytime I please. Don't think you can get away with being a supreme dictator just because you're . . ." Words totally failed her. What was he?

I already answered that. Deliberately he used the intimate form of communication that his race used with their lifemates. He bent his head to the vulnerable nape of her neck, unable to resist the temptation. *I am Carpathian, your lifemate.*

At once hungry flames danced over his body. His gut clenched hotly, and he closed his eyes to savor the taste and feel of her skin. To savor the feeling of intense hunger. His larger, stronger body bent over hers, slowly forcing her to lie across the bed beneath him. She was very delicate, very fragile beneath his exploring hands as he imprinted her for all time deep within his soul.

"Lucian." His name came out a soft, whispered plea, almost as if she were asking him for help.

Lucian lifted his head and stared down into her enormous eyes. She looked confused, drowsy, and very, very sexy. "I am not hurting you, angel, only giving in to a tremendous need I have to feel you."

She reached up to brush at his hair, a small smile tugging at her full lower lip. "Yes, well, I noticed. I just think this is a little dangerous. I'm still trying to get used to the idea that you're not human. You tell me all this interesting science-fiction stuff, and I hear what you're saying, but my mind doesn't want to put together all the facts. You're positively scary, Lucian."

"Not to you," he denied, his voice lazy as he bent to find her throat with his mouth. She tasted so good. Felt so good, her skin like satin. "I have been unfailingly gentle with you." His mouth followed the perfection of her skin down her throat and across her collarbone. She was so very delicate. He didn't see how anything so small could hold together such a perfect package.

"You're always in such perfect control. I can't imagine you not in complete control. But then you look at me, and . . ." She closed her eyes as his mouth wandered lower, pushing aside the thin material of her top so he could touch more skin.

"You were saying?" he murmured against the inviting swell of her breast. "I look at you?" His teeth scraped gently, erotically over her sensitive skin, and she heard herself gasp even as her arms cradled his head to her.

What had she been saying? He was still in control. Even now, while she lay in his arms and could feel his body burning for hers, hungry for hers, he was in complete control. She turned more fully into his arms, her body pressing closer to the enormous strength of his. What would it feel like to belong? Really belong to someone? Not to be afraid all the time? When she was with Lucian, she was never afraid.

Lucian felt her body, soft and pliant, molding itself to his. He pushed the offending cloth farther from her skin, exposing her small, perfectly molded breasts to the cool air. To his dark, possessive gaze. To the heat of his mouth. She really was a miracle, everything about her. Her body moved restlessly, and he shifted his weight to pin her more fully beneath him, needing to feel every inch of her imprinted against his skin. He lowered his mouth and tasted her breast, his tongue swirling lazily, teasing her nipple into a hard peak.

He could hear the ebb and flow of her blood rushing through her veins, calling to him, beckoning with a sweet invitation. He murmured her name softly, stroked her skin, tracing each separate rib, finding the indentation of her small waist. In his ears was a dull roar, and the beast within him lifted its head and roared for release. Roared to claim what belonged to it.

Jaxon sensed the change in him. It was in the hard possession of his hands, the sudden aggression of his body. For the first time she was afraid. She caught his thick black hair in her fists and made a small sound somewhere between submission and protest. "Lucian." She whispered his name like a talisman, knowing he would always protect her.

At once he raised his head. Her breath caught in her throat. Behind the depths of his eyes crouched a primitive animal; she could see it, the red flames in its eyes, the heat and hunger gathering into a fierce conflagration. Her heart thudded wildly. "Lucian." She tightened her grip in his hair, two large handfuls, holding on for her life.

"It is all right, angel," he said tenderly. He kissed her throat gently, lingering over her wildly beating pulse. "I could never hurt you. You are my life, the air I breathe. I may sometimes act more animal than man, but I am truly a man after all."

"But not human." Jaxon's voice was a mere thread of sound.

"Not human," he agreed. "A Carpathian male, very much needing his lifemate at this moment."

Jaxon was suddenly acutely conscious of her disheveled clothes. "I think it would be best if you removed yourself from my bedroom."

"Best for whom?" Amusement tinged his voice. "Not me." Very gently he arranged her black top to cover her creamy skin. "Do you have any idea how much you mean to me?" He shook his head. "It is not possible that you could know."

She was afraid to breathe. Her entire body was crying out for his, completely betraying her saner self. "Lucian, I really need to be alone for a while."

"So you can deny that you want me?"

"Absolutely," she agreed readily. There was no reason to deny it. He was lucky she wasn't experienced. She might just be ripping his clothes off. The idea took her breath away.

He arched an expressive eyebrow at her. "It takes my breath away, too," he murmured against her throat, proving he was a shadow firmly entrenched in her mind.

She wanted to be annoyed with him. He had no right to listen to her every thought. But she found herself laughing. It just seemed so intimate, lying on the bed with his arm curved around her waist, his black eyes moving over her with such stark hunger in them. "You're so bad, Lucian."

Jaxon closed her eyes tiredly. It felt good to simply lie there and be still. Not think. Not do anything but feel his warmth and strength. "I'm so tired. It must be close to dawn. Why are we always talking until dawn?"

"So you grow tired and sleep all day while I am at my weakest. It is a good way to keep you chained to my side." Lucian stretched lazily "I intend to sleep here with you, so settle down and do not try to argue with me."

Jaxon thumped his shoulder, then shifted to lay her head on it "I wasn't going to argue with you. Why ever would you think that? I never argue."

Lucian smiled at her. She was so small, it amazed him she was such a strong person. "Of course you do not argue. What was I thinking? Go to sleep, honey, and allow my poor body to rest."

"I'm already asleep. You're the one gabbing."

Lucian concentrated on safeguarding the estate. He found he was more than a little distracted with Jaxon snuggled so close to him, her body fitting perfectly into the curve of his. She thought him so controlled, and perhaps it was true in every other matter—every matter other than Jaxon. He was not so sure of his ability to protect her from his own needs and hungers.

"Lucian?" The drowsy note in her voice sent his gut clenching into a ball of fire that was spreading like molten lava.

"Go to sleep." He draped his arm over her, completely engulfing her. Of their own accord his fingers tangled in the thick mop of untamed hair. His own voice was husky with need.

"Don't you sleep underground or something? I know you don't use a coffin, but this seems too normal for you." Her voice held suspicion.

Lucian hesitated. There could be no untruths between lifemates, and he had always been careful to tell her those details of his life she asked about. But this. What was he to answer? "Go to sleep."

At once Jaxon tried to lift her head. Lucian didn't appear to notice. His arm lay firmly in place. "Tell me, Lucian, or I'm going to bug you all day."

He sighed. "I thought you didn't like hearing all the gory details of my existence." His fingers were moving in her hair gently, a tender caress that warmed her heart as nothing else could.

It was the way he touched her, the way he looked at her, Jaxon decided, as if she were the only woman in the world for him. And he was beguiling. A dark sorcerer impossible to resist. Like right now, his mouth skimming the top of her head, the way he inhaled her scent as if he were taking the essence of her into his own body "I'm beginning to be rather fond of your fantasyland, Lucian." The smile left her voice, and she became very serious. "I want to know everything about you. Not all at once, maybe, but eventually, everything."

He lay there, his body tight and hot and uncomfortable. He should have been in a burning hell, but instead he was filled with joy. Her words moved him, melted his insides, so that the demon within him was safely leashed. He knew he would have her, he knew he would never allow her to escape him, yet he never believed she would grow to love him for who he was, what he was. Maybe it wouldn't happen, but Jaxon did want to know him, his reality.

Lucian's hand moved to the nape of her neck, his fingers curling around it. "To rejuvenate our bodies, such as when we have suffered mortal wounds or used much energy to heal another, the soil of the earth welcomes us. But it is not strictly necessary to sleep within the arms of the earth. It is safer, for little harm can find its way to us there." Again he hesitated, unsure how she would take the next piece of information.

Jaxon thumped his chest lightly with her fist. She didn't bother to open her eyes and frown at him, considering her gesture enough of a reprimand. "Tell me."

"Normally we sleep differently than humans in that we shut down our hearts and lungs and lie as if dead. But that is a dangerous thing to do in a setting such as this one. Beneath this house I have a sleeping chamber. If something should happen and my safeguards failed, then it would be much easier for an adversary to destroy me here than in my sleeping chamber, where they cannot find me."

Jaxon shoved his arm aside and sat up, her hair spilling wildly around her face, her eyes enormous. "Why aren't you doing what you're supposed to be doing? I'm not going to be thrilled waking up next to someone who looks dead."

"I will not sleep in the manner of our kind, Jaxon. We

are bound together. We must touch minds frequently, or it is uncomfortable, even dangerous. Your mind is used to the touch of my mind. Without it you would feel intense grief, much more intense than a human could withstand. Carpathian emotions are extremely strong, Jaxon, due, no doubt, to our longevity. I cannot exactly describe what you would feel, but I cannot take such a chance with you. There is no need for it. I will sleep in the way of your people."

"Why don't you sleep like we do all the time?"

He sighed and deliberately pulled her once more into his arms. "You talk too much, when you should be sleeping."

"You've been doing that, haven't you? Sleeping beside me like a human instead of doing what is good for you," Jaxon guessed shrewdly. "That's why you look tired sometimes. Your body doesn't rest this way, does it?"

"No, it does not rest." He sounded somewhere between exasperation and laughter.

"Go to your sleeping chamber or whatever it is you call it," she demanded.

"I cannot be apart from you."

"If your heart and lungs are shut down, then you can't possibly feel anything," she said logically.

"You are trying to take care of me again," he pointed out, wishing his heart didn't react quite so strongly to her concern. In all the endless centuries he had endured, he could not remember a single individual, other than his twin brother, Gabriel, who had worried about him. And that hadn't been the same.

"Someone has to take care of you. You don't," she replied. "I mean it, Lucian. I can see how tired you are. Please go where you can sleep properly."

"Not without you."

There was a small silence. "I can go there?"

"Yes," he said slowly. "I told you, it isn't in the earth.

153

It is below the basement but not in the soil."

"If I woke up, I could just walk out of there? I don't think I'm claustrophobic, but I'd hate to trapped somewhere."

"I can show you the way. But, Jaxon, you must not think I'm dead. If you wake without me, before the sun goes down, your mind will play tricks on you. I will look dead and feel dead to your touch. You cannot allow your mind to trick you into doing anything foolish. Lifemates often end their lives rather than exist alone after they are bound together. You must promise me, should you wake, you will not leave the house, and if it becomes unbearable, you will call out to me persistently in the way of our people."

"You can hear me while your heart and lungs are shut down?"

"Most cannot. But I am not most. If you are suffering and you call to me, I will hear you."

"Then let's go." She said it determinedly.

"You are certain you wish to do this? It is not necessary."

"Yes, it is. You need to sleep and stay strong and powerful for all that weird stuff that you do. I'm getting used to it, and I'd miss it if you couldn't do it anymore."

Lucian lifted her easily as he rose straight off the bed into the air, cradling her in his arms. "Close your eyes, angel. You know how you hate my manner of travel."

"The speed thing."

"Exactly." His voice was infinitely tender.

She closed her eyes and snuggled more deeply into his body, her heart pounding nervously. There was a rush of wind and sense of traveling through time and space as they maneuvered the intricate passages to his sleeping chamber far below the house.

As he laid her on the bed, Jaxon looked around her in awe. It was beautiful, nothing like the cave she had imagined it to be It was a room with furniture and candles and crystal rocks that reflected the dancing flames, projecting intriguing shadows. Its fragrance was soothing, and Jaxon found she could lie beside him without fear.

Lucian leaned over her, his hand tracing the beloved lines of her face. "Sleep well, angel. If you dream, let it be only of me." He bent his head and found the silken heat of her mouth one last time, staking his claim, his intentions, moving the earth for both of them. Even as he lifted his head, he commanded she sleep, a deep sleep undisturbed until the sun sank from the sky.

Only when he was certain the safeguards were in place and he had sent word to the wolves to guard the property did he allow the breath to leave his body and his heart to cease beating.

Chapter Seven

Jaxon fought her way up through layers of thick fog, emerging with a pounding headache and a sick feeling in her stomach. In the darkness of the chamber she could not tell whether it was night or day. Not one speck of light seeped through the room's thick walls. She lay very still, deep within the earth, trying to sort out what was happening. She could feel Lucian beside her. His body was cold, and he had no discernable heartbeat, no rise and fall of his chest. It was eerie lying there beside him, knowing he wasn't even breathing.

For a moment she felt as if she were suffocating at the possibility of his lying dead beside her, but he had prepared her for just such an event, and she forced logic into her panic-stricken brain. What had awakened her? Instinctively she knew she had been programmed, *commanded*, by Lucian not to wake up until he did.

It took her a few minutes to shake off the fog. Even so, her headache refused to disappear along with it, almost as if the air was too thick to breathe. Sitting up, she pushed at her thick hair. Her stomach lurched crazily. She pressed both hands against her stomach and went very still. Drake. Was it Drake? Something evil was lurking close to them. Something malevolent. Something ugly lying in wait for them. Stalking them.

She glanced down at Lucian. He was such a perfect specimen of a man. He was amazingly beautiful, sensual in a purely masculine way. She touched his long black hair, pushing it from his forehead with caressing fingers. Drake was not going to hurt him if she could help it. She knew if she called to him, he would awaken, but she had confidence in her own abilities, and Lucian was far safer beneath the earth, where no one would find him until he was at full strength. Resolutely she slid from the high bed and padded barefoot across the floor. It was pitch-black in the chamber, but her night vision was phenomenal.

The door was heavy, and it took all her strength to open it. Even then it seemed difficult to walk through it. It was much like walking through quicksand or a heavy bog of some kind. Jaxon hurried through the narrow passageway, noting that it slanted upward, twisting and turning through bedrock. At last she came out into the basement. But she could see no evidence of a door. Then she discovered it concealed neatly in the rock. The feeling in the pit of her stomach was getting stronger. Something was definitely stalking them.

She ran lightly through the kitchen up the stairs to her room. Hastily she threw on a pair of slim black jeans and a navy police academy sweatshirt. It was an old favorite she often wore for comfort. Again she considered waking Lucian, calling to him as he had told her she could, but she dismissed the idea. Even through the heavy drapes in her room she could see that the sun was not quite out of the sky yet. He needed all the rest he could get. And if he wasn't at full strength, he could possibly be hurt. She didn't know enough about him yet to determine what would happen if he awakened during daylight. The thought of him melting or something was laughable but unpleasant all the same.

She put on her tennis shoes, strung field glasses around her neck, and found her favorite Browning. If it was Drake, he wasn't going to get to Lucian. Jaxon glided silently from window to window, studying the surrounding grounds, taking care not to expose herself on the one side she knew could be seen from the distant bluff. She heard the lonely cry of a wolf, and a few moments later a second answered it, but it didn't sound as if they were hunting or had been disturbed in any way.

Jaxon decided whatever it was could not make an assault on the house from the woods side without some warning from the wolves, so she concentrated on the courtyard and the front entrance. Outside the high wall she caught a brief glimpse of something moving. Not enough of a view to make an identification, but enough to be certain something was out there.

She made her way midway down the winding staircase where the balcony with the glass door was. She slid it noiselessly open and rolled out onto the deck, hidden from view behind the railing. At once the terrible precognition hit her fiercely, making her physically ill. She knew she was on the right track. Why hadn't she called for backup? Because she couldn't explain Lucian's absence to anyone. And she couldn't have the police department snooping around.

Cautiously she raised her head and surveyed the front of the estate. She lifted the field glasses to get a better view. At once she saw the arm and leg of what appeared to be a large male. He was moving along the wall of the estate and came into full view as she watched. Brought up close by the binoculars, he was a frightening sight. He looked like a giant, and his head was somewhat misshapen, almost like a bullet. His eyes were dull and lifeless, his teeth blackened and sharpened to ugly points, and his entire expression was the blank mask of insanity.

He slammed his palms repeatedly against the high stone wall, and each time sparks would explode and smoke would rise. He would scream and pull his palms away, only to move one step farther along the wall and try again, with the exact same results. The wall couldn't possibly be electrified, yet it seemed that way, crackling with life every time the stranger attempted to touch it. He was persistent, not in the least deterred by the fact that he was being burned.

Jaxon stood up to climb onto the railing, wanting access to the roof. She was too short; her fingers missed by several inches. Irritated, she glared up at the eaves. There had to be a way up if she just took a minute to think about it. She didn't want the strange person out of her sight. He was up to no good, and he gave her the creeps. As she turned, her body automatically adjusting her weight to keep centered, she glanced at the sky to judge the setting sun.

Too late she saw a spinning silver web coming at her from above, sparkling out of the clouds like a net to encase her. Fear slammed into her. *Lucian!* It was automatic, calling for him, reaching for him, almost a compulsion, certainly not a thought of her own. Except on her job, it was nothing she would ever do in her life—think to call another for aid. The strange glittering net stopped in midair, hovered there for a moment, and then dropped harmlessly to the ground below.

Jaxon felt her small body lifted by unseen hands to the safety of the balcony floor. She actually felt his hands around her waist. At once she was forced backward, the hands pushing her right into the house. The sliding door closed firmly and latched solidly. She placed both palms on the thick glass and peered below at the strange person resolutely testing the strength of the wall's defenses. Instead of using his hands, he was now slamming his entire body against the hard surface, and sparks were flaring in the waning light all around him.

He looked up at her, his dead eyes meeting her gaze, and his actions became more frantic, battering his body even harder and more determinedly than ever. Jaxon could only stand there helplessly, locked in place, while far below her point of safety the scene of horror unfolded. As the sun sank, the stranger began emitting growls, digging at the earth beneath the fence and casting anxious glances skyward.

Her heart thudded as she saw the tall, elegant frame emerge from the heavy brush on the north side of the house. Lucian walked neither fast nor slow, his immaculate charcoal-gray jacket emphasizing the width of his shoulders. His hair was flowing around his shoulders, his eyes glittering in his still face. He stopped only feet from the gate and waved a hand. At once the sparks ceased, and the stranger realized there was no protection on the property. The gates began to swing open.

Jaxon's attention was caught by the ominous appearance of dark clouds moving swiftly through the sky. Something was terribly wrong. She tried to open the door, afraid for Lucian, afraid he wouldn't notice the danger from above when the creature on the ground was trudging toward him with such purposeful steps. She banged on the glass helplessly, tried to turn to run downstairs, but she was unable to move more than a couple of feet. Swallowing hard, she pulled out the Browning, praying Lucian hadn't installed bulletproof glass.

In her mind she reached desperately for him. *Lucian, above you! Something's coming, and it's far more evil than what you're facing now. Let me help you!* Nothing could happen to him. Nothing could ever happen to him.

She felt instant warmth, reassurance flowing into her mind. For a brief moment she even felt his arms around her, holding her close. Jaxon placed a hand on the glass, the Browning in her other fist, and watched the easy, fluid way Lucian walked. He moved with total confidence, total assurance, his head up, his long hair flowing behind him. He took her breath away. As she watched, his hand came up almost casually, and above him the black roiling clouds dispersed as if they had never been. Something dropped to earth, a twisted, writhing, reptilian body with wings.

"Oh, God," Jaxon whispered aloud, all too afraid of what it was. She bit her lip hard in agitation.

The strange man had nearly reached Lucian, swinging a heavy spiked ball on the end of a chain. The ball whistled harmlessly through space as Lucian disappeared from Jaxon's sight for a split second. When he reappeared, he was behind the huge stranger. She watched in horror as the stranger's head tilted to one side, a crimson smile appearing around his throat like a necklace. The head wobbled grotesquely, then slowly slid off the shoulders, spraying a trail of red in all directions. The body toppled over and hit the ground as the head bounced and rolled away from Lucian's legs.

The reptile sprang at Lucian so quickly it was a blur of claws and teeth. The tail lashed back and forth like a whip, and the beating wings were creating a windstorm, stirring up leaves and dirt like a smokescreen. Jaxon's scream of warning caught in her throat, nearly choking her. Lucian seemed to stand completely motionless, his face expressionless, calm, even serene, as if he were simply admiring the view around him. Jaxon aimed the gun at the hideous lizard. The creature seemed to hit an invisible wall before it reached Lucian, and it shrieked as flames erupted all around it. Charred flesh peeled in layers from the lizard. The carcass split into pieces. Jaxon could hardly believe her eyes when a man emerged from the peeling flesh as if from a cocoon.

161

The vampire flew backward away from Lucian, while tree branches and rocks whistled through the air, aimed directly at him. Lucian flowed across the ground, going from stillness to motion with unbelievable speed. Jaxon felt she was watching a merciless predator, a killing machine, a jungle cat with rippling muscles to bring down its prey. At fast as the vampire retreated, throwing obstacles into his path, Lucian was faster. The debris never touched him, deflected with casual ease by his mind as Lucian overtook the undead.

At the realization it could not escape, the vampire turned its head and looked up at Jaxon, hatred in its eyes, cunning and malevolence on its face. The glass of the sliding door began to bulge inward toward her even as Lucian plunged his hand into the chest of the creature, extracting the pulsating heart. Jaxon leaped backward, away from the door, her gaze riveted on the scene below.

Lucian dropped the heart some distance from the writhing body and glanced toward the sky. At once clouds gathered overhead, more and more of them coming to his bidding. Shocked, Jaxon watched him orchestrate the storm. Lightning arced from cloud to cloud in a brilliant display. He opened the hand that had extracted the heart, and a fiery ball dropped from the sky into his palm. For one moment the orange flames danced over his skin, reflected in his black eyes; then he tossed the ball onto the heart and waved his hand, spreading the flames.

Noxious black smoke rose into the sky. In it she could see images of death and darkness, violent, misshapen creatures hissing and crying out to the heavens. They slowly evaporated in the smoke, and the rising wind carried them away. Fire raced across the ground, leaping from one body to the other, incinerating the two creatures for all time, erasing all evidence of their existence, as if they had never been.

Jaxon watched as the glass door smoothed, as rain began to lash at the windows of the house, and outside Lucian raised his head and looked at her. Her heart thudded uncomfortably. At once she knew the barrier imprisoning her within the house was lifted. She lay the gun and binoculars on the top step and hurried down the winding staircase to the first floor.

Lucian terrified her—the power he wielded, the fact that he could destroy life so easily, that he could command the very heavens to do his bidding, that he could hold fire in his hand and not be harmed. Yet she wanted to touch him—no, she *needed* to touch him—to know he had not suffered one single scratch.

Lucian came striding into the house, tall and powerful and dangerous beyond her imagination. His face was expressionless, calm, as always in complete control. But something in the way he moved gave him away, and she faltered in her headlong rush toward him, coming to a halt just inside the living room. Lucian continued to move quickly, never breaking stride, flowing across the room like water, only his eyes alive with something she had never seen before.

"Lucian." Her hand went defensively to her throat.

He didn't respond, merely caught her fragile wrist in an unbreakable grip and continued walking down the hall, taking her with him to his den. As they entered, he waved a hand, and flames sprang to life in the rock fireplace. He turned in one motion, his fingers wrapping around her throat. He stepped toward her, locking her against the wall, trapping her with his taller, heavier frame.

Jaxon's heart missed a beat, and she could only stare up at him with wide eyes. He suddenly looked like the dangerous predator he really was.

"You will never defy me like that again and place yourself in danger." His voice was so soft she barely caught the words, yet she recognized the iron, the command in

it. His black gaze moved over her face, brooding, possessive, gleaming with that extra unknown quality that made
her heart pound in fear. Abruptly he lowered his mouth
to hers, and her heart stopped completely.

The very earth rocked beneath her feet. She felt his immense strength in the fingers curled around her throat,
felt the hard aggression of his body, and knew his sudden
resolve. She should stop him—she had to stop him—yet
his body was hot and heavy with need, and his hunger
was swamping her, overwhelming her. She was going up
in flames right there with his mouth fastened on hers and
his hand threatening to choke the life out of her as punishment for her needing to protect him. Unable to think
clearly, she made a small sound of protest, even as her
body relaxed into his.

"Listen to me, little love." He framed her face with his
large hands, resting his forehead against hers. "You do
not yet love me, I know. But you are a strong woman,
and even facing the monster in me, your first thought was
to see to my health. I am frightening to you only because
you do not fully comprehend what I am.

"You are my life, my only reason for existence, my
heart and my soul, the very air I breathe. I have lived
without joy for nearly two thousand years, and in the
short time we have been together, you have made every
one of those dark, endless minutes worth it. There is no
way for you to fully comprehend the depth of my feelings
for you at this time—I understand that—but you will
have to try. You belong with me. I know this absolutely,
without a shadow of a doubt. And my feelings will only
grow stronger with the passage of time."

His fingertips moved over her beloved face, found their
way to her hair to tangle in the silky strands. "I need you
completely, Jaxon, for all time. I need you safe and protected so that I never wake again with the knowledge that
you have placed your life in danger. And you would, over

and over. It is not defiance; it is in your nature to protect others. And when I say I need you completely, you must know that I need your body desperately."

There was fear in her eyes, in the telltale pounding of her heart. "I've never been with anyone, Lucian, and you're very overwhelming." She bit her lower lip, not wanting to fail him, wanting to be there to take away the terrible hunger building in his eyes, in his body. She had almost wanted to see him a little bit out of control, yet now she could see where that would lead. Lucian was going to have her. She wanted him, yet she was afraid of the dark intensity within him. He seemed so tranquil, yet the fires smoldering beneath the surface were dark and deadly. She sensed them, knew she was unleashing something powerful she could never stop.

Lucian's dark eyes searched hers, held her gaze. "Before I do this thing, before you are mine for all eternity, I want you to know that I know I can make you happy in this existence, that there is no other who can do so, and that I will move heaven and earth for you if that is what I need to do."

His black gaze found and captured hers. She saw the terrible hunger so strong in him, so stark and raw and alive with desperate need. The sane part of her knew he was saying something important, something she should analyze before she dared succumb to the dark, beckoning fire, but it was too late. Her arms were already sliding around his neck, and she was giving up her mouth to the sheer domination of his. Heat and fire. A volcano of such need rising seemingly out of nowhere. His need, her need—she couldn't tell the difference. Couldn't tell where he began and she left off.

Lucian's skin was hot and sensitive, far too sensitive to feel fabric brush against it. He needed Jaxon's soft skin pressed close to him, not the annoying cloth barrier between them. Nothing would ever be between them again.

His resolve was complete, total. She would never again be in such danger. She belonged to him, had been made for him, his miracle, his to love and protect. She was more than his life. She was his soul.

He thought away his shirt—an easy accomplishment. But it was his hands that caught the hem of her blouse and lifted it slowly over her head. She was so beautiful, she took his breath away. It was his breathing that was out of control, his heart that was racing so quickly. Or was it hers? He couldn't tell anymore. Only that she was hot, silken fire, and he needed to burn. Was already burning. His hands found their way to her skin. So soft. So perfect. The feel of her was almost more than he could bear. He had waited so long, never once believing she existed for him. He had existed in that black, endless void without hope, without the thought of light. Without the possibility of Jaxon. Was she real?

His mouth fastened on hers, hot and hard and hungry, sweeping her into another world where there was only Lucian and his hard muscles, the touch of his hands, the aggression of his body. He was everywhere, swamping her, in her mind, in her heart. His hands were touching her intimately, exploring every inch of her. His mouth was sheer magic, so that her world narrowed to pure feeling, so that there was no way to think, only to feel.

Lucian lifted her easily, his mouth still on hers, so that she had no real awareness of anything but him. There *was* nothing else for her, he knew. His mind removed the last barrier between them—the rest of their clothing—so that when he took her down to the oriental rug on the floor in front of the fireplace, he knew she felt the thick carpet against her already sensitized skin. He lifted his head to look at her, to watch the firelight caress her face. She was so beautiful, simply looking at her actually hurt at times.

Her large eyes were gazing at him with an enticing invitation, sexy yet innocent in that she didn't really know

166

what she was agreeing to. His world. His woman. His true lifemate for all eternity. Deliberately he bent his head to find her soft mouth, to taste the silken heat so addicting to him. She was his. The reality of it was more than he could comprehend. Her skin was soft, felt like satin. The shape of her curves, the lines of her body, the perfectly proportioned form. She was a miracle to him, and he worshiped her leisurely. His mouth wandered over her throat, so vulnerable to one such as he. With others she was careful, yet with him she was so trusting.

He found the swell of her breast, heard her gasp as he indulged himself, as he lost himself and the world around him in her body. Her waist, so small, so perfectly designed, the triangle of tight blond curls below beckoning him. He inhaled her scented call, the wild, untamed need rising to match his own. His teeth nipped at her inner thigh, easing her legs apart, while his hand found moist heat, a welcoming to the hunger in his body.

Jaxon heard the soft sound escaping from her own throat as Lucian began a slow, intimate exploration, finding her every secret place. He took his time; he had learned patience over the centuries, and he had waited for this moment for so long, he intended her first time to be perfect for her. His mind was firmly merged with hers so she could feel his rising need, a tidal wave swamping him, hot lava pouring through his body where his blood had been. She could feel the painful ache, and the total pleasure he took in the erotic things he was doing to her body. She found his long hair, wrapped her fists in it to hold on to as her body began to wind tighter and tighter with need.

The world seemed to dissolve around her as little ripples of pleasure started deep inside her and spread until she was clutching at him for anchor. Lucian loomed over her, his shoulders wide, the muscles of his arms and back defined and taut from the effort to go slowly. He eased

Christine Feehan

into her, inch by slow inch, until he met the thin barrier
of resistance. She was so tight and hot, he was going up
in flames. His hands caught her small hips. Even now, at
this moment, with his body urging him to bury himself
deep within her, with a roar in his ears and a red haze of
desire in his mind, he realized just how small she was,
how fragile she seemed in his hands.

"Lucian." She whispered his name, and he bent to take
her mouth again, surging forward as he did so. Her soft
gasp was caught for all time at that first taking, that first
merging of body and mind.

"Relax for me, angel," he instructed softly, leaving a
trail of fire from her throat to her breast. He waited for
her body to stretch to accommodate his size, to become
used to the feel of his invasion. "You were created for
me, the other half of my soul." His teeth moved back and
forth over her pulse. He whispered softly to her, sweeping
resistance from her mind, so that there was only acceptance of his every need.

Jaxon's nails dug into his back as white-hot pain lanced
through her, then gave way to something dark and erotic
as his teeth sank deeply into her. His hips surged forward,
and he was sweeping her into a world of sensuality unlike
any she had ever imagined. His mouth, feeding on her,
was intimate and sexy, and she cradled his head to her,
offering her breast, wanting him to take the very essence
of her life into him for all time. His body moving into
hers in long, sure strokes, each deeper and harder than
the last, creating such a friction of heat that they were
both on fire, a single, living, breathing flame. His tongue
stroked across the small pinpricks on her breast, and he
moved within her faster, surging deep to find her very
core.

His palm cradled the back of her head, and in his mind
he built the need, thought it, became need, until he was
the only thing she could think of. Jaxon had to quench

168

that terrible urgency that was in the red haze of his mind. He held her head close to the heavy muscles of his chest, and immediately a small wound appeared there. Lucian pressed her mouth to him, his mind controlling hers, needing her to drink deeply from the dark well. The feel of her mouth feeding on him was like nothing he had ever experienced. Her body, hot and tight, was velvet surrounding his, a fiery sheath that tested the limits of his control.

While she drank, Lucian very softly recited the ritual words once more. He wanted this, the rightness of it, the completeness. This was his true lifemate for all eternity, and he wanted the ceremony to be exact, so that there was no chance she would escape him. No chance that harm could come to her. "I claim you as my lifemate. I belong to you. I offer my life for you. I give to you my protection, my allegiance, my heart, my soul, and my body. I take into my keeping the same that is yours. Your life, happiness, and welfare will be cherished and placed above my own for all time. You are my lifemate, bound to me for all eternity and always in my care."

He would reside in her for all time, would know immediately should danger threaten her. And she would reside in him, anchoring him so that the beast within had no chance to be unleashed on the world.

His body was going up in flames. He could feel himself fast losing his control. At once he removed the compulsion for her to feed, certain he had given her enough blood for a true exchange. With the ritual complete—their third blood exchange and their mating—he allowed himself the indulgence of losing himself in her body. He buried himself in her, over and over, feeling her heat, her fire, taking him in, cleansing the darkness from his soul. All those empty centuries, all the dark deeds, necessary though they might be, all the missing pieces—she was somehow putting him back together again. The ecstasy of her body was almost more than he could stand. He felt her muscles clenching around him, tighter and tighter, spiraling him ever more deeply into that fiery vortex, milking him so that he was exploding, shattering, taking her with him into the unknown.

Jaxon clutched at Lucian for security, for a safe haven in a storm of such sensation she was shocked by it. She had no idea she could feel this way, no idea her body was capable of such things. Lucian was lying above her, careful to keep his weight from crushing her, his body still locked firmly within hers. It was sexy, erotic, and terribly intimate. She savored the taste of him in her mouth, a slightly coppery flavor, masculine and addicting. She lay beneath him, staring up at him in wonder.

There was a memory in her mind, of her mouth moving over his chest. Even as she tried to catch it, the fleeting thought brought her to instant awareness of the hard thickness of him buried deep within her body. He was moving gently, almost as if he had to move, as if the feel of her surrounding him was more than he could bear passively. His hands framed her face. "You are so beautiful, Jaxon, so truly beautiful."

She moved against him, her body as hot and restless as his, as in need as his. The carpet beneath her skin brushed at her like fingers. His mouth was moving over her body again, his tongue swirling over her breasts, his masculine being reveling in his ability to take her over and over, to indulge himself.

She was heat, silk, everything he could ever want. And she wanted him with the same urgent need he had for her. He watched the firelight play over her body, caressing the shadows and lingering on the creamy lines of her small frame. He watched his body moving in and out of her, the erotic sight heightening his pleasure even more. He bent his head to the tip of her breast because he could, his hands stroking her small waist and flat stomach. All the time his hips moved slowly, leisurely, building the heat between them until they could both once more go up in flames. He wanted it this way, slow and long and easy enough to last for all time. He wanted to live there in the safe haven of her body, where miracles really did happen.

"Lucian," she said in breathless wonder, her hands sliding over his shoulders, soothing him.

He was gentle with her, loving, ensuring her pleasure, yet at the same time she could feel him watching her closely, waiting for something. Waiting for her to condemn him. She caught that thought from him before he could censor it, and at once she raised her head to find his mouth with hers, wanting to wipe away his fear of her displeasure. Lucian couldn't think that he had hurt her, that she might never be able to forgive him. What they were doing was beautiful and right. She felt that in every cell of her body. How could he think otherwise? How could he condemn himself when he had been so gentle and careful of her?

"I do not want you to loathe me, angel." He bent his head to kiss her vulnerable throat. "I have searched your memories, your heart and soul, and have found no evidence of hatred—not even for your worst enemy. It is the one thing that gives me hope."

She wrapped her arms around his head as his body began to move with more aggression, with harder, faster strokes. Her body seemed to find the same rhythm as his, rising to meet his so that she could feel him deep within her, a part of her. She needed to hold him close as she felt the building of a firestorm, flames whipping from him to her and back again, higher and higher, rushing through their bodies, a fierce conflagration finally exploding into a thousand fragments, raining sparks down upon them.

Lucian rolled over, taking her with him so that she lay atop him. The firelight danced over them, yet the air seemed to help cool their bodies. His hand pushed at the wild blond hair falling around her face so that he could look at her. "You are mine, you know." He made it a statement.

Her body certainly knew it. She felt him in every cell, alive, living within her. She smiled, her hands caressing the heavy muscles of his chest. "You were angry with me for going outside, weren't you?"

"I do not honestly think I could be angry with you," he said thoughtfully. "You are my life. My miracle. I *feared* for you, and I did not care for the feeling. I have never known fear. I hunted and destroyed, went into battle a thousand times, and I never knew this emotion. I know it now, and I do not like it." His hand was back in her hair, stroking, twisting strands, his fingers occasionally finding the nape of her neck to massage her. "It is in your nature to protect others. You are very different from what I envisioned once I knew you existed."

Jaxon lifted her head. "Really? Just what was your vision?"

He smiled into her dark eyes. "I have a feeling my answer could get me into trouble. I think I will remain silent."

"Oh, no, you won't. You tell me all about this wonder woman." She thumped his chest for emphasis.

"The women of my race are tall and elegant with long black hair and dark eyes. They would never go hunting a vampire or ghoul or even a madman, especially when asked by their lifemate to stay within a certain area. And before you consider them downtrodden, these women do this because they have complete faith in the ability of their lifemate to protect them. You go rushing out headlong, your first thought for my safety instead of your own. I am the most powerful hunter our people have known, yet you think to save me from one such as a ghoul." He smiled and reached to kiss away her frown. "I am not complaining, angel. I am merely stating a fact that I have come to understand."

"Tall? Elegant? What does that mean? What do you mean by 'elegant'? Just because I'm short doesn't mean I can't be elegant. I wear jeans because I like them, and they're comfortable. Long black hair may be beautiful— it is on you—but there's nothing wrong with blond hair. Or short hair, for that matter. It's very practical to care for." She sounded indignant.

His hand was moving in her hair. He loved her hair, the silky, wild strands that went in every direction. He found himself smiling again for no reason. Jaxon didn't care that the women of his race might stay safely indoors while the men went out to hunt. She cared that he had described them as tall and elegant with long black hair. He found that rather amusing. Jaxon was Jaxon, a small powder keg prepared to save the world. No one would change that, least of all her own lifemate. She had to be accepted for the person she was.

Lucian's decision to bring her over to the Carpathian race stemmed from his knowledge of her nature. It was the only real way to protect her from harm. He would sleep when she slept; he would always be aware of her every movement. He would be in her, with her, if anything or anyone threatened her. It was the only path left to him if he wanted to allow her to remain exactly who she was; yet his decision might very well cause her to despise him.

"What is wrong, Lucian? Are you sorry you made love to me?" Suddenly Jaxon was uneasy. She wasn't experienced enough to know if she had pleased him or not. She thought she had, but maybe not. He was intensely passionate. Maybe she couldn't sate his hunger. After all, he was a completely different species.

"How could I ever be sorry for doing the one thing I have wanted more than anything in the world? Just for your information, angel, I intend to make love to you a few more times before this night is done. And no one else could ever satisfy me. There is only you for me. Not any other woman. Ever. I do not want tall elegance or long black hair. I have grown rather fond of your short blond hair and small, perfect body. You will not be getting rid of me easily."

Jaxon smiled and lay her head once more on his chest. Deep inside her where she had felt so wonderful, she became aware of a slow, torturous clenching and unclenching of her muscles. She pressed a hand to her stomach and lay very still, trying to assess what was happening. Was this normal? It felt like cramps—no, worse than cramps—something alive moving within her body, spreading to every organ.

Lucian's hand was on the nape of her neck, easing the tension from her suddenly taut muscles. He was very still, as if he sensed something was wrong. He didn't ask her what it was. He didn't say anything at all. He simply held her close in his arms, protectively, possessively.

Chapter Eight

Jaxon lay quietly in his arms, staring up at Lucian's face with wide, dark eyes. Haunted eyes. Terror-stricken eyes. "I feel sick all of a sudden." She sat up abruptly, pushing at him futilely to put distance between them. The terrible burning in her stomach was increasing with each passing second. Increasing and spreading like wildfire throughout her body. "Lucian, something's really wrong." She reached for the phone on a small end table.

Lucian leaned around her and took the receiver from her hand. "It is the conversion taking place within your body." Once more his voice was totally without expression. "Your body must rid itself of its human toxins." He spoke in his soft, matter-of-fact voice.

Jaxon jerked away from him, her eyes enormous. She pressed both hands to her stomach. It felt as if someone were taking a blowtorch to her insides. "What did you do, Lucian? What did you do?"

Fire rushed through her body, her muscles contorted, and she found herself falling back to the floor helplessly

175

in the throes of some kind of seizure. Lucian was there before her, cradling her close, his mind sharing hers so that he bore the brunt of the horrific pain as wave after wave rushed through her. Jaxon could only cling to him, terrified, as the agony crawled through her body.

It seemed to last hours, yet in minutes the pain began to wane. Little beads of sweat covered her skin, and she felt sicker than ever, exhausted. "The fire, Lucian. I can't stand the fire. It hurts. Everything hurts." Even her eyes hurt.

He waved a hand, and the flames were gone. A cooling breeze moved through the room, fanning her skin. Her nails dug into his arm. It was starting again. He felt it in her mind, the swelling pain twisting at her insides, clawing at her. Lucian was appalled at the strength of the seizures that lifted and slammed down her small body. Without his arms around her she would have been crashing onto the floor. This spasm was worse than the last one, her muscles knotting and clenching beneath her skin. She tried to say his name, to whisper it as she did when she needed an anchor, but nothing would come out, not even a croak. Inside her mind she was screaming for him.

Lucian surrounded her, body and mind. He sent himself seeking outside his body and into hers. Her organs were reshaping, her tissues and cells contorting. He made every attempt to ease her pain, but Jaxon was very slight, very small, and the force of the seizures was tearing at her body, her muscles so strained they were hard knots. He breathed with her, for her. He held her when her body rejected its human remnants and she vomited over and over. He washed her face, removing the beads of blood she had sweated from her forehead, and rocked her when the wave of agony receded.

Jaxon lay passively, conserving her energy. She was no longer fighting the pain, and her mind was carefully blank. Her eyes widened, and she looked at him helplessly, hopelessly when the next seizure began to take hold. Lucian found himself swearing between his teeth in the ancient language. He waited until he was certain the vomiting was over, the last toxins removed from her body, before he could safely command her to sleep.

Once she slept; he carefully cleansed her body, then cleaned all evidence of her torment from the room. Very gently he picked up her, cradling her against his chest. She felt so slight, so delicate, her bones so fragile. He buried his face in her hair, tears swimming close to the surface, burning his eyes. He carried her through the basement to his sleeping chamber and placed her in the middle of his bed. She looked like a small child under the sheet he drew carefully over her.

Lucian sat down and watched her for a long time, his dark eyes brooding. When she woke, she would wake as a full Carpathian, needing blood to sustain her life. She would be unable to walk in the sun, her skin and eyes far too sensitive to stand the light. Would she look at him with loathing, with revulsion?

He waited another hour wanting to make certain she was sleeping peacefully, before leaving her. He dressed himself as he glided up the stairs and through the house. The night was cool and clear, the wind fresh on his face. He breathed it in, the tales it told of the night. With three running steps he took to the skies, winging toward the heart of the city. He needed blood enough for both of them. His prey would be those ne'er do-wells who roamed the city in search of victims, thinking themselves safe and powerful in the darkness. But he could see them as clearly as if the sun were shining brightly.

He landed on the sidewalk, walking without missing a stride, a tall, elegant man dressed in a charcoal-gray suit. He looked very wealthy, at odds with his surroundings. He glanced neither left nor right, acting as if he heard nothing, yet he heard everything, even the low murmur of conversation coming from the projects on the other side of the street. He heard the whisper of footsteps behind him. One pair, then a second. The footsteps separated, his attackers coming at him from either side. These were the people he had often used over the centuries, the ones who tried to assault him in the hope that he had cash on him. He always allowed them to attack him before he sentenced them; he always made certain of their nefarious intentions, though it was easy enough to read their minds.

He read their thoughts, knew their plan, knew which of the two was the leader, the more vicious, the one who would attack first. He continued to walk, neither fast nor slow, looking straight ahead, simply waiting for them to make their move. He was halfway down the street, just coming up on a small alleyway between the apartment houses, when the leader rushed him. The man was large and strong, wrapping an arm around Lucian's head, driving him into the alley. Lucian cooperated, going in the direction the leader took him until both attackers were out of sight of any eyes that might be watching from the windows.

He whirled around, knocking the knife from the leader's hand, catching the man in his enormously strong hands, stopping both assailants with a soft command. The two thugs stood waiting for his attention. He drank deeply from each of them, uncaring that both would be weak and dizzy. It always took tremendous self-control to leave men such as these alive. At times, when he read their depraved minds, he found it nearly impossible. But he told himself he was a guardian of the Carpathian people; the human race had its own set of laws.

Lucian didn't bother planting a plausible memory for either of the two attackers. They would remember attempting to mug him, and then they would have a black void of time and experience that no amount of trying would help them fill. He left them there in the alley, lying on the ground moaning, unsure what had happened to them.

When Lucian returned, the house was cool and dark. These days Lucian loved to return home. To Jaxon. Nearly everything in the house was something he had picked out of her memories, things she loved, colors she found soothing. Art pieces she had seen and admired. Even the stained glass, incredible works of art his brother's wife had created, had been made especially for Jaxon. Woven into each piece was a strong safeguard for the house and a soothing invitation of welcome and warmth for those who dwelled within. Francesca was a true healer, and, even in her art, her gift came through.

In the sleeping chamber he shed his clothes and gathered Jaxon into his arms before issuing the command to awaken. The conversion was complete, and she had rested for nearly two hours. He wanted any confrontation over before the next rising. Jaxon stirred, moaned softly as if in memory, and then he felt her heart slam hard. She was fully awake, refusing to open her eyes and face the truth of what had happened. He felt his own heart skip a beat; his breath caught in his lungs. This was the moment. She would have to confront what she had become. He would have to confront her rejection of him.

Lucian held her in his arms, watching the expressions chasing across her face. Jaxon's impossibly long lashes fluttered, then lifted, and he was looking into her large dark eyes. He saw no condemnation what so ever. She simply looked up at him. Very slowly she raised a hand and rubbed at the frown he didn't realize was on his face.

"What have you done this time?" she asked.

His hands moved over her face, brushing her hair from her delicate cheekbones. "I think you already know."

"If it's what I think it is, I may have to resort to violence."

She was doing it again, not dealing with something her mind wasn't ready for. Instead the pad of her index finger was rubbing a little caress over his mouth. "Don't look so worried, Lucian. I'm not made of porcelain. I'm not going to break. You look as if the world has come to an end. Although, I have to tell you, it did hurt like hell, and when I'm feeling a little stronger, I might have to retaliate."

"I love you, angel, and I would not have put you through the suffering of a conversion had it not been necessary."

Jaxon was shaking her head. "Don't say *conversion*. I don't think we should go there right now. *Conversion*. Sounds like a a movie I once saw. It had vampires and icky things in it. This really disgusting creature bit the heroine and then gave her his blood." Her voice faltered for a moment, and he felt her tremble, but she went resolutely on. "It transformed her into a vampish sex maniac. She ran around sucking men's necks and killing little children. Not really my thing. At least not the killing of little children. I don't know about sucking men's necks." A fine tremor ran through her body.

His hand was stroking her hair, one arm locking her possessively to him. "I would never tolerate your sucking other men's necks, so we can dispense with that worry."

"I'm so glad. Although, maybe I would have liked it," she tried to tease him.

That was one of the things he admired so much about her. She was frightened, her heart was beating faster than normal, but she was holding on, being brave. His respect for her continued to grow. "I am sorry, angel, but you will have to get over your disappointment if that is the case. I am discovering I am a jealous man after all."

She snuggled into him, subconsciously seeking comfort. "You look like a man with complete confidence, Lucian. I can't believe you would be jealous. Besides, no one else wants me."

His eyebrows shot up. "You do not notice how men fall all over you? Even that silly young one who disobeyed your orders by going into the warehouse and making such a fool of himself—you thought his heroics were for self-promotion, but in truth he wanted you to notice him."

"No way." Jaxon was shocked, and it showed. "He had political pull, and he used it to get on my team even though I was totally opposed. He wasn't ready, and he wasn't a team player. He wanted glory and headlines. Publicly my unit is as anonymous as possible, but within the ranks it's known as the best. Benton definitely had promotion—not me—on his mind," she declared certain of her facts.

Lucian bent his head to gently brush the side of her mouth with his. The light touch made her heart somersault, and she felt the answering jolt in his. His lips had barely skimmed hers, yet she felt the heat curl in the pit of her stomach.

"That is what he appeared to be like, but it is not what was in his mind. He wanted to stand out, wanted you to notice him."

"He certainly went about it in an interesting way. I noticed him all right. He almost got Barry and me killed." Her voice betrayed her rejection of Lucian's assessment.

"I was there, honey. I read his mind accurately. You wreak havoc among the males in your department, and now, unfortunately, you will do so even more."

Jaxon laughed softly at him. "You are smitten with me, aren't you? No one wants me. They just think I'm dynamite at my job, which I am," she said without false modesty.

"You are surrounded by men all the time where you work. It is improper for a Carpathian woman to be unprotected in the company of men."

Now her eyebrows shot up. "Lucky for me, I'm just a plain little human woman who works for a living."

His hand caressed her hair, then moved to stroke her soft skin before returning to the untamed blond strands that so intrigued him. "Not any longer. I am no modern man, angel. I believe strongly in the duties I have sworn to carry out. You are my true lifemate, my heart and soul, the light to my darkness. I do not think running around seeking danger is what I want for the light to my darkness. Think what it would mean to the world, my love, if something were to happen to you. I have held out against the darkness for more centuries than I can say, but if something happened to you, I would truly become a monster. Even the hunters in my family would find it impossible to track and destroy me."

"I don't think so, Lucian. You forget, I'm getting used to being in your mind. You wouldn't become a monster. You're just trying to get me to do what you want."

"So you think you know me." His voice was softer than ever.

At once Jaxon frowned and moved to sit up cautiously, testing her body for its responses. "That's just it, Lucian. I don't know you, and you don't know me. I don't even know how I got here. I don't know how I've allowed you to take over my life. And now this. I don't know what you've done, but I know it's not something I want, and you didn't bother to consult with me one way or the other. Is that part of being old-fashioned? Born centuries ago? The little woman doesn't have a say in her own life?" Her hand crept defensively to her throat. She wasn't the same at all. She could feel the difference. Reality was creeping in whether she wanted it to or not.

She was in bed stark naked with a man she knew relatively nothing about. He wasn't even a man. He was some powerful predator she found sexy. Gasping, she shoved at the solid wall of his chest and, grabbing for the sheet, wrapped it around her. "I don't know you at all. I can't believe I slept with you."

Lucian's face was more sensual than ever, a slight, puzzled frown making him so attractive, Jaxon wanted him outlawed on the spot. "Do not modern-day women sleep with their husbands?"

"We aren't married. I didn't marry you. I would have known if I had done that. I didn't, did I?" She shoved a hand through her hair, sending it flying in all directions, then had to grab hastily for the sheet slipping so precariously. She glared at him, daring him to smile at her predicament.

Lucian found that his centuries of self-control stood him in good stead. He kept his features completely expressionless when he wanted desperately to smile with the joy flooding his heart. She melted his insides, turned him into something gentle, when he had been so certain there was no chance for him to feel such things. He wanted to wrap his arms around her and kiss her until her eyes went dark with desire and her body went up in flames with his. "What do you think a lifemate is? We are married in the way of the Carpathian people. We are bound for all eternity, one to the other, body and soul."

She jumped out of bed, trying to be dignified with a sheet swirling around her like a toga, bunching at her feet, preventing freedom of movement. "There you go again with words like *eternity*. See? That's exactly what I'm talking about. We're not in the least bit compatible. And I don't sleep around. You've done something to me. Some black-magic trick. Voodoo. I have a few morals. I don't sleep with just anyone, you know."

A smile hovered dangerously close. Lucian's black eyes gleamed at her, moving over her with a slow, burning possessiveness that said more than any words could possibly express. "I am not just anyone, Jaxon, and I am more than grateful that you do not 'sleep around.' " He moved then, a sleek jungle cat stretching lazily.

At once her heart was pounding overly loud and she

was backing away from the bed, her eyes wide in her face. "You're asking me to be something I'm not, Lucian. You didn't give me a chance to think about things."

"What things? What was there to think about? I must rest in the ground. I cannot do so if you are not beside me. You have a penchant for getting into trouble."

At once her dark eyes flashed fire. "That's it! I've had it with you. You don't even seem to know what you've done. You show no remorse at all. I'm the one who has to do all the compromising, except there is no compromise. You simply decide I'm going to do something, and then I do it. And it hurt like hell!" With that parting shot, she stormed from the bedroom. The hem of the sheet trailing behind her caught on the edge of the door and brought her up short. Jaxon simply allowed the sheet to flutter to the floor, giving Lucian a last glimpse of her soft, pale skin and beautiful curves before she disappeared from his sight.

Lucian stretched again, reveling in the feel of his strong muscles, in the way his body felt so alive. He wanted her again. He would want her for all time. The day could never come when he was fully sated. He was smiling, unable to stop. She was such a perfect miracle to him. Right now, when most women would be hysterical at the thought of conversion, she was giving him hell for being an arrogant Carpathian male. Lucian knew she was going to have to come to terms with what she had become, and it wouldn't be easy on her, but it had been necessary to ensure her continued safety. Jaxon was not a woman to be put on a shelf. She would always be in the thick of things, no matter what he decreed. Once Lucian had accepted that fact, accepted her personality, her protective nature, he had taken the only course open to him to prevent disaster.

He padded on bare feet across the room and stooped to pick up her discarded sheet. He smiled again. It had never occurred to him he would ever experience jealousy, yet he found he didn't like the idea of other males being close to her. He didn't even want them thinking about her, fantasizing over her. More than that, he didn't want her to smile at them with her innocent, sexy smile, or to touch them in the way humans often did one another. Living with emotions was an interesting experience. Worse, now that Jaxon was fully Carpathian, her ability to attract males would increase. Her voice would become more alluring, so memorable that those hearing it would want to hear it again and again. Her eyes would draw men to her—as if they didn't already. Lucian sighed and shook his head.

He moved through the house and up the stairs to her room. Drawers had been yanked open so she could grab some clothing. Jaxon was in the spacious bathroom. He could hear the shower running. Lucian touched her mind very gently. She was panicked and trying to calm herself with normal human activities. There were tears in her mind, running down her face. At once he found himself needing to be with her.

But the door to the bathroom was firmly locked, and she had placed a rolled-up towel at its base. In spite of everything Lucian found himself smiling again. She had no real idea of his true power. He could mentally command her to open the door. One touch would burst it open. He could open it a thousand ways. His solid frame shimmered for a moment before it became insubstantial, transparent, then dissolved into mist. The droplets streamed through the keyhole of the door and poured into the bathroom, mixing with the steam from the shower.

Lucian stepped out of the fog, his muscular frame solid once more. He could see Jaxon clearly through the glass shower door. She was leaning her forehead against the wall, the water pouring over her head and down her back. She looked beautiful, pale, and fragile. She took his breath away. Silently he slid into the tub and reached for her, turning her into his chest with his strong arms, giving her no chance to protest.

"I cannot bear your tears, my love. Tell me what you want me to do, and I will do it. Anything. You are the only thing in this world that matters to me." His hands framed her face to tilt her head up toward his. He bent to taste her tears. He ached inside, his heart clenching with actual pain.

Jaxon felt his reaction to her tears and knew it was genuine. He was distressed by her sorrow. His mouth moved over hers, back and forth, a gentle, persuasive caress. At once she could feel her body's reaction, the way her heart found the rhythm of his, the way her blood began to heat, to pool, to make demands. That brought a fresh flood of tears. She wanted him, wanted to be with him this way, Lucian holding her so protectively, so tenderly. He was enormously strong, yet he was so careful with her, so gentle. She loved that about him, loved the way he needed her, hungered for her, wanted only her. But she didn't want to want him. She didn't want to want anyone.

"I want you to want me," Lucian whispered, reading her mind. "I want you to know me the way I know you." His mouth wandered to her neck, her soft throat. "I know everything about you, and I am madly in love with you. *Love* is not even a strong enough word for the way I feel about you. Take the time to get to know me, Jaxon. Try for me, angel. Just try."

His mouth was creating a world of heat and colors, a place where only the two of them existed. His hands were moving over her body with exquisite care.

"I'm like you now, aren't I?" Jaxon whispered softly against his chest.

His fingers found the nape of her neck, moved through her hair, his touch possessive. "You are Carpathian, honey, with all the gifts of our people. The earth calls to us, the wind, the rain, the heavens above. It is a beautiful world. We can run with the wolves, fly with the raptors, swim in the rivers with the fish if we desire. I can show you wonders never seen by the human eye. You can do things so incredible, you will know joy beyond anything."

She let him kiss the tears from her face, let his rising hunger become hers. There was madness in what was happening, but it no longer mattered to her. She couldn't change what was. She couldn't undo what he had done. And she couldn't hate him for doing it. Jaxon wanted to lose herself in the dark passion only he could provide. She wanted him needing her so desperately that she would never have to face what she was.

Her hands moved over his body, tracing each defined muscle. Lucian caught her head in his hands as she moved closer to him, her mouth moving over his wet skin, catching little beads of water on her tongue. His body was tightening to a painful ache, making urgent demands, when all he wanted was to comfort her, to tell her how much he loved her for not condemning him. He wanted to hold her in his arms and let her cry, if that was what she needed to help her face what had taken place within her body. "You are not here to serve my needs, angel. I am here to serve yours. Let me hold you. Ask me questions."

Sheer terror shimmered for one moment in her eyes, then was lost in a sultry blaze of sheer sensuality. Her hands were moving over his hips, delving into the defined muscles of his buttocks, exploring his thighs. "I want to feel alive, Lucian. I want to feel I have some power, some control over my own world. I just want to *feel*." Her hands found the hard, thick evidence of his desire, her fingernails stroking lightly, her hands taking pleasure in learning the shape and texture of him.

Lucian's head went back, his eyes closed. Even with the

sheer ecstasy of her fingers caressing him so intimately, he merged fully with her mind, seeking to find her greatest need, her greatest desire. She had pushed out all reality, anchoring herself with thoughts only of him: how much she loved to be with him, how she loved to watch his eyes go from ice-cold to molten heat, the way his body hardened yet he remained so incredibly gentle. Her thoughts stole his breath, his heart. She admired his courage, wanted to take away the bleakness of his past existence, and she was determined no one would harm him. She wanted him to be at peace, no longer forced to destroy the terrible creatures loose in their world. She wanted to please him, and she worried about her inexperience.

The air rushed from his lungs as her mouth—silken, moist heat—closed around him. She could draw on his erotic fantasies, could feel what she was doing to him. Jaxon had lost herself in her newfound power, and Lucian was reacting with swelling desire, hot, hard hunger. His teeth actually clenched together. She found the rhythm of his hips, reveled in the helpless way he moved into her. Time was lost. Reality was lost. Jaxon had disappeared, and in her place was a siren, a temptress testing her ability to steal his self-control.

Lucian bunched his hands in her hair and dragged her up to him to find her mouth. She was moving against him, her breasts tantalizing him; her hands stroking and inflaming. His burned a trail of fire from her throat to the creamy swell of her breasts. His palm found the tight blond curls at the apex of her thighs and pressed close to find damp, welcoming heat. His fingers moved to test her readiness and found hot velvet clenching around him, found her needing him with the same urgency he felt. Her breath was coming in shallow gasps.

"Hurry, Lucian!" Her breathless cry sent a shaft of piercing joy sweeping through him. She did need him; no other would do for her. He was her true lifemate, and her body cried out for his. He wanted all of her. Her mind and heart as well as her body and soul. And her mind was filled with hot, hungry need of him.

He caught her small waist, lifted her into his arms, and settled her over him like a perfect sheath for a sword. A sound escaped from one of them—him or her? Neither knew which was Lucian, which was Jaxon. She was tight and perfect, and he filled her completely, holding her in his strong embrace. Jaxon circled his neck with her arms, leaning close to him, skin to skin, heart to heart. She closed her eyes and allowed the beauty of their joining to take her far away, until she was spinning into space, free-falling with Lucian, wanting it to last for eternity. Just the two of them in their own private world of erotic fantasy.

The way he held her was so right. Gentle, tender, yet moving deeply within her, each stroke creating a fiery friction that left both of them reaching endlessly for more. Lucian bent his head protectively over hers, surrounding her with love and warmth and comfort even as her body surrounded his with such perfect rapture.

Jaxon felt her inner muscles tighten, the feeling building and building, the pleasure almost more than she could bear. Her teeth found his shoulder; she was gasping for breath, for sanity, trying to prolong the moment even as her entire body was splintering, fragmenting, spinning out of control. Lucian's mind was firmly merged with hers. He could feel her body's reaction to his, and it triggered his own white-hot explosion, intensifying the feeling for both of them. He could feel the ripples of aftershock, her body contracting and releasing around his.

He turned her so that the water cascaded over both of them. Jaxon clung to him, not wanting to give up the completeness of being one. Lucian simply held her protectively in his arms, needing to comfort her. Eventually she lifted her head and gazed into his black velvet eyes.

She looked so fragile, so vulnerable, he was afraid she might break.

"I am with you, Jaxon," he whispered softly. Very gently he began to separate their bodies, feeling almost bereft. "You will never be alone again. I reside in you as you will always reside in me." He cradled her gently in his arms.

"I can't think about it, Lucian. If I try, I go crazy."

"That is all right, angel. What do you expect of yourself? Instant acceptance? No one could easily accept such a thing. It is a dark gift. We live in a beautiful world, yes, but we must pay a high price for the special talents we are given. And your lifemate has responsibilities that place you in dangerous situations. I would change what I am if I could—the dark angel of death, my people call me—but I am a hunter of the undead, and I fear I always will be."

Her wide eyes flashed with sudden anger. "They call you that? 'The dark angel of death'? How can they be so terrible when you've given them so much? What right do they have to judge you?" She was instantly protective of him, a young tigress, and he had a sudden vision of her with their children.

The thought made him want to smile. Instead, he turned off the water and carried her out of the shower. Once she was standing on the tiles, he enveloped her with a large towel. Pulling the edges together, he drew her close. "I am an ancient Carpathian male with tremendous knowledge and power. My people know how dangerous that combination is. We are predators, my love, and can turn at any moment when we are without our lifemates. Most males turn after far fewer centuries than I have existed."

She glared at him. "Don't you make excuses for them. I've been in your mind, and you're no more a killer than I am."

He laughed; he couldn't help himself. She was so innocent, even now, after all they had shared. She could never be what he was, a predator with a thin veneer of civilization and tremendous discipline. She was light to his darkness, his savior, his miracle, and she couldn't see it. She wouldn't look at herself through his eyes.

"The dawn is approaching, Jaxon." He knew it without glancing at the time; his people always knew the exact moment of sunrise or sunset. "Come with me to the sleeping chamber."

Lucian felt her instant reluctance, the sudden dread seizing her. That made it real in her mind, too final for her to accept. He held out a hand. "Walk with me." He said it softly, gently, his voice like velvet.

Jaxon stared at his hand, not wanting to go with him, as if somehow by staying in the main part of the house she would remain human. She felt torn, wanting to remain, yet not wanting to hurt Lucian. Very slowly, hesitantly she put her hand in his. His fingers closed around hers, warm and sure. "You will always be safe with me, Jaxon. If you believe that, you will get through this."

He tugged until she was beneath the protection of his shoulder and he could wrap his arm around her. They moved together through the house, down the wide spiral staircase, through the kitchen, and into the basement. He felt her hesitation as they entered the narrow corridor leading down to the sleeping chamber. It was there in her mind, the thought of running back up the stairs. Lucian merely tightened his arm, bending his head to brush the warmth of his mouth against her temple in a small gesture of encouragement.

"In all the centuries of my existence, Jaxon, I have never met a woman such as you." His admiration and love for her was in the soft purity of his voice. Deliberately he matched his breathing to hers, his heart to hers so that he could regulate her panicked pace to a calmer one. Easily he moved in her mind, stilling the chaos, a light touch to bring a measure of tranquillity, of acceptance, easing her into the difficult transition.

Lucian was careful not to take away her free will, but he could not bear her suffering. It moved him as nothing else in his life ever had. He would have done anything for her, anything to protect her. He had the ability to erase every terrible memory from her mind, wipe out her past entirely. He had the capacity to ensure she would accept being a Carpathian, believe she had always been one, yet he knew it was wrong. Still, the idea lingered in his mind. He despised himself for allowing her to suffer, for causing the physical pain of the conversion and now her agony of attempting to accept what he had wrought.

"I would hate that. Eventually you wouldn't be able to live with the lie, Lucian," she said quietly.

He glanced down at her, his black gaze loving. She was looking up at him with wide brown eyes, a hint of laughter in their depths. "You didn't think I would learn to read your mind so easily, did you?" She shook her head. "No, you didn't think I would *choose* to read it." She was smug about catching that bit of knowledge.

He opened the door to the chamber and stepped back to allow her to enter first. It pleased him that she had chosen to read his thoughts. It was an intimacy between lifemates, the sharing of thoughts and feelings without words. A private path for two. "You continually astonish me," he admitted. And she did. She amazed him with her ability to adapt to every new situation. Just the fact that she could smile was astounding.

Jaxon held on to the towel, looking around rather desperately for something to put on so she wouldn't feel so vulnerable. Lucian held out an immaculate white silk shirt, and she slipped her arms in it. Her long lashes swept down, veiling her expression as he began to button up the front of the shirt, his knuckles brushing against her bare skin. "What was that creature that was throwing itself against the wall? It wasn't a vampire, was it, because it seemed incredibly stupid."

"It was a ghoul. The walking dead. Not undead, like a vampire, but a minion of the vampire. A servant. A puppet. As I told you, the vampire can use a human to do his bidding during the day while he rests. The ghoul lives only to carry out the vampire's wishes. He is fed by the blood of the vampire and the flesh of the dead."

Jaxon gasped and covered her mouth. "I don't know why I ask you questions. You always say something wild. And it's not as if I don't know you're going to do it. I just wade right in and ask anyway." She shoved a hand through her hair, sending damp tendrils in every direction.

Lucian automatically reached out to smooth her hair back into place. "A ghoul is dangerous because it never stops until it is completely destroyed."

She nodded, turning the information over and over in her mind. "What about the wall? What kind of security system do you have in it? Did it ever occur to you a child might try to climb on that wall?"

"If a child attempted to climb the wall, absolutely nothing would happen," he answered. "The wall only reacts to evil."

She nodded again, biting down on her lower lip. "Naturally. Of course. Why would I think anything else?"

"Come to bed, angel," he invited softly.

She wasn't looking at him, her eyes carefully studying the surrounding walls. He had been meticulous about the construction of this room, ensuring that it appeared to be a replica of a bedroom aboveground. Lightly he touched her mind, wanting to correct whatever might be wrong. It took great effort to prevent a smile from showing on his face. Her reaction had nothing to do with the room, nothing to do with her conversion, and everything to do with his naked body and the things they had done together.

Lucian glided to the bed and covered his lower body

193

with a sheet. "Are you going to walk around the chamber for the entire day?"

"Maybe," she answered, touching the walls, running her fingertips over them to feel the texture. "How far underground are we?"

Lucian shrugged his powerful shoulders, a casual ripple of muscles, his eyes suddenly watchful. "Do you have a problem being beneath the earth?" He was a shadow in her mind and knew she had no anxiety over being underground. She was reluctant to get into bed, afraid of sleeping, of waking, afraid of facing the truth.

She glanced at him, more comfortable now that his nakedness was covered. Her behavior made no sense to her. Why did she want to be with Lucian so desperately? It was so unlike her. He had been honest with her from the first about who and what he was, yet she had simply gone along with everything he said, everything he did.

"You are my lifemate, Jaxon. You were born the other half of my soul. Your body and mind recognized me. Your heart and soul cried out for mine. It is the way of our people."

"I'm not Carpathian." She said it defensively, her hand going protectively to her throat. "Why would it happen?"

"It is as much a mystery to me as it is to you. All I was told was that some human women with psychic powers are truly lifemates to our males." He softened his voice deliberately, evoking a soothing, tranquil calm. "Obviously it is so." He was once more merged fully with her, slowing her heart and lungs, allowing her to find the strength to cross the floor and slide into bed beside him.

Lucian wrapped his arms securely around her, pulling her small body into the shelter of his larger frame. She relaxed into him immediately, his touch calming the rising tide of terror sweeping through her. She felt battered emotionally and physically. She had so many questions but didn't want them answered, afraid of her own reactions to what he might tell her.

"I just want to go to sleep, Lucian," she said, her head snuggled against his shoulder. "Can we just go to sleep?"

He felt her holding her breath. She didn't want to sleep; she wanted to run away. He brushed the top of her head with a kiss, his fingers moving tenderly in her hair. "Sleep, angel. You will be safe with me." He took control, sending her into a deep sleep immediately so that she would have no chance of fighting the command.

They would not sleep in this chamber, or this bed, this night. Her body needed rejuvenation; it needed the healing only the soil of the earth could offer a true Carpathian. Lucian had no intention of forcing her to face that particular reality of their existence. He was her lifemate; as such, he could do no other than to see to her health, to her happiness. But he wanted to spare her the details he deemed unnecessary for her to learn at such an early stage.

He lifted her slight body into his arms, then concentrated on the wall to the left of them. The wall shifted to reveal the narrow stone passage leading deeper into the heart of the earth. He followed it downward until he came to the rich, dark soil bed he had provided within the rock. Waving a hand, he opened it. Then he floated into the bed, cradling Jaxon's slender body to him. Safeguards in place, the wolves roaming free, he closed all doors so that his lair was secret from any intruders. Again he placed safeguards at each door, along the passage itself, and above them in the rock bed. Only then did he send Jaxon into the deeper sleep of his people, stopping her heart and lungs so that she lay as still as death within the earth. As he waved a hand to command the soil to pour over them, he sent his own body into Carpathian sleep. His heart stuttered for a moment, then ceased to beat. The soil continued to pour over them until it was all in place, undisturbed as if it had lain there for centuries.

Chapter Nine

The sun moved slowly across the sky. The house up on the hill remained silent, the beautiful stained-glass windows reflecting the rays of light back toward the sun. Inside it was hushed, quiet, the air itself stilled, as if the house were alive and waiting for something. As the sun began to sink, deep within the earth a single heart began to beat. Lucian scanned the area around his estate even as he opened the soil above them. All was quiet. He floated from the earth back to the comfort of his sleeping chamber. He lay Jaxon on the bed, at the same time waving a hand to light the candles. The dancing flames lent soothing shadows and scented herbs to the room.

Lucian inspected Jaxon's body carefully to ensure that not one speck of soil remained, that she would awaken clean and refreshed. He sent himself seeking outside his body and into hers so that he could examine her internal organs and see for himself that she was completely healed. Only when he was satisfied that all was well did he release her from the sleep of Carpathians into the lighter sleep of mortals. He felt her take her first breath, heard the first beat of her heart. His hands went to her small waist beneath the thin silk of the shirt so that he could feel her soft satin skin.

He felt the instant surge of heat racing through his own body in answer, and he stretched lazily. She was with him. She would be with him at each rising. He pushed the shirt from her stomach and bent his head to taste her skin. His hands followed the sweet curve of her hips. He was becoming very familiar with her delicate bone structure, the lines of her body. Her skin was warming beneath his wandering hands and mouth. He moved lower still, wanting to taste her, wanting her to awaken to the erotic pleasure only he could provide for her.

She was hot, flowing honey, so soft he wanted to crawl inside her. He knew the moment she woke, the moment she was fully aware of him, of what he was doing, of the rising tidal wave of hunger rushing through her body like a fireball to match the molten lava racing through his. *Lucian!* She cried out his name in the intimate way of their species, her body hot and restless and aching with need. Burning for him. She needed him. Needed what he was doing to her, needed the feel of him hot and hard and thick inside her, relieving the terrible building storm. Her body rippled with life, with such pleasure that she cried out his name again, her hands clutching at his hair to try to drag him up to her.

At once he blanketed her body with his own. Her entrance was a hot, creamy invitation to him. As he pressed against her, slipped inside her tight sheath, she gasped as her body reacted again and again, spiraling outward, contracting and gripping. Then he was driving into her, hard and fast, his hips riding her into a firestorm that kept building higher and higher.

Jaxon was clutching his arms, her face against his chest. She felt the beckoning heat of his skin, heard his heart beating, the inviting rhythm of his pulse. She nuzzled his chest almost helplessly. Her mouth moved over his skin. Her body clenched around his, making more demands. Her teeth nipped his chest right over his pulse. She felt it leap in response, felt him thicken even more within her, hard and heavy, his hips surging forward to bury himself even deeper. Her tongue swirled over his pulse. Once. Twice.

God, angel, do it. I need you like this. His voice whispered in her mind, over her skin, sexy, low, pleading with aching need.

He was wild now, savage in his intensity, his body frantic for hers. All of hers. Her tongue swirled again, and he groaned, burying himself again and again in her fiery sheath. *Jaxon. Please.* His hands cupped her small hips like a cradle so he could drive forward in long, hard strokes.

There was so much pleasure, Jaxon allowed it to wash over her, to consume her. His pulse was fascinating. She heard his husky cry, felt his mind merge solidly with hers, so she felt the white-hot lance of lightning whipping through him as her teeth sank deep and the essence of his power, his ancient lifeblood, flowed into her. She felt what her body was doing to his, the hot fire surrounding him, gripping him tightly. She felt the intensity of his pleasure, so deep, so real, his desire for it to last for all time.

Her tongue stroked across his chest, closing the tiny pinpricks, just as the muscles in his body tensed beneath her hands and her own body was fragmenting, taking his with hers. She heard her own voice, a sound in her throat, soft and husky. She tasted him, the terrible hunger in her sated as her body throbbed and burned, exploding into the night to become part of time and space.

Jaxon found herself looking up at him, her dark eyes wide with shock. She couldn't believe the things her body was capable of. She couldn't believe what she had just done so willingly. She wanted her body to reject the nourishment, but it savored it, the taste of him in her mouth, on her lips, like an addictive nectar. She pushed at the wall of his chest, determined to get away from him so she could think. His gaze smoldered, black velvet, dark and dangerous, moving slowly over her face. There was stark possessiveness in his eyes. Hunger. Dark desire. He bent his head to trace the soft column of her neck with his tongue. "I am not certain this rising will be long enough to sate my hunger. Again. I want you again."

"You can't possibly!" she gasped, but he was already stroking her body, keeping her restless and aching for his.

"We are not bound by any limitations," he whispered softly, seeking the creamy hollow of her throat. "I have much to teach you."

Hours later, Jaxon settled into a chair in Lucian's den. Her body was deliciously sore, still sensitive from his endless possession. He had been in turns gentle and tender and wild and untamed. Always looking at her with hungry eyes. Only when he realized she was exhausted did he carry her upstairs to the shower, where he washed her with far too caressing hands. Right now she wasn't certain she would ever be able to look at him again. Trying to be nonchalant, she shook out the newspaper and glanced rather idly at the different headlines. Her eyes widened in surprise. "Samuel Barnes died yesterday."

Lucian paused in the act of working on the computer. He had been doing his best to give her some space, accurately reading her mind. His Jaxon was shy with him even after the erotic hours they had spent together. One eyebrow shot up as he looked at her over his shoulder. "The banker?" His voice was strictly neutral.

"Yes, the banker, Mr. International Grab-all-the-Headlines Banker. He just died in his house. An employee found him and tried CPR but wasn't successful. I suspected he was a major player in the drug trafficking going on in our city, but I could never get anything solid on him."

"And he died how?"

Jaxon's enormous eyes regarded him steadily over the top of the newspaper. "They don't suspect foul play. There's no evidence of that." All at once her voice was suspicious. "You didn't know Barnes, did you?"

"Jaxon." He said her name softly, intimately, his voice wrapping her up in satin sheets, effectively stopping her heart. "You are not accusing me of anything, are you?"

She found herself blushing for no reason at all except the way he was looking at her. Lucian was synonymous with control. He might be deadly, but he was quiet about it. He never seemed to allow anything to affect him. Until he looked at her. She could see his terrible hunger smoldering just beneath the surface every time his dark gaze rested on her. He was so sexy, merely looking at him stole her breath. Right now wasn't the time to dwell too deeply on everything that had transpired between them. She felt she was doing fairly well, holding on to her sanity by her fingertips. She was effectively putting off facing the truth about what Lucian had done with his "conversion" and what she had done since then with him. Carpathian women must be sex maniacs, because the real Jaxon was definitely not. She shook her head, determined to stay on track. Would Lucian have known Barnes's connection with her? What was she thinking, anyway? How could Lucian possibly know about Barnes? She couldn't accuse him of anything. "No, of course not."

She watched him turn back to the computer screen. He seemed very intrigued by his work, although she had no clue what he was doing. Once she saw that he received e-mail from Gabriel, his twin. Two of them like this in the world! *That* was a scary thought.

She went back to her reading. On the second page was

a small article about a car going off a cliff. The occupant did not survive. She stiffened when she read the name. This was too much of a coincidence. "Lucian."

Instantly she had his full attention. She loved that about him, as if everything she said and did was of the utmost importance to him.

It is. His voice whispered intimately in her mind, a caress of sound that brushed at her insides until she had to wrap her arms protectively around her stomach, where butterfly wings seemed to be fluttering endlessly.

Jaxon gave him her most intimidating glare. "You stay out of my head, weird one. I'm the only one who gets to read my thoughts." She frowned suddenly. "Can all you people read each other's thoughts?"

He shrugged, a casual rippling of his muscles that seemed to make her stomach somersault even more. "Yes and no. It isn't quite the same as with lifemates. There is a standard path of communication for our people, and more private ones are established if blood is exchanged. I can read Gabriel's mind and always could, but who would want to do so now? All he thinks about is Francesca. Well, Francesca and the girls. Skyler is their ward, a young teenager once badly abused. She is human, a psychic. And they have a little daughter now, not yet a year old. Gabriel guards her with good reason, but still, he has turned into a fussy old man."

Jaxon burst out laughing. "I can't imagine anyone looking like you acting like a fussy old man."

"I do not know how Francesca puts up with him." Lucian reveled in the fact that he actually experienced affection for his twin. It was not the memory of affection or wanting to feel affection, but actual deep emotion. Jaxon had done this to him. His Jaxon. His miracle. His gaze rested on her possessively. She was fast turning his world upside down.

Everything was different. Every time he looked at her,

his heart melted around the edges, and he went soft and warm inside. He could watch her for all eternity and never tire of the sight. She had a dimple that appeared unexpectedly out of nowhere, then melted into her smile. Her eyes held laughter when she teased him. She *teased* him. It was a miracle that anyone would dare to do so. She thought nothing of it, giving him as bad a time as possible at every opportunity. He loved the way she moved. She was small but perfectly proportioned. She was quiet and flowing, all grace and femininity, yet she thought she projected an image of toughness. Everything about her made him smile—everything, from the top of her head to the tip of her toes. Especially her sassy little mouth. He loved her mouth. Each time he looked at her, his body made instant, urgent demands. He reveled in that, in the hot, hard hunger one glance at her could produce.

A wadded-up newspaper came flying at him, and he picked it rather absently out of the air.

"Are you listening to me? I was just thinking how great it is that you hang on my every word, and now you sit there like a lump, staring off into space. Where are you?" Jaxon asked.

"You were not saying anything."

"I was, too." She was not above telling a small lie just to prove he wasn't listening. She looked at him indignantly.

He had been some distance from her, sitting at the computer, but now he was towering over her like some avenging angel. "You did not say a single word," he reiterated. He looked amused and tolerant. He looked like a lazy jungle cat stretching. He had that look that she knew was more dangerous to her than any other. He seemed to get around her defenses so easily. He turned her insides to molten lava and sent erotic images dancing in her head.

She sank back against the cushions and waved a hand

at him to ward him off. "That speed thing you do has got to go."

He arched an eyebrow at her. She wanted to touch his beautiful face with her fingertip, trace each eyebrow and the shadow along his jaw. Very carefully Jaxon put her hands under her and sat on them, her eyes completely innocent. He had better not be reading her mind at that precise moment. She glared at him just in case he *was* reading her mind, to show him she meant business.

"You have such a way with words, honey."

She liked to watch his eyes. They could go from ice-cold obsidian to glittering jewels in a matter of seconds. "I do, don't I?" She looked pleased.

"I am not certain I meant it as a compliment," he pointed out with a grin.

"There was an accident reported in the paper." She changed the subject with a little sigh.

"So you said."

"*Another* accident. A man drove his car over a cliff. The state police think he just drove straight off the road. There were no skids marks at all."

"And the significance of this is?" he prompted.

"The man worked for Barnes. It's just too much of a coincidence that they both died so suddenly. Maybe the drug cartel was annoyed with him over something. I'll have to do some digging around. If I could just know for sure you'd be safe from Drake while I went out to work . . ." She trailed off, looking up at the ceiling as if she would find her answers there.

A slow grin softened his mouth and added warmth to his eyes. "So, you are the one keeping me safe. I thank you, lifemate, that my safety is always such a top priority with you. It shows how important I am to you." He had successfully ended any chance of insubordination on her part over the issue of safety. If she worried about him now, he would simply bask in the knowledge.

"You would think that. You have a most annoying arrogance about you." She sniffed indignantly. She had to pull her hands out from under her bottom to snatch up the newspaper. "I simply don't want the publicity of some big shot like you getting murdered on my watch. I have my reputation to think about, you know."

"Speaking of reputations, who is Don Jacobson?"

She looked shocked. "How did you know about Don?"

"You were talking to him last evening on the phone, and this rising you were thinking of him."

"There really aren't any secrets from you, are there?" She didn't want to think about how often she had fantasized over Lucian. How right at this very moment she was thinking thoughts that brought a hint of color to her face.

Lucian wasn't about to be distracted. "Who is he?"

"I grew up with him in Florida. Before Drake goes on one of his killing sprees, he always returns to where it all started. It's some kind of ritualistic thing. He goes over the entire training course several times, camps out, almost as if he's playing hide and seek with the new recruits. No one has ever actually spotted him, and he's never killed anyone there, but he leaves signs to taunt them all with how superior he is."

"Florida is clear across the country."

"It doesn't matter. He always starts there. I was hoping maybe he was still there when I called Don. It was a long shot, but I had to try it. We might have caught him at an airport or stopped him in a car on his way here. No such luck. Drake has scouted your royal palace, just as you expected him to. Now I have to stick around and protect you from your own arrogance."

"I am very happy I am an arrogant man. It pleases me you have a reason to 'stick around and protect me.'" Lucian reached out and cupped her face in the palm of his hand with exquisite gentleness. "You did not answer to my full satisfaction who this man Don Jacobson is to you." His voice was very soft and intimate.

"I don't need to explain him." He was wreaking havoc with her insides, melting her like butter. Just looking at him made her feel weak and shaky. "It's getting hot in here," she complained. "You didn't turn on the heater, did you?"

"Carpathians can regulate their own body temperatures."

She nodded. "Of course they can. Why didn't I think of that?"

Lucian leaned into her so that the heat of his skin touched her through the thin material of her blouse. He swept back strands of her platinum hair. "You do feel a bit on the warm side." He was frowning as he checked her forehead. Touching her skin was addicting. The more he did it, the more he needed to do it. "Think about feeling cool, angel, and it will automatically be so."

She pushed at the wall of his chest. Who could think about cool when he was standing so close to her? "Get away from me, Lucian, and stop looking at me that way."

"How am I looking at you?"

"You know," she accused and deliberately caught up the rest of the newspaper. "Go away. If you touch me again, I'm going to break into a million pieces."

"I merely wish to kiss you," he murmured innocently, his voice velvet soft and deliberately seductive. He lowered his head to touch the pulse beating so frantically in her neck with the heat of his mouth. He felt it jump beneath his exploring tongue. His fingertips caressed her skin, pushing aside the thin ribbed cotton of her shirt to slide along her delicate collarbone. She felt like satin to him, unbelievably soft. At once need rose, sharp and urgent. He leaned his weight into her, forcing her smaller frame back into the couch. He cupped the fullness of one breast in the palm of his hand while his mouth took possession of hers.

He breathed her in, took her scent into his body. She was small beneath his wandering hands, so perfectly formed, a miracle of soft skin and silky hair. Even as his body made its demands and he felt her acceptance, her need and willingness to assuage his hunger, he sensed her exhaustion. She was still sore. He should have taken more care with her, as small and fragile and inexperienced as she was. He had been far too demanding of her. Her knew better; he had been just that little bit out of control.

"I am sorry, honey. I should have been more careful of you." He kissed her temple, then stroked a hand through her silky hair. "I can heal you," he offered.

"You didn't hurt me, Lucian," she protested immediately, blushing at the thought of what he had done, the pleasure she had experienced. "I like the way my body feels." *As if I belonged to him.*

You do belong to me.

She loved that, the intimacy of his velvet voice whispering in her mind to her alone. Their secret world of heat and darkness. She would never be alone again. Never have to face the monsters in the world alone again. Jaxon knew she was looking up at him with stars in her eyes, and it irritated her. She looked away from him, pretending to find the newspaper more interesting.

Lucian laughed softly, a man's amusement at finding his woman shy after hours of making love. Jaxon's long lashes lifted for a moment to chastise him before she returned to her reading. Almost at once she spotted the next article, her body going ramrod stiff. "Listen to this, Lucian. James Atwater apparently shot himself in his own home. He left a note saying he couldn't live with himself anymore after taking so many lives at the direction of Samuel T. Barnes. He actually named Barnes. No way would Atwater suddenly have an attack of conscience. He isn't like that. This has to be a purge in the ranks. These guys must have made a mistake, and someone higher up the food chain ordered the hit. Whoever took them out did a good job to get the coroner to rule the deaths from natural causes, accident, and suicide. The reason I got on to Barnes in the first place was his association with Atwater. Atwater was a straight-up killer."

Lucian's hand tangled in her hair, running the strands between the pads of his thumb and index finger repeatedly. A series of small beeps sounded for a moment, then ceased. Jaxon found her pager on the coffee table. "It's the department, Lucian. I have to call in."

"We have not had that discussion yet," he said lazily, following her to the phone.

He walked so quietly, he gave her an eerie feeling. "What discussion?" She was punching in the numbers quickly from long habit.

"The one where you tell me you are going to quit the force and stay home with me."

"Oh, that one." She laughed "Don't count on it."

Lucian could hear the answer on the other end, the flurry of activity, then the captain's booming voice. At once he knew something was wrong. He moved close to Jaxon, his large frame protective against hers, his arms circling her waist. "What is it, Daryl? Just come out with it," she said softly.

Lucian could hear the words as if the man were in the room with them. Stark. Ugly. "I'm sending you an escort to take you and Daratrazanoff to meet us at your old apartment building. Drake struck again, Jaxx, and it's bad."

Lucian was in her mind, and he felt her go very still. Even the air around them stilled. Jaxon hunched into herself, trying to move away from him. Firmly Lucian locked his arms around her protectively, his grip unbreakable. He refused to allow her to escape him either physically or

207

mentally. *I am with you, angel. We can face anything together*.

"Tell me," Jaxon said softly into the phone, her fingers wrapping around the cord until her knuckles turned white, betraying her nervousness.

"Mrs. Kramer, Jaxx. Drake murdered her. And the couple in the apartment next to yours—Tom and Shelby Snyder. He killed them." The captain cleared his throat. "He also took out the old man in the apartment two doors down from you." They could hear his fingers snapping. "Come on, John, what's the old guy's name?"

"His name was Sid Anderson. He was seventy, and he wrote the most beautiful poetry I've ever read," Jaxon supplied softly "Carla and Jacob Roberts? What about them?" Her voice was a whisper. She could hear screaming inside her head, over and over, yet her voice sounded as calm as ever.

"We're looking for them now," Daryl Smith told her in a tight voice. "So far we haven't found them."

"They're alive then," Jaxon said. "Drake would never change his methods. He's very angry, and he's punishing me. The message is, get rid of Lucian or he'll take out everyone who ever mattered to me. Try Carla's mother. They go there often. Put them in a hotel or something. Drake will go after them for sure. He likes things finished. Thorough. I'll meet you at the apartment building."

"Wait for your escort."

I have my own personal security team. Tell him not to waste the manpower, Lucian said in her mind.

"Lucian has good people, Daryl. Don't bother to send anyone over. We'll make it without trouble. Fifteen minutes."

"It isn't pretty, Jaxx."

"It never is." She slowly replaced the phone in the cradle and turned to lay her head against Lucian's chest. Closing her eyes, she stood quietly in his arms.

"Do not even entertain the notion that you should leave me, Jaxon. I feel your sorrow and fear in your mind. You believe if you leave me, he will stop. But it is not an option. It will never be an option. Drake is responsible for these crimes, not you."

"He won't stop, Lucian. As long as he knows I'm with you, he will keep on killing. Everyone I know is in danger because we're together."

He caught her chin firmly in his hand. "They are in danger because a sociopath is on the loose. It has nothing to do with you. He has fixated on you, but you are blameless. You cannot let this monster dictate your entire life. He's baiting a trap, not punishing you. I will find him. I promise you, I will find him."

Her large eyes searched his face for a long time. Tears shimmered in the depths, threatened to spill over, glistened on her long lashes. "He could kill a lot of people before we find him He's highly trained, Lucian, and he's cunning, very cunning. He blends in with his surroundings, he can wait for hours without moving just to get that one shot at his target. He doesn't know right from wrong He'll kill a child just as easily as a man or a woman."

"I will remove his presence from your life, Jaxon. That is my promise to you, and I always keep my promises." He took her elbow. "Come on, angel. The chauffeur has arrived."

"You sent for him that fast? No phone? Carrier pigeon perhaps?"

"He happened to be in the neighborhood."

"I'll just bet he did," Jaxon answered him, walking with him toward the door. Her feet felt like lead. She had seen Drake's work before, and each time, along with the horror of his latest crimes, the memory of the murders of her mother and brother was branded anew in her mind.

The limousine was waiting at the gates, the chauffeur

standing by the open door. "Good evening, Jaxon, Lucian." The man tipped his hat, a slight smile on his face. That humor didn't reach his eyes. They were watchful, wary, compassionate.

"I think an introduction would be in order," Jaxon suggested dryly.

Lucian nodded. "This is Antonio. He is the son of Stefan and Marie. They are friends and family to one of ours, Aidan Savage, and his lifemate, Alexandria. Antonio has many special gifts."

Is he like you? It was becoming easier to communicate in their intimate way, and she found it convenient when they weren't alone.

You mean, is he like us? No, Antonio is human, as are his parents. The members of his family have voluntarily served Aidan Savage for hundreds of years. Few humans are allowed to know of our existence, but they have done so throughout history, mother to daughter, father to son.

Jaxon held out her hand to Antonio. "It's a pleasure to finally meet you. Has Lucian explained to you who Tyler Drake is and just how dangerous he can be?"

Antonio winked at her. "Lucian is always explicit when he gives his orders."

"Just be careful." Jaxon slid into the car and was comforted when Lucian's large frame moved protectively in beside her. He felt solid and right.

Lucian curved his arm around her shoulders. "Do not waste your time worrying about Antonio. Your protective streak is growing."

I couldn't bear it if he was killed because of me.

Antonio is highly skilled, angel, and he is under the protection of our people. No one will kill him easily.

Jaxon shook her head, fought back tears, and stared sightlessly out the window as the sleek car raced through the night toward death and hell. Her personal hell. Reading her thoughts, Lucian pulled her in close to him, his dark head bending over hers protectively, his mouth brushing the top of her head. She felt his love radiating out to her, enveloping her, filling her until the terrible pain threatening to overwhelm her lessened. She didn't understand how Lucian could do it, but she was grateful. She knew what she was going to see. She knew and cared about each one of Drake's victims.

I am with you. Stay connected to me.

She swallowed hard and nodded. The car was pulling up behind the squad units, detective cars, and the coroner's van. Even as she slipped from the car, the sickness hit her gut; she smelled the odor, the sickly sweet odor of death.

Breathe, angel. Listen to my heart, and let your body use mine to regulate your heart and lungs. You are never alone. We are in this together.

Jaxon nodded without looking at him, allowing her body to tune itself to his. It helped to take away the rolling in her stomach. Or maybe Lucian was doing something to prevent it. However it was done, it helped tremendously. She tried to stay toward the outside of the sidewalk, a small barrier between Lucian and the rest of the world, but he had other ideas. He swept her easily beneath the protection of his shoulder, his much larger frame squarely blocking her from the prying eyes of the gathering of reporters. Antonio took up a position on the other side of her, successfully sandwiching her between them.

She didn't protest, knowing it was useless. As they entered Mrs. Kramer's apartment, Captain Daryl Smith came out to meet them. "Jaxx, it's messy in there. You know his work better than the rest of us. Take a look around, and see what you can tell us."

Antonio had stopped at the door, not wanting to intrude on the crime scene. Jaxx pulled on gloves and gave Lucian one long look of anguish before turning to the task at hand. Lucian's watchful eyes never left her small figure. He saw it all through her eyes. Felt her emotions. These were her friends. These people mattered in her young life. He caught glimpses of memories she tried hard to suppress. Mrs. Kramer laughing when Jaxon slipped in the doorway, grabbed at the back of a chair, and landed on her bottom anyway. Jaxon, who was always so graceful. Mrs. Kramer had teased her about it often, holding it over her like friendly blackmail.

He wanted to wrap her up in the protection of his arms and take her for all time away from this place of death and misery. He wanted to erase every painful memory from her heart and mind. Jaxon said nothing at all. When others murmured things to her, she barely seemed to register that they had done so. She concentrated totally on the crime scene, careful not to miss the smallest detail. She went from room to room, a mask of professional detachment on her face, pale yet composed. Jaxon, the consummate cop and protector of people. His Jaxon.

He could read the thoughts of those around him, pick up the various conversations in every room, the halls, and even outside. Jaxon had the same ability now. She knew which of her colleagues feared to speak with her, which ones worried for their own families, which ones thought her a robot without emotion. It went on and on, the bombardment of sympathy and blame, blood, and death, from apartment to apartment.

The memories. Shelby Snyder baking her a birthday cake and bringing it over. Tom fixing her sink and banging his head, water spraying over his face as Shelby and Jaxon laughed at him. He took it good-naturedly, as he always did. Night after night with Sid, talking poetry because she couldn't sleep and neither could he. She had been so careful, never appearing in public with any of them, even sneaking into Sid's apartment at prearranged times. She had told Sid Anderson about her background.

He was the kind of man who inspired confidence. Sid's death was a terrible blow to her.

Lucian watched it all, felt her strength, her resolve, the weight of responsibility so heavy on her shoulders. His admiration for her grew. Her brain analyzed every piece of data. She didn't shirk from the grisly results of Drake's madness; these victims had been her friends, which made her all the more determined to catch him. She was physically ill, her stomach in knots, her head pounding, and he heard her screaming in her mind, yet her face was calm, and she never once turned away from examining the gory scenes.

Daryl Smith followed her over to Lucian as she moved out of the last apartment, removing another set of gloves. "So, what do you think, Jaxx?"

"He hit Mrs. Kramer first. He was waiting for her when she came in from shopping. The groceries are still sitting on her table. She always put her groceries away immediately. He entered through her bedroom window. It was locked, but Drake had no problem with it. He used his knife on her. It's his favorite weapon, up close and personal. I counted eighteen deep stab wounds and several shallower wounds. He took her eyes before he left. His standard trademark." She frowned. "It was him . . . but not exactly."

"What does that mean?" the captain asked.

Lucian was in her mind, and he felt her puzzlement. "I can't tell you exactly, but he's different. Still, it was definitely Drake. I think he went to Carla and Robert's apartment next and found they weren't home. Angry, he slashed up their bed in a killing rage. From Carla's apartment he went to Tom and Shelby's. He caught them in the shower together. He stabbed Tom fifty-eight times and Shelby at least eighty. There's a lump on Shelby's head. He probably hit her and knocked her out as he was killing Tom. His rage increased as he murdered them. I

213

can tell because the stab wounds they received after they died are deeper and more savage. I believe the medical examiner will agree with me on that. He took their eyes and he carved up their bedroom. Clothes, blankets, mattress, even the carpet. He entered their apartment through the rear door. They hadn't locked it. It looks as if he just walked right in with no problem."

Jaxon suddenly reached out to Lucian, the first public gesture she had made toward him. She was exhausted without hesitation his fingers laced, warm and solid, through hers. And he was right. She didn't feel alone anymore. *I am responsible for so many deaths, Lucian. I feel as if my soul is black.*

You are not responsible. Hear me when I say this, Jaxon. Tyler Drake murders people because he is a sick man, not because of you. If it was not you he had fixated on, it would be another.

Her mouth curved in a semblance of a smile that never had a chance of reaching her eyes. *You're sure of that? You don't know what it's like to know that people you care about are dead because the only crime they committed was being your neighbor. Lucian, I don't want this to touch you.*

I have been judge and executioner for nearly two thousand years. I have destroyed so many I cannot count that high, nor would I want to. I am a predator, honey. You are a sweet, compassionate angel. A miracle. My miracle.

Thank you. She said it simply, meaning it.

I love you, angel, Lucian said in his black-velvet sorcerer's voice, and *he* meant it.

A ghost of a smile touched her mouth before she resumed her assessment for her boss. "Drake went to kill Sid after that. There's a smear of blood in the hall beside Sid's door. I'll be willing to bet it's Shelby's. Blood never bothers Drake. Sid answered the door. He never looked through the peephole, although I cautioned him numerous times. He was a wonderful man. He trusted everyone. He played with children in the park, taught them chess, spent half his monthly check on food for the kids in the neighborhood. He gave them things to do and a place to go when their parents weren't home or when there was trouble. He didn't deserve what Drake did to him."

Lucian felt her falter then. She crumbled inside, her silent screams louder than ever. On the outside she appeared calm, but she was sick, fighting back the nausea gripping her. Immediately he wrapped his arms around her, turning her against his chest. His heart matched the exact rhythm of hers. *You are not alone, never alone. Drake can never separate us. You can reach for me over time and space, and I will be with you.*

I can't bear this. Sid was so sweet. You would've liked him. Tom and Shelby were nice people. They had no children, and they treated me like a daughter. Their only sin was that they liked me. And you met Mrs. Kramer. There was no one nicer. This is all because of me. If I hadn't gone to your house, let them publish our engagement in the newspapers, Drake wouldn't have done this.

Drake is totally responsible, honey, not you. He was patient, repeating it over and over, wanting his words to sink in.

He'll get to you. He will. You and Barry. She stiffened, her eyes suddenly wide with terror. "He's going after Barry, Captain. Drake will do it—I know he will. He'll access your computers, torture someone, I don't know how, but he's going to go after Barry. Drake's different now. I can't explain it—I just feel it. Something's wrong with all of this. In the past he always killed because he perceived others as a threat to his family. This was rage. This was because he *wanted* to kill. Part of him was Drake, because he performed like Drake, he took their eyes, but he wasn't exactly the same. He doesn't kill with this kind of rage. He's different." She shook her head. "I have to get to Barry. He isn't safe."

"No one knows where we stashed Radcliff," Daryl protested. "I want you to go to the station and write up your report. Every detail. We need it, Jaxx."

"Someone knows where he is. There's a paper trail. There's always a paper trail. You think he can't find Barry? It's what he does. I'm going to him." She was absolutely firm.

"He can't find him," the captain reiterated.

"I could find Barry," Jaxon said confidently. "Lucian, we have to protect him."

"You go back to the station, Jaxon," Lucian said softly, his voice as mild as ever. That voice that no one could ever resist. "I will go with Captain Smith to get Barry and bring him to safety. Antonio will go, also, so there is no need to worry about protecting me. I will keep him safe, Jaxon." The black-velvet voice was gentle. "You will be safe at the station, and I will concentrate on picking up Drake's trail."

She clung to his hand, knowing he was right, but afraid it was just what Drake wanted. Afraid Drake was using the threat to Barry as a trap to lure Lucian out into the open. She felt so sick inside. "I don't know what I would do if something happened to you, Lucian."

He brought her hand to the warmth of his mouth. "Nothing can harm me, angel. Go to the station where it is safe, and allow me to do this small thing for you."

"Drake is different, Lucian. I don't know how, but it changes everything and makes him much more unpredictable. He is a monster, a true monster, with every skill of our best fighters and all the cunning of wild animal. Our engagement must have driven him over the edge."

"He was already over the edge," Lucian said quietly, deliberately allowing his voice to drop an octave so that it soothed and calmed her. He walked with her to the squad car. "I will stay with you until I see that you are safe within the station house where no one can harm you. Then we will go to Barry."

"You have to hurry, Lucian. Drake could be stalking him right now." She was anxious, but his voice held that strange, mesmerizing effect that made her feel as if everything would be all right.

Daryl Smith cleared his throat, determined to protest. He had allowed Lucian Daratrazanoff onto the crime scene because Jaxx clearly needed him there, but that he be allowed into the middle of a police crisis was going too far. But there was something dangerous about Lucian, something powerful, and it wasn't his money. The eyes were too watchful, the face too still. Smith was frankly wary of denying the man anything.

Daratrazanoff turned his head toward the captain, almost as if reading his thoughts. "Of course you want Antonio and me to come along with you." He spoke quietly, his voice so low Smith barely heard him, yet the words penetrated to his deepest soul. He *needed* Daratrazanoff with them. It was imperative that he be there.

"Yes, of course, Mr. Daratrazanoff," the captain invited.

"Please call me Lucian," he replied almost absently. His full attention was once more directed at Jaxon, the only person who really mattered to him.

Lucian held the door open for her. He had deliberately chosen to escort her to a car whose driver had been particularly sympathetic in his conversation with some of the other officers. It was a small thing, but she did not need to feel uncomfortable with one of her peers who was secretly afraid to be seen in public with her or who held her accountable for Tyler Drake's actions.

Jaxon kept her head up, her face a blank mask. The flashes from news cameras were going off in all directions. She didn't look at any of them as she slipped into the car.

Antonio and Lucian got in on either side of her, effectively walling her in, protecting her from prying eyes. She stayed close to Lucian, to the warmth of his body, to the warmth of his heart.

We will find him, honey.

But we can never bring them back, can we? Tears filled her voice, her mind, her heart.

Lucian wanted to weep for her. She didn't deserve this. She was so young and compassionate, totally the opposite of what he was. Monsters didn't come after *him;* they wanted her. Human and Carpathian alike, they wanted Jaxon. He hadn't elaborated on the story of vampires, because she had enough guilt weighing her down. But vampires were once Carpathian males who had chosen to lose their souls after centuries of bleak hopelessness. And just as the Carpathian male searched for a lifemate, vampires searched the ranks of humankind for women just like Jaxon. Her presence in the area attracted them.

Vampires were solitary creatures for the most part, trusting no one, vain, cunning, and evil. They were incapable of loyalty, though sometimes they banded together in the hopes of eluding or even destroying a hunter in the area. Other times a master vampire, one ancient and skilled who had survived as the undead for centuries, took on as apprentices the newer, younger vampires just turned. They used them for menial labor, as pawns to sacrifice, as a front line to achieve their ultimate goals. Jaxon had attracted more than one vampire to the area by her presence alone.

Lucian had hunted and destroyed three such vampires the humans had mistaken as serial killers before he had made his claim on Jaxon. He had established his home, watching her, reading her likes and dislikes, finding out all he could about her before he approached her. If she knew vampires were coming to her city because of her, she would be capable of terminating her life to protect others. He could not allow such a thing. If she knew the whole truth, she would suffer even more than she was suffering at present, and he could do no other than protect her. He was her lifemate and responsible for her happiness, health, and complete safety.

Lucian and Antonio escorted her up the stairs to the police station, opening the door and waiting until she was inside. "Remain indoors with all these officers until I return with Barry," Lucian said. "And this time, angel, I expect you to do as I say. I will not be pleased if I come back to find you have left the safety of this building."

"I won't," she assured him, clinging to his hand. "Just be certain nothing happens to you. Or Barry. Bring him back, Lucian."

"I will." He bent his head to hers, his mouth finding hers with incredible tenderness "I will return quickly."

Chapter Ten

Jaxon pressed both hands against her stomach as she watched Lucian stride away. She felt sicker than ever. Close to Lucian, she could control the terrible feeling, but with him gone, it was growing stronger. She walked slowly through the familiar hallway, waved to a couple of people who greeted her from the bullpen, tried to reply when others patted her shoulder and murmured their sympathy.

There was a roaring in her ears, jackhammers pounding in her head. Resolutely she continued walking, but her desk felt as if it were a million miles away, her legs rubbery. The ability to hear so acutely was a terrible curse. Her fellow officers were all discussing the murders; on every floor she could hear the various conversations. She didn't want that—didn't want to know what people thought of her part in the carnage.

She admitted to herself that most of what she overheard was kind and sympathetic, but that didn't lessen the pain. And she had never sought pity from anyone. As she sat down, her stomach lurched again, and the feeling of evil nearly overwhelmed her. She was aware of eyes on her, unable to keep from staring. She wanted desperately to be alone, to weep and throw things, to scream, to sit on the floor in the bathroom, hugging the toilet, and be sick. Instead, she made herself spread her notes out on her desk. The pictures would come later. She couldn't face them now.

It wasn't easy being without Lucian. She had been with him nearly every moment since waking up from the warehouse disaster. Now, when she needed him most, needed his comfort, he had gone to save her friend. He was in danger because of her. She rubbed the heel of one hand against her throbbing head.

I am not in danger, angel. That is impossible. You should know that by now. Be still, and allow me to take away your headache.

It's enough that I know you're there if I reach out to you. And it was. Jaxon felt comforted, safe. She felt he was holding her in his strong arms. *Bring Barry back safely, Lucian. I still have that feeling, the one that means Drake's about to do something terrible.* Her stomach was a mess, clenching and knotting in outrage.

We are close to the safe house where the captain says he has Barry stashed. I am scanning the area around us continually, and all is not right. I feel the intrusion of evil, yet it is not the same as what you were feeling in the apartments.

Jaxon closed her eyes tightly, trying to shut out reality, if only for a moment. If Drake already knew where Barry was located, the chances were more than good that it was far too late to save him. She could only hope that Daryl had called ahead to warn the officers guarding Barry that Drake was on a killing spree and was stalking them.

She bent over her notes, trying to focus, trying to read the words, but the ink all seemed to run together. How was she going to generate a decent report if she couldn't even read her own work? It took several minutes before she realized she had tears in her eyes. Swearing silently to herself, she jumped up and began to make her way down the hall to the bathroom.

Every step she took only increased the terrible precognition of death. Small beads of sweat broke out on her forehead. *Lucian?* She reached for him desperately.

I am here. His voice was tranquil and soft, more soothing than ever, a mesmerizing tool that instantly calmed her.

He's killing someone right now. I feel him. Please get to Barry.

It is not Barry. Your captain is talking to Radcliff on the phone. We will be there in minutes. There is a presence, but I am not certain it is Drake. It does not feel the same as what is in your mind when you replay your memories. Similar, but different.

Like in the apartment?

No, not even that. We are here now. I will protect Barry from this monster. With that last assurance Lucian broke off their merge.

She thought about that, the abruptness of his departure. He never did that, never separated from her as he had just done. He always did it slowly, almost reluctantly, his presence lingering so that she felt him, not always certain whether he was really gone or still a shadow remaining in her mind. This was different. He was completely gone, and she actually felt a loss. For the first time she knew what he meant when he talked about lifemates and their urgent need of each other.

With a sigh she pushed open the door to bathroom. At once the feeling of darkness and evil overwhelmed her, and she doubled over, clutching her stomach, retching violently.

An arm curved around her waist, and Tom Anderson helped her into the bathroom and away from all the watchful eyes. "You'll be okay, Jaxx. Let's get you some water."

Tom had been a loyal member of her unit for a long time, so she let him help her, although she found it humiliating that he should see her this way. She had trained with these men, fought beside them, led them. She needed their respect if she was going to work with them. Splashing cold water on her face helped ease the gagging in her throat, but her stomach was in knots as tight as ever. The feeling persisted. Drake was busy this night. Barry? She couldn't bear it if Barry was killed.

"I'm sorry about all this," Tom said. "But Radcliff is tough. No one is going to get to him easily. Besides, they have guards all over the place."

"Thanks, Tom," she murmured softly and bent to take a drink of water. It hit her then. The feeling was far too strong for the distance between the stationhouse and where Barry was located.

She straightened up, pressing a hand to her stomach, turning to look over her shoulder at Tom. "He's here."

"What? Who? Who's here?"

"Drake is here. Somewhere in the building, in this building." She pushed past Tom and began to move swiftly down the hall toward her desk.

"Are you nuts? Jaxx, this is the police station. He's the most wanted man in these parts. Do you really think he's that stupid?" Tom was whispering, trying to protect her from her overactive imagination. He didn't blame her, but he didn't want anyone else to witness her breakdown.

Jaxon didn't answer him; what was the point? How could she explain? She just knew it. She knew things. She knew Drake was in the building, stalking more victims, people she worked with. Maybe stalking Tom himself. Her desk drawer contained a gun and a spare clip. She pocketed the clip and moved around Tom. "Just stay here in this room. He won't come in here where there're so many witnesses. He's probably targeted every one of you in my unit."

"Are you sure about this?" Tom was beginning to believe her. Jaxx might have gotten sick, but she was as steady as ever. There was that look in her eye, the one that always kept their butts out of trouble. "You think he's here?"

"I know he's here. You're in terrible danger, Tom. Stay here and call the others in our unit and warn them. Anyone in the building should come here. It will be safer if you're looking out for one another. I'm going to hunt him."

"Not alone, you're not." Tom was appalled. "Not only would the captain and Radcliff kick me to hell and back, but that fiancé of yours would be likely to break my neck. He's no one to mess with, Jaxon. He said to keep you safe."

"Shut up, Tom, and do what I said. This is Drake we're talking about, and no one else knows him like I do." She was halfway down the hall, heading for the stairs. Above her was the second story. It was night, and not too many officers would be on duty, but two homicide detectives, the vice squad, and several uniforms were roaming around up there. Below her, on the basement level, would be only two officers, maybe three, and perhaps a handful of prisoners waiting to be transferred to the overnight cages.

"You're not thinking straight, Jaxx. You're a cop. Be a cop. You can't round us all up and put us in a safe place while you hunt. Get organized."

Jaxon shoved an impatient but rock-steady hand through her hair. "You're right, Tom, thanks. I think I just wanted to face him."

"Let's do it right then."

Jaxon nodded and moved back down the hall to the phone. "Call them in then, use our code, and get everyone a radio." She tapped her foot as Tom did as she ordered, anxious to get moving. When the group was assembled, she looked them over carefully, ensuring Drake hadn't penetrated their forces. "We sweep the building. Tom, take them to the top. Look at everything, no matter how ridiculous. The air vents, under desks, anyplace he could fit. He's incredible at hiding out in the open without being detected. Each of you should have a number and count off regularly so that he can't join you. No one go off alone, and never forget he's a highly trained killer. You can't hesitate to kill him, because he won't hesitate to kill you. Start upstairs, and don't leave anything to chance. I'll keep in touch by radio. I'm going to the basement to see what's going on down there. Does anyone know the exact prisoner count?"

"A drunk driver, a couple of petty thieves, and we have Terry Stevens down there waiting for transport."

"And the officers?"

"Two—Kitter and Halibut," Tom replied.

"Let's do it then," Jaxon said. "Be careful. He's extremely dangerous."

"Take someone with you, Jaxx," Tom insisted.

"I'm just going to make sure everyone's all right down there. I'll get Kitter and Halibut to look with me." The basement was a maze of pipes, file cabinets, and the cages. Jaxon had a strong feeling about the basement. There was every possibility that Drake was upstairs, but she seriously doubted it. She was not going to allow one more friend to die simply because he worked with her or spoke with her.

This had started with her. She couldn't remember a time in her life she hadn't known Tyler Drake. He had been more of a constant in her life than even her own father or mother, yet that had become a destructive, twisted, obsessive force. Drake had killed her father to take his place in her life. Her mother and brother had been destroyed so he could have her to himself. She was the one who had to end his killing spree once and for all.

Jaxon dismissed the others from her mind as she started down the stairs. She moved silently, not allowing even her clothing to whisper of her presence. With each step her stomach tightened even more. She was on the right track. The lighting was dim on the stairs and worsened when she arrived at the bottom. It didn't matter. Her eyesight was now phenomenal.

Lucian? She reached out to him before she really thought about it, before she even knew she was going to do it.

He was here, angel. We found two of the officers dead in their patrol car. They were stabbed several times.

She was silent for a moment, thinking about his revelation. *Are you positive it's Drake?* She couldn't be wrong. How could she be? Was it possible after all this time that she was losing whatever special sense had been granted her to detect when evil was close? Perhaps she was suffering the aftereffects of being in proximity to so many murders.

It feels the same as before, at the apartments. And their eyes are gone. The strange thing is, I cannot get his scent. I am unable to track him that way. I noticed it at the apartment building. There was nothing for me to trace.

What happens when you scan? You always seem to know where everyone is.

Several people are inside, but I cannot tell who they are. No one is conversing. A television is on. I am going inside.

Be careful, Lucian. It's a trap. Drake wants you dead more than anyone else. Everyone else is nothing to him. It's all to get you.

No one will see me, honey, if I do not wish it.

Just be careful. She allowed the mind merge to slowly slip away. The feeling in the pit of her stomach was as strong as ever. Something evil was lurking in this building, stalking her friends, and she had to believe it was Drake. Perhaps Drake had been at Barry's safe house already in an attempt to draw them away from the station.

Jaxon kept moving, her senses flaring out to locate the officers, the prisoners, and, with luck, the intruder. She became aware of movement around the corner from her position. Staying close to the wall, without a whisper of sound to betray her, she inched her way closer toward the slight brushing noise ahead of her. As she stepped forward, a lump on the ground to her right caught her eye. She paused. The terrible darkness was growing within her. Drake was here, and he had already killed.

Lucian? He is here. She made her way to the dark bundle slumped across the floor. She could see that the man was dead, the uniform punctured with a dozen stab wounds. The head was at a peculiar angle. It was Halibut. His eyes were gone. Drake's trademark.

You are certain? His voice was the same. Calm, tranquil, comforting in its soft steadiness.

Absolutely. I'm standing over a body right now. I can feel his presence.

There is something wrong, love. He is here, also. There is the taint of power here. Can you feel it there?

I'm not certain what you mean.

It would be the same faint feeling of power you experienced when you sensed the ghoul's presence, and later the vampire. It was at the apartments, too. A trace is here, also. But I no longer think Drake is in either of these places. I think we are dealing with puppets programmed by a vampire, clones of Drake to carry out his deeds. I think any humans who have memories of you are the ones in danger.

Jaxon was on the move again. She didn't know Kitter very well, just to say hello in passing, and none of the prisoners knew her other than Terry Stevens. Stevens was a habitual criminal, a street dealer well connected with a great lawyer. If the intruder was in the basement, as she thought, and Lucian was right, it would be Stevens in the most danger. He had had many encounters with Jaxon.

You could be right. It does feel different, but it felt different at the apartment building too. Does that mean Drake is dead? What are we dealing with?

Just get out of there. I will be there when I dispose of this one. I cannot leave these humans to face the danger this thing poses. I do not want you to face such a powerful being, either.

I'm a police officer, Lucian. I don't run away because something gets dangerous. There are prisoners down here and another officer. I have to get them to safety.

I have no time to argue, angel. The killer is striking as we speak. I am going to the aid of the human, and it would put you in danger if I forced your compliance. Stay merged with me at all times so I can give you any help you need. Lucian's soft voice held more than his usual gentle command; it held a compulsion to force his will upon her, to ensure she would do as he said.

It was weird to be in two places at once. If she wished, she could "see" through Lucian's eyes as he glided silently through the building, unseen by humans. She watched two uniformed men pass right by him and not even notice he was there. He was a blur, really, using his ability to move with impossible speed. The door burst open for him with one blow from the flat of his palm. Lucian was facing a being that looked exactly like Tyler Drake.

Jaxon's breath caught in her throat. *It's him. That's Drake!*

Drake's arm was on a downward swing, a bloody knife clutched in his fist. Lucian's mind placed a barrier between the knife and Drake's intended target. The knife fell harmlessly to the floor. Jaxon caught a brief glimpse of Barry Radcliff as Lucian glanced at him in passing.

Barry's hands were slashed, as if he had attempted to ward off the attack. There was a streak of crimson across his right biceps and a spreading stain on the right side of his shirt.

Even as Lucian was leaping toward Drake, something distracted Jaxon—not a sound really, more a movement of air. She whirled around, bringing up her gun as she did so. Drake was almost on top her, his eyes gloating and mad. He had a knife in his hand. Jaxon could see the blood on it, the blood staining his hands. She fired three quick shots, straight at his heart, as she flung her body to one side, rolling under a desk and coming to her feet on the other side.

All three bullets had struck him in a small pattern over his heart. He seemed to hesitate and swayed for a moment, a sickly, taunting grin pasted on his face. Then he began to come toward her again. She fired off two more rounds, this time going for his forehead, dead center, afraid he was wearing a bulletproof vest. Two red holes blossomed in the middle of his forehead. Again he paused. Blood trickled down, then gushed in a steady stream, running down his face, into his eyes. But he continued to smile at her, his expression never changing, and he started toward her again.

"Kitter? You in here somewhere? It's Jaxon Montgomery. Halibut's dead. Drake killed him. Answer if you're alive," Jaxon called out. She was moving to keep furniture between Drake's advance and herself. She was trying to maneuver him away from the cages holding the prisoners.

"I've got you covered," Kitter yelled back. "Freeze, Drake! You take one more step toward her, and I'll blow you away."

Drake didn't act as if he heard. His eyes never wavered from Jaxon. He didn't blink or attempt to wipe the blood away. He kept moving forward. Kitter fired his weapon, the shots so close together they sounded simultaneous. He swore as he saw the back of Drake's head disintegrate but the man kept moving forward. "What the hell? Jaxx? What's going on?"

"Get the prisoners out of here, Kitter. Take Stevens out first. I think he's in more danger than the others. Go on, hurry up."

"He must be on something. . . ." Kitter muttered, confused.

"Do what I say. Get the prisoners out." Jaxon gave the order in her no-nonsense voice, snapping Kitter back to the reality of their problem. It was easier to deal with moving the prisoners than with the impossibility of a man with half of his head blasted away, stalking another officer.

Lucian, tell me what to do. She didn't dare try to "see" through Lucian's eyes. It was too distracting with two Drakes in two separate places. She was disoriented enough.

At once he was there. His breath was hers, slowing her breathing so that she was relaxed and in complete control. His heart regulated hers to a normal, steady pace. His warmth flooded her body with reassurance and complete faith. *Focus on him, angel. Look directly at him. He cannot harm you from a distance. Do not look away from him no matter what is happening. Remember, you are no longer human with human limitations. You are a Carpathian with all the abilities of a Carpathian. You can dissolve into mist if the need arises.*

Jaxon was gliding with the same ease of the Carpathian people without really being aware of it. She moved quickly and silently, skimming around a file cabinet as the thing that was supposed to be Drake continued to stalk her. She kept her gaze fastened on the bloodstained abomination. She could feel Lucian pouring strength into her, filling her with confidence and power.

As she stared at Drake, flames began to dance along

his skin, licking over his arms and shoulders, his chest, even his head, so that his hair smoldered and blackened. At once the air smelled of burned flesh. Horrified, Jaxon tried to turn away.

Stay calm, Jaxon. Stay focused. You must defeat this one. He is an instrument of the undead, and nothing will stop him from his appointed task.

She found she could not look away. *Lucian, please. I can't kill someone like this.* The cry was wrenched from her deepest soul. Drake was not fighting back; he was merely howling in a high-pitched, steady, almost unearthly cry. The sound grated on her ears, tore at her heart. Drake continued coming toward her, each step fanning the flames higher until he was engulfed by them.

I know you cannot, my love. You are the light in my life. You are not killing him, Jaxon. I am destroying what is already dead. I am the dark angel of death and have been for over two thousand years. The responsibility is mine.

Jaxon couldn't look away from the gruesome sight. The hideous creature was burning yet still stalking her. Parts of him began to fall to the floor in ashes as the flames burned cleanly through him. She noticed the fire did not spread to the floor or to any of the shelves Drake banged into as he followed her around the basement. She was aware of the officers crowding down the stairway, yet they seemed unable to enter the room. She could hear them frantically trying to get to her to help.

Tears streamed down her face as she watched the blackened ruin of a man finally crumple into a heap of flames. Even on the ground the thing tried to reach her, extending itself toward her. *Lucian, please stop. It can't live now,* she cried, desperately afraid she would never rid herself of the memory.

It must be totally destroyed, my love, or it will rise

231

again and again to be used by its creator. I am sorry. I know this is difficult for you.

Jaxon could feel his deep regret for having to use her for such a distasteful thing—killing from a distance, employing her eyes—but he didn't relent, holding her in place until the creature was literally a pile of ashes. She slumped to the floor the moment he released her. Her hair was damp with sweat and clinging to her face. She was shaking. For a moment she closed her eyes, grateful that she could. How could Lucian have lived day after day, month after month, year after endless year, forced to endure such hideous torment? Her heart went out to him even as it went out to the creature he had destroyed.

Lucian, a shadow in her mind, allowed himself to take a breath, allowed his heart to beat. He should have known how Jaxon would react. With compassion for him. She thought of him and his bleak former life, not of what he had just done, destroying another and using her to do it. He concentrated on her, closed his eyes, and savored his own personal miracle. *Jaxon.* She was a clean, fresh wind blowing the stench of death from his mind.

He turned his head slowly to once more look at the heap of ashes beside Barry Radcliff. Barry was still alive, a surprising testimony to his will to live. Ghouls rarely failed in their appointed tasks. Barry had fought the creature off long enough to give Lucian time to get there and destroy the creature. Lucian had slowed Barry's heart and lungs to prevent the officer from bleeding to death while he disposed of Drake's clone. Now he bent over the human.

Is he going to live for sure?

Lucian found himself smiling. Jaxon had no idea how quickly she was gaining strength. She touched his mind so easily, using their private, intimate channel as if she had always done so. She was becoming accepting of the changes in her body, the power she was gaining. She was a woman with tremendous control, and she utilized the special talents of the Carpathian people almost without realizing it.

There is no doubt. I have stopped the bleeding. The main problem will be damage control. Barry will only remember being attacked by Drake. I will plant it in his head that it was a copycat attempt. You must make it clear that the same occurred there.

One of the officers shot the ghoul, puppet, clone— whatever you want to call it. He nearly shot its head off. He saw me shoot it, too. Three times in the heart, twice in the forehead. Kitter hit it twice in the back of the head. He knows it didn't go down.

Try to find him as quickly as possible. I will plant a story in the confusion. Things often look different than they are.

And the ashes at both places?

There will be ashes only at the police station. He will have escaped from here.

The timetable is all wrong.

That can be dealt with. They have to believe it was the same man who attacked at both places, and now he is dead. He doused himself with some chemical rather than be taken prisoner. When the ashes are examined, they will back up your story. I cannot come to you, as I must take Barry to the hospital and ensure that our timetable holds up, but I will be with you at all times.

Jaxon slowly got to her feet and made her way toward the stairs. She was so tired. The clamor of the officers trying to get to her made her realize that only a minute or so had passed, yet it seemed forever. An eternity. The door jammed on the stairs suddenly gave way, and policemen spilled down the stairs. She leaned against a wall and allowed them to surround her. Just the human company provided a measure of comfort.

She wanted to be held. As soon as the thought crossed

her mind, she felt Lucian's arms around her, holding her close to the warmth of his body. The illusion was so real, she stood perfectly still, savoring the feeling of being part of someone else. The men were touching her, checking to make certain she wasn't injured. She could hear them all talking to her at once, but it was just a blur of sound to her.

Tom Anderson shoved the others out of the way. "Give her some room. Jaxx, are you all right?" He gave her arm a little shake. "What happened down here?"

Jaxx swallowed hard. The stench of burning flesh was offensive. "Hell happened down here, Tom. It wasn't Drake. Some copycat—I don't know. He looked like Drake, and his M.O. was close enough that he fooled me, but it wasn't Drake."

"Kitter said he shot him twice, blasted away the back of his head. He said you shot the guy at least three or four times, and he didn't go down."

Jaxon nodded. "Kitter did hit him. I'm sure of it. I saw blood. I rarely miss, but he just kept coming." She caught sight of Kitter and moved to stand directly in front of him, her wide, chocolate eyes capturing his. "He acted as if he was on drugs. Something powerful, didn't you think so?"

Lucian's power was flowing through her. Jaxon could feel him inside her mind, feel him taking control of Kitter. The officer nodded slowly, thoughtfully. "I don't see what else it could have been. I've seen some ugly things with perps on PCP. I hit him, but he didn't even blink."

Jaxon released the man's gaze. She felt the flood of information, the story passed through her to Kitter, and she was awed by Lucian's powers. He did it so smoothly, so efficiently, with seemingly little effort. For the first time she really allowed herself to think about that and what it meant.

There is no need to find new reasons to fear your life-

mate, honey. His masculine amusement almost made her smile. *You already have plenty of reasons in your imagination. If I was going to turn vampire and prey upon the human race, I would have done so already. You are the light to my darkness. It is no longer possible for me to turn.*

You don't need to turn to prey upon the human race. You've been doing it for years. Centuries. You're always getting your way.

Jaxon immediately had the impression of a wolfish grin, a predator's flash of white teeth. She even heard him growl very low. *Show-off.* Resolutely she turned back to the problems confronting her. Her colleagues had examined the ashes and were crowding around her again, demanding answers.

She held up a hand for silence. "I don't know what happened. One minute he was coming at me with a knife in his hand and blood all over him, and the next we could hear you on the stairs. He said something, but I couldn't really understand it. I think it was something like no one was going to take him alive or words to that effect, but I'm not really sure. It all happened so fast. He had some kind of liquid he doused himself with, and, just like that, he set himself on fire. It was horrible. I thought about shooting him to end his misery. I think I'll hear him screaming for the rest of my life."

"Did you see this, though? There's no body—nothing left at all. Nothing but a pile of ashes. People don't burn like that. And there's no burn marks on the floors or anywhere else," Tom pointed out.

"He burned fast, too," Jaxon said. She shoved at her hair. "I want to go sit down somewhere. It's been a hell of a night. Has anyone heard from the captain yet?"

"Dispatch just called in and reported they received a message about fifteen minutes ago that Radcliff was attacked by some maniac. Radcliff fought him off, but they took him to the hospital. Two officers in a patrol car were killed on the scene. The perp got away. Could be the same as our boy. They thought it was Drake."

"Does anyone know how Barry's doing?" Jaxon asked anxiously. She was so tired she stumbled on the stairs, and Tom slipped an arm around her waist to help her.

"I'll call the hospital, Jaxx. You sit down before you fall down. You took a big chance going down there alone. And how did the door get jammed? We had to break it down. The thing's in pieces." Tom pointed it out to her to prove his point, then helped her to her desk. When she glanced with distaste at the notes spread out before her, he hastily gathered them up. She didn't need to look at the reminders of her dead neighbors and friends right now. "Let me get you a glass of water."

"Thanks, Tom. It's been one long night." She appreciated his thoughtfulness.

Tom handed Jaxon a glass of water and watched as she drank. He had always thought her beautiful, but now there was something more. She had a mysterious, ethereal quality to her. And her voice was so beautiful, he could listen to it forever. Her eyes were classic bedroom eyes. He had heard the description before, but he'd never really known what it meant until he looked into her eyes. She moved with a flowing grace, innocently sexy. He had a difficult time keeping his gaze from devouring her.

Jaxon flashed a smile, completely unaware of the havoc she was creating. Tom was watching her so closely, she was embarrassed. She ran her hands through her hair. "I look awful, I know. A complete mess."

She looked so vulnerable, he had the urge to gather her up and protect her for all time. Without meaning to do it, he settled his hands on her shoulders, intending to massage the tension from her. Before he could do so, a cold wind swept through the room, an icy draft of ominous warning. When Jaxon and Tom looked up, Lucian was looming over them.

At once Jaxon could barely breathe. There was something wild and untamed in him, something dark and dangerous in the depths of his black eyes. Not rage. Icy death. When he looked at Tom, Jaxon was suddenly afraid for the man and not really certain why. "Lucian?" She said his name softly, a whisper of inquiry.

Lucian didn't turn his head toward her, but he stepped close so that his body was firmly between hers and the police officer. He smiled, almost pleasantly, but it looked like the smile of a hunting wolf. "I do not believe we have met. I am Lucian Daratrazanoff, Jaxon's fiancé." He extended his hand, his black eyes fathomless, dark pools capable of mesmerizing. His voice was as soft and gentle as ever. "You must be Tom. Jaxon has spoken of you often. I appreciate your looking out for her." He stepped forward and whispered softly. Tom nodded several times, smiling in return.

Jaxon's heart was beating so hard, it terrified her. She couldn't fault Lucian's courtesy, yet his show of power, right out in the open, had rendered everyone in the squad room utterly silent. They were policeman, detectives, hardened cops used to dangerous situations, yet something about Lucian stopped them dead in their tracks. That frightened her. Had she escaped Drake, only to attach herself to someone worse? Lucian certainly had enough power to be worse. What was it in her that brought out the worst in men?

Nothing, angel. You are the perfect woman for me. I am a Carpathian male and cannot be anything other than what I am.

She was reaching up to try to comb her hair into some semblance of order, a nervous habit she couldn't help. She felt at a great disadvantage, looking so disheveled. Lucian caught her hand and carried it to the warmth of his mouth, his gaze suddenly centering solely and completely on her.

Do not, little love. You are beautiful just the way you are. At once the ice in his black gaze heated to a black-velvet hunger, to a blatant love he didn't bother to hide from her. His touch was extraordinarily gentle as he drew her under the protection of his shoulder.

"Thank all of you for helping to look after Officer Montgomery and for trying to end this nightmare that refuses to leave her life. You are all very loyal to her, and I appreciate that, as I know she does. If there is ever anything we can do to repay such loyalty, please do not hesitate to tell us. Barry Radcliff will be moved to an undisclosed location as soon as they are finished with him in the emergency room. He is going to be fine. He put up quite a fight before we got there. Whoever attacked him must have heard us coming and run. He was gone before we had a chance to catch him."

He bent his head to brush a kiss on the top of Jaxon's head. "I am going to take Jaxon home. It is nearly dawn, and she is exhausted. She can return this evening to finish her report. The doctors have said it is imperative she rest, so I can do no other than to see that she obeys. I am sure your captain will understand."

There were a few derisive snorts over that. "Don't count on it," one of the detectives said. "He's never what you call understanding."

Lucian smiled appropriately, but his eyes had gone flat and cold when his gaze turned away from Jaxon and rested on the speaker. "He will have to be."

Harold Dawkins stared defiantly at Lucian. "Jaxon, I need to talk to you in private for just a minute. You understand, Mr. Daratrazanoff—police business."

Lucian shrugged casually, a small smile curving the edge of his mouth. Instead of softening the touch of cruelty there, however, the smile only served to make him

238

look more imperious, more dangerous than ever. A warrior of old, untamed and savage.

Jaxon reluctantly left the shelter of Lucian's body to follow Dawkins across the room. "What is it, Harold? I'm exhausted, and if the captain doesn't understand that, too bad." Harold Dawkins had worked with her for several years. He was nearing retirement and always looked upon Jaxon as a daughter.

"Who is this guy? What do you know about him? He isn't even from this country. I think he's dangerous, Jaxx. It's in the way he moves, the way he holds himself. You don't see through all that European charm. He could take you off to some foreign land and hide you away where no one could ever help you. There's been too many cases of that kind of thing."

"Seriously, Harold, I don't think that's going to happen." Jaxon tried not to laugh as she patted the older man's arm affectionately. Lucian did rather look the type to secret her away in a harem. "I'm not some sweet victim who can't defend herself. As it is, Lucian thinks I'm a bit of a lunatic. He says I own an arsenal."

"I wish you'd listen to me, Jaxx. Don't rush into anything. Take some time before you commit yourself. This guy is . . ."

"My fiancé, Harold. He only looks scary. He's really a teddy bear," she lied. Lucian reminded her more of a huge wolf, lean and mean and highly intelligent. Except with her. He was always unfailingly gentle with her. She wanted to defend Lucian. He had saved Barry. He had protected the human race for centuries. But she couldn't say that, couldn't explain to Harry that Lucian had dedicated his life to the safety of others.

She turned back to Lucian, who immediately walked across the room to her side. He enveloped her small hand in his, bringing her palm to his chest to hold it over his heart as they walked out of the station house together.

Chapter Eleven

"You are very easy in the company of men."

Jaxon glanced up at Lucian's face. His voice was velvet soft, with no inflection whatsoever. His features were free of expression, yet as harsh and relentless as the wind, carved in granite, yet so sensual he took her breath away. For some reason butterfly wings brushed insistently at her stomach, and she was instantly nervous. She made herself shrug casually, annoyed that she would react so to his simple statement. "I work with men all the time. I trained with them. Grew up around them. I don't even know very many women." Now she was irritated because she sounded like a defiant child. She had no reason to feel guilty. She hadn't done anything wrong. He was the one acting like a jealous husband.

She bit at her lip. He hadn't exactly *acted* that way; he was just so intimidating. Power clung to him, and he looked dangerous. So much so that sweet Harold had thought to warn her against him. Maybe Lucian didn't mean anything by it, maybe it was merely his accent that made his words sound so frightening. Or his lack of expression. She glanced up at him again as they moved together to the waiting car. Antonio was holding the door, open, and, for once, he wasn't smiling. He was shaking his head at her as if she had committed some grave sin.

"What?" she burst out, glaring from one man to the other. "What?"

Lucian's hand came down on the nape of her neck, exerting enough pressure that she automatically climbed into the limousine.

"She is trouble, this one," Antonio whispered loudly enough for her to hear.

Jaxon waited until Antonio was behind the wheel of the car and they were moving swiftly toward their home. "I am not. What does that mean? Those men are my friends, my colleagues. I work with them."

"That is why the older gentleman took such care to tell you I was a dangerous man, one you had no business being with? I heard him quite clearly warning you away from me." Again there was no inflection in his voice, only that soft, velvet whisper of trouble.

"Well, what do you expect when you stand there looking all intimidating and scary like a Mafia enforcer or a hit man or something? You need to look more . . . I don't know, more something."

"Foppish?" he supplied softly, a hint of compassion escaping into his voice.

"What kind of word is *foppish*? Antonio, have you ever heard of *foppish*?"

"Antonio cannot hear us," Lucian pointed out.

Jaxon was busy stabbing at various buttons. "Which one of these things makes it so he can? You use mind control so easily, Lucian. Are you controlling me, too?"

Very gently Lucian laid a hand over hers to still her frantic fingers. "Be calm, Jaxon. You are suffering needlessly. I do not control your mind. If I did so, you would

241

not be placing yourself in danger at every opportunity. Believe it or not, I am working at finding a balance with your nature. Carpathian males are not easy with other men around their women. That is a simple fact. There is no need to fear what is natural. My emotions are new and raw, but I would never harm you or someone you care for."

"Well, I am not Carpathian, so you'll just have to get used to it," she muttered rebelliously. "And I'm not afraid of you." In the close confines of the car, with his hand covering hers, his thumb sliding back and forth in a caress over her wrist, it was difficult to think of anything but Lucian. "I'm a cop. Those men are my partners. We watch each other's backs. It's how I live, how we all survive." In spite of her determination not to, she found herself explaining.

"I knew there was a reason I did not want you to continue in your chosen profession," Lucian said without expression. He leaned down to her, his palm finding her chin to force her head up. "I do not like to see you in danger. It is more than my heart can stand. Add your sorrow and the guilt you heap upon yourself, and my heart knows what it feels like to break. If another man, human or not, decides to look upon you with desire and then places his hands on you, I have a wish to lose my control for just a few minutes."

Jaxon found herself managing a small smile at his complete sincerity. "Did you make Tom think I looked like a wrinkled old crone or something?"

"It was a temptation." His hand slipped to the nape of her neck and found several tendrils of hair to caress. "I had a primitive urge to discourage him from coveting you."

She blinked up at him suspiciously. "I don't want to know what you mean, so don't bother to explain."

A slow smile warmed the black ice of his eyes. "You are beginning to know me."

"Thank you for saving Barry. The glimpse I caught of him, he looked to be in bad shape. I know it must have been difficult destroying the ghoul there, helping me, and working on him all at the same time." She could feel his exhaustion. It didn't show on his face, but it was in his mind. He was extremely tired. He had used tremendous energy tonight. Even someone as powerful as Lucian could get tired.

She was certain she was tired, too, but it manifested itself more as sorrow. It was almost too much to comprehend the loss of so many of the people she knew and cared about. For a moment the reality of it all touched her mind, and she couldn't breathe, her lungs refusing to work properly. "If the man at the apartments wasn't Drake, and the one at the station house wasn't him either, who were they, and how did they know exactly what Drake did to his victims? How would they know whom to kill? And why would they even want to kill them, Lucian?"

"There is only one answer, angel." Lucian's voice was more expressionless than ever. It made Jaxon glance up at him in apprehension. "There must be a vampire involved here, a master vampire, one of the ancients. It is a creature capable of such things."

"It has Drake? Is he dead?" There was almost a hopeful note in her voice.

Lucian shook his head. "More than likely Drake is still out there somewhere, probably puzzled by these murders. The vampire has read your mind, picked the details out of your head, and that is why you knew something was wrong. The details were not exactly Drake. The vampire created his ghouls and sent them out with orders to kill whoever had fond memories of you."

Jaxon's fingers twisted together, and her stomach

burned, a hard knot of pain. "Why? What would he accomplish?"

Lucian's black gaze moved over her, fathomless, moody, possessive. "Precisely what he did. Pain. Vampires thrive on other people's pain. He must have caught you out in the open, away from the protected property, and read your memories. He could not have hidden his taint of power from me had I been close."

Jaxon felt as if he had punched her hard in the pit of her stomach. The feeling was so real, she actually hunched over, dropping her head into the heel of one hand. "So *I* did this. Just by going out of the house, I caused all this to happen. Basically that's what you're saying, isn't it?"

Lucian's arm slid around her slender shoulders. Her pain was radiating from her, enveloping him so that he felt almost as sick as she did. "Of course not, Jaxon. You cannot ever think you are responsible for the sick actions of others."

Jaxon ducked out from under his arm, unable to bear the contact. She was struggling just to breathe. "Lucian, have Antonio stop the car right now. I need to get out. I'll walk the rest of the way. It isn't that far."

"It is almost dawn, my love." He said the words softly, without inflection, apparently neither for nor against her decision.

"I can't breathe in here, Lucian. Stop the car." She wanted to run as fast as she could—whether from herself or from everything that had happened this night, she didn't know. She knew only that she had to be out in the open. "I need to be alone. Please just stop the car and let me walk by myself back to the house. I have to be alone."

Lucian's black gaze moved over her face once more, brooding, suspicious. His mind moved in hers. He read Jaxon's need to alone, to be in the fresh air, to be able to breathe freely. There was such chaos in her mind, she was having trouble breathing.

At once the car rolled to a stop, and Jaxon realized Lucian had commanded Antonio to come to a halt. Instantly she was out of the car and running, leaving the asphalt behind, taking to the open meadow leading to the hills and the south side of the estate. She ran parallel to the road until the car went around a bend and disappeared from sight. Instantly she switched directions and ran up the hill, away from the house and toward the bluffs. Twice she had to stop, leaning over as her body protested the terrible crimes committed simply because someone knew her. What was she? A monster magnet? Some hideous thing inside her drew out the demon in others. She didn't pay the price; some innocent bystander always did.

Jaxon had heard the conversations throughout the apartment building and in the squad room. The murmurs, the silent condemnation. Most of her friends were afraid to speak to her, none of them wanted to be seen with her, and all of them were terrified for their families, and rightly so. This latest carnage was worse than anything Drake had ever done before. This vampire was capable of mass killing in two places at one time.

She continued running as fast as she could. As the trail became steeper, she stumbled occasionally, tears streaming down her face, clouding her vision. Jaxon had no clear thought in her head; she really didn't know what she was going to do. Only that this killing couldn't continue any longer. Her father. Her mother. Her beloved little Mathew. The entire Andrews family, even poor Sabrina, just home from college on a break. Then her neighbor, Carol. Sweet Carol's big crime was watching the sunrise every morning, and she died because she enjoyed sharing the experience with her neighbor. And now all these other innocent victims.

She was sobbing as she clawed her way up the steep rock to the top of the bluff. Just as she pulled herself up, the earth rolled and bucked beneath her feet like a roller coaster. Overhead black clouds swirled and roiled, boiling like a cauldron. Lightning arced from cloud to cloud, slamming to earth in white-hot jagged bolts, the thunder nearly deafening her. She screamed as she ran for the cliff's edge. If there was no Jaxon, there would be no need for Drake to kill anyone ever again.

She tried to run with the earth rocking beneath her feet, hurtling her body toward the edge. Just as her lead foot stepped off into empty space, a thick arm caught her around her waist and lifted her completely off the ground.

"Lucian." She whispered his name, clung to him, her only sanity in the madness of the world. Her slender arms circled his neck, and she buried her face in the comfort of his shoulder.

His body was trembling; she could feel it. She lifted her head and saw stark terror burning in the depths of his eyes. He lowered his head and took possession of her mouth even as the heavens opened above them and poured rain onto the earth.

"I need you, Jaxon." Each word was enunciated softly. "You cannot leave me alone in this world. I need you." Whips of lightning sizzled and danced all around them. Thunder cracked and boomed. "You cannot leave me alone."

"I know, I know," she whispered back, pressing closer, an offering in the midst of the world crashing down around them. "I don't know what happened, what I was thinking. I'm sorry, Lucian. I'm sorry."

"You do not have to say that. Never say that." His mouth was moving over hers again, hot and needy with fear and rising desire. "I have to know you are here with me."

"I am here. I won't leave you. It isn't you." She was crying, her hands sliding under his shirt to touch the solid reality of him. He was real, and he was her only comfort, her only sanity. She had hurt him; she felt it radiating from him, deep and intense, along with the terror gripping his soul. She lifted her head to meet him kiss for kiss, giving herself to him, wanting only to comfort and be comforted.

Lucian was consuming her, devouring her, his mouth everywhere, the rain on her bare skin, on their bare skin. He had removed their clothing so quickly, so easily, with a mere impatient thought in his mind.

It took Jaxon a few moments to realize he was enraged, the terrible ferocity of the storm reflecting the blackness of his mood. But his enormously strong arms held her with such gentleness, it turned her heart over. "I need you with me, angel. You still do not see, no matter how often I try to tell you, to show you." All around them the earth moved and split, great gaping cracks in the rocks. "Without you I have no reason to live. I need you. Really need you. Put your legs around my waist." He whispered the command to her even as his teeth were scraping over her frantic pulse. "Right now, Jaxon, I need you, need to be inside you, need you surrounding me with your heat and light. I need to feel you are safe and alive and nothing can harm you."

He was everywhere, his hands exploring, inflaming, his body so hard and aggressive, taut with terrible need, terrible hunger, that Jaxon obeyed him almost blindly. His hunger was intense, the storm increasing rather than waning, a true barometer of his urgent desire.

"You cannot leave me alone to live in an empty world with no light or laughter. You cannot leave me alone."

His voice was raw, his beautiful voice raw with his fear and relentless hunger for her alone. His hair was soaked, the thick ebony strands hanging down his back. He looked wild and untamed. He looked what he was: dangerous and unpredictable. Yet Jaxon wasn't afraid. She clung to him, needing him with the same urgency, wanting only to feel the strength of his arms, of his possession, his body moving in hers, his mouth feeding at her breast, his soul anchoring hers in this chaos.

Her legs slipped around his waist, and she eased her body over the hard length of him. He filled her instantly, making her gasp with the unexpected pleasure. The storm intensified, lightning slashing through the gray sky. The sun tried valiantly to rise, but the ominous, swirling black clouds were thick and dark, preventing the light from penetrating to their sensitive skin. Still, Jaxon felt the first prickling of unease at the muted light. Tears were streaming down her face, her eyes burning, her lungs gasping for air from the strangling sobs wracking her as they clung to each other in a wild tango of life-affirming love.

His arms were like steel, holding her safe, his body moving aggressively in hers, yet he was so heartbreakingly tender, his mouth warm and loving on her skin. "Stop crying, angel. You have to stop now," he whispered against her rain-soaked hair. "We can get through anything as long we are together. I cannot ever be without you. You are the air I breathe. You are in my soul, my heart. Look into my mind, into my memories, see my life, empty and endless without you. You could never contemplate such a thing if you knew the way I needed you. I cannot be alone again."

"I didn't know what I was doing," she denied.

He believed her. Her mind had been so chaotic, so filled with sorrow that she was running blindly, without real thought. Not once had she been thinking about destroying what she had become. Her thoughts had been centered solely on the tragedy. He found he could take a real breath, forcing air into his lungs, allowing his heart to beat once more. "You will never do such a thing again." His hips were moving in a rhythm to match the ferocity of the storm.

Jaxon found her tears slowing as fire spread through

her body, spread through his. Flames leaped higher and higher, reaching toward the heavens, reaching into the clouds above them so the jagged bolts of lightning danced with them, through them. She heard her cries blend with his as they exploded together, clinging to each other like two frightened children as their hearts and lungs worked frantically to keep pace with their soaring bodies.

Jaxon lay against him, huddling as close to him as possible for comfort, unable to control the storm of tears any more than she had been able to control the firestorm of need sweeping through both of them. She felt his body tremble, shudder, and his arms clasped her more tightly than ever. She felt his tears in his mind, the agony of fear, the mounting terror as he realized what she had nearly done.

Then it was Jaxon providing comfort to Lucian, framing his head in her hands, covering his face with kisses. "I didn't mean to do such a foolish thing, Lucian. It wasn't because of you or what I am. I wasn't thinking properly. It had nothing to do with us. I just couldn't bear bringing so much death to so many families."

"Jaxon, Jaxon," he said softly, his pain tearing at her. "What am I going to do with you? And how many times must I remind you that you are not the one responsible for these deaths? You do things so impetuously, without thought. You think to throw away such a beautiful, important life, even though you would not have died had you gone over the cliff."

She blinked up at him. "What do you mean?"

"Had I not caught you or merged with you to float you down or stopped you in some other way than I did, had you really gone over and your body hit bottom, you would have suffered terribly with broken bones and internal injuries, but your body would not permit your death any more than mine would. Our people often sustain mortal injuries, but the earth heals us quickly."

She pressed her face against his chest, unwilling to talk about it anymore. It was too difficult to assimilate the information he was giving her with her mind in such chaos. Only then did she realize that her skin was beginning to tingle in spite of the fierce storm blanketing the area and dulling the effects of the rising sun. And the burning in her eyes was increasing with each passing second. She put a hand over her eyes as he allowed her feet to touch the ground. It felt as if a thousand needles were brushing at her eyes with murderous tips. She bit down hard on her lower lip and burrowed her face closer against his chest. "Lucian, about that speed thing you like to do? Now would be a perfect time."

Lucian could also feel the effects of the sun on his skin despite the dark clouds veiling the sun. Scooping Jaxon into his arms, he moved with his preternatural speed so that space swirled around them and the rain lashed at the empty air left in their wake. Lucian entered the house from the second-story balcony and kept his hold on Jaxon until he had glided through the house to the lower chamber, where the sun's rays could not possibly reach them. Only then did he allow the storm to begin to subside.

"What are we going to do?" Jaxon asked. "How can we stop all these deaths?" She looked around the room for a robe.

Lucian handed her one, easily reading her mind. He picked it out of the air while Jaxon was blinking up at him with her large, trusting eyes. She slipped her arms into the thick cotton and pulled the lapels together. Her eyes remained steadily on his face. *You could use a robe, too.*

He shook his head at her modesty but obligingly fashioned another robe, one far larger and longer, just to please her. He could that see she relaxed once his body was covered. He had to turn away from her to hide his smile. Jaxon was pacing back and forth across the floor, unable to be still with all the adrenaline pumping through her. "Tell me what we're going to do, Lucian. How do we stop this monster from killing everyone I care about?"

"We have two choices," he said softly, his voice forever tranquil, helping to calm the overload of nervous energy coursing through her veins. "We can stay here and attempt to draw out the vampire. It will not be easy. He is old and knows who I am. He will send his ghouls and other dark creatures to fight us before he shows himself. And he will expose himself only if he believes the advantages are his and very great."

Jaxon shoved a hand through her wet hair, found her hand was trembling, and hastily placed it behind her back. Twisting her fingers tightly together, she did her best to look composed. "And the other choice?"

"We can leave this city. Go far away and hope our enemies follow us, drawing them away from your innocent friends. I believe Tyler Drake will come after us. It is possible the vampire will, also. There are very few human women like you. He will not want to wait to try to find another. It is possible he was already on your trail when I found you and believes I have unfairly taken you from him. If that is the case, he will follow us."

"If he doesn't, we leave everyone unprotected." Jaxon sounded forlorn. "I don't understand, Lucian. What is in me that attracts such monsters to me?" She turned to look at him, unaware of the raw pain in the depths of her eyes.

Lucian met her gaze squarely, steadily. *He* was a monster. A dark monster that had lived for more centuries than even most of his kind. He had committed crimes, was responsible for countless deaths. He had searched the world over for her, he would never allow her to escape him, never give her up, never let any other take her from him. What was the difference between him and the others who so desperately wanted her? Is that how she saw him? As a monster?

Christine Feehan

Jaxon threw her arms around him and held him close to her. "You are not a monster, Lucian. You are kind and honorable and a good man. Don't even put yourself in the same category with someone like Tyler Drake or that evil thing you call a vampire."

He bent his head over her, holding her tightly to him. She didn't know him as well as she thought she did. He held so much power, he had been named monster many times over the centuries. Jaxon had read his mind. It amazed him that she had done so and not even noticed. She made him believe his soul was not damned for all eternity, that his deeds would be judged with compassion. She made him believe in miracles.

He whispered to her that he loved her, using the ancient language. He whispered to her in his mind, unable to say the words aloud and have her turn away from him. His hands moved through her hair possessively. "I have learned the meaning of the word *fear*, angel. It was no easy lesson and one I do not ever wish to repeat, but is has given me a small glimpse of the hell you have endured in your young life. Choose, Jaxon. Do we leave a trail for the vampire to follow? Lure him away from your friends? Or do we stay and fight here?"

He was asking her opinion. Jaxon blinked back tears. It was true she didn't know him all that well, but she caught glimpses of his mind each time he merged fully with her, and she had seen enough to know he was a master at planning battles. Most of all, it mattered that he would ask her opinion.

She thought carefully about each plan of action. "I think it's too hard to protect everyone. We can't be with them during the day, so they're vulnerable to Drake and any creature the vampire decides to create. If we go, I don't see what good it will do for the vampire to attack people here. We should think of a place we can lay out an ambush and easily defend." She suddenly noticed she

252

was shivering uncontrollably, her hair soaking wet, while he was standing there perfectly groomed in his robe. She glared up at him. "Why are you dry and I'm soaking wet and shaking with cold?"

Lucian took her hands in his and rubbed them gently to warm her. A faint smile touched his sculpted mouth. "Think of being warm and dry. Picture it in your mind. Hold the picture in your mind of your hair dry, your skin dry, your body warm." He merged with her, stilling her tumbling thoughts, helping to build the image of warmth and dryness.

Jaxon withdrew her hand from his to reach up and touch her hair in awe. "I did that? Just like that? No blow-dryer, no towel?"

"Just like that." The smile was once more inside him, blossoming strong, filling him with joy. She brought back his first days as a fledgling trying to learn the things that came so easily to the adults of their species.

"Can I do all the things you can do?"

He nodded slowly, watching her face through half-closed eyes. He looked lazy, yet Jaxon had the feeling he was totally alert.

"What would you like to learn how to do?" he asked.

"Now?" She ran her palms along her arms, aware of the way her skin had resisted the rising sun.

"Your skin will become tougher, Jaxon. Eventually you will be able to watch the sunrise as long as you wear dark glasses. You should make it a habit to carry them with you wherever you go. That way if you are caught out in the morning or need to rise early, your eyes will be safe from the rays of the sun. I am an ancient—we feel pain much more intensely than do the younger members of our species—yet I can go out in the early-morning hours with little trouble. It is one advantage the hunter has over the vampire. The vampire cannot rise until the sun has truly set. He cannot see the sunrise ever."

"Are we really helpless in the afternoon?" A soft note in her voice betrayed her fear.

His hand found her silky hair, then slipped to the nape of her neck, his fingers slowly massaging to ease the sudden tension from her. "Our bodies are lethargic at that time, it is true, but we are not entirely without means to protect ourselves. I am extremely powerful, angel; there is no way you will come to any harm, I would never allow it."

Jaxon moved into his arms, holding him tightly. Staying a shadow in her mind allowed him to see how his world, so alien and different, so filled with myths and superstitions, with violence and creatures of the night, seemed a very terrifying place to her. Lucian locked his arms around her. "Should we ever have need of help, Jaxon, my brother is always near."

"I hate to disillusion you, Lucian, but your brother lives in Paris. I saw his address. That isn't just around the corner, even by your standards."

"If your need was great, he could do as I did from afar, seeing through your eyes—lend you his aid, his strength, even destroy an enemy threatening you."

The thought of any other man crawling around in her mind was instantly abhorrent to her. Why she didn't mind Lucian reading her every thought, why it seemed natural, she didn't comprehend, but she knew she would be reluctant to have anyone else discover the things about her he had.

Lucian was absurdly pleased with her thoughts. She was normally so easy in the company of men, which bothered him more than he had realized. He wanted her to want him, *need* him, the same way he needed her. Not because the ritual had joined them together and their bodies cried out to each other, but because *he* was important to her. Lucian. No other. Still, she was reluctant to read his mind, explore his memories or the person he was. Lifemates learned about each other quickly by exploring each other's minds, yet she persisted in shying away from such things.

"You look sad." She put a hand on his arm and touched his mouth with a fingertip. "Your eyes, Lucian. Sometimes you look so sad, it breaks my heart. I know you must find me a great disappointment because I can't do the things the women of your race have always done, but I'm trying. I really am."

"You could never disappoint me, angel. Do not even allow such a thought to cross your mind. Every moment I spend with you brings me great joy." He moved her smaller, slender body toward the bed by simply crowding her with his larger, heavier frame. The sun was moving in the sky; he could feel it, feel the effects on his already tired body. "In your learning, I can experience the joy of each gift all over again."

Jaxon climbed onto the bed almost absently, biting on her lower lip in deep thought. "I don't want you to be sad for me. Is that it? Don't pity me, Lucian. I couldn't stand that."

He dragged the thick cotton robe from her body even though she made an attempt to hold it around her modestly. His own robe was left on the floor in an untidy heap. His arms swept her backward so that she landed on the bed, her large eyes staring up at him. "How could I possibly feel pity for a woman who has Lucian Daratrazanoff as her lifemate? He is quite handsome—I have it on good authority. Sexy. *Hot* is the term I believe was used."

Jaxon knew a blush was covering her entire body. His hands were moving over her skin gently, a leisurely exploration, as if he couldn't quite keep from touching her. She closed her eyes and gave herself up to the feeling of his hands on her body. "He is hot, but he's also quite arrogant."

"He has beautiful eyes," he murmured, his mouth finding the corner of hers, teasing, skimming, his teeth nipping tenderly. "You like his eyes."

The pleasure he gave her was indescribable. She could think of no words to explain the sensations sweeping through her body. Warmth. Happiness. Lucian was indulging himself, tracing his hands over her skin for the sheer delight of it. He shaped the creamy swell of her breasts, took tremendous enjoyment in feeling the way her nipples pushed pleadingly against his palms. He bent his head to place a kiss in the center of her throat. His hair slid over her breasts, an exquisite torment.

Her hands came up to cradle his head. Her legs shifted restlessly. She loved the way he wanted her. She could feel it in the touch of his hands, almost as if he were worshiping her body. She could feel the warmth of his breath as he moved over her, his tongue finding the pulse at her throat. Her heart somersaulted, and her body clenched in anticipation. She felt her breasts ache with the need for his touch, felt the creamy dampness as her body called to his. His mouth found her breast, the feeling so exquisite she heard herself moan softly. His hands were at her waist, her hips, stroking over her hipbones. It wasn't enough. It could never be enough. She reveled in the way he touched her with such perfect care. There would never be another who could ever reach her the way he did, the way he lived inside her. His black gaze was on her as he slowly inserted two fingers deep inside her, pushing gently.

With her fists clenched in his long wild hair, she gave up her body to the total ecstasy only he could provide her. His took his time, bringing her again and again to hot, rippling fire. Through it all, she wanted more. She needed more. She wanted his mouth on her skin and his body filling hers. She wanted her blood flowing into him, connecting them, making them one and the same. They could never really be apart—she understood that now, knew she always had to be with Lucian. Whatever he had done to bind them together had worked. She could not bear the thought of separation from him anymore. And the fire between them only seemed to grow hotter and more out of control the longer they were together.

She cried out when he joined them together, her breath exploding from her lungs. She needed more than his body surging, so thick and hot, in hers. She needed. *Needed.* His chest was over her face, his hand cupping the back of her head, holding her against his heart. *You need, angel, and I provide. Taste me, I am yours. Taste me. You are so hungry, and you need to feed. You need only me. I tasted so perfect, honey, remember?* The whisper was soft and seductive, brushing softly in her mind. An invitation. An enticement. Pure seduction.

Her mouth moved over his skin. She felt his body clench. *I need this, angel, the way you need it. I need you to do this.* She could feel it in his mind, the terrible anticipation, the dark desire, his entire body waiting with such urgent obsession. He needed her to do this as much as she needed to do it. *For me, Jaxon, for me. I want this as I have never wanted anything. You need this, too.*

He was everywhere she was—in her mind, in her heart, in her body, in her very soul. He needed, and she could do no other than provide. Her mouth moved of its own accord over his skin, without compulsion, with only the thought of pleasing him, providing for him. She felt the way his body clenched when her teeth nipped his skin and her tongue swirled around to ease the ache.

You have to do this by yourself this time, he was pleading with her even as his hips were surging forward in a wild rhythm of fierce possession. He moved over her, around her, in her, wanting to flow through her.

He was swamping her with such erotic need, Jaxon was consumed with it. She felt her incisors lengthen as she sank them into his skin until they were connected in every way. White-hot whips of lightning arced through his body and into hers. She heard his voice echoing her name in her mind. Intimate. Sexy. Wild with passion. She felt the blazing heat of his body moving in hers as he thrust forward, burying himself deeper and deeper with each sure stroke.

He tasted wild. He tasted hot and exotic. He was addicting. His blood flowed through her veins with his ancient power, filling her starved cells and flooding her body with such a storm of dancing flames that she had to give in to the demands for relief. She felt herself fragmenting, exploding, seeking to take him with her as she clung to him tighter and tighter, spiraling outward.

Use your tongue to close the pinpricks. I want to feed. I want all of your taste in my body. I want to savor you for all time. His voice was a dark sorcerer's weapon, a black-velvet beguilement she couldn't possibly ignore. Whatever he needed, she would provide.

Whatever you need, I provide. And you need this. His teeth found her pulse and sank deep. Beneath him, Jaxon moaned softly, her body tightening around his in a convulsion of heated pleasure. She gave herself up to him completely, immersing herself in his passion, in the hot ride of his body, his bunching muscles, the pull of his mouth, the flames engulfing both of them.

It went on forever, for an eternity, until Jaxon thought she might die with the beauty of it. Of them. She held him, cradled his head, savored the sensation of his hair against her sensitized breasts. He thrust into her again and again until she was drowsy and sated, completely satisfied, totally complete.

Very, very gently Lucian allowed their bodies to disengage. The sun had risen; even deep within the sleeping chamber, he knew its exact position. Looking down at Jaxon's heavy lashes, the beauty of her face, the aftereffects of his lovemaking, he knew she didn't know or care where the sun was. He bent his head to brush her lush mouth with his. "*Je t'aime*, angel." he whispered softly as he commanded her to sleep. It was the last thing she heard, the words she carried with her as the air left her lungs and her heart ceased to beat.

Lucian opened the floor of the sleeping chamber and floated down to the deep, beckoning soil with his lifemate. She lay in his arms, her beauty captured in her stillness as he opened the earth and took them to rest.

Chapter Twelve

A discordant note filled the silence of the earth beneath the sleeping chamber. Beneath the layers of dirt a slow, deadly hiss seeped through the dark, rich soil to permeate the air above it. It traveled around the estate, filling the grounds with menace. Lucian's black eyes snapped open, and he lay with his leaden body listening to the sounds of the insects and animals. A rat scratched for sustenance somewhere close by. A wolf murmured to its pack brother in annoyance. What was the sound so out of place with the rest of the universe that it would reach into the very bowels of the earth and awaken him?

The crackling of the stone wall told him an intruder was testing the strength of his safeguards. Lucian lay quietly listening. He reached out to the alpha pair of wolves, warning them not to touch any meat or food that was thrown to them by an outsider. He warned them to care for the other members of the pack, the young, silly ones that liked to defy authority. In his mind was the clear warning of poison, the death of the pack. He directed the alpha pair to take their brethren deep within the forest, where guns could not reach them. The male bared his fangs and issued a warning growl, alerting the pack.

Satisfied, Lucian continued to listen. The intruder was persistent. He learned he could not get through stone wall or gates. He was climbing a tree, avoiding the back of the estate because of the wolves. No doubt he could see that his "gift" of tainted meat had not been devoured, and he dared not try to make his assault near the cunning beasts. Lucian closed his eyes and sent himself seeking outside his body. He became as light as the air itself, traveling as pure energy, breaking free of the soil. He moved through the narrow passageway up into the cellar and then the kitchen.

As always the heavy drapes prevented any sunlight from intruding into the interior. As pure energy, he moved easily through the house until he was at the vantage point of the balcony. Francesca's beautifully detailed stained glass masked the brilliant light so that he had a good view of the intruder making his approach to the house. Finally. The one who had destroyed Jaxon's family. But was this the man? Lucian waited until the face swam into view through the thick foliage.

Disappointment sent Lucian's silent snarl shimmering in the air. This intruder could not possibly be Tyler Drake. He was wearing a dark blue suit and a silk tie. Lucian observed the ease with which he climbed the branches of the trees overlooking the stone wall. The man was whispering into a two-way radio. "No one seems to be home, but getting in isn't going to be easy, not if we don't want to tip them off they have company."

Lucian's mind was working quickly. For several centuries he had been asleep deep within the earth, and many things had happened to his people while he lay locked within the soil. He had heard rumors of a society of human hunters who believed themselves to be scientists.

They claimed to have evidence of the existence of vampires and vowed to destroy them. So far, few humans took them seriously, so they were determined to capture a live vampire. The only problem was, they seemed unable to differentiate between a Carpathian, a vampire, and a human with extraordinary gifts. Could members of that vampire-hunting society have found him?

He decided the best way to get his answers was to allow the intruder or intruders into his home. After all, the sun was beginning to sink. If they wanted to prepare a surprise for him, he was more than willing to oblige. He moved up close to the stained glass and concentrated on his safeguards. He wanted to rid the house of the lethal traps and spells only on the outside to allow the estate to be penetrated. It shouldn't be so easy that they would become suspicious, but he wouldn't want them to be discouraged and give up too soon.

Having done what he could, Lucian flowed through the house, the basement, and the narrow passage carved through rock to the sleeping chamber, then below to his earthen lair. He returned to his body deep within the healing soil. It required intense energy to flow free from one's body, and he wanted the rejuvenating soil to strengthen him.

He put himself to sleep, relying on his inward alarm system to tell him when the intruder had actually violated the sanctity of his home. It took the man well over an hour after the sun went down before he managed to make it into the main yard. From there he opened the gate for two of his colleagues. When Lucian felt the disturbance, he came awake slowly, waving a hand to open the earth. The vibrations of violence echoing through his home were amplified by the stained-glass safeguards Francesca had wrought. It disturbed the soothing tranquillity of the house.

Beside him, without his consent or command, Jaxon

inhaled. Her heart began to beat, and she moaned softly in distress. Lucian would never have believed it if someone had told him her built-in alarm system would be enough to disturb her sleep so soon after her initiation. Fledglings did not often awaken at the mere presence of evil. He merged with her before she could open her eyes, his intention to send her back to sleep.

Don't! She said it sharply, her lashes lifting, her eyes blazing with fury. "You lied to me." She pushed his body away from hers and looked around her.

Lucian could feel her rising nausea as she realized she was in the ground, not in the sleeping chamber. When he would have comforted her, she held up both hands to stop him. "I don't want you to touch me. You buried me alive, Lucian. You buried me and let me believe we were sleeping in a normal bed."

"Jaxon," he said softly, persuasively. "I did not *lie*."

She tried to scramble out of the hole in the earth. "Call it whatever you like, it was still a sin of omission," she hissed over her shoulder.

But when Lucian caught her around her waist and pulled her back to him, she didn't resist, rather went very still. She was pale, her skin clammy, and he could feel her heart pounding. "Someone's in the house." She clutched her stomach, knowing they were being stalked. "I thought you said nothing could get in."

"The intruder is human. Actually, if you listen, you can hear more than one. They are spreading out now, searching the upper story. I allowed them entry to the premises to see who they are. It is always best to know your enemies." His voice was soft and winning, wrapping her in warmth and tranquillity. "I did not allow them access to your room. I did not want them touching your things."

She swallowed her anger. "That's supposed to make me forget all about what you've done? I'm so angry with you, Lucian. Right now I hate the way you're so calm and unemotional. How many more surprises do you have in store for me?"

"I presume you are alluding to our resting place, not the intruders."

She thought about hitting him, but he was built like an oak tree and more than likely she would end up with a bruised fist. "Where are my clothes?" she asked between her teeth.

"Your usual feminine garb?" When she steadfastly refused to look at him, Lucian shrugged with his casual strength. "Your clothes are in your mind. Seek and ye shall find." Deliberately he floated from the hole in the ground. It was a little more than eight feet deep. Jaxon could not possibly get out of her own accord.

You want to bet? Furious, Jaxon stood up and examined the walls of their grave. That was how she thought of it. Their grave. She swore repeatedly in her head, calling him every name in the book as she paced off the area. The walls were impossible to climb.

You need help? It was an infuriating male taunt.

"Not on your life. I'd rather stay down here with the worms than ask for your help," she snapped.

Lucian waved a hand down his body and at once was clothed in black jeans and a black T-shirt. His long black hair hung loose and shone like a raven's wing there in the darkness. It suddenly occurred to Jaxon she could see as well as if the sun were shining on them far below the earth.

She tilted her chin. If he could do it, she could do it. All she had to do was think about being dressed. Picture it in her mind. She closed her eyes to block out everything else. It took a few moments to clear the fear of spiders and creepy crawlers out of her thoughts before she began to build an image of what she would wear. Lace underwear, the comfortable kind, her favorites. Slim cotton blue jeans and a thin cotton ribbed top. Black, to suit her mood. When she opened her eyes, she was astonished that she had done it. She was fully clothed. With the exception of her shoes. She had forgotten shoes.

Jaxon had to push down the beginnings of a smile. It was amazing to be able to do such a fantastic thing. Immediately she thought of cleanliness, her hair and teeth, her body, ensuring she was as clean as if she had spent a long time in the shower. Then she began to inspect the gravelike cubicle.

She could hear the hearts beating upstairs, the sound of footsteps as intruders moved through the house. She heard the air moving in and out of their lungs. When she glanced up at Lucian, he was grinning at her with that infuriating male taunt. "I will return to help you out of there after I dispose of our guests."

He actually turned around and sauntered away from her. For a moment her breath stilled in her lungs. She wanted to cry out after him to come back, but her pride wouldn't allow it. She wasn't afraid of spiders. Not really. Her ears picked up the sound of something scratching around somewhere close by. Too close. Okay. Rats. *There are rats here, Lucian. I won't put up with rats.*

I am certain you can manage until I return. He sounded smug. *At least I know you are safely stuck there instead of trying to shoot someone. If any rats come around, try talking to them.*

They're probably related to you, she sniped. Hands on her hips, she turned around twice, trying to figure out how she could manage on her own. She *would* get out, and she *would* shoot someone, preferably Lucian. How did he do it? How did he manage to float the way he did? Did she have to picture herself floating to the top? She tried it, but nothing happened. She tried two short hops. Still nothing.

Lucian's laughter brushed at her mind like butterfly wings. Could she possibly strangle him? If she thought about strangling him, would it work? She knew exactly where he was. In the kitchen. He was moving silently, not a single footstep audible, but she knew where he was. When he breathed, she breathed. How did that happen? How did she suddenly need him so much, need the touch of his mind to hers, just so she could breathe?

She was very still for a moment, waiting to see what Lucian would do next. She did not want him confronting intruders without her, but she knew that was his intention. Suddenly she was smiling. How did something float? It wasn't that hard. It was lighter than air. So light it just moved through space, drifting upward toward the sky. In this case, more toward the floor of the sleeping chamber, but she'd take what she could get because . . . *Ha! I did it!*

She felt his hand brush her face, his touch tender. Inside she was suddenly warm, as if he had praised her. She felt his smile in her mind. *I knew you would. Now just stay put while I ask these gentlemen their reason for visiting.*

Jaxon rolled her eyes heavenward. *That sounds like something I'd do—just sit around twiddling my thumbs while you go serve our guests tea.*

Tea was not my first choice, but then, it has been a long while since I was expected to entertain with civility. There was an edge to his voice, as if the thin veneer of civilization had worn through and the velvet gloves were coming off.

Jaxon found she was shivering. *Don't do anything rash. I'm a cop, remember? We arrest people for breaking and entering. They're already going to jail. Maybe they're reporters looking to get the scoop on the love nest of the local billionaire.*

Stay clear until I have them under control.

Jaxon was already racing through the passageway into the basement and up the stairs leading to the kitchen. *You're already in control, Lucian. I'm more worried for them, not about you. I can feel the weight of your . . .* She searched for a word to describe it. Nothing. He wasn't angry. There was no rage. He smoldered with menace, yet he was tranquil, even serene. Nothing disturbed him or shook his complete confidence in his own powers.

They pose a danger to you, angel, not to me.

You are reading their minds.

That is so. Our guests are from out of state. Do not worry so much, my love. I will do nothing to embarrass you or harm your status as a police officer.

I just want you to know I will arrest you in a heartbeat if you lay a finger on any of them.

His laughter was soft and sensual, brushing at her mind and body like the touch of his caressing fingers. *My beloved angel, I would never be so crass.*

Her heart almost stopped at the drawling menace she caught beneath the surface. She knew him now. She knew he was more lethal at that moment than when he had so casually destroyed the vampire who had tracked him to his home. What had he said? *They pose a danger to you, not to me.* Of course he would remove any threat to her. He believed she was his heart and soul. She felt his tremendous need of her. He would never allow anyone or anything to threaten her.

Lucian, I know you handle things differently in your world, but this is my world. These men are human. They must be handled within the boundaries of the law.

I am the dispenser of justice, my love. I will not destroy them at this time.

She felt her heartbeat return to normal. He wouldn't lie to her. She had visions of him incinerating them right there on the carpet. How would she explain another pile of ashes to Barry Radcliff or Captain Smith?

Lucian knew her exact whereabouts, how close she was to coming up the stairs. He put on a burst of speed, and found the first man in the spare bedroom. Seizing him by the neck, he sank his teeth deep into his jugular and drank. The intruder had no chance to struggle, no way to move in that iron grip. *Be silent. You will obey.* The soft voice instantly quieted the man, and he was passive in the enormously strong grip. Lucian simply dropped him to the floor and left him there, evaporating into mist so that he streamed through the hall and into the next room.

The second man, the one in the dark blue suit, choked back a cry of alarm as Lucian suddenly materialized in front of him, seizing him in a grip of steel, brutally going for his neck to drink deeply. *You will obey. Be silent.* His enthrallment was complete. Both men would do his bidding day or night, hear his call, and complete appointed tasks. He allowed the second man to drop to the floor, dizzy and weak from blood loss. Stepping over him with a hint of contempt, he flowed through the house toward the turret, where the third man was examining old papers in Lucian's private desk.

The beast in him was allowed reign for a brief moment while he savagely took his fill. These men had come to kill his lifemate. By rights he should have ripped their hearts out. He had important work in store for them, but that did not mean he had to treat them with human civility. In his world, there was little room for such niceties.

At his command the three men followed him along the upstairs landing. All three were pale, and one of them staggered a bit, but they moved as he directed, with pleasant smiles on their faces. They would do anything for him; they needed the touch of his mind and the sound of his voice. They lived to do his service. Jaxon was charging up the steps when she spotted the little parade and paused in the middle of the staircase. She looked so apprehensive, Lucian found himself smiling.

"I found our guests wandering around upstairs, Jaxon, but they are going to act like gentlemen callers and visit with us in the sitting room. I am rather old-fashioned in some ways. The casual American style of allowing guests access to their entire homes is beyond my scope of entertaining. You gentlemen do not mind, do you?" His voice was very soft, very pleasant.

All three shook their heads, murmuring various agreements to his suggestion. Jaxon studied them for a moment suspiciously, but when they appeared normal, she preceded them down the stairs and led the way to the small cozy room off the foyer. The three men waited politely for her to be seated first. At once Lucian sat beside her, his fingers curling around hers.

"Perhaps you would like to introduce yourselves," Lucian invited softly.

Jaxon glanced at him nervously. The men were sitting calmly, not in the least disturbed by the fact that they had been caught outright trespassing. They were all in suits, and, if she wasn't mistaken, all three were armed.

The man in the dark blue suit appeared to be the spokesperson. "I'm Hal Barton. This is Harry Timms and Denny Sheldon."

Lucian nodded politely, as if people prowled around his home uninvited every day. "This is my fiancée, Jaxon Montgomery. Jaxon, these gentlemen are here from Florida and have an interesting business proposal for me."

Jaxon arched an eyebrow, her expression frankly skeptical. "You came all the way across the United States to break into Lucian's house to make him a business offer?"

Lucian sat back and smiled. All three men were nodding solemnly. Hal Barton took up the banner once more. "Actually, yes. We thought if we could beat the security system and break into Lucian Daratrazanoff's house, he might listen to us and back our revolutionary new security system. We designed it, but we don't have the funds to mass-produce and market it."

Jaxon turned her head and met Lucian's black eyes with her dark brown ones. "This is totally brilliant. Such short notice, too. I'm truly impressed." She turned back to the three men. "What did he offer you for lying to me? Freedom from prosecution? I'm a cop. Did he mention that?"

Hal Barton shook his head. "You don't seem to understand the idea. If we can get Mr. Daratrazanoff to back us, we can make an incredible amount of money. We could all be millionaires. We have a great product."

Jaxon tried to touch Barton's mind the way Lucian was able to. His "scanning," as he called it, not the intimate way she merged with Lucian. Such intimacy required taking blood. Her heart jumped, and she hastily banned the thought from her mind. She didn't dare think too closely about what had transpired between Lucian and her the night before. As long as she didn't actually think too much, everything would be all right. As she tried to scan the man, Barton seemed as if he were being totally honest with her. Jaxon sighed. It was so improbable. Grown men couldn't really be that stupid.

Money often makes people do things they would not ordinarily do.

You can read their minds much better than I ever could. Do you really think they're telling us the truth? Jaxon ran both of her hands through her hair. This all felt wrong. These men should never have broken into her home. And she had felt the vibrations of violence when she first awakened. She had known. She always knew when someone was violent in nature. Their signals had been strong enough to awaken her. Now she felt none of that. *Could someone else have been in the vicinity?*

No one, Lucian said with soft authority.

Jaxon shook her head. Her life had become totally bizarre. The people in her life were totally bizarre. What did that say about her?

Lucian's palm cupped the nape of her neck. *That you are a very tolerant woman.* His voice caressed her, ran over her like the touch of his fingers, in the same way his thumb slid over her soft skin along the edge of her shirt.

"You have to admit, we were able to penetrate your security system," Hal continued eagerly with his pitch. A frown crossed his face. "It was more difficult than I imagined. I've never run across anything like it before."

"I designed it myself," Lucian replied. "I tinker a bit."

Jaxon sighed and stood up. "I'll leave you to it. Otherwise, I'd feel bound to arrest everybody." *You included.*

None of it made any sense to her. When the three men jumped to their feet respectfully, she was more suspicious than ever. With a wave of her hand she dismissed them and sauntered out of the room. Lucian never made mistakes. Never. He had said they were a danger to her, not to him. That meant *she* was in danger. They had come to her home with the intention of harming her, not introducing some alarm system to Lucian. What had he done to bring this act together so quickly? And what was he planning to do? Surely he wouldn't kill them?

In the kitchen she fixed coffee, determined to get fingerprints. She should have arrested them first thing, and then she would have known immediately who they were and what they were up to.

In the sitting room, Lucian found himself smiling. That was Jaxon's mind, quick, intelligent. No one was going to fool her for very long. *Fingerprints.* She thought like the detective she was. He leaned toward the three men. "You were sent here to kill Jaxon. You know how wrong that is. She must live. She is the only thing standing between you and certain death." For one brief moment he allowed them to see him—his power, his fangs, shapeshifting before their horrified gaze into a beast with flaming eyes and the need to devour, to kill.

Paralyzed with terror, they sat ramrod stiff. He had implanted their story, controlling their beliefs for the short period Jaxon was in the room. She was becoming far too adept, and he was taking no chances that she

271

would read their intentions. "Hear me now, all three of you. At all costs, you must protect her life. You will return to the two men who sent you here, and you will do whatever it takes to ensure they never send another to harm her. If you should fail, there will be nowhere on this earth that I cannot find you. I will destroy you. Go from here, get on a plane, and rid Jaxon of these two threats to her life."

His voice was impossible to disobey. He had taken their blood. He could monitor them easily from any distance. He would know the moment their bosses were dead or if they sent others after her. Lucian walked them to the door and watched them leave. He was firmly entrenched in their minds. They would remember only his orders. They would experience them as a great need, always uppermost in their minds.

He turned when he sensed Jaxon's approach. She had always been light on her feet, but now, with his blood running in her veins, she was as quiet as a born Carpathian. She was carrying an enormous tray with four cups of coffee on it. She was so small, the tray looked as if it overpowered her. He took it from her. "What are you doing?"

"You know what I was doing. Getting fingerprints. But you hurried them out of here as soon as you realized I didn't buy your ridiculous story. If you're planning on fooling me, Lucian, you're going to have to get better at lying."

He grinned unrepentantly. "I did not tell an untruth."

"No, you had *them* do the lying and even went so far as to make them believe their absurd story."

"You were not planning on drinking coffee with them, were you?"

"Naturally, I would have been polite."

"You cannot drink this stuff. Jaxon, you are not human. Your body would reject it. You cannot do things like this."

"I figured it might make me sick. But you've eaten meals before, haven't you?"

Where had she learned that? Lucian turned away from her large brown eyes and glided back to the kitchen. She was learning things far too fast. She wasn't ready yet. He wanted to ease her into his world gently, slowly. She was already immersed in violence and death. She didn't need her initiation into the Carpathian way of life to be as bad. Most of their people lived calm, productive lives. She was moving easily within his mind, picking out random memories. He wasn't ready for that. He had things, terrible things, in his past. How could someone in modern times ever understand what it was like in those horrible times? Enemies everywhere. Blood and death and sickness surrounding them. Women and children murdered. How could Jaxon understand the depravity of the true vampire, the evil it was capable of inflicting on humans? The threat the undead held for the species that was Carpathian?

The same way I know the other things. I see them from your memories. Her voice was soft and beautiful, almost loving. Certainly caressing. It nearly stopped his heart and took away his breath.

"Do not drink coffee or eat any human food. You have recently undergone the conversion, and your body would not simply rid itself of the contents. Instead, you would feel tremendous pain." He could not allow such a happenstance. It was difficult enough to watch her endure the things outside of his control.

Jaxon watched him place the tray on the counter. "So tell me what you don't want me to know. Who were those men, and why did they come here?"

Lucian dumped the contents of the coffee mugs into the sink and rinsed them out. "What does it really matter? They are gone, and I doubt they will return."

"It matters if you placed yourself in danger for me." She touched his arm because he wasn't looking at her. Lucian was always so straightforward.

He looked down at her hand against the thickness of his arm. She held quite a bit of power in such a delicate hand. He covered her fingers with his palm, holding her to him, keeping the physical connection between them. "They are human, Jaxon, and I am of ancient blood. It would be difficult for me to place myself in a position of danger. I have knowledge and skill and gifts far beyond their capabilities. No, I did no such thing."

"But they were a threat to me." She made it a statement.

"We are leaving this house, honey. I do not wish to have any of your belongings lost to you, should there be an intruder while we are away, so I will remove the things you value highly and place them in the sleeping chamber. Antonio will keep an eye on the house while we are gone."

"Those men were a threat to me," she insisted stubbornly.

He transferred his hand to the middle of her back, applying pressure to move her out of the kitchen. "We have only the night to make this departure. We must find a place that will be safe from the sun and one that is easy to defend. The idea is to lure those who wish to pursue us into a trap, not to get caught out in the open."

She went with him, fitting easily beneath his shoulder as he moved, her walk matching the rhythm of his. "We can talk while we're moving my things."

"Persistence is not always a virtue, Jaxon." He tried to sound stern, but he admired the way she was able to figure things out for herself.

She grinned up at him teasingly. "Of course it is. It's the only way to find out things you'd rather I didn't. So they threatened me. How in the world were you able to turn them into such sweet men with only money instead of mayhem on their minds?"

"I took their blood."

She blinked several times in amazement. "But I didn't hear anything. And I was right behind you. How could you accomplish so much so quickly? They were all in different rooms. You can't possibly be that fast, can you?"

"Yes, I can, if I sacrifice elegance for speed. I am an ancient, honey. It is easy enough to do such things. By the time you came up the stairs, I was already in control of them. It was easy enough to plant the story in Barton's mind and instruct the other two to believe and remain silent."

"Why? Do you know why they want me dead?" She was gathering up the few treasures she had. Photos of her mother and brother. Little Mattie's favorite blanket. Her fingers automatically rubbed at the thin material lovingly. It was obvious to Lucian she did it often.

He swept a hand through her hair. "After his death, it was one of the few things that gave you momentary comfort."

She brought the blanket to her face and inhaled deeply. She could still catch Mathew's scent after all these years. "He was so little, so funny. His eyes would dance with such mischief when he was trying to be a joker. He was so cute, Lucian. Sometimes I can hardly bear to think of him. It still hurts as much as if it just happened. Everyone said time would ease the pain, but when I think about it, it's still sharp and ugly and so terrible I can't breathe."

He pulled her into his arms, removing the blanket as he did so. At the same time he took the distressing memory from her and replaced it with her determination to find out who their guests had been and what he had done to handle the situation. Very quickly Lucian folded the blanket, knowing the association with pain touching the material carried. The woven strands held the boy's cries,

275

and Jaxon, as sensitive as she was, could not help but feel them. He could not stand the agony entrenched so deeply in her heart. Lucian saw no need for her to suffer continually when he could so easily stop it.

Jaxon blinked and put a hand to her throat. What had she been thinking about? Something had distracted her when she was so determined to find out what was going on in their home. Lucian must have seriously wanted to keep the truth from her. She reached for her jewelry box. "Why did those men want to kill me, Lucian? And this time give me a straight answer."

"I did not ask them straight out." He took the jewelry box out of her hands. It contained her mother's jewels, beautiful gems. He had seen them. Rebecca Montgomery had come from money. She had diamonds, rubies, emeralds, and star sapphires set in necklaces, earrings, and bracelets. Jaxon never wore them, only looked at them.

"You didn't need to ask them straight out," Jaxon observed. "All you had to do was look into their minds." Her dark brown eyes were challenging him.

Lucian shook his head. "In all the centuries of my existence, I have never had anyone question me as you do. When I determine something needs to be done, I simply do it. No one questions me."

"You are not God. You can't always be right." Her eyes flashed at him with a warning hint of her temper.

"I would not presume to be God, but I am fully aware of the tremendous responsibilities I have been given and the gifts bestowed upon me in order to accomplish the tasks set to me. I am able to weigh problems without personal anger or any other emotion clouding my judgment."

"That is setting yourself up as judge, jury, and executioner, Lucian. No one has such a right."

"You are mistaken, angel. Throughout history many of my kind have needed to be just such a being. It is not easy, and the toll on our souls is tremendous, but we have accepted the responsibility in order to protect both our people and humankind. I am what I am, and I cannot change what went before or what is now. When anyone threatens our way of existence, we do our best to remove their memories without violence, but should the need arise, we have no choice but to fight back. We also have the right to walk this earth. The same being created us in the same likeness. We were given many challenges and trials, and we have accepted them."

"What if someone completely innocent discovers your existence, and you can't erase their memory? Do you believe you have a right to take that life?"

A small smile touched the corners of his mouth. "In all the centuries of my existence, such a thing has never happened. If a being discovered us and could not be controlled, I would imagine a good reason existed for such a phenomenon. I would do much investigative work into the matter. I could not render a judgment at this time without much more information."

"How terribly convenient for you." She found herself following his tall figure back down the stairs to the lower story.

His black gaze swept over her, in no way perturbed. "Sarcasm does not suit you all that well, angel. I must admit I have a weakness for your sassy mouth, but sarcasm over so great an issue is beneath you."

She flushed. It *was* unfair of her to be so judgmental. In her line of work it was easy enough to be put in a position of having to shoot or not shoot in the blink of an eye. In a way, that could render her judge, jury, and executioner, too. She had never had to face a decision like that, but she knew a couple of officers who had chased a suspect, had the suspect turn with something shiny in his hand, and had made the decision to fire. Neither officer had been able to accept that they had shot an unarmed teenager. One committed suicide, and the other quit the force and still battled with nightmares and alcoholism. How would she have handled a life filled with such dark decisions? Her mind shied away from the question.

"I'm sorry, Lucian. You're right. I'm glad I'm not you and I've never had to live your life or make your decisions. Mine have been difficult enough." She rested a hand on his arm. "Really, I mean it."

"You do not have to apologize to me, Jaxon. We are making tough decisions very quickly that affect more than just our lives. I know this is difficult for you, and, after all, you still do not know me so very well."

Only some time later did Jaxon realize that Lucian had not given her any of the information she had requested. She still had no idea why the three men had invaded their home or what they wanted. Or what Lucian had really done to handle the situation.

Chapter Thirteen

Lucian took care of the wolves first, helping Antonio crate them and ready them for travel. With his calming touch, the wolves were quite willing to take a trip back to the wilderness, into the Canadian forests. Lucian appeared unhurried as he carefully prepared each animal, paying special attention to the alpha pair. He looked deep into their eyes, exchanging something wild and primitive Jaxon was certain she would never understand but thought extremely beautiful. Tears formed in her eyes as she watched how gentle he was with the animals. Lucian continually astounded her.

As they watched the truck pull away from the estate, Jaxon reached for his hand, experiencing a sense of sadness watching the creatures go. They belonged with Lucian. Wild and untamed. "You wouldn't have to send them away from you if you weren't with me."

At once Lucian's entire attention centered on her. He bent his dark hair over her blond, one arm curving around her small waist. "You are my life, the only one who matters to me. I can live without the wolves. I can live without my people and outside my homeland, but I cannot live without you. This was our decision together. We are not leaving our home for all time, rather taking a small working vacation. The wolves would be uneasy outside their natural environment without me. If someone else should try to poison them and I was not here to advise them properly, some of the young ones might eat the tainted meat."

Her dark brown gaze moved over his face. "Those men fed the wolves poison?"

He tugged at her hand to get her walking beside him toward the long white limousine. "Actually, yes, they did."

Antonio handed her into the car. She smiled up at him rather absently, turning over the information in her mind. "And you let them go? That doesn't sound like you. Where are we going? We aren't taking this monstrosity wherever we're going, are we? I own a little car. It gets great mileage," she added hopefully.

Lucian leaned toward her and whispered softly in her ear. "We do not need a car when we leave, angel. We are simply drawing attention to ourselves for the moment."

A small smile found its way to her mouth. "This car definitely draws attention."

"Is that not the idea? Tyler Drake will know we are leaving. That is imperative. And the undead must be aware of our every move."

"But are we actually taking this limo all the way to our destination, which, by the way, I haven't been told? Do you even know it for certain?"

The car was moving with silent swiftness through the streets toward the police station. "I own property up on the border between Washington and Canada. We will be able to set up housekeeping there with no problem."

Jaxon shook her head but refrained from pointing out

that she had misgivings about being in the wilderness with Tyler Drake hunting them. They had already discussed it. She knew Lucian believed Drake would be easily handled, but he didn't realize the extent of Drake's training. Tyler Drake was human, but he was an extraordinary human. And the only thing that now mattered to Drake was likely killing Lucian. It would be impossible in hand-to-hand combat, but not from a distance. She believed Drake capable of killing from a very long distance—much longer than Lucian might suppose. Drake was an excellent shot and equally adept at making remote-controlled bombs.

Jaxon turned her face away from Lucian to stare out the window at the passing streets. Even in the night the sidewalks were alive with people. She was familiar with the patterns of their lives. The ebb and flow of crime according to time, weather, and month had always been her focus, her life. Now she felt out of sync with that world she had known. She could hear things she had never heard before, a barrage of sounds from insect chirps to whispered conversations. Sometimes the assault on her ears was almost more than she could bear before she remembered how to turn down the volume. She was aware of things she had never noticed before. Textures. Colors. Little everyday things like the brush of hair against her cheek. Hearts beating. The rush of blood in veins. The bark on trees. The way the wind blew through foliage.

There was a growing restlessness in her that she had never experienced. A wild, untamed spirit that seemed to be spreading, demanding more from her, demanding things she had no knowledge of. She had known the night as a time when many crimes occurred under the cover of darkness, yet now it called to her seductively, whispered to her continually. *Embrace me. Embrace me.* She belonged in the night. It enfolded her within its darkness as in the softest of blankets. The stars overhead were like glittering diamonds, a kaleidoscope of amazing beauty.

The car pulled into the police station parking lot, and Antonio courteously opened the door for them. Feeling embarrassed and hoping none of her friends would see her, Jaxon hastily slid out of the limo.

Lucian caught her hand, preventing her from surging ahead of him. "Follow my lead, angel. This is where we spread rumors so that those we want to trail us will do so."

She nodded and walked with him into the station. As always, Lucian commanded immediate attention. She didn't think he was manipulating anyone; it was simply the way he carried himself. Tall and straight with complete confidence. Dark and dangerous. Mysterious. Old World. Gothic, even. A dark lord or prince. He automatically commanded respect. Even the captain came out of his office immediately, hand extended. To Lucian. Not to her. She shook her head and allowed the conversation to flow around her. She even spaced out a bit until she heard the word *marriage*. At once she blinked to bring the two men into focus.

To her horror, Lucian was telling Captain Smith that they had married quietly and he was now taking her away. He admitted they were hoping Drake would follow them and thus any copycats would be headed off before they could strike. The official version would be that they had gone off for a secluded honeymoon. The captain was to drop it around the station house that they had headed to Lucian's hideaway along the border. The captain actually hugged her while he murmured his congratulations and admonishments to be careful. Jaxon had the odd feeling she was living in a fantasy world, a Dorothy in Oz effect.

We aren't married. She said it firmly because it was the one thing she knew absolutely to be true.

Of course we are. What do you think lifemates are? He

refuted her testimony with the causal finesse of a swordsman.

We aren't married, she repeated stubbornly. This time she flashed him a warning with her dark eyes.

He grinned at her, a mischievous, little-boy, all-too-sexy grin that instantly melted her heart. *I recall the ritual ceremony in vivid detail. If you do not, I will be happy to repeat it. The ritual is binding in every way.*

She lifted her chin at him as they reentered the limousine. "For you, maybe, but I'm human, remember? I get married. That's the way *we* do things."

"You wish, maybe, but reality is an altogether different thing." He sounded very male, very smug.

Jaxon sat beside him in silence, smoldering. It wasn't that she was angling for a wedding ring. Or a wedding. It was the idea that he was always right that was so galling. *Thought,* she reminded herself. He *thought* he was always right. Officially, they were not married, so that made her technically right. She relaxed, feeling rather smug herself. Let him think she was wrong.

You are very much married to me, Jaxon. Make no mistake about it. A little thread of iron ran through the soft velvet of his voice, as if he thought she was considering jumping ship and hotfooting it away from him.

Deliberately Jaxon shrugged carelessly. "Think whatever you like, Lucian. Obviously we aren't going to come to any agreement on this issue. What are we doing now?"

"We are ensuring we have made enough of a spectacle of ourselves that everyone in town has seen us or heard of our departure. And because you are so adamant, we will leave a paper trail as well."

"What does that mean?" She was suddenly suspicious of his soft, melting voice. He sounded too pure and beautiful. He just had to be up to no good.

"Carpathians leave as few paper trails behind as possible. Things like passports have a way of turning up as incriminating evidence a few hundred years later. Now, with computers, it is even easier to find oneself trapped in a maze of paperwork. We do not like to create documents unless they are for property or money or businesses we continually leave to ourselves upon our timely 'deaths.' It is one of the reasons we travel often from continent to continent if we are not in our homeland. People find it impossible to identify us as other than our own sires, perhaps, fifty or sixty years later."

She laughed softly. "I guess I deserved that answer. I just had to ask. What are you doing now?"

"Marrying you in the way of your people. There is a man who can do so, a judge I know, and he will arrange the necessary paperwork. Money and influence work wonders even at this time of night. Of course he will be understanding, with so many crimes happening so quickly around us. The news can be leaked to the papers tomorrow, which will further our cause."

Her eyelashes swept down to conceal her expression. "I hope you're kidding."

The long white limousine was already parked at the curb as if Antonio had received his orders and was waiting. She sat back against the leather seat, her face hidden in the shadows. Lucian touched her cheek with gentle fingertips. "This ceremony means much to you." He made it a statement.

"Not really." Jaxon tried to be as casual as he had been. So what if, like nearly every girl in the world, she'd dreamed of a white wedding dress and a church filled with family and friends? Her family was dead, and most of her friends were going that way also. Any guests attending her wedding would be taking their lives in their hands, just as the man who performed the ceremony would be. She was already shaking her head. "I don't want to do this. Drake would retaliate before he followed us."

Lucian studied her averted profile for a moment before

nodding his agreement. At once the car slid back into traffic and headed for their home. She was correct. Tyler Drake would indeed perceive anyone who helped with their marriage ceremony as a threat to his fantasy world. Lucian let his breath out slowly. There were many things in Jaxon's memories he didn't fully understand. A human ceremony to him did not have the same beauty and completeness about it that the Carpathian one held, yet he could not put her longing out of his mind. Someday, he vowed, she would have her ceremony in a church, surrounded by friends and family, just like the picture he had caught in her mind. For now, all he could do was pull her close to his warmth and hold her in his arms.

In their house he left behind a rough, partial map of his property deep within the Cascade Mountains, along with three black-and-white photographs of the old ornate hunting lodge he had purchased. Prominently displayed was a note written in his flourishing handwriting. An analyst would have said it was Old World, bold, and the writer a dominating male with complete confidence in himself. The note was allegedly to Antonio, detailing instructions on the care and management of the estate in Lucian's absence. Antonio was quite familiar with his instructions.

Lucian caught Jaxon's hand and led her to the privacy of the enclosed backyard. "Are you ready? We must leave soon if we intend to travel this night."

Her eyes were suddenly wary. She had been far too quiet during his preparations, not once asking him anything. Her silence worried him far more than her questions would have.

"I don't know why, Lucian, but I'm getting the distinct impression we aren't taking the limousine after all."

"No, we travel much faster and more safely on our own. Antonio will pull the car out of the driveway and head toward the airport while we take off."

"And we're going to . . ." She trailed off, looking at him expectantly.

"Fly." He said it softly.

Jaxon swallowed the lump that was suddenly blocking her throat. Somehow she had known. Somewhere along the line she had realized they wouldn't be boarding an airplane or driving through the state in the white limousine. She wasn't certain what had tipped her off; perhaps simply being able to read Lucian's mind. Maybe she was sharing his mind more often than she was aware.

She realized she was twisting her fingers together nervously and immediately put both hands behind her back. He thought she could do this. He *expected* her to do it. He was treating the idea of flying as an everyday occurrence. "Like superman?" Her attempt at a smile fell flat.

"Not exactly. Clouds are moving in—a perfect cover. I will help you dissolve into mist, and we'll use the drafts to move through the air."

Her heart slammed hard in her chest. Her teeth bit more deeply into her lower lip. "Mist sounds a bit difficult to start with. Why don't we try something easier?"

"Such as?" Lucian prompted gently.

"We can use our feet. You know, just start walking down the highway and stick our thumbs out." Again she attempted a smile. But the rapid beating of her heart betrayed her.

"Look at me, angel." He turned the full force of his black eyes on her. "You trust me. You know you do. I would never ask you to do anything you could not do. You are very capable of doing this."

She was nodding, aware he was right, but at the same time, the thought of her body dissolving into drops of mist was terrifying. "Couldn't I try something else first? Something easier?" Her fingers twisted together nervously, but she stood resolutely.

Lucian hesitated. Mist would be easy to move quickly

through time and space, streamlined, fast, unseen by even the undead in the dark of night. "Mist takes the same amount of energy to create as shape-shifting into owls or birds of prey with tremendous wingspans. It is essentially the same."

"How can our bodies be squeezed into the tiny little body of a bird?" Her voice was trembling. She heard it but could do nothing about it. No matter how much she wanted to accept this, she was finding the idea terrifying.

Lucian swept his arms around her. "I can help you, Jaxon. Will you trust me to do that for you? I can make the acceptance easier."

Her first reaction was to shake her head firmly, her teeth grinding so hard on her lip that a small bead of blood appeared. The idea of someone else controlling her was not to her liking, but when she made herself take a breath, she felt differently. This was a part of her life now. Like it or not, she was no longer human. She was Carpathian. There was no going back, only going forward. She had to learn to do this somehow. And she was not going to be able to control every situation.

Lucian watched as she gnawed nervously at her lower lip. The sight was enough to tear at his heartstrings. His palm slid around the nape of her neck, his fingers sliding over her skin, her pulse. Of their own accord his fingertips stroked her blond hair soothingly. He bent his head to hers, his mouth finding hers with ease, his tongue swirling a healing agent over her full lower lip even as he took the essence of her blood into his body.

"Just to help me, to calm me down," Jaxon said softly. "I don't want you to take over my mind entirely."

His hand moved lovingly over her face. Taking over *was* a temptation. It wasn't that he begrudged the time. He had used up a good portion of the night getting the wolves ready for transport, preparing them for the disturbing separation the pack would have to endure. He

Christine Feehan

would spend every minute of this night allowing Jaxon as much time as she needed to accept what must be done. To accept the tremendous gifts she had inherited. Still, he was tempted to take control of her mind, to eliminate her fears, so that she would cease to suffer so needlessly. He really had trouble bearing her pain.

As if she was touching his mind and reading his thoughts, she forced a small smile. "I can do this. I know I can. If I do it this time with your help, I know I can do it by myself the next time. It would have come in handy when I was facing that ghoul at the police station. I could have just evaporated."

"You will feel an incredible sense of freedom, Jaxon," he said softly, and he merged his mind fully with hers. At once his calmness was hers, his tranquil mind centering hers. He built a picture in her head, in his.

Jaxon felt her body begin to fade—well, not fade exactly, but begin to become light and airy. She wanted to grab his hand and hold on tightly. He was an anchor in her mind, and, immediately, as her terror began to rise, she felt the warmth and strength of his arms creeping around her. Except there was no Jaxon anymore. She was vapor, a colorful mist like rainbow prisms. Droplets in the air. Surrounding her was Lucian. Not flesh and blood, bone and sinew, but diamondlike specks moving swiftly to protect her as they began to move through the sky.

It was unexpectedly exhilarating. Terrifying but exhilarating. They streaked skyward, right up toward the clouds. Jaxon had never experienced anything even close to the feeling. Power flowed through her and out into the night sky.

She was aware of the sights below her, although not in the same sense as seeing them through her own eyes. Rather, she was seeing them through Lucian as they streaked through the sky. They were moving far too fast and she was too inexperienced to be able to focus on any one thing below them. Each time she became at all distracted, Lucian's mind centered her, holding the picture of mist uppermost in her mind. It was easy for him, second nature, so much so that he was no more aware of the mechanics of shape-shifting than of walking. For Jaxon it was an energy-draining yet wild ride.

By the time Lucian called a halt, Jaxon was so exhausted she was barely able to resume her own form. She was swaying, her skin so pale it was nearly translucent. Without Lucian to hold her up, she would have simply collapsed onto the ground. She had no idea where she was, and she really didn't care. All around her was forest, thick stands of trees and dark, lush vegetation. They were in a mountainous area, steep and wild. The wind was blowing fiercely through the branches and leaves, creating a whistling that sounded curiously like a moan.

Jaxon felt light, almost insubstantial, in Lucian's arms. He eased her down to the ground so she could rest her back against a broad tree trunk. "You did exactly right, my love. Shape-shifting is not nearly as alarming as it first appeared, is it?"

Clasping her knees, she shook her head, dizzy and swaying, her head almost too heavy to hold up. She was hungry; hunger beat in her like her a pulse, like her heart. It pounded in her ears, throbbed in her veins. It was a sickness consuming her. She could hear Lucian's heart beating strongly, beckoning her. The ebb and flow of blood moving through him, his life force like the sap moving through the trees. She could smell his scent calling to her, his very essence beckoning her. She felt the heat of his skin radiating outward toward her, surrounding her like a silken web. She needed the feel of him, strong and powerful, holding her close to him.

Lucian bent to her. The sound of the blood rushing through his veins, bursting with hot, sweet life, tormented her. Without looking up at him, Jaxon pushed at his chest with the palm of one hand. She didn't want him to see the loathing of her own need in her eyes. It was just that she was so weak, so drained of energy. She had never felt as tired and insubstantial before. She could get her craving under control if he just would move away from her and give her space.

What you are feeling is very normal, little love. You need to feed. His voice brushed at her, soft, seductive, deliberately intimate.

I know exactly what is wrong, Lucian. To you it's perfectly normal. To me it's abhorrent. She was too tired to speak aloud, to fight for her humanity. *I want to sleep for a while. Can we just find a place for tonight?*

Lucian straightened slowly. He knew they were being tracked. The one following them was a distance away, careful to keep from putting himself in Lucian's path. Lucian felt a strange blankness in two areas several miles from them. Only those of power could manage such a thing. When a Carpathian scanned a region for life-forms, very few could successfully hide their presence. Lucian was an ancient. He was sensitive enough that he could feel the absence of life as clearly as he could feel life itself.

"Listen to me, honey," he said very softly, his voice so gentle and tender her heart fluttered. "Our plan is working very well. To the north and west of us, two lesser vampires are tracking us across the country. Another, much more powerful being is following, also. I can detect the taint of him but cannot find his exact location without going out to face all three of them."

Jaxon raised her head and looked up at him with her large eyes. She was so tired, she had to reach for her voice. "Not alone, you're not. If you go, I go. Come on then, Lucian. Do your mind-control thing. It's the only way I'm going to be able to eat. Or feed, or whatever disgusting way you say it." There was resolve on her face, in the depths of her eyes.

Lucian immediately felt an answering response in the region of his heart. She was totally exhausted and overwhelmed by all the new things she was having to face, yet she rose to the occasion the moment there was need, overcoming her natural aversion to their feeding habits. She knew she needed to be at full strength in order to aid him and was determined to do whatever was necessary to accomplish this.

Before she could change her decision, Lucian acted, merging their minds fully, taking control, commanding her to come to him, to take what she needed from her lifemate. Jaxon rose with one fluid movement, sensuous, sultry, a full-blooded Carpathian temptress. She moved toward him without a sound, like flowing water, graceful and beautiful. The dark night could not hide her incredible beauty, the whiteness of her teeth, the scent of her, her flawless skin or shapely body. Lucian heard a soft groan escape his throat as even there, in the moonlight, with enemies approaching from all directions, the sight of her made his body tighten with urgent demand.

Her small frame, soft and pliant, moved restlessly against his, warm satin skin melting into his heavier muscles. At once his clothes felt confining and coarse against his sensitive skin. Her fingers brushed at him as she slowly unbuttoned his shirt, seeking contact with his warmth. Slender arms wound around his neck as she pressed closer. His heart picked up the rhythm; his gut clenched hotly. She was moving so seductively against him, he thought he might not be able to stand it. She whispered something soft against his chest, her breath warm on his heated skin. Her mouth moved upward over his throat to the pulse beckoning in his neck. Her tongue swirled once, twice, her teeth skimming, nipping, scraping until his body was a taut, urgent demand so hot and needy he found he was having a difficult time concentrating on scanning the area.

Angel, you are going to kill me if you do not feed now. His voice was husky, betraying the desperate need he had of her.

At once he felt the white-hot lance of pleasure-pain slashing through his body, turning his insides to molten lava. Ecstasy rushed through him like a fireball, spread like a wildfire as his blood flowed into her. They were connected for all eternity. He closed his eyes and savored the way his body felt, hot and hard and uncomfortable yet swamped with wave after wave of pure pleasure.

In all his existence he had never felt sexual desire or enjoyment when he took or gave blood. With Jaxon he couldn't separate the two. He was not certain he could ever stand by and watch her feed from another man. The thought of her gliding seductively up to another male, her arms circling his neck, his head thrown back to allow her to find his pulse beating strongly, sickened him. Her mouth moving over someone else's skin, her tongue touching, teasing, her teeth sinking deeply, connecting the two of them—the image swam alarmingly in his mind for a moment.

A fierce growl escaped his throat, and his eyes glowed hotly, red flames leaping in their depths. Jaxon's tongue swept across the tiny pinpricks to close them, and she looked up at him. "What is it?" There was a hot, coppery flavor in her mouth, addicting and subtly masculine. She put the back of her hand to her lips and wiped surreptitiously, willing her stomach not to rebel although her mind was screaming at her in denial. She blinked up at Lucian, trying desperately to appear normal. He had enough worries without always trying to placate her fears.

Lucian swept his arms around her, holding her to him tightly. "You are the most important person in my world."

"I'm also turning out to be the biggest baby in the world. I can't believe how afraid I am of everything." She attempted a laugh, but they both knew she was telling the truth. "Usually I'm really cool under fire, Lucian. I don't know why I'm acting so silly."

"Do not do this, Jaxon. Do not apologize to me when I am the one who made this decision for you. You have had much to learn and cope with in a short space of time. You are learning things that are completely foreign to you. I think you have done remarkably well under the circumstances." His hands came up to caress her hair. "I have no quarrel with the way you have accepted the extraordinary things I have demanded of you, and I am exceptionally proud of you." He leaned close. "Can you not feel the way I feel about you? You have been in my mind enough to do so."

"I think I'm still afraid to look too closely. I'm still getting used to the new me," she admitted almost shyly.

"Perhaps you would learn more of yourself if you saw yourself through my eyes instead of your own," he suggested, his voice black-velvet persuasion.

A slow curve touched her soft mouth. "I'm beginning to believe you're just the tiniest bit prejudiced in my favor."

His eyebrows shot up, an elegant, Old World, lord-of-the-manor gesture she found endearing. "That could not be true. You are the most beautiful, desirable, courageous woman in the world. It is a fact."

She nuzzled his chest, savoring his warmth and strength, the way he comforted her in a world she no longer understood. "I'd be willing to bet your brother doesn't think that. He probably thinks Francesca is the most desirable woman in the world."

"He has never had my superior intellect or my discernment," he replied solemnly.

Jaxon found herself laughing. "I'll be sure to tell him when I finally meet him."

Lucian shrugged carelessly, a casual ripple of muscle

and sinew that made her think of a great jungle cat stretching lazily. "I have told him so on many occasions, but he fools himself into thinking he knows more than I."

At once she was laughing aloud, her young voice soft and carefree, floating in the wind. "He does that, does he? More and more I think I should meet him. The two of us might find we share the same point of view."

His fingers ruffled her hair in a caress before tugging the silken strands gently. "I do not believe I shall ever introduce you to him."

"I have a feeling I will meet your brother very soon. It is obvious to me you care a great deal about him. In the meantime, what do we do about our company? You can tackle the big guy—I don't want any part of him. The lesser ones seem more up my alley." She was looking up at him expectantly, her dark eyes clear and serious. She expected to go into battle with him, was fully prepared to do whatever he told her.

Lucian bent his head to kiss her inviting mouth. She moved him. It was that simple. The way she was so certain she would help him. She was a bright light to him, warming him where nothing else ever could. It was amazing to him that she could still be so determined to help him when she knew his power, his abilities. She didn't want him fighting alone.

Her long lashes fluttered down to conceal the expression in her eyes. "You never should have been alone all those years." Her chin lifted. "We're a team now."

Lucian found himself smiling at her. "Absolutely." Ordinarily he would have gone after the two lesser vampires to remove that threat, but with Jaxon in jeopardy, he would never take the risk of leaving her alone while he went into battle. "It is no small thing to fight a vampire, honey. The ghouls you faced were nothing compared to a vampire. Even one who has just 'turned' is very formidable. Remember, they were male Carpathians at full strength for centuries. They have acquired tremendous knowledge and skills during that time. As vampires they maintain a certain tainted strength. All of them must be considered extremely dangerous."

She nodded solemnly. "I'm not looking forward to this, if that's what you think. I wouldn't mind werewolves—I can do the silver-bullet-in-the-heart thing. I'm a great shot. Do silver bullets do any good on these creatures?"

"We are not going to fight them at this time. We are not ready. We want the full advantage. Let them come after us. They must seek shelter soon. I know these mountains, and they do not. We can travel longer in the early dawn than they can. We will pick our battleground and wage our war when we are completely set."

He wanted to call the lesser vampires to him, to destroy them immediately as he knew he could, but he was well aware of the other out there, waiting, bloated with skill and the knowledge of centuries spent as a vampire. He was a foul creature, wholly evil, using mortals and immortals alike for his own dark purposes. He would be aware that Lucian was capable of calling the lesser vampires to him. He would know that Lucian would be well aware of the undead tracking them and would expect Lucian to deal with them.

"Are you saying that just to keep me from going after them with you? I learn fast, Lucian, I really do. Just tell me what to do."

"You will learn all too soon, Jaxon. It is easy to read my mind when we are merged. The information you seek is there for you at any time. Right now, we must continue with our journey. We must have shelter before the sun rises too high."

"Am I holding us back?" she asked anxiously.

"We have plenty of time, Jaxon. There is no hurry. We are high in the mountains. I know this area intimately. Before we go down into the cities, Carpathians always search out the high reaches. The Cascade Mountains are fire and ice—a perfect home for ones such as us."

Her eyebrows rose. "I'm going to pretend I didn't hear that. Fire and ice? I don't like the sound of those words."

"You should. They describe you."

"They do not!" She was indignant.

He laughed softly, an intimate, sexy sound that immediately sent a rush of heat spiraling through her body. "You are fire right now, my little love, and you are ice when you are under fire."

She blushed for no reason she could think of except for his voice. It was the way he talked, his accent, the black-velvet sorcery that could make her feel as if she was the only woman in the world, the only one down through the long centuries. It was in his voice, in his eyes, the way they went from ice-cold to smoldering heat in a blink. He made her feel intensely desirable. He *had* to have her, *had* to be with her. Everything she said, everything she did, was of great importance to him.

Lucian leaned close to her, one arm slipping around her waist so he could pull her slender body into the heat of his. "I make you feel that way because it is so, not because my voice is magic."

She touched a fingertip to his mouth. "You are magic, Lucian."

His body tightened in urgent demand, and for the first time his heart slammed painfully in his chest. He heard something in her voice that had never been there before. She didn't say she loved him, because deep within her mind she didn't believe she did. Her soul bound her to him; she had no choice but to accept that. Her body cried out for his; he was well aware of their physical chemistry. But he had expected a long battle for her heart.

Yet there it was. Four little words that should have meant nothing, yet he heard it. Soft. Shy. Unaware, even. *You are magic, Lucian.* It was in those words—the surrender of her heart into his keeping. He held her to him, a tiny package of dynamite, closing his eyes to savor the moment. It would be etched in his mind for all eternity. Jaxon with her ridiculous name and small, feminine build, with all the courage of long-forgotten warriors.

"You are safe in my care," he whispered, his mouth at her temple.

She was content to be held. Even with the sun so close to rising, with the wilderness surrounding them and enemies chasing them, she felt totally protected. He held her for a few minutes, relaxing in the cool of the mountains before the next leg of their journey.

Chapter Fourteen

The view was breathtaking. Jaxon perched on the top of a flat rock and surveyed the cascading waterfall pour down the cavern wall in a rush of white foam. Lucian had once more stopped their flight, this time deep within a cavernous mountain. She was under the earth before she had time to think about the layers of granite and dirt above her head. The cave was huge, the pools deep below the falls giving the illusion of tremendous space. Crystals hung in long spears of color sparkling like diamonds. She could see as clearly as if it were daylight. She was very tired but strangely happy.

As they had made their way across the sky, Jaxon managed to maintain the mist by herself without Lucian's aid. He had remained fully merged with her but had allowed her to be the one to hold the image firmly in her mind. On the first leg of their journey she had been apprehensive and very much aware of what they were doing. It seemed wholly unnatural. The second time she had accepted the method of travel as expedient and much easier to maintain than she had first thought. She had found her body relaxed and her mind calm as they streaked across the sky together. It was tiring, no doubt about it, but she realized it was like any other effort: It required only practice before she perfected it. Now she wanted to try other things. Wolves. Birds. Everything. Anything.

But it could all wait for a better time. She was too tired, and, aboveground, she was aware the sun was rising. Just before they had entered the cave, her eyes had begun to sting as if pricked by a thousand needles. And the crazy thing was, she had been only mist, with no skin, no eyes, nothing for the sun to touch. Yet she had felt it, and it had been distinctly uncomfortable.

She sat cross-legged on the huge, flat boulder overlooking the series of pools. Above and to her left the long waterfall filled the chamber with a deafening roar. Jaxon was becoming adept at turning down the volume of sounds and now did so with ease. It was good to be sitting on something solid where she felt safe and far from the rays of the sun.

Lucian was setting his safeguards to ensure they were not disturbed. She wasn't certain exactly what he was doing, but she knew he was powerful enough to protect them from anything that might come their way. She drummed her fingers on the rock surface, wishing she had access to a telephone.

"Why?" The sound of his voice startled her.

Jaxon turned to see him gliding toward her. The way he moved took her breath away. "I thought I'd call back to the captain and make certain nothing had happened since we left."

His hand unerringly found her hair. "You are still worried about Drake." His voice was soft with compassion.

She nodded. "I know it's probably best that we left, especially if we really are being trailed by . . . vampires." She stumbled over the word, the idea to her still something out of a Gothic tale! "But I can't help feeling as if I deserted everybody."

"Drake will follow us, honey," he said gently, his fingers tracing the delicate line of her collarbone. "I know he will. There is no reason for him to hurt anyone else."

"I just wish I could be certain we did the right thing," she said worriedly.

"Merge with me," he invited softly.

Jaxon hesitated for a moment only because his mind was becoming so familiar, so natural, so much a part of her. She was slipping in and out of it constantly, her mind often reaching for his even without conscious thought. It was disconcerting how much she craved being a part of him. Lucian waited patiently, never hurrying her decision, simply watching her with his dark, fathomless eyes. Jaxon allowed her mind to melt into his. At once she felt safe, sheltered, loved. She felt power and confidence. A sense of completeness.

Antonio? All is well with you?

Jaxon was startled. The mental path Lucian used to contact the man was completely different from the one he used with her. She found Lucian's hand, weaving her fingers through his.

Yes. And you and your lady?

Both of us are fine. She is worried that Drake has retaliated.

All is quiet here. I am keeping a low profile, expecting him to visit your home tonight. Tell her not to worry.

Thank you, Antonio, and good day to you.

Jaxon found herself smiling at how old-fashioned and courtly Lucian managed to sound even in thought transfers. "Can he contact you anytime?"

Lucian shook his head. "No, although I am certain I would feel his anxiety if he were in a situation where his life was threatened. His family has served Aidan Savage's family for hundreds of years. They are human but well-versed in the ways of our people. To my knowledge they are among only a handful of humans trusted with the knowledge of the Carpathians' existence. Antonio is an exceptional young man. I consider him a friend."

"Are you sure the main vampire followed us as well?"

"Absolutely, Jaxon. He broke off from our trail earlier than did the two lesser vampires, but he has followed. No doubt he thinks we are unaware of him. He will know I am conscious of the two following, but he has a very high opinion of himself and his ability to hide from me."

"Perhaps it's because he deserves it," she suggested quietly.

Lucian arched an elegant black eyebrow at her, a lofty gesture that spoke volumes silently.

Jaxon burst out laughing at his arrogance. "What?" she demanded. "Isn't it conceivable that he has managed to stay alive for centuries because he's really good at being a vampire? Maybe he's more powerful than—"

"I know you are not going to say more powerful than me." His voice dared her to challenge him.

She pushed at the wall of his chest, completely unafraid. "Isn't it possible?"

"Absolutely not."

"You really believe that, don't you?"

"I know it, angel. There is no vampire as powerful. I have great control, tremendous discipline, and I have learned what others have not. Only my brother Gabriel comes close to having the knowledge and abilities I possess."

He was not bragging, he spoke matter-of-factly, unconcerned with his power. He accepted it as he had accepted everything else in the world around him. It simply was.

"What if you're wrong? What if you underestimate him?"

Lucian shrugged with lazy casualness. "I can underestimate him easily enough without being less powerful.

301

Some vampires are quite cunning, all are ruthless and wholly evil. I am certain this one has lived long and acquired much knowledge. It will not do him any good. It is my duty to destroy him, and I will do so."

"How did you hold out for so long when so many other males have turned?"

Lucian touched her face with gentle fingertips. "I would like to say that I knew you were going to be born and I held on for your sake, but the truth is, I did not believe I would be so rewarded. I met a man many centuries ago. Some say he was the Son of God. Others say he did not exist, and still others say he was merely a good man who lived an exemplary life. I know only that we walked together one night and talked. I touched his mind with mine. In all the days I have walked on this earth, I never met another such as he. He was like me yet different. He was like a human, yet different. There was only goodness in him. Only that. He knew things no one else knew. He was gentle and compassionate. I had already lost my ability to feel, yet when I was in his presence, I was comforted." Lucian sighed softly and shook his head. "He asked me if I could have anything in the world granted to me, what would I ask for. I replied, a lifemate for Gabriel. He told me Gabriel had a lifemate and he would find her, but we would have to hold out far longer than any other of our kind. I knew he meant that, without my aid, Gabriel would not survive so long a time."

"And you believed him?"

"You do not understand. This man could not tell an untruth. He was not capable of deceit. I made a promise to myself I would never allow my brother to go the way of the undead. Much was asked of us—the constant killing of our own kind, the isolation the hunter must endure. Gabriel was different; he felt emotions far longer than was normal for our males. I believe it was because his lifemate was alive. She is one of our people. We were moving so

302

often, hunting and destroying and battling, Gabriel missed finding her. Eventually I pretended to become vampire when I knew my brother was close to turning. My doing so prevented him from having to make kills, which is dangerous to those close to turning. He had to hunt *me* instead. After years of battling me and chasing me across the continents, Gabriel managed to lock us both in the ground." His slight smile was rueful. "A miscalculation on my part. Gabriel actually managed to surprise me. It was only by chance that we surfaced before his lifemate chose to meet the dawn."

"You did all that for your brother." Jaxon was awed by his sacrifice. He told the story casually, in a few simple words, but she was still a shadow in his mind, and she saw his painful memories clearly. The details were vivid, the carefully constructed scenes of death and mayhem planned meticulously to convince his twin, a man who was lethal and well aware of what a vampire kill looked like, that he had turned. It had been a difficult existence, to say the least.

"Even when I could no longer *feel* such an emotion, I knew I loved my brother and that he had followed my lead. It was my decision to fight for our people and battle the Ottoman Turks and destroy the undead. Gabriel followed me and remained steady and loyal throughout his life. He deserved happiness. It was my duty to ensure it came to him."

"Whose duty was it to ensure yours?" she asked softly.

He smiled at her instant defense of him. "I was given tremendous gifts, honey. I was strong and better able to hold out against the gathering darkness. And even more than that, I had touched the light as no one else had ever done. I could not forget that moment, touching a mind so pure and beautiful, so completely good. It was a gift I could not turn my back on. I never had a choice to lose my soul after that. I would never turn my back on something so completely of the light. I knew the truth. I knew we were here for a purpose and that our lives counted for something."

She shook her head. "You amaze me, Lucian, how little you ask for yourself."

He laughed then, a soft sound of love. "I would never give *you* up, Jaxon. You are everything to me. You are the only thing that matters now. Believe me, my love, I am no saint, no martyr. I would no longer ask for your presence in my life, I would *demand* it."

His gaze was suddenly hot, a dark intensity centering solely on her. It made her feel hot and achy, a curling excitement blossoming deep within her.

Jaxon shoved impatiently at her hair, the action lifting her breasts beneath the thin material of her blouse. "Why have I so easily accepted our relationship when before I would never allow anyone close to me?"

"Even before you were converted to our blood, your heart and soul were still the other half of mine. Once I spoke the ritual words, we were finally bound together as one." He turned up her hand to kiss her knuckles in a tribute. His tongue licked the inside of her wrist. It was sexy and intimate. "We belong. We are complete now. You are the light to my darkness. I am the predator, and you are compassion. I need you just to be able to feel emotion, to see the colors in the world, to enjoy each day and night. You need me to protect and cherish you, to be certain of your happiness. It is not exactly the same relationship as that of humans; it is more intense and continues to grow so as the years go by." His gaze burned over her possessively, his fingers sliding along her thigh, massaging her knotted muscles.

"You believe that? That we were destined to be together even before birth? That I am really the only woman in all the centuries you existed who was for you? That there is only you for me?" Jaxon could barely breathe, could barely get the words out, all too aware of his palm sliding between her legs, pushing against the core of her right through the fabric of her jeans.

His black eyes smoldered at her, a sexy, brooding look that melted her insides. "Do you?" He pushed harder, rubbed, caressed until a soft moan escaped her throat.

She thought about the question for a few minutes, turning it over in her mind before answering. Did she believe they were meant to be together? She couldn't imagine her life without him. She, who had never shared her life with another human being, wanted to never leave his side. She wanted to share his mind, his memories; she wanted the feeling of belonging always. And when she touched his mind, she found an intensity burning there, a need of her as elemental as breathing. He thought only of her, no other woman. She had touched no memories of another woman. She was his life. Very slowly she nodded. "It must be your bad influence on me, but I can't imagine life without you anymore."

"It is a good thing, angel, so do not say it as if it is a fate worse than death." He bent his head, his teeth nibbling at her shoulder. "Take off your blouse, Jaxon. I'm so hard and hot, I think I may explode." He leaned closer, his mouth against her ear. "I want to taste you, wet and wild and hot for me. You are—I feel it."

Jaxon loved him hot and hard for her. Loved hearing him admit it, that soft hitch in his voice, a slightly husky note that caught at her insides. She slipped her top off obediently and tossed aside the lacy scrap of bra, spilling her breasts out under the heat of his gaze. She watched his shirt follow her bra and helplessly leaned over to taste a small bead of sweat on his skin. His body trembled.

"Lie back, honey, and stretch your hands over your head." He gave the instructions softly, but there was nothing soft in the way his black gaze moved over her.

Jaxon's heart leaped, but she lay back along the flat

rock, her arms stretching past her ears until her hand connected with a long, thick stick. She wrapped her fingers around it and held on, knowing it was what he wanted. It left her breathless, stretched out under his hot gaze, her body an offering for him. Little beads of sweat were running along her rounded breasts, into the valley between them.

Lucian tossed his pants aside and caught at her waistband to slide the material from her body. The tiny curls beneath, already damp with her invitation, caught his attention. "I think about you like this all the time. Open your legs for me, angel. Invite me in." He was hard and thick, aching with the urgency of his own need.

Jaxon spread her legs wide, deliberately slowly, a carnal enticement, tightening her grip on the piece of wood in anticipation of his reaction. He looked so big, so desperate for her body. It was incredibly sexy, and she was rather shocked at herself that she felt so uninhibited. "You have no idea how much I want you. Touch me, Lucian. I need to feel you touching me." Her tongue touched her lush lower lip; her nipples were hard peaks beckoning him.

He stroked her leg, her thigh, his fingers lingering in her damp curls so that her body jumped, her hips arching toward him. Lucian smiled, his teeth very white. "Do not let go, angel. I want you like this, just like this, open to me." Watching her face intently, he inserted a single finger into her hot, wet core. At once her body clenched around him, velvet soft, tight. He felt her response, her muscles gripping his finger. He pushed deeper, watched her gasp her pleasure. "I know how tired you are, Jaxon, so you just lie there and let me make you feel good." He brought his finger to his mouth, his tongue capturing the juices. Lucian inhaled, taking in her spicy scent.

Her eyes darkened, trembling with a terrible need. "Lucian." There was an ache in her voice.

His answer was to lift her legs to his shoulders, his tongue stroking a hot caress along the tiny curls. She cried out, the sound husky, needy, a soft, wordless plea. His tongue probed deeply, plunged and retreated, in a wicked game that brought her to mindless rapture. Her body tightened, spun out of control, fast and furious, catching her unaware in a shattering series of earthquakes.

Lucian dropped her legs to his waist and thrust his throbbing, aching shaft against her hot, moist entrance, watching as he slowly began to push into her. She was small, tight, and so hot he shuddered with pleasure as her body took more of him, inch by slow inch. She was spiraling again, her body going up in flames, colors dancing and spinning, gasping for air, for mercy. "More," he said softly. "You can take all of me. I belong here, inside you, my love. I belong." His sanctuary, his haven.

He began to move, thrusting with long, hard strokes, driving deeper, welding them together, building the friction at a furious pace, unrelenting in his need. He indulged himself, taking her body for his own, giving her his body without reservation, bringing her again and again to shuddering ecstasy. He felt the building heat, could feel the endless clenching of her muscles around him, tight and hot, gripping and milking until he was no longer in control, until her body took his soaring with her.

Jaxon was exhausted, unable to move, her eyes closed, her body rippling endlessly, tight around Lucian, holding him inside her. He leaned forward, his tongue catching the bead of sweat on the tip of one breast. The action sent her body rippling again, but she was so tired she could only lie beneath him, going up in flames. He lay over her, breathing her in, her small body swallowed by his. Their hearts beat as one; their lungs labored together. Jaxon slowly allowed her fingers to loosen her hold on the wood, her arms falling limply to her sides. She couldn't find the energy to hold Lucian to her; she could only enjoy the sensations his mouth at her breast was producing. They lay together, their bodies entwined, his mouth nuzzling gently on her in silent worship. She slid into a hazy, dreamy state and was shocked when he stirred, reluctantly pulling his body from hers.

Lucian sat up, his arm curving around her shoulders to lift her, cradling her close. They had made it to the cave just as dawn was breaking. Aboveground, the sun would be climbing high now. Because Jaxon had expended so much energy her first time flying, she had been tired when they arrived. Their lovemaking had been long and rough. He could feel her exhaustion beating at him. "We should seek rest."

Her heart jumped wildly. There was no sleeping chamber here with a cozy bed. She knew he would bury them both deep within the earth and make no apologies. The idea was unsettling even as tired as she was. "I'm very different from other Carpathian women, aren't I?" She sounded sad. It bothered her that she couldn't readily adjust to all the necessities of her new life.

He found her mouth with his, his tongue dancing with hers, searching, probing deeply, loving her, reassuring her. His eyes were glittering possessively as he lifted his head. "You are different in a lot of ways, angel, but not in the ways you think. Our women would never hunt the vampire with their lifemates as you wish to do. Hunting the vampire is more than a wish to you. If it were only that, I would have denied you the opportunity. It is a need, a part of your personality, your nature. I can only accept you as you are, not as I would have you be, quiet and secure within my safeguards. That is the only difference that in any way calls for me to compromise."

She shook her head in denial, then nuzzled his chest, her eyelids drooping. "I'm a cop. I've always been a cop. It's who I am."

"You are my lifemate, not a cop. When we hunt, we hunt together, but you will follow my lead." He made it more than a statement; it was a command, an order. He said it with centuries of authority in his voice.

Jaxon leaned against him, pressing her petite body into the sheer masculine strength of his. If he wanted to give her orders, it didn't really matter. She would never go out hunting vampires without him. The idea was terrifying. She had led her share of men because she was brilliant at what she did. But she could concede leadership in the hunt for vampires to Lucian. He had been battling the undead for centuries and was a master at it. "All right, Lucian, just get it over with. Let's go to sleep before I fall over."

Lucian found her mouth again tenderly. "You will be safe, my love."

"I know I will," she murmured, her mouth against his neck, her long lashes sweeping down. "I just don't want to know the details. I'm finding some things are best left alone."

"You are safe within my care," he repeated, wanting her to believe. And she would always be safe. He *cherished* her. His every thought was of her. He would have done anything to make her transition easier, but he also wanted it to be at her pace. He bent his head to hers slowly, his smoldering gaze on her soft mouth. He ached for her. Even with the sun rising higher and higher and his body turning to a leaden weight, he still ached for her. He kissed her gently, leisurely, as if he had all the time in the world to savor her.

Jaxon relaxed against him, giving herself up to the wonder and magic of his mouth. It was the last thing she remembered, the last thing she took with her into her sleep. *Sleep well, angel. Take me with you deep into your dreams. You will not awaken until I command you. You will have no fear of the earth and its welcoming arms.*

Lucian's mouth captured her last breath as she suc-

309

cumbed to his demand that she sleep. His gut clenched hotly, every muscle in his body taut all over again. She was so beautiful, so perfect. He would never get used to the idea that she put his desires, his safety, and his happiness before her own. She watched out for him, worried about him, needed him. A soft groan escaped. She thought only good of him; she didn't have the sense to be afraid. It didn't occur to her that he would be capable of mass destruction should anything ever threaten her. She trusted him implicitly. She had complete faith in him. She had no idea what that did for him. For centuries, the very people he had dedicated his life to protecting had feared him. Jaxon had every reason to be afraid of him, of the changes he had forced on her, yet she gave him her trust, and this filled him with humility.

Lucian? Gabriel's voice startled him. It came from far away. *You have need of me?* The sun was already set where Gabriel dwelled, and night was upon him.

I have a need, but not of you, Gabriel. Is all well with you and Francesca and with Skyler? What about little Tamara? Tamara, Lucian knew, was still very much at risk.

Jacques and Shea Dubrinsky, the Prince's brother and his lifemate, have arrived to help us in finding a way to keep Tamara alive. She is doing very well. Skyler is quite brilliant, but you know that. She misses you but is happy that you touch her mind often. Francesca is much happier with Shea here. Shea has developed a formula, and it seems to be helping.

I will come to you should there be need, Lucian assured him unnecessarily. He had not yet told Jaxon about the terrible reality of having a much-wanted child and watching it fade away despite everything the healers could do. He, like so many other Carpathians, was counting on Shea, Francesca, and Gregori to find answers to why their kind lost so many females soon after their birth, threatening the continuation of the species.

I thank you for that. You worry for your lifemate.

I will protect her. I can do no other.

I will aid you should there be need. Gabriel made the identical offer instantly.

Lucian smiled, grateful that he could feel the intensity of his love for his twin brother, not just a remembered emotion, but one heartfelt and real. *I know you would come, Gabriel, and I will call should I have need. Francesca and the children have a greater need at this time. Jaxon and I are followed by three of the undead. Jaxon fears them less than the human monster we are attempting to lure.*

Perhaps she has good reason to fear the human. Watch yourself. I could leave now and be there on the next rising.

Thank you for the offer, but you are needed there. I can take care of these evil ones with no problem.

And the human?

Do not start, Gabriel. It is bad enough to have my lifemate think such a puny one could defeat me. I do not need you to side with her.

Soft laughter met his statement. The hour of the day was beginning to tell heavily on Lucian. He was an ancient and very susceptible to the effects of daylight. His body needed the earth. He set more safeguards and his warning system in place to keep humans and immortals alike from their resting place. Gliding out of the cavern of pools, Jaxon cradled in his arms, Lucian followed a narrow tunnel leading deeper beneath the earth. He avoided the molten pools and found rich, dark soil teeming with healing, rejuvenating minerals and opened a bed several feet under its richness. As he floated into the beckoning arms of the earth, he focused his attention on scanning the surrounding areas. He held Jaxon to him, curling his body around hers protectively. He went to sleep with a smile of satisfaction touching his mouth.

311

*   *   *

The sun tried valiantly to bathe the mountains with light, striving to reach through the heavy foliage to the ground below. At noon, when the sun was at its highest point, the winds began to pick up. Clouds gathered, moving in from the south. By four the clouds were heavy enough to dim the light of the sun. At five the wind was strong enough to bend the trees and throw the branches into a wild frenzy of dancing. Deep beneath the earth, in the very bowels of the mountain, Lucian stirred awake.

He moved the soil above him easily and stretched with lazy pleasure, his fingers unerringly finding the silken strands of Jaxon's hair. She lay perfectly still, her face pale, no discernible heartbeat in her body. Gently he extracted himself from where their bodies lay entwined. He floated to the surface and stood quietly for a moment, debating. He did not want her to awaken and find him gone while she lay buried in the earth. She was not ready for such an experience. Yet his command had sent her to sleep, and she should not wake until he gave the order. Technically. A ripple of unease touched his mind. Jaxon was strong and intelligent, a force to be reckoned with already, and she was but a mere fledgling. She had proven to him time and time again that she always did the unexpected.

He turned his head slowly, his mind settling on the battle plan. The most important thing to do was to find the master vampire's lair. Now, before the sun had a chance to set, he would be locked in the earth. He would know Lucian was hunting him, and the vampire would be snarling beneath the mountain, counting the seconds until he was released. As Lucian moved upward through the caves and tunnels, he intensified the storm, stalling it over the mountains to aid him in his quest. With the clouds so dark and full, his eyes could take the light without the help of dark glasses.

He exploded into the sky just as the clouds burst open and rain poured down in silvery sheets. He began his search, sending his senses miles throughout the sky to scan the surrounding area.

The vampires themselves would be difficult to detect. Small things were more likely to give them away: an inordinate amount of insects, bats uneasy within their normal setting, a multitude of rats gathering together. The vampires would be spread out and unknowing of each other's lair. The master vampire would secret himself far from the others, not trusting his safety to anyone. The undead thrived on the pain and suffering of others, were wholly evil and capable of nothing but deceit and treachery. They would never trust each other with such important information as the location of their resting places.

He found a faint taint of power in the mountain to the north of his position. It was an indication of one of the lesser beings. No ancient would make such a mistake. Lucian proceeded away from the area to widen his search. A slight disturbance among the bats gave away the second vampire. He was using a cave high up in the southern tip of the mountain. He turned his attention to the west and east.

Jaxon was aware of nothing at all. But then a dark, oily thickness, insubstantial really, began to penetrate the layers of earth to find its way down to her. It seeped into her pores and saturated her mind, moved through her body to take possession of her heart, squeezing hard like a hand massaging. One beat. A second. Jaxon woke with sweat pouring from her body, with heavy earth surrounding her. She could feel every inch, every foot of soil and instinctively knew precisely how deep she was buried.

Lucian knew the exact moment Jaxon awakened. He was truly astonished by her built-in radar system, by the intensity of their connection, that allowed her to override his command to sleep. Admittedly he was not using his full power, but Jaxon was not his puppet, and he would never treat her like one. He waited, a quiet shadow in her mind to see her reaction. If it was necessary, he could strike swiftly, taking control of her.

At first the sound of her heart was like thunder in her ears, such a roaring it was nearly deafening. Her throat was closed, suffocating her. There was no air to breathe; she was buried alive. Instinctively she brought up her hands to try to scratch her way out of her grave. Her mind was a chaos of screams and panic and fear. But the thick, oily darkness invading her soul was overpowering, pushing aside even her panic. Something was out there, malevolent, dark and evil, something lurking in wait for . . . *Lucian.*

Her heart stopped for a moment, then began to beat. It was hot beneath the earth, but her mind was still and calm, able to function and compute. There was a way to move this dirt. Not move through it, but actually move it. Lucian had done so when she first discovered they slept beneath the earth. What to do? She needed to think it through. It took tremendous discipline to ignore her mind telling her she couldn't breathe with the layers of soil crushing her, suffocating her.

She formed the picture in her mind, precise, meticulous in every detail, the earth opening all the way to the surface, a large enough area that she could escape the confining space. To her surprise and intense relief, the soil above her parted neatly to reveal the high ceiling of the cavern. Slightly shocked, Jaxon drew in great gasping breaths, filled her lungs, and lifted her face to try to get some relief from the vicious heat. She was awake again despite Lucian's command to sleep. What had been strong enough to call her?

Jaxon floated to the cavern floor, sheer elation carrying her to the heated pools. She began to run along the narrow passageway. Only one thing could wake her, only one need. Something was fixating on Lucian, threatening him in some way. She felt that dark malevolence, felt the greedy evil reaching out with unseen hands, poised to strike. *Lucian, you skunk. So much for sharing the hunt with your partner. You thought you'd just take care of the problem while I was sleeping, didn't you? You cad. You're in great danger.* The tunnel was branching in all directions. It was frustrating trying to remember which passage led where.

Great danger? I do not believe I would use the word great, *my beloved lifemate.* There was not one iota of remorse in his voice. If anything, there was a thread of mocking male amusement.

That soft sound set her teeth on edge and made her more determined than ever to find her way out of the maze and help him. She closed her eyes and concentrated on Lucian. The scent of him, the heat of him. His energy and power.

It amazed her, the amount of information flooding to her immediately. She knew the way out instantly, unerringly. She knew exactly where he was and what he was doing. She sensed he was seeking the lair of the master vampire, that he was moving slowly, quartering an area he found suspect. As she moved swiftly through the mountain, working her way toward the top to the entrance, she cast her net into the skies to search also. Her body was like a tuning fork for something evil.

More toward your left, Lucian. She relayed the information automatically without thinking about it. He would have known the moment she awakened, she was certain of it. He had probably aided her in stilling the chaos of her mind. She was grateful he hadn't interfered, allowing her to open the earth herself. Even as she moved ever upward through the massive bulk of the mountain, she frowned. Perhaps he had helped her even then. *You're close to the entrance. I can feel his loathing, his rage. He is very close to you, Lucian.*

I have it. What do you think you are doing? As always Lucian's voice was gentle and calm. He was tranquil in the midst of extreme danger.

She caught a glimpse of a solid granite wall, seemingly undisturbed for centuries. As before when she "saw" through Lucian's eyes, it was disorienting. Jaxon stumbled and caught at the rock passageway for support. *Be careful, Lucian. He knows you're there. He's watching you somehow.*

He is locked in the earth until the sun sets. And the sun is very close to setting. You did not answer me. What are you doing?

Coming to help you, of course. It's called backing up your partner. She explained the concept sweetly, enunciating each word in her mind. *Perhaps you remember it. I seem to recall you worked with your brother, so you must have known how to work together. We're partners. It means you don't run off and leave without the other one's knowledge.*

Soft laughter brushed at her mind. Lucian couldn't help himself. She filled him with warmth in any circumstance. He surveyed the cliff wall carefully. *As you have the habit of doing?* He breathed the words in her mind even as he began to move in a peculiar pattern, his feet finding a rhythm centuries old. It was an ancient safeguard, not especially strong and set mainly as a delaying tactic. It required little effort but a great deal of time to unravel. He glanced skyward. He would never get to the evil one before the sun sank from the sky.

It didn't make any difference to him. His pace remained the same, steady so that he made no mistakes, a deliberate, precise set of movements designed to negate what the vampire had wrought. Lucian was not deceived by the primitive structure of the safeguard. He had infinite patience and even more confidence. The only worry he had was Jaxon. She would not stay idly by, safe somewhere, while he hunted and destroyed the undead. She was determined to aid him.

Don't worry, Lucian, I am learning quite a bit from your memories. All you have to do is direct my actions as you did your brother's. I am quite capable of doing what he did. There was no hesitation in her voice. She considered it a duty, a responsibility. He had no doubt she meant what she said.

The first safeguard had been neutralized. He began the more complicated regimen of dismantling the trap set for unwary hunters. This pattern was a much more intricate and difficult one. He had not seen it used before, but that mattered little to him. It was an illusion hiding the entrance to the cave, an illusion using a deadfall and more to guard the opening. As he began to unravel it, the granite creaked and moaned in response. A shower of boulders fell from above him to crash in the spot where he was working. Lucian merely leaped to one side, the movements of his hands continuing despite the assault from above. As the avalanche showered down, increasing in strength and size, Lucian simply took a moment to provide himself with an invisible shelter to deflect the rocks.

Jaxon gasped, feeling the hatred and anger issuing in waves from beneath the earth. She was still some distance from the site, moving toward him, yet the malevolence the creature was projecting made her physically ill. She knew Lucian was in grave danger from the malicious monster, that it was bending its mind and powers, its will toward destroying Lucian. The closer she got to its lair, the more fouled the air became. It was thick with poisonous, noxious gas, a toxic combination of evil and hatred that threatened to choke her. It was directed at Lucian, the cloud even thicker where he stood, so that no air could displace it despite the wildness of the wind.

Christine Feehan

She could feel how calm Lucian was, with no panic, no sense of haste, just his tranquil mind working at a steady pace to unlock the opening to the lair of the hideous abomination that waited within with dripping fangs and murder on its mind. Even trained as she had been to work through pain and discomfort, Jaxon knew she never would have been able to force herself to enter the realm of the undead had it not been for Lucian.

Nothing seemed to bother him. He acted as if he didn't notice the noxious odor, the thick, poisonous gas creeping around him. He simply worked quietly and efficiently. Jaxon made a concentrated effort to do the same, using Lucian as an anchor while she moved within the field of evil gas.

Approach from the south, angel. He will sense your presence, and you will feel his triumph. He will perceive you as the weak link he can escape through. He knows I cannot possibly reach him in time to confront him in his lair, so he will come after you, thinking to delay me with his traps. You must be ready for him. Once he is in your vision, you cannot lose sight of him. Do you understand me? If you are to do this thing, you must do exactly as I tell you.

This monster scares me to death. So, believe me, whatever you say goes.

He will try to capture you. If he cannot and he sees he cannot escape, he will be very dangerous and will certainly attempt to destroy you.

I trust you, Lucian, Just tell me what to do to delay him long enough for you to get to him. Jaxon's heart was pounding now, and she deliberately took a few calming breaths to steady herself. She had successfully opened her earthen grave on her own. She had to believe that. She had moved through the mountain with incredible speed, following the mental path Lucian had left behind to guide her. She was streaking through the sky in the form of insubstantial mist, again holding the image in her own mind, even as she spoke with Lucian. She could do whatever he needed her to do. This was no different than police work. She had to look at it that way. Her partner needed back up.

You could remain safe, as you should. Lucian made the suggestion gently, almost absently, as he unraveled the second lock. At once huge scorpions boiled out of a tiny crack that was just beginning to form in the rock. It was a thin gap, but great sheets of the poisonous insects welled out of the opening, spilling over one another, extending their tails at Lucian in an effort to reach him.

Jaxon choked back a cry of alarm as she caught the impression of the creatures from Lucian's mind. They moved much faster than she had thought possible. And they were very ugly and frightening. It was Lucian's soft laughter that relaxed her, allowing her to continue to her appointed spot. He never changed, never appeared disturbed by anything the vampire threw at him. It had all been done before, all been seen before. Lucian reacted to the swarm of insects with his lightning-fast reflexes, rising into the air, breathing fire as if he were a dragon, destroying the swarm in a smoking pile of ashes.

It is merely a ploy to slow me down, he sent the assurance to Jaxon.

It could be a fairly deadly ploy. Jaxon shimmered into solid form on the south side of the mountain, taking deep breaths to remain calm. At once she was sorry. The air was so thick and noxious, she felt sick. It was better than insects, though. If a swarm of giant scorpions had spilled out of the mountain to greet her, she would have gone running for cover instantly.

You are much braver than you think.

I hope you're right. She knew exactly what he was doing now. He was the one holding the merge, not she. She touched his mind occasionally, but Lucian was the one to stay linked, a shadow in her mind. He was unraveling the next lock, reversing the vampire's intricate pattern, his eye on the setting sun.

She felt the vampire reaching for her, trying to swamp her with fear, with terror. Jaxon remained immune, able to block out the waves of fear in the same way she had the poisonous gas the creature was excreting into the air. Jaxon simply held fast to Lucian, wishing desperately that she had a gun or two, even though she knew bullets wouldn't do much good against the undead. A weapon would still give her a sense of security, and she needed that right now. The sun was sinking fast.

At once the wind picked up, the storm increasing in strength, becoming violent, hurtling branches and foliage in all directions. Now the mountain erupted, spewing hot lava at Lucian, the mixture shooting into the sky, seeking its target. The molten, spewing, fiery rocks forced Lucian to take cover. Jaxon held her ground, scanning the skies, waiting quietly for the fiend to show himself.

The creature burst from the ground only a few feet from her, with no real warning, flying straight at her with outstretched talons. With dirt raining down on her, Jaxon had only a split second to react, saw only jagged brown teeth and red-rimmed eyes and razor-sharp claws coming at her. She hurtled herself to one side, rolling away, careful to keep her eyes on the hideous creature. It wasn't easy, moving so fast and keeping her gaze fixed on the monster. He was grotesque, the most loathsome thing she had ever seen. The vampire's breath nearly knocked her out. He reeked of decay.

The undead whirled around, his arm extended toward her, lengthening, growing before her horrified stare, thin and misshapen, reaching to grab her. She forced herself to remain completely still, trusting in Lucian. At once she felt incredible power flowing within her, through her. The vampire nearly reached her with one long fingernail. It was grotesquely twisted, long and ugly, a dull yellowish gray. It came within an inch of her skin. Smoke curled up black and strong, and the nail withered black, hissing in the cold night air. The charred blackness spread like wildfire, racing over the gray hand and up the gnarled arm. The vampire screamed, the high-pitched sound hurting her ears.

Jaxon stood her ground, not moving an inch, staring at the monster. His eyes were black empty holes, his nose gone, flesh sloughing off his bones. He hissed at her, an ugly sound of hatred and defiance, a promise of retaliation. Flames erupted on the creature's body, breaking out all over as it rose, screaming, into the sky. The rains pouring forth from the clouds seemed only to add fuel to the flames.

The vampire raced away from Jaxon, moving across the night sky in a fiery streak of orange and red. Jaxon sagged against a thin tree trunk, her legs rubbery. The monster was fleeing, terrified of Lucian's power. Even as she allowed her breath to escape, she felt the next ripple of evil in the air.

Chapter Fifteen

Lucian! Do you feel that? The others, his friends, have come to aid him. Jaxon cried out the warning, her eyes anxiously searching the sky in an attempt to spot the fleeing vampire. If the others had arrived to aid him, the master vampire would certainly return to fight.

The undead do not have friends. Each is out for his own gain. The master vampire will use the others to wear me down. The others can be used by us.

How? What do we do?

They are seeking you, my love. They wish to find a woman to remove their sins and recover their souls. It is impossible, but they will not accept that.

What should I do?

There was warmth filling her mind, strength pouring into her Lucian was close by; she could feel him.

Just look beautiful and sexy. Choose one to be flirtatious with, but do not allow either to touch you, not even a slight scratch. Keep both of them in sight at all times.

And my big he-man will come and rescue me? She was

annoyed, and it showed in her sarcastic tone.

His laughter was soft and sexy in her mind, brushing at her skin like gentle fingers. *They will most likely fight each other and save me the trouble. I will be waiting for the strong one.*

Then you think the ancient one will return.

Three against one? He will like the odds and come immediately.

Two. There are two of us. She was even more annoyed with him than ever.

A vampire would never expect a woman to participate in a battle, angel. It is not done. Our women are filled with compassion, not with a penchant for violence.

She wanted to stay irritated but found herself laughing instead. *Then he's in for a surprise, huh? But you think I have a penchant for violence? I've been incredibly sweet-natured, while you've been arrogant and impossible.*

You do not understand the difference between arrogance and confidence, but I will teach it to you.

I can't wait for the lesson. Jaxon's alarm system was working overtime now, the air becoming thick with waves of malevolence.

She searched the skies above her as she moved away from the trees so she had plenty of open space for maneuvering. It was strange to be facing an enemy as depraved as a vampire without so much as a weapon. For a moment her confidence wavered, but instantly she felt Lucian moving within her, strong and assured. He was very close by; his presence was too strong for him not to be near. That made her feel better, and she had his memories of many battles to draw on. While she waited out in the open under the drizzling sky, she examined as many of his encounters with the vampires as possible, paying close attention to the strategies Lucian had used with his brother. One of them often lay in wait while the other drew their enemy to them. Lucian was basically employing the same strategy.

A chilling wind blew through the very middle of the storm, settling close to earth only yards from where Jaxon stood. A tall, gaunt man shimmered into view. He was remarkably elegant and courtly-looking, his clothes impeccable, not at all what she had expected. He was rather pale, and his teeth gleamed at her when he smiled. He was handsome and compelling, much different from the others of his kind she had encountered. Watching his every movement closely, Jaxon searched his features for hidden signs of depravity.

He has only recently turned, angel, Lucian informed her softly. *Do not listen to his voice with a human ear,* he added as a caution.

The vampire bowed from his waist. "Good evening, ma'am. This is an unseemly place for a woman to be alone." His voice seemed soft and musical.

You are hearing him as he wishes you to do so. He can manipulate with his voice alone.

It was Lucian's voice that allowed her to unmask the undead and his illusion of soft gentleness. Lucian's voice was purity itself, the sound so perfect it was almost not of the world. Now, in contrast, the vampire's tone grated like fingernails on a chalkboard.

Jaxon tilted her head a bit coquettishly. "I happen to like the peace of the mountains. Even in the storm, it is beautiful up here. Where did you come from? Is there a town nearby?"

The vampire moved slightly, a stirring of strength, his eyes glittering and red-rimmed. "Where is the one who would protect you?"

Jaxon shrugged. "He often leaves for long absences. One of power challenged him, and Lucian doesn't like to be challenged."

An elegant eyebrow shot up. "Lucian? You have named

one long thought dead. This cannot be. Lucian is vampire. All Carpathians know this."

"I know only that he calls himself Lucian and says I am to stay with him always. He doesn't treat me the way I thought he would."

"Tell me what your name is."

"Jaxon." She moved away from him, shifting to one side and back to maintain distance as he glided forward. She moved with grace, with feminine, sensuous gestures that kept the vampire's attention centered directly on her. Her stomach was knotting, clenching and unclenching. She made a concentrated effort to keep her hands at her sides. She felt Lucian in her mind, strong and powerful and completely confident. There was no way she could be anything but confident herself. They were one being, one mind, and one heart and soul.

"Who are you?" Jaxon sounded excessively flirty. She felt Lucian wince and stopped herself from smiling.

The vampire bowed again, his manner as courtly as ever. "I am Sir Robert Townsend."

Jaxon widened her eyes to stare up at him in feigned awe. "You're a knight? For real?"

Overhead, the tree branches shook and trembled. From the top of the trees a second male descended. This one was as tall and thin and pasty as the legendary Dracula had been described. When he smiled, his teeth appeared jagged and stained. His eyes were flat and cold yet glowed a fiery red. His gaze was on the other vampire. "Good evening, Robbie. I hope you are not regaling the young lady with your lies, trying to impress her with false titles."

A slow hiss escaped Townsend's throat. Red flames began to dance in the depths of his eyes. "Leave this place, Phillipe. You are not wanted here. The lady and I are talking. Go and find yourself your own woman."

The newcomer smiled, a grim challenge, very clearly a warning. "I have tolerated your presence, Robbie, only because you could be of use. But now I have what I have searched for, and you are more trouble than you are worth. I say to you, be gone."

Townsend hissed again, a growl rumbling deep within his throat. He took a step closer to Jaxon. She was careful not to be caught between them. It would be difficult to defend herself against two of them; she would much rather face one at a time. Her insides were trembling with the realization of the monsters she was facing. *Not human.* They were evil, two of them stalking her and a third somewhere unseen. Close. She could feel he was close.

"The woman has come here to be with me, Phillipe, not with you. I have put up with your ridiculous ego for far too long."

Jaxon sent Sir Robert Townsend a dynamite smile, lashes sweeping down. The tip of her tongue came out to moisten her bottom lip, calling attention to its lush fullness.

Phillipe snarled and leaped at the younger vampire, flying through the air with incredible speed, faster than Jaxon expected. She had seen the memories in Lucian's mind, but the real thing was terrifying. The two vampires came together in a clash of fangs and claws. The sight was horrifying. As they fought each other, they continually shifted shape, one animal after another, hideous growls issuing from their throats.

Jaxon stayed very still, unable to look away from the two writhing bodies covered with fur and rippling with everything from barbs to horns. It was something out of a horror film. Blood sprayed in wide arcs. Instinctively she leaped back out of range of the poisonous liquid. She bit her lip hard, focusing on the pain to keep herself from being mesmerized by the scene.

The only warning she received was the sudden slamming of a vise around both her ankles, and abruptly she was being sucked beneath the ground. Without conscious thought Jaxon dissolved into droplets of water. Afterward neither of them knew who had done it, Lucian or Jaxon, only that evaporation had been uppermost in her mind, in their mind. Jaxon shot into the sky, streaming upward into the bank of thick mist and fog Lucian had immediately provided for her to merge with. From her vantage point she watched the battle unfold, watched as Lucian materialized for a brief second only to dive beneath the soil and move like lightning through the earth toward the fleeing master vampire.

The two lesser vampires were raking each other with teeth and claws. Crimson blood was spraying in all directions. Overhead, lightning arced from dark cloud to dark cloud and then slammed to earth in jagged bolts At once Jaxon smelled charred flesh and saw sparks erupting all around the two vampires. One screamed, a high-pitched cry of terrible pain, and when the smoke and sparks cleared, Jaxon could see the creature dragging itself across the ground, a huge gaping hole through its chest where its heart had been The searing heat from the lightning bolt had cauterized the monster's flesh, so there was no poisonous blood, but she sensed it was still dangerous.

The second vampire, Sir Robert Townsend, lay motionless, smoke still rising from his chest, where an identical hole had incinerated his heart. Jaxon studied Phillipe as he crawled across the ground moaning and hissing. The sound hurt her ears. Being mist, she had no way to muffle the noise until it occurred to her to turn down the volume. Part of her was still locked with Lucian, monitoring his progress as he hurtled through the earth after the undead. She tried not to be distracted, concentrating on what to do about Phillipe. He should have been dead, lying motionless along with Townsend.

Perhaps the lightning bolt didn't hit his heart straight on. If any part of it is still functional, he can repair himself. Do not allow him to burrow into the soil.

She recognized Lucian's confidence in her, and it gave her the sense of partnership she needed with him. Jaxon focused on the vampire. He was indeed, reaching for handfuls of mineral-rich soil and packing his gaping wound. Using Lucian's memory as a guide, she centered her energy on the sky above her, felt the power moving within her. Even as she did so, a part of her found the beat of the vampire's heart. It was unlike that of a human being. It seemed cold, dead, with no real rhythm, rather a sluggish, irregular flow of fluid through the chamber. She gathered together the electrical particles in the air, moving them with her mind, shaping them into a fiery orange and red ball. When it was large enough for its purpose, she focused on Phillipe. At her silent command he turned his body toward the sky, far too weak from his hideous wounds to fight the compulsion. The ball hurtled from above and struck him, searing easily through his chest and incinerating his heart in one blow.

Jaxon found herself sitting on the ground several yards from the two bodies. She was exhausted and pale, unable to find the strength to stand. It had taken unbelievable energy to use her mind to accomplish such physical tasks. And she knew from studying Lucian's memories that she was not yet finished. Both bodies and any evidence of the battle and all droplets of blood had to be completely obliterated.

She was suddenly aware of hunger moving through her body like a living, breathing entity. Her cells were crying out for sustenance, for replenishment after her sleep, after the battle, after using such energy

Do not! The order was sharp in her mind.

It took Jaxon only a moment to realize that her weakness and hunger were affecting Lucian's own abilities. She immediately thought of power and strength, of love and achievement, leaving no room for anything else in her mind. She found, as she did so, that her own strength returned. She was able to once more gather the particles of electric energy together and direct them to the bodies, leaving only fine ash to be scattered by the wind. Every droplet of blood was found and eradicated, all evidence of the existence of vampires or Carpathians banished. When it was over, Jaxon sat in the open meadow with the cleansing rain pouring down on her upturned face and the wind driving out all thoughts other than supporting Lucian in his battle with the most evil monster of all.

Lucian knew as he tracked the vampire through the newly dug tunnels that the vampire was extremely dangerous. This one was old, an ancient of incredible skill and power. He had eluded justice for many centuries and would not be easy to kill. Without thinking, he instructed Jaxon in the same way he had always instructed Gabriel. *Get ahead of him. He is moving up toward the surface again. He will attempt to rise approximately four hundred yards or so from the rock outcroppings to your left. You must drive him back toward me.*

No problem. Jaxon had no idea what she was going to do to stop the creature from surfacing, but if Lucian said it had to be done, then so be it. She streaked across the distance, judging where they were by the vibrations beneath the earth. If she listened, she could hear the ground groaning at the touch of the tainted being as it pushed its way through. She actually felt the dirt under her feet shift and knew the vampire was racing toward her to get to the surface far away from Lucian.

Jaxon went skyward, sending a sheet of fire sweeping the ground, flaming everything in its path. She knew she scored by the shriek and noxious odor that followed, then the sudden silence, as if the thing had burrowed back into the earth. Just to be on the safe side, she directed down flames as long as she could before sheer exhaustion sent her reeling to earth.

Something was wrong. Lucian had pulled away from

their mind merge. She was left alone in the silence of the storm. Too tired to move, Jaxon couldn't summon the necessary energy to join with Lucian. Without warning, tentacles erupted all over the ground, great spiked arms like those of an octopus but sharp and pointed like spears. They broke the surface everywhere, reaching, writhing, searching for her. Jaxon leaped up, sheer terror lending her the strength to move, when one wrapped around her ankle. She stared down at it in horror. Even as she did so, the appendage withered, shrunk, and fell harmlessly away from her.

Jaxon whirled around and almost ran right into a tall, gaunt man. He was youthful at one moment, ancient the next. He looked handsome, then hideous and evil. He smiled at her. "I trust you are finished with your pitiful attempts to harm me. It is impossible. I am much too powerful. In the end, my dear, you will pay for your sins against me." His voice was pitched low. It might have seemed beautiful to other ears, but to Jaxon it was an assault.

She moved slowly, keeping her hands down and at her sides. She had to avoid the searching spearlike arms yet keep her gaze fixed solidly on her enemy. And he was her enemy. As sweet as his voice sounded, as gentle as his face tried to appear, Jaxon knew this was a monster without honor, without soul. She tilted her chin, her body as still as the mountains around them. Inside herself she found a calm, tranquil pool and simply stayed there while the shell that was her body faced the vampire.

He smiled at her, his teeth gleaming like needles. "You think that he will come for you, but I have ensured that he is trapped for all time beneath the earth. You will do as I say, and I will take that into account in my dealings with you." His voice was mesmerizing, powerful.

Jaxon kept her eyes fixed on him, the tension all at once draining from her body. She began to laugh softly. "You can't possibly believe that your voice can make me believe the impossible, can you? Lucian is not trapped in the earth. He is everywhere, all around you." She waved an arm, and the ancient hunter sprang up at every point, east, west, north, and south. He was in the clouds above their heads and leaning against the rocks with lazy indolence. Lucian, tall and handsome, his black eyes glittering.

The vampire whirled around, his long black cape swirling like a magician's. Jaxon took the opportunity to put a little more distance between them. The large head of the undead began to undulate in a reptilian manner, a long, slow hiss escaping him, betraying his anger. The red-rimmed eyes settled on her like a suffocating cloak of malignancy. "You think to frighten me with your childish tricks." He waved his arms, and the images faded away as if they had never been. Even as he did so, scorpions erupted out of the holes the octopus arms had made. Scores of them blackened the earth, making the surface of the soil itself seem to be moving toward her. She could hear the clicking as the horrible insects rushed at her.

Jaxon tried to leap skyward, but something oppressive forced her back down. It seemed there was no escaping the swarm coming at her, their stingers poised and ready. For one beat her heart slammed painfully in her chest, and then she relaxed, smiling sweetly at the vampire. "We are reduced to this then?" She waved a hand, and the thick onslaught of scorpions wavered, began to turn on one another, and thrust their stingers into one another. "It's amusing but rather silly."

"Come to me." He held out his hands to her.

Jaxon's eyebrows shot up. "Just like that? You think to win so easily? I don't think I want to make it that easy. You would never fully appreciate me." She was trying to ignore the stains on his daggerlike nails. The sight of the dark brownish color turned her stomach How many humans killed? How many hunters had he destroyed? How much innocent blood was on his hands? "I'm not so easily won." She knew Lucian would come. *Knew it.*

Jaxon wanted to reach for him, to merge her mind with his, but she was too exhausted. She conserved her energy, certain she would need it soon enough. Whatever the vampire had done to trap Lucian, to delay him, would never hold him.

The wind rushed at her, a whirling minitornado that pushed and tugged at her, attempting to drive her toward the undead. The beauty of his face was beginning to disintegrate, his features going gray and slack, the flesh hanging loosely, as if he couldn't quite be bothered to keep up appearances. The bones of his skull were far more prominent now, his eyes sunken into dark, merciless pits. "You will do as I command."

"You think?" Jaxon began to laugh. "Do you know who he is?"

The vampire stirred, a rippling of his cloak, a gnashing of his teeth. "It does not matter. He will die like those who have come before."

"You really don't know, do you? How funny. He is Lucian. The ancient. The most famous of all hunters." She said it softly, sweetly, her voice nearly as gentle and pure as that she had heard Lucian use.

The vampire went very still except for a sudden pronounced tick under his left eye. "Lucian is long dead, I have heard it said. But I do not believe it. It is also said he is one of our kind. *That* I believe."

Jaxon shrugged, a delicate, feminine gesture. "Nevertheless, it is Lucian, and he is a hunter unsurpassed by any other." She lifted her arms just as she felt the connection with her lifemate once more, the complete merging, the strength pouring into her. She caught impressions of a terrible struggle, still fresh in his mind, yet he had been the one to wither the appendage when it had first claimed her, he had aided her in building illusions even as he fought for his life. Again she waved her arms, encompassing the entire surrounding area as she addressed the vampire. "Can't you feel his presence? Can't you feel him? He is everywhere, all at once. All around us. There is no way to defeat one such as Lucian." As she waved her hands, images of Lucian once more appeared in all directions, lined up like paper dolls, standing tall and straight, leaning lazily against the rocks, reaching up toward the clouds, arms dangling at his sides.

"Enough!" the vampire hissed, his voice grating and cracking with his smoldering anger. "I will not be swayed by your childish tricks. Repetition is boring. I am not amused."

"I was not attempting to amuse you," Jaxon said softly. "I was attempting to warn you. There is a difference."

The images of Lucian began to move, at first merely swaying back and forth with the wind, then actually circling, their feet picking up a peculiar dancing rhythm. Immediately the vampire focused on Jaxon, his lips pulling back into a snarl. "How dare you attempt to trick me!" The voice cracked and broke, all gravel and chalkboard. Saliva sprayed into the air as he spat the words at her.

The vampire glared at her, his eyes narrowing to focus on her throat, his expression grim and hateful as he deliberately closed off air to her lungs. Or attempted to. Jaxon merely felt the brush of his evil hands as he tried to strangle her from a distance, but then the grip was gone, and Jaxon watched the vampire's eyes widen in horror, his hands flying up to protect his own throat.

All around them the clones of Lucian began to laugh softly. "You know better than to lay your hand on the lifemate of another. The law is clear and ancient and as old as time itself. I remember you now. Matias. You fought in the battle against the Turks but deserted when the sun began to rise. You sought the earth far too early, and I knew then I would face you in our own battlefield."

The vampire was struggling to remove the invisible hands around his throat. His face was turning purple. All at once he dissolved, only to appear directly behind Jaxon, his arms attempting to whip around her, claws poised at her neck like a knife. The talons hit something solid and snapped off. His arms touched empty space.

Lucian spoke. "You can try, but you know it is futile. I would never allow my lifemate to be touched by one such as you."

Even as the clone spoke, the vampire was struck from behind, the blow delivered with enormous strength, the hand crashing through ribs, tearing through muscle and sinew straight toward the vulnerable heart. The vampire roared with pain and anger, whirling around to face the hunter, abandoning his hope of using Jaxon as a hostage. Some impenetrable force field surrounded the woman, and he had no time to examine it for weaknesses. Right now his life was hanging in the balance. As he turned, he raked out with his poisonous claws, uncaring where he struck, only seeking to inject venom into his adversary. Lucian was not behind him. Facing him were clones, or the illusions of clones. Ten of them standing like statues, no expression on their faces, no movement to betray if any were really alive.

Blood was pouring out of the gaping wound, and the vampire knew if he attempted to take to the air, the hunter could trail him easily. He had no choice but to make a stand and fight his way free. He stepped away from the woman and the compassion and sympathy in her large eyes. Looking at her hurt him, made him weak. She believed him already defeated. He was great and powerful and would not be lessened by a lifemate's belief in the hunter's abilities. Even as he told himself that, he knew he believed himself already defeated by Lucian. No one could destroy or escape such a powerful hunter. It couldn't be done.

Matias swore aloud, the sound of his voice crass and ugly in the clear air the wind of the storm had brought. He heard that jangle, the discordant note he could no longer prevent, no longer control. He saw himself clearly, the flesh sliding from his bones, the jagged, bloodstained teeth, and empty, dead eyes. His head swung from side to side in a desperate attempt to shake the truth from his sight. "Stop it! You are doing this to me, playing tricks in my mind. Is that how you defeat your enemies? Lucian the great. Lucian the powerful. You do not face us as is honorable. You use tricks and illusions."

One of the clones to the vampire's right bowed slightly from the waist. "Do you think to chastise me, old one? You have no honor, and there is no honor in facing one such as you. It is a complete waste of my time."

The vampire's poisonous blood was pouring into the ground, spreading out, searching for victims. It moved slowly, relentlessly toward Jaxon, inching its way as it soaked the ground, seeking her feet. The vampire swung around in a wide circle, allowing his blood to spray in a wide arc so that the droplets would be carried on the wind.

At once another clone lifted an arm and waved his hand casually to still the wind so that the poisonous drops fell to the ground. The paper dolls that were Lucian kept their carefully expressionless masks. Nothing seemed to touch them, to shake them.

The vampire screamed in frustration and hatred, whirling around faster and faster so that he stirred up the wind to a wild twister, blowing with hurricane force at the line of clones surrounding him. The figures shimmered into transparency but never quite dissolved completely. The attack came from above, the bird plummeting from the sky directly over the vampire, into the very core of the cyclone.

Jaxon covered her ears as the shrieking took on new

heights, scraping so hideously that she wanted to cry. Tears burned her eyes and tangled in her lashes. She wanted to run, to dissolve into mist and hide in the thick bank of fog. She had complete faith in Lucian, knew he would destroy the ancient vampire, but the unfamiliar sounds and sights of such a battle were terrifying.

Even as the thoughts entered her mind, she felt reassurance and warmth pouring into her. It was odd how much they were connected, how Lucian could be fighting for his life yet still know exactly how she was feeling and seek to soothe her. She knew she loved him at that moment. Really loved him. She wasn't obsessed or crazy or hypnotized. If there was a choice to be made, she would always choose to stay with him, not because of their intense chemistry, but because of who he was. Lucian. Thoughtful and kind and loving. She truly loved him.

The vampire slipped out from under the bottom edge of the whirling tornado, flying straight at Jaxon with his talons curved and sharpened, razor-edged. She stared at him impassively, although her heart was pounding. He intended to rip her heart out, to use her to destroy Lucian, his only real chance for revenge. His gaunt face was slashed with crimson lines; around his neck was a ring of ruby blood. Where his eyes had been were empty, lifeless sockets, bloody pits ravaged by the destroyer.

Even as the vampire launched himself at her, hatred and loathing issuing from his throat, malice in every line on his face, Lucian quietly materialized in front of her, a solid form, immovable, impenetrable, as still as the mountains around them. It happened so fast, the vampire had no time to turn, no time to counter. It impaled itself on Lucian's outstretched hand.

Jaxon turned her face away from the awful finality of that scene, but the sucking sound and the shrieks would echo for a long time in her head as Lucian extracted the heart of the creature and tossed it some distance from the body. There was no hatred or anger in Lucian, no remorse or guilt. There was no contempt or disgust or feelings of any kind that Jaxon could detect. He simply carried out his responsibility, separate from his emotions. It took her a few moments to realize he had not had access to emotion for centuries, and in battle his mind simply functioned as it had for over two thousand years.

Jaxon was so exhausted she could barely stumble her way to the rocks, where she could sit and escape the river of poisonous blood soaking the ground. She didn't want to see the vampire's body as it flopped and writhed on the ground, forever seeking its pulsating heart. She kept her face averted as Lucian gathered energy from the skies to direct straight to the heart so that it incinerated the organ into fine ash. She felt the heat from the white-hot ball of flames sweeping the ground to cleanse the earth of poisonous blood, knew the exact moment it destroyed the body.

The wind scattered the ashes and took the noxious odor far from them. Lucian walked over to her and sat down so that their bodies were touching. "It is done."

Jaxon heard his voice, soft and gentle as always, and when she looked up at him, his features were the same, beautifully masculine, rugged, perfect. Still, Jaxon felt his exhaustion, the hunger beating at him that he kept at bay with his strict discipline. It was there in his mind. She also found the reason for his delay in getting to the surface. The vampire had devised a trap, crude but effective. As Lucian had raced through the tunnels hollowed out by the vampire, a pack of rats had rushed behind him, attacking, biting, sent to slow him. As he fought them off, the tentacles shooting above ground had swarmed over and around him, pinning him in the earth long enough for the viper to inject a compound of poison into his system.

Jaxon gasped, her heart slamming hard at the explosion

of pain she discovered in his memories. It was a lethal poison, a complex mix the vampire had manufactured that moved with speed throughout the nervous system, causing excruciating pain as it ate at the cells, gobbling them up as it replicated itself. It had taken Lucian a few minutes to slow the poison, analyze it, and manufacture the antibodies necessary to drive it from his system.

"I can't believe you were able to do that," she said, awed. "How can anyone do that? Drive the poison out of his own body?"

"It is not unusual for our people to do such things. Sometimes it is done by pushing the poison out through the pores. This was more like a battle—indeed, in the midst of a battle—because the poison was a combination of several very lethal compounds. Rather extraordinary for a vampire to concoct. I am sorry I had to disconnect, but you would have felt the pain, and that I could not allow." His arm circled her slender shoulders. "Besides I knew you would handle things aboveground until I was able to reach you."

"You monitored me even though I couldn't tell what was happening to you," she said with some annoyance. "That's how you helped me, isn't it? How come you know what I'm doing when we aren't merged together? I ask just in case the information comes in handy some-day—for instance, when I get tired of your arrogance and decide to have a flaming affair. Or better yet, when I want to make certain you aren't running around on me." She was running her hands over his body to assure herself he was fine.

His hand cupped her chin so that he could look into her enormous eyes, eyes that held a hint of the fire within her. "You seem disturbed, honey." His voice was a drawl-ing, teasing caress.

"Absolutely I am," she vowed, but she had to look away from him or she would have burst out laughing.

Either that or kiss him. "You 'allow' me to be your partner, but you wrap me up in cotton wool as if I were a porcelain doll. I should know what's happening to you all the time, just in case you have need of me."

"I understand your nature, angel, probably better than you understand it, and I'm willing to provide you with everything you need to make you happy. But you have to understand, I will never allow your life to be placed in any real danger. If I cannot adequately protect you in a situation, you are not to be there. That is all there is to it. You are not to be there." He said it softly, gently, like a lover. His voice made her heart somersault and set butterflies fluttering in her stomach.

She sighed and shook her head, knowing she was lost. He didn't understand fairness, equality. He understood she was a woman. *His* woman. His nature demanded he protect her. To him, "compromise" meant she could be with him, even aid him, but only under specified conditions. Jaxon shook her head again before dropping it onto his arm. "I'm tired, Lucian. I've never been this tired before. How many hours before the sun rises and I can get some sleep?"

"You need to feed, my love. We both need to feed. To do the things we did requires tremendous energy. You do not have the stamina for such battles. You are very . . ." He trailed off when her head snapped up and she glared at him.

"If you say *small* or *little* or anything stupid like that, I'm going to show you that penchant for violence you say I have."

His long lashes swept down for a moment, concealing the laughter in his eyes. He felt that was far more prudent than revealing it. "I think we should get out of here and find prey."

She covered her face with her hands and groaned. "Did you have to use that word? You probably did it on purpose just to make me crazy. I don't hunt *prey*. People are not *prey*."

His immaculate white teeth gleamed at her. "I like stirring you up, honey. You have this one expression that does something to my insides." He stood up, a rippling of muscle and power, holding out a hand to her. "Come on, we have a long way to go this night. And do not feel too much pity for ones such as these." He waved his hand to encompass the ground where the three vampires had been slain. "This was the one who orchestrated the killings in the station house and went after your partner, Barry. These beings are without souls. They are wholly evil. I can feel your sorrow, my love, and I ache for you. I cannot bear it when you feel so sad."

She slipped her hand into his. "I'm fine, Lucian. I really am. There's just so much depravity in the world, so many sick people."

He brought her hand to the warmth of his mouth. "Not here. Not where we are."

Chapter Sixteen

Lucian returned to the underground cavern, entering silently. He had fed well, knowing Jaxon was in great need of sustenance. His first duty, his first *need*, was to provide for his lifemate. He had found several campers miles away from them and had drunk long and deep so that he could provide for Jaxon.

She was standing on a flat rock overlooking a pool. It was hot in the cave, and she had clothed herself in a long gossamer skirt that wrapped loosely around her slender figure, clinging here and there, giving him intriguing glimpses of her shapely legs when she moved. She wore a thin blouse knotted beneath her breasts, leaving her midriff bare. Little beads of sweat trickled down the valley between her breasts in invitation.

Lucian allowed his body to respond, hard and hot and needy. He glided across the cave, his shirt floating to the floor as he made his way to the rock and came up close behind her. Without touching her he bent to whisper close to her neck, "I can feel your hunger beating at me." His voice

341

was soft, seductive. His hands came down on her shoulders, moved lightly down her arms, traced the sweeping line of her back to her waist. Bare satin skin. He caressed the small of her back, the line of her hips beneath the gossamer skirt, moved his hands around to trace her buttocks—to find she wore nothing beneath the filmy material.

His breath caught in his throat, molten lava moving through his blood, spreading heat and fire to pool low in a hard, throbbing ache. She leaned into him, tilting her head back, exposing the vulnerable line of her throat, thrusting her breasts upward invitingly as she reached back to circle his neck with one arm.

"Smell my blood, angel, calling to you. I'm hot and hard, and I need you feeding." He needed the feel of her mouth on him, the erotic sensation of her sharing the essence of his body, his life.

Lucian circled her body to cup her breasts, to feel the weight of them through the thin fabric of her blouse. Only the small knot kept them from spilling free into his palms. "I want you, my love, right now," he whispered against the nape of her neck, one hand slipping down to follow the curve of her hip, to find the slit in the gossamer skirt so he could shape her leg, trace her thigh, move his hand to find the damp heat beckoning in the nest of tiny curls.

She moaned softly, his need merging with hers, his erotic images dancing in her mind, heightening her own desire, heating her blood. She pressed back against him, feeling the hard length of him, picking up the seductive rhythm of his fingers as he delved deep into her secret velvet sheath. Heat and fire. Flames licking over her skin. Her body coiling tighter and tighter. His desire pounding like a jackhammer in her head, in hers. She was aware of his hand at the knot beneath her breasts, the material suddenly gaping open, spilling her aching breasts into view of his hungry eyes. One hand found softness, his thumb caressing her nipple into a hard peak.

"Do you want me, Jaxon?" he asked softly, his voice husky with need.

"Very much," she replied, barely able to force the words out of her throat. "I need you, Lucian, need you in me, your blood flowing into me, your body in mine." And she did. More than anything, she needed to feel his body taking possession of hers. The heat of the cavern was in her body, all around her, the need for his blood in her mouth. She wanted him like this, hard and hot and hungry for her. She wanted those images dancing in her mind for all time.

She bent her head back even more as he leaned over her body, her arm bringing his head closer so that she could find his throat, his thick, muscular neck. Unerringly she found his pulse, pounding erratically, the telltale evidence of his intense desire. Against her back she could feel the heat of his skin, the muscles of his chest, the slamming of his heart in synchronization with hers. She arched her breast more fully into his palm, her hips finding the rhythm of his fingers. Her mouth moved over his pulse, breathed warm seduction, and felt it jump beneath her swirling tongue. She pressed back against him to feel him thick and hard through their clothes. Her teeth nipped, scraped, teased. She smiled when he groaned and offered her his throat, his palm grinding harder into the softness of her breast, his fingers stroking deeply. Her body clenched seductively around his fingers, taking him deeper, pushing against his hand for more. She moved in restless, wanton invitation against him.

She answered his tremendous need in the ancient way of their people, sinking her teeth deeply so that white-hot lightning danced through his body, through hers, lashing at them with fiery strokes. He groaned again, the sound, erotic and husky, tearing from his throat as her hips moved against his hand, her body shuddering with pleasure. The feel of her mouth was driving him crazy. His slacks were far too cumbersome against his sensitive skin, growing tighter and tighter as his body swelled with need. She fed sensuously, her body undulating against his, her buttocks pressing against him, the friction an enticement, a temptation.

She turned then in his arms, closing the pinpricks with a flick of her tongue, her hands at the buttons of his trousers, knuckles brushing his hot skin. His fist found her hair and clenched it tightly while he closed his eyes and threw back his head, savoring the freedom as he sprang free, hot, throbbing, thick, and hard. Her nails raked him lightly, her fingers moving over him in the exact way his mind anticipated. Her hands glided over his waist, his flat, hard belly, thumbs hooking in his trousers and pushing them down his thighs. The feel of her hands was driving him crazy. The very air around them was heavy with their combined scents, with the intensity of their hunger.

With his mind firmly in hers, she knew what he wanted, what his body was demanding, what was driving him over the edge. Lucian's body shuddered as her tongue caught the beads of sweat rolling down his belly, following the trail to find him swelling even more. He was velvet over iron, hot and needy.

Jaxon's mouth was tight and moist and perfect as he thrust helplessly over and over, his fists clenched in her hair. When he looked down at her, the sight was so erotic, her blouse open and her breasts thrust forward, her nipples hard and erect, the filmy skirt nearly transparent, its slit exposing her leg and thigh. Her hands were moving over him, never still, cupping his weight, delving into the firmness of his buttocks, running up and down the column of his thighs. She looked exotic and beautiful and was giving them both such exquisite pleasure he thought they might go up in flames.

He had to tug her to him, bring her against the hard strength of his body, hold her tightly so that he could feel every inch of her satiny skin. She was delicate beneath his exploring palms, fragile, a perfectly formed woman, and he had every sweeping line, every curve, committed to memory. He found himself murmuring to her in the ancient language, words of love, of commitment, words he had never spoken to another being in the eternity of his existence.

Words for her. Words only she gave meaning to. He loved her, every inch of her, worshiped her, mind and body and soul. His hands were gentle as he laid her down, finding a soft bed on the rich soil, using her gossamer skirt for a sheet. The sight of her lying there looking so trustingly, so lovingly up at him took his breath away. Time and space fell away. In his world there was only Jaxon. Her need of him, her hunger for him, was in her dark eyes, on her face. It was in her mind. Wherever he led, she intended to follow him, a willing partner.

Lucian bent his head to her breast, savoring the feel of her creamy skin. He wanted this night for lovemaking. Maybe the next rising also. He wanted the luxury of taking her again and again without hurry, with no fear of interruption. He wanted time to show her, tease her, please her. He wanted her to know the full beauty of their life together. Make love to her again and again. His hands moved over her legs, her thighs. "Do you have any idea just what you mean to me?" His black gaze moved over her face, inspected her body, his eyes hot and smoldering with desire.

She smiled then, loving the way his eyes devoured her with such hunger, such intense need. His body was hard and taut, burgeoning with urgent demand. His hands stroked her thighs, shaped her hips. He turned her over easily, exploring the clean line of her back, her tiny waist and firm buttocks. Lucian bent over her, blanketing her smaller frame with his. His teeth nipped her shoulder, his hands skimming along her ribs, the softness of her breasts, the curve of her hips, the smooth line of her rounded bottom. He caught her hips, lifting her so he could pull her back against his throbbing shaft. Just the feel of her satin skin, the shape of her body, sent molten lava spreading through him, flames dancing over his skin.

"I want you, angel, right now," he murmured softly, his black-velvet voice washing over her like his hands worshiping her body.

He pushed against her, rubbed closer, his hand once more finding moist, damp heat beckoning him, ensuring him she was ready. He pressed against her creamy entrance, hot and slick. She was tight, her channel gripping him as he pushed deeper, invading her body with his, his hands holding her hips still as he buried himself again and again, long, hard thrusts of sheer ecstasy.

Colors danced behind his eyes. His heart pounded. His hips thrust forward aggressively. His teeth held her shoulder with the ancient dominance of the Carpathian male. Fire raged through him, over him, so much pleasure it was almost more than he could take. She moved then, her body so delicate and soft and feminine, the complete opposite of his. He shared his pleasure with her, the building, sweeping firestorm that threatened to engulf him.

Jaxon pushed back against him, making a small sound of submission, indulging the growing wildness in him. They were both spiraling out of control, her body winding tighter and tighter, his hips thrusting forward in a frenzy, welding them together, closer and closer. She caught every desire in his mind, adjusted her body instinctively to accommodate him, just as he did for her. Her body seemed to tighten, to clench, then ripple with fiery release. His hoarse shout was muffled against the smooth skin of her shoulder. It was like an explosion of color and light, the earth itself moving under them.

Lucian gathered her to him closely, pressing his large frame tightly into hers while waves of sensual pleasure washed over them, through them. They were both covered in beads of sweat. He sipped several, following the line of her spinal column to the small of her back.

"You are so beautiful, Jaxon." He breathed the words more than saying them, his lungs working overtime. He rested his forehead between her shoulders, his body still buried deeply in hers.

He wanted to stay there for all eternity, in her mind, in her heart, in her body. His hand moved around to unerringly find the swell of her breasts. "Everything about you is so perfect—the way you feel against me, the way you move, your taste. I do not understand how I could have lived all those endless centuries without you. How did I do it?"

Jaxon pressed back against him, on her hands and knees. Where only weeks earlier she would have been embarrassed by the position, now it was beautiful, sensual, erotic. She listened to the sound of their hearts beating in perfect unison. He was everywhere, surrounding her, swamping her with his masculinity, his enormous strength. The feel of his body over hers, in hers, was, frankly, very sexy. "I love this, Lucian. I really do. Every single moment with you."

Reluctantly he withdrew, lying back, rolling her with him to bring her up on top of him. His black eyes smoldered with intensity. She was so beautiful. He wrapped his arms around her, wanting to maintain closeness between them. "No one other than you has ever teased me before."

"You have that look." She lifted her head so she could look into his eyes. She loved his eyes. Tenderly she traced his mouth. "Sort of scary. I imagine most people are intimidated by you."

His eyebrows shot up. "I do not intimidate people," he said.

Jaxon burst out laughing. "You intimidate people all over the place, and you do it on purpose."

Lucian lifted her in one smooth move and was on his feet with fluid ease. He tossed her without ceremony into a sparkling pool.

Jaxon came up sputtering, her dark eyes laughing at him. "Are we going to stay here for a while?"

He nodded, his smoldering gaze caressing her body beneath the shimmering water.

Jaxon smiled at him, a siren's invitation. "I do like the way your body responds so beautifully, Lucian."

"So do I," he answered, his voice a whisper of seduction. "I think we will stay here in this cavern for a few risings. A honeymoon."

"We aren't married," she pointed out.

"Of course we are. The Carpathian ritual is binding, my love, more so than the human ceremony. There is no word for divorce in our society. It is not an option." Although his tone sounded mild, there was nothing mild about the smoldering passion of his hungry gaze.

She shrugged one white shoulder. "You're married, then, not me. I was human when you started all this."

"Then I will have to do something to make you realize you are well and truly bound to me for all time." His white teeth flashed at her, gleaming menace like those of a predator.

Jaxon had just enough time to get off one little yelp before he was diving through the air, slicing cleanly through the water, and coming after her. Laughing, she tried to swim away from him, only to be caught by strong hands at her waist and pulled up against his body.

They spent three nights in the glittering cave, three nights of paradise, indulging themselves in each other: talking in low, intimate whispers, making love all night, flying through the sky as owls, shape-shifting into wolves so Lucian could share the joy of running free in the forest with Jaxon. They spent every moment together, holding hands, laughing, just being in love.

Their ultimate destination, the old lodge Lucian had purchased, was made of huge logs with high-beamed ceilings and an open landing on the second floor. It was rustic but quite beautiful. Someone had built the house with loving hands and lived there long before it had been used as a hunting lodge by some rich sportsman. Lucian merely waved a hand to dispel any dust and grime that might have accumulated. She was grateful to see no deer antlers or stuffed wildlife decorated the place. The idea of so many animals slaughtered for sport made her sick.

The furniture was interesting, in good shape, and rugged, as befit a lodge. Jaxon wandered through the rooms, wondering what was wrong with her. Her stomach was clenched in knots, and she couldn't dispel the feeling of death and violence from her soul. She wished they were back in the cave, in the cleansing pools, where the stench of violence couldn't seem to reach them.

The lodge was built overlooking a lake, with trees all around, grasses and ferns everywhere. It was an unbelievably beautiful location, far from civilization, the nearest neighbors several miles away. Jaxon wanted to feel as if she was in a honeymoon cabin, but the cavern with its crystals and pools was much more to her liking. The lodge made her uneasy, as if, perhaps, she was feeling an echo of things long dead. Was it the animals slaughtered for sport? Was she now too sensitive for a hunting lodge? Had something terrible happened here in earlier days? Was it possible a previous owner of the lodge had committed a crime in his beautiful but remote home and the house still vibrated with violence?

She walked through the large structure, able to admire the architecture without liking the lodge at all. Jaxon found herself shivering despite the fact that she could easily regulate her body temperature. Running her palms up and down her arms to warm herself, she knew her trembling had nothing to do with really being cold. "Do you feel peculiar in here?" she asked softly, not wanting to hurt Lucian's feelings if he loved the house.

Lucian had been watching her alertly, a shadow in her mind. He could feel her increasing uneasiness, yet there was no real echo of evil in the lodge. He glided in his graceful, silent way to her side, wrapping an arm around her shoulders. "What is it, honey? You are afraid here." He knew she had a curious built-in radar system when it came to trouble, yet he felt nothing. Just to be on the safe side, he scanned their surrounding area. The closest human was a mile or so away, a solitary hiker. He was staring down at the lake, watching for otter, his mind occupied with the wildlife. He was humming low, the sound vibrating softly in his mind. A group of humans was several miles away in a cabin. They were laughing, playing some kind of game together. There were campers in three other locations, all within a day's hike of the lodge, yet they appeared to pose no threat to anyone. He picked up no thoughts of violence in any of the humans near them, and certainly there were no vampires or ghouls in the area. He would have known immediately.

"I don't know what it is, Lucian, only that this place gives me the creeps. It feels haunted in here."

His eyebrows shot up. "Ghosts?"

Her elbow nudged him in the chest, her dark brown eyes censuring him. "Very funny, Lucian. And don't tell me your best friend is a ghost. I don't want to know."

"I have never met a ghost," he reassured her with his most charming grin. "I like this place. It is very remote, affords us privacy, the view is beautiful, and we are right in the middle of one of nature's mountains born of fire and ice. What more could we want?"

Jaxon allowed him to pull her body back into the protection of his. He was warmth and strength. She could feel him washing through her, enveloping her, but the uneasiness remained. She didn't like the lodge, and she didn't know why. "Do you already have a secret sleeping chamber?" Even as she asked it, she was trying to do as he did, scanning the lodge itself, looking for something hidden, something that might be making her nervous. No one had been there since Lucian had last visited the place. Not even a camper or hiker had discovered it. She knew Lucian would have caught that immediately, and she felt no echoes of another whatsoever. Since she disliked the idea that someone had purposely killed wild animals just for the sport of it, that must be the answer to why she was so uneasy, Jaxon decided.

"This mountain has many chambers beneath its surface. We can readily make use of them for sleeping. Study the layout in my mind and know where they are so you are never caught without several escape routes."

She received a flood of information, marveling at how precise it was. Lucian was a walking map, detailed and perfect, and he transferred information to her in the same way he had always transferred it to his twin. She laughed softly. "Do you still do that?"

"What? Share my knowledge with Gabriel?" Lucian grinned a little sheepishly. "It was the one thing, even as I masqueraded as a vampire, I could not stop myself from doing. Even then, if I learned something new, something of value, my mind automatically touched his. But he did the same thing."

"And you still do." She made it a statement. She had studied the path in his mind he used to communicate with Gabriel. There was a wealth of affection there. Lucian didn't realize the extent to which he was tied to his twin. It was just natural to him, as it was natural to Gabriel. Lucian and Gabriel were so close, Jaxon was certain she could just as easily reach Gabriel, even though she had never exchanged blood with him.

"Are you a city girl, Jaxon?" Lucian teased gently. "Are these trees and wide-open spaces too much for you?" He was still aware of her uneasiness and attempting to use humor to put her at ease.

They walked together out onto the huge wraparound porch that on one side jutted out over the cliff. The view really was breathtaking. Jaxon rested both hands on the railing and leaned over to look at the drop below them. Snow blanketed the ridges above them and dotted the canyon below. The trees looked frosted and decorated in the crisp night air. It was beautiful. The air was cold and crisp and smelled fresh and clean.

Lucian's much larger frame trapped hers against the railing. "So? Is that it? You miss those tall buildings and the sounds of traffic?" He swung her around, sweeping one arm out to encompass their surroundings. "I give you all this, and you prefer the city?"

Jaxon laughed and reached up a hand to his shadowed jaw—just as his body jerked. A spray of crimson showered her head and shoulders, and Lucian slumped forward, an enormous rag doll with the stuffing knocked out of it. He was so large he took her with him straight to the deck, covering her. It was only then that the sound caught up and she recognized the whine of a bullet.

Her heart in her throat, she maneuvered out from under his lifeless form. She knew immediately that Drake had found them. He must have flown a plane and gotten there ahead of them. She had no real idea her brain was computing the information; she could only hear herself screaming over and over, although no sound escaped. On her knees she examined Lucian. There was no pulse, no sign of life. He lay without moving or breathing, his heart and lungs utterly motionless. It took a moment to still the chaos in her mind enough to realize that there should have been far more blood than there was. Lucian had stopped his heart to minimize the blood loss! Time slowed to a crawl. This man was her life, the air she breathed. He was not dead. Lucian had said he could not be killed, and she had to believe he was not. He was trusting her to do whatever needed to be done.

What is it? What am I supposed to do? she cried out to him, wanting to weep, to scream, to throw things. She had to save him.

How bad is it? The voice came out of nowhere, in her mind, on a strange mental path she had never used before. The tone was as calm as the one Lucian often used. It served as an anchor to quiet the terrible panic gripping her, that voice so like Lucian's.

Jaxon realized that the far-off voice was Gabriel's. He had known the moment Lucian was hit, the same as she had; he had felt the same terrible emptiness, a black void unlike anything she had ever faced before.

Breathe, Jaxon. My brother is not dead. He needs you now. You will have to heal him quickly. He will need blood.

Tell me what to do. I don't have very much time. Drake will be making his way here. I don't know how long it will take him. Tell me now.

You have to make yourself light and energy. Concentrate on nothing else; your body must fall away. Enter Lucian's body and find the damage. Repair it from the inside out. You must have had some medic training. Francesca, my lifemate, is a healer. Describe what you see to me, and she will instruct you. I know this is far beyond your capabilities, but you have no choice.

I can do this, Gabriel. Lucian won't die! She meant it. If she ever did anything in her life right, this would be it. She would save him, whatever it took.

Allow me to hold the mind merge between us. You will

need all your strength to heal my brother. I will be with you. You are not alone.

There was no time for conversation. She had to hurry. She blocked out the knowledge that Drake would be stalking her, even now covering the distance between them as rapidly as possible. Jaxon followed the instructions Gabriel had given her, took the images from his mind. She closed her eyes and stilled the chaos and panic, the silent screaming, the horror of seeing Lucian lying pale and lifeless on the deck. She blocked out the blood in her hair and on her clothes. Her world narrowed to a tranquil, calm pool where she became as light as air. Bright. White. Pure energy. She moved slowly in her bodiless state, merging with Lucian, moving through his body until she found the entry wound at the base of his skull. The bullet had severed the spinal cord, a clean path in and out, sheering off everything in its way. Jaxon's heart pounded, her breath coming in gasps at the extent of the damage. She had no idea how to repair such a terrible wound.

Francesca will guide you. Keep the image in your head. Trust her, no matter how difficult it gets.

There were so many veins and arteries and pieces of flesh she couldn't identify. She had to force her mind to remain calm when she knew her body was shaking and every fiber of her being was terrified. This could not happen. Lucian was her life. After her lonely existence, afraid to have a friend, let alone a family, he had turned her world into something beautiful again. He had given her back her dreams, treated her as if she were the most wonderful woman on the planet. He was a great man, a man who fought demons and protected others without any thought of reward. He would not die.

You will not die. Her command was every bit as strong and authoritative as any Lucian had ever delivered.

Steeling herself, she began the grim business of putting his insides back together. It was like a jigsaw puzzle, the pieces tiny fragments. She couldn't think she might be making a mistake; she had to believe that voice whispering in her mind, telling her what to do. She had to trust that Lucian's brother loved him the way she did and would do anything to save him. She worked meticulously, unhurriedly, keeping the knowledge that Drake was stalking her in the back of her mind, where it belonged. She could only concentrate on what she was doing.

You will live, Lucian. She whispered it over and over in her head like a litany. Wherever he was, she would be there with him. The idea of being without him was intolerable.

She was not a doctor, not a nurse. She had little knowledge to aid her. The paramedic training she had received had covered wounds, but nothing like this. She was in awe of the unknown Francesca, her ability to know exactly what to do, how to repair such devastation. Carpathians worked on wounds from the inside out, aligning, rejoining, cauterizing, inspecting to ensure infection could not set in.

In her bodiless state, Jaxon was completely unaware of the passage of time, of anything other than the task at hand. *You will live,* she whispered fiercely in her mind. *I won't let you die on me, you arrogant jerk. I told you he was trouble, but, oh, no, you couldn't listen to a woman, could you, big shot?* She recited words in her mind even as she worked at a steady pace, following Gabriel's voice. It was a weird method: relaying to Gabriel what she saw, Francesca sharing his mind and relaying back to Jaxon through her lifemate exactly what to do.

When Francesca was certain every detail had been attended to, she instructed Jaxon to remove herself from Lucian's body and provide him with blood. Jaxon found herself sitting on the deck with her lifemate's body lying beside her. She was exhausted, her body swaying with weariness. Gently she bent over Lucian. *Wake up, my love. You need to wake up now.*

355

He lay lifeless, so white it terrified her. Jaxon reached for Gabriel. *He isn't moving, Gabriel. I did something wrong. Maybe I described something incorrectly, and Francesca gave me the wrong advice.*

Stay calm, Jaxon. You have done wonderfully so far. Do not panic. Remind him that Drake is stalking you. Reach for him with your entire mind. He will hear and awaken. Gabriel was very calm.

Jaxon took a deep breath and let it out slowly. *Lucian, I am in terrible danger. Feel my fear. Wake up.* She watched his chest. When nothing happened, she caught at his arms and shook him gently. *Wake up, you arrogant male. I'm in danger here. Your job is to get off your butt and rescue me. Francesca says you're all better. Wake up!*

She bent over him just as his eyelashes fluttered. One arm whipped up to catch her to him, to pull her down to him. *He shot me.*

'I'm glad you comprehend, Sherlock. He's on his way right now. He could be here at any second. You need blood, Lucian."

He was doing a quick assessment of his injuries before he scanned the area. *You are right, Jaxon. He is very close.* His hand came up to caress her hair, then moved to the nape of her neck. His mouth moved over her throat to find her pulse beating steadily if a little too fast. His tongue stroked once unhurriedly, preparing her for the shock of his teeth sinking into her. She cried out, her arms stealing around his head to cradle him to her. Then she closed her eyes and relaxed. This was Lucian. Injured he might be, even severely, but he could stir her blood and make her feel completely safe under any circumstances.

Already weak, she found herself drowsy, fading, slipping into a dreamlike state. Her arms fell away from him to her sides. She slumped against him, unable to hold herself up, uncaring that it was so. She heard him murmur her name, heard the love in his voice as he closed the tiny pinpricks in her throat. His hands were gentle as he moved her to a more comfortable position. *You called me an arrogant jerk, Jaxon. That was not very nice. Your bedside manner needs to improve immensely.*

You're lucky I didn't kick you. You scared me to death. And just remember, Mr. Arrogance, it was a human that nearly did you in.

I knew you were the type of woman who would say "I told you so." Despite the weariness in his voice, there was a hint of laughter.

If she had the strength, she might have hit him, but she was far too tired to make the effort. She lay slumped on the deck, unmoving.

I knew you had a penchant for violence, he teased.

Jaxon felt it then, her stomach clenching in a hard knot. *He is here.*

Yes, my love, I know. Do not worry. This monster will never harm you or anyone you love again. His voice, his beautiful, black-velvet voice, was as tranquil as ever. He did not tell her, as he saw no need, that he was incredibly weak and that Gabriel with Francesca was aiding him from a distance, their combined strength pouring into him.

You must be careful this time. Her words, even without her voice to speak them aloud, were slurred in his mind.

Sleep, my love, and do worry about me.

No! Her protest was sharp. *Do not try to force me to sleep. I must be aware in case you have need of my help.*

Lucian did not point out that she was too weak to fight her way out of a paper bag. He sat up carefully, not wanting to undo all the repairs Jaxon had so meticulously made. He needed several days of sleep in the rejuvenating soil before he would be back to his full strength.

Drake was only a few yards away now. Lucian could hear him as he moved through the brush toward the lodge. He waited, sitting beside Jaxon, one hand tangled in the mop of wild silky blond strands he loved so much.

This was the one then, the monster who had taken control of Jaxon's life at such an early age. Tyler Drake. Lucian could feel her tension, although she tried to conceal it.

Lucian sent her a wave of warm reassurance before he turned his attention to the approaching monster. He sent his voice, the perfect weapon, out into the night. "You will come to me unarmed, Drake."

There was no way to disobey that voice that could so easily enthrall. Under compulsion, Drake moved out into the open, both hands empty and in plain sight. His eyes were restless, blinking rapidly, repeatedly. He was sick, his mind twisted, his thought processes unnatural. Lucian realized then that he had thought Drake a camper or hiker because the man wasn't actually thinking of killing anyone. He wasn't planning it. He considered himself a good man, a man who loved his child.

"You have caused Jaxon much sorrow in her life, Mr. Drake," Lucian said quietly, his voice gentle. "I can do no other than ask that you no longer walk this land with her. You must go to a place where one much greater than myself can pass judgment on you."

Jaxon's slight body was trembling visibly. She was far too weak to sit up beside her lifemate. She lay on the deck with her head in Lucian's lap and his hands in her hair. She touched Lucian's mind, found him tranquil, at peace. Even with one such as Drake, he felt no anger, no sympathy, no remorse. He carried out his responsibility without emotion, as he always did. She slipped into his mind, allowed his peace to wash over her, through her. She didn't hate Drake, and she didn't feel sorry for him; she only knew that Lucian had to destroy him.

Lucian stared at Drake, unwilling to utter the command aloud for Jaxon to hear. Drake brought his hands up to his throat as he began to fight for air. Lucian concentrated on the man's chest. Inside the man, his heart was shutting down, chambers clogging as his blood thickened. Veins collapsed, arteries shattered, and Tyler Drake shuddered and went down abruptly, sitting on the snow-covered ground, then toppling over to lie still.

Jaxon could only stare in astonishment, half lifting her body in astonishment. That was it? After years living in torment, she couldn't be free so easily. So quietly. She glanced up at Lucian. *Is it over? He's really dead?*

Lucian wrapped his arms around her protectively. "He is dead," he said out loud, knowing she needed to hear the words spoken.

Jaxon closed her eyes and slipped back toward the deck, fainting for the first time in her life. Lucian moved with his preternatural speed, his arms cradling her head before it could hit the wood. She wasn't going to be very happy with herself for fainting.

Exhausted, Lucian allowed Gabriel to do most of the work as he gathered energy particles from the sky and sent them flaming into Tyler Drake's body. When there was nothing left but ashes, he lay back beside his lifemate, pillowing her head on his shoulder. It was only then that he noticed she was covered in his blood. The last thing he wanted was for Jaxon to awaken in that state. He was going to have to concede to her that he might have been a little arrogant where Drake was concerned. She would never let him get away with anything less.

Right now you need to go to ground. That was Gabriel, acting as if his twin needed to be taken out behind the proverbial barn.

Gabriel, easily picking up Lucian's thought, gave a rather rude snort of derision. *I do not think that will happen anytime soon. Francesca says get beneath the earth immediately, and take your lifemate with you. She has given far too much of her strength in healing you.*

Lucian shook his head as he gathered Jaxon into his arms. Gabriel had to have the last word. He was like that.

Only because I am always right.

Chapter Seventeen

Jaxon curled up on the small sofa right in front of the fireplace. She wore only a thin robe, her small rebellion against the coming event, and the warmth from the flames felt good. She also liked the way fire light flickered and danced on the wall, bringing out the wood trim's golden hue. She was nervous, striving for normalcy, and needed something to keep her from thinking too much.

Shaking out the newspaper, she began to scan it, reading as a policewoman, looking for any stray detail that might be of use in any of her open cases. Often some odd item in the paper could help bring together pieces of information in police work.

Finding an article on the second page, she could hardly believe her eyes. She recognized three names, attributed to three great humanitarians. *Hal Barton. Harry Timms. Denny Sheldon.* The three men who had "visited" their home so recently. "Lucian, have you read the paper this evening?"

He glanced at her, his black eyebrows raised in inquiry.

"What now?" He hid his smile, knowing exactly what she was doing, what she was trying to avoid.

"I wonder. It seems your three friends, the ones who broke into our house and wanted you to invest in their foolproof security system, have become rather wealthy in their own right."

"I am glad for them. They will not need my money after all."

"They never did. I'm not a moron, you know. You did something to them, didn't you? What did you do?"

Lucian's black eyes were laughing, but his voice was innocent. "What could I have possibly done? You were there. What does the article say?"

"The three of them worked for a couple of 'businessmen.'" Her large brown eyes were boring into him. "Ha! Probably drug lords. I'm right, aren't I?"

She was altogether too smart. Staying one step ahead of her for the rest of their lives was going to require effort. Lucian shrugged, a secret little smile tugging at the corners of his mouth.

Jaxon found him altogether too sexy. Likely he was always going to get away with far too much. "Anyway, these two 'businessmen' apparently met with a sailing accident and left their companies to the three of these guys, who now seem to be running the businesses legitimately and giving huge profits to charity. According to the reporter, they were investigated thoroughly, and the police are convinced they're completely legitimate."

"Good for them. And this is somehow worrisome to you? You must explain this to me."

She glared at him. "You are so innocent, aren't you, Lucian? You know what? I don't want to know what you did. It's probably illegal."

"You said they were investigated thoroughly."

"Very convenient. No one would know if you did anything, would they?"

361

Christine Feehan

"Angel." Lucian's voice was soft and gentle, perfectly innocent of any mischief making. "They live completely across the continent. I do have limitations."

"If you do, I haven't noticed them yet," she answered and shook out the paper again, raising it high to cover her face.

Lucian laughed softly. "I think you are just suffering prewedding jitters."

The paper rustled warningly. "I am not nervous."

"Yes, you are. I am in your mind, honey. You are very nervous. I must say, it is an interesting phenomenon, when you are already irrevocably bound to me. We have been together under the worst circumstances, and you know you are sealed to me, so why are you so apprehensive about a little ceremony?"

"I'm not nervous." It was a blatant lie. "Lucian, I don't know why you're insisting on this ceremony anyway. You said we were already married. That's enough for me. And weren't you worried about paper trails? I thought you said Carpathians had to be careful about such things."

"You are trying to squirm out of it," he accused her. "But it is not going to work. I have been in your mind, and I saw how much such a wedding means to you."

Jaxon carefully folded the newspaper and set it aside. "Lucian, look at me." When he turned to face her, she locked her gaze with his. "It *meant* a great deal to me, Lucian. Now I know it isn't the wedding that counts, it's what the wedding means. I know we belong together, and your ceremony, although terribly sexist, is as binding as a human ceremony."

"More so," he said softly.

She smiled. "Maybe."

"But still, the human ceremony is quite beautiful, and my brother has come all this way with his wife to stand beside me. I have endured his stupid grins and gloating manner long enough. He believes you have me wrapped around your little finger. You will go through with this, Jaxon, just to pay for that alone."

"Maybe we could go hide out in the mountains, Lucian." Jaxon stood up and went to him, wrapping her arms around his waist, pressing up against him suggestively. "Someplace where we can be alone."

He turned immediately and took her into his arms. "You are blatantly trying to seduce me into missing our wedding and disappointing our guests. Shame on you, angel. And I am so susceptible to your charms." His voice held that husky note of desire that always took her breath away.

"Many charms," she corrected, turning up her mouth to be kissed.

He obliged her, bending his head to her instantly, his mouth moving slowly, thoroughly over hers. His mouth was hot and moist, his tongue dancing with hers suggestively. Her fingers brushed at his long, thick ebony hair lovingly, then slid to his shirt to push it from his shoulders, letting her burrow against his skin. "I don't care if all our guests miss us. I want you, Lucian."

"You cannot wait a few hours?" he teased her. "I made love to you just this rising."

Her eyes darkened, and she allowed her robe to slip from her shoulders. "Let's have more hot, crazy sex, then. It works for me."

His dark eyebrows shot up, but he obediently waved a hand so the room's door lock snicked into place. His body tightened painfully, hard and throbbing in anticipation. "You are, after all, my lifemate, and I can do no other than to keep you happy." His clothes floated to the floor immediately.

Pressed as she was against him, Jaxon found the thick evidence of his compliance thrust temptingly against her bare breasts. She cupped him in her hand, her fingers sliding, caressing, stroking until his breath slammed out of his lungs. "It seems to me, since I'm being so demanding, that I should help you out . . . get you in the mood." Her breath was deliberately warm on him. She blew softly, gently, her tongue stroking curling heat along his length.

A rough growl escaped from his throat. Jaxon laughed softly. He was pushing against her. "I'm not quite sure what you want," she teased.

His fist bunched in her tousled hair. "I will make myself perfectly clear," he murmured softly. "Open your mouth."

He threw back his head, arching more deeply into her as her mouth, hot and moist, closed tightly over the most sensitive part of him. Her tongue teased and danced as her hand tightened to slide over him again and again. "Jaxon," he groaned, forgetting the wedding, the guests, everything but her mouth and her hand.

Reveling in his reaction, Jaxon forgot she was deliberately seducing him, the haze of his pleasure echoing in her own mind. She wanted him so much she couldn't think clearly. This was no longer a ploy to distract him but a necessity.

"Are you ready for me? You have to be ready for me," he bit out between clenched teeth.

She lifted her head slowly and smiled at him sexily. Very deliberately she slid her hand down her body, drawing his attention to her breasts, her narrow rib cage, her stomach. She heard his breath catch as he watched her fingers disappear between her legs. She moved, a sensuous ripple of her body, then withdrew her fingers to hold them up to him. Glistening. Hot.

Lucian bent his head and drew her fingers into his mouth, his black eyes burning over her. Without any further preliminaries, he simply lifted her into his arms. Jaxon wrapped her legs around him and began to settle over him, taking him into her body inch by exquisite inch until he filled her, stretched her. "All of me, honey, take all of me," he whispered in encouragement. Her breath came in small, needy gasps as she took him into her sheath, hot and slick and so tight he was shuddering with pleasure. It was her desire, her need, that drove them now, and Lucian let her set the pace.

He watched her ride him, her body supple and strong, her arms around his neck, her skin, caressed by the firelight, glowing. She began to hasten the rhythm, tightening her muscles, clenching and gripping until he was as breathless as she. One hand caught her small bottom, pressing her to him as he began to move, thrusting into her again and again. Fast. Furious. Hard, hot sex. Just what she wanted, what he wanted.

He caught the back of her head, brought her face to his, thrusting his tongue wildly into her mouth. His mind thrust into hers, sharing his excitement, the taste of her, of him, sharing the intense pleasure and passion of her body, of his. They moved together in perfect unison. The firestorm burned hot and bright through both of them, sending them soaring, clutching each other, hearts nearly exploding with the shared pleasure.

Jaxon laid her head on his shoulder, holding him deep within her. "I love you. I know I do. Let's just run away together, disappear for a while, Lucian, just the two of us, like it was in the cave."

Very carefully he lowered her to the floor, separating their bodies. His hands framed her face. "You really are afraid of marrying me." He kissed her gently, tenderly.

Her long lashes swept down to conceal her expressive eyes. "It isn't marrying you, Lucian, it's the wedding. It's turned into such a big deal!" she wailed. "Everyone's going to be looking at me. And I don't even know half the guests. You have all these big shots attending. Aidan Savage from San Francisco. Desari, the famous singer, singing at my wedding. How did that happen?"

Almost automatically, without any real thought, Jaxon

cleaned and clothed her body in the way of Carpathians. She was still struggling to regain her breath and lower her heart rate.

Lucian's eyes lit up with pride. She had accepted her new way of life as she did everything—embracing it quickly, passionately. He matched the rhythm of his breathing and pulse to hers and easily regulated them. Then he responded mildly to her concerns.

"Desari's lifemate is Aidan's twin brother, Julian. When I asked Aidan and Alexandria to attend, along with Antonio, who is practically a member of the family, Aidan asked if we would like Desari to sing. Apparently she and Julian were visiting. From what I understand, she is very nice." He added his own clothes, then smiled when Jaxon raked a hand through her hair, once more tousling her short, silky cap. "And you do have most of the police force attending."

"I'm certain Desari is very nice, Lucian, but she's *famous*." Jaxon tried not to kick him in the shins. He was being far more difficult than usual. And he looked gorgeous—someone who deserved a tall, elegant, beautiful woman. "And it isn't most of the police force, just my coworkers and friends. I don't want strangers looking at me."

"You will be beautiful in your wedding gown, angel. A dream." He said it sincerely. "My dream. I find you very beautiful and incredibly sexy."

She glared at him. "I have never worn a pair of high heels in my life. I'll trip and break my neck." She wrung her hands.

He shrugged with his casual grace, took possession of her left hand, and turned up her palm to place a kiss in the exact center. "Why would you wear something uncomfortable? Your gown is long. Wear whatever you like beneath it."

"And when you take off my garter in front of the entire

crowd, they can all see my elegant tennis shoes." She pulled her hand away and nibbled nervously at her nails.

He sensed she was close to tears. His arms circled her small body and brought her into the protection of his chest. "Honey, there is not going to be a problem with your shoes. Wear your tennis shoes until we need to remove the garter, and I will ensure you have on your elegant high heels when the time comes."

"What if you forget?"

He bent to brush her temple with the warmth of his mouth. "I never forget anything important to you, Jaxon. You must have learned that by now." His mouth found the pulse in her neck, felt it leaping beneath her skin. "You must know that."

She was nodding, her face buried against the heavy muscles of his chest. "So who else is coming to our wedding?"

"The mayor. A few others you know."

"I wasn't asking about them. I was asking about *your* friends. Our wedding is taking place in the middle of the night to accommodate your people."

"*Our* people," he insisted. "Naturally, Desari's brother and his lifemate are attending, and another member of her band—Barrack and his lifemate, Syndil, who is also in the band. The only other person whose name you might recognize is Savannah Dubrinsky, the magician. She is the lifemate to one of our greatest healers and vampire hunters and the Prince's right hand man, Gregori. They might attend also."

"I'm *not* doing this. I'm not. Those people are famous. And what's this about a right-hand man to the Prince? He sounds important. Why would he come?"

Lucian laughed softly. "Angel, I am considered rather important in our world. Gregori is of my lineage, and he is attending our wedding out of respect. The Prince would have come, also, but he is not in the States at this time.

367

Naturally Gregori would represent him if they can make it here in time. Savannah, by the way, is Prince Mikhail's daughter."

Jaxon was shaking her head at him. "Don't tell me any more. I can't take it. You really do have all that money, don't you?" She made it an accusation.

"Money means nothing to our people, Jaxon. It is used only to make things run smoothly in the present time period."

She thumped his chest with a clenched fist. "Still, all those people sound so important. Why are they coming? You need to tell them to stay home."

"Actually, I am interested in meeting Desari and her brother, Darius. I am related to them. And it just so happens that Gregori is my younger brother by a thousand years or so. I gave him much advice when he was a fledgling and would very much like to see how he turned out."

"Your relatives?" she said accusingly. "They're all related to you? Your family? Really, Lucian, I don't think I can do this."

"Of course you can, angel. I will be right there beside you. Together. In your mind, in your heart. And, technically, we are already married, so they are all related to you, too. When this is over you will *feel* that they are your family. You will know that *we* are family. You will love this, angel. It's your dream wedding."

She managed a nervous smile. "Sometimes the dream is better than the reality, isn't it? This sounds terrifying."

"This from the woman who helps me destroy vampires and ghouls and runs around like a maniac chasing criminals?" His fingers tangled in her blond hair. "Settle down, angel. Francesca is coming down the hall to help you dress."

"Kiss me now, Lucian, or I might run for it."

He made absolutely certain he did a thorough job.

* * *

The wedding was out of a fairy tale. Barry Radcliff walked Jaxon down the aisle, and she didn't see a single face to make her nervous as she walked slowly toward the altar. Her eyes remained locked with Lucian's. He looked tall and handsome and impossibly courtly. Beside him was his twin, looking every inch an Adonis. Still, she would have known the difference between them anywhere, anytime. Lucian took her breath away. As she approached on Barry's arm, she knew this was right. She loved Lucian, and she would for all eternity. They were two halves of the same whole. And now, after all these lonely years, he was giving her a family too.

With her eyes held captive by his smoldering black gaze, Jaxon put her small hand in his large one without hesitation, fully prepared to make their vows.

DARK PRINCE

Raven Whitney is a psychic who has used her gift to help the police track down a serial killer. Now she is determined to escape the glare of recent publicity for the peace and quiet of the Carpathian Mountains. Despite her own emotional fatigue, Raven finds herself connecting psychically to another wounded individual somewhere close by.

Prince Mikhail Dubrinsky is the leader of his people but, as his ancient Carpathian race grows ever closer to extinction, he is close to giving in to the heavy weight of loneliness and despair.

Then a female voice enters his mind and tries to console him. Intrigued, Mikhail becomes obsessed with finding this unusual human female. From the moment their minds touch, Raven and Mikhail form a connection.

But there are those who incorrectly view all Carpathians as vampires, and are determined to give their extinction a helping hand . . .

978-0-7499-3747-8

DARK DESIRE

Seven years ago, Dr Shea O'Halloran experienced an unexpected and horrendous pain unlike anything she had ever known. It felt as if she were being tortured. Eventually the pain disappeared, but Shea never forgot. She has since devoted her life to trying to understand the cause of the rare genetic blood disorder that is slowly killing her.

The answers to some of Shea's questions start to reveal themselves when she is approached by two men, who accuse her of being a vampire. Shea runs for her life and – following a feeling she can't explain – her desperate wanderings lead her to Romania.

The ancient one known as Jacques Dubrinsky can explain. Seven years ago, Jacques was captured, tortured and buried alive by several humans and a Carpathian betrayer. The years of extreme pain and lack of sustenance that followed have nearly driven Jacques insane. He has been using what is left of his powers to psychically draw Shea to the region. But is Shea to be his healer . . . or his prey?

978-0-7499-3748-5

DARK GOLD

Alexandria Houton will sacrifice anything to protect her
little brother. But when they both encounter an
unspeakable evil in the swirling San Francisco mists, Alex
can only pray for their deliverance . . . And out of the
darkness swoops Aidan Savage, a being more powerful
and more mysterious than any other creature of the night.

This ageless Carpathian male has saved them both from a
hideous fate. But is Aidan truly Alexandria's salvation . . .
or her ultimate betrayer? And if she surrenders to Aidan's
savage, unearthly seduction is Alexandria in danger of
sacrificing more than her life . . . ?

978-0-7499-3749-2

DARK MAGIC

Savannah Dubrinsky is a mistress of illusion, a world-famous magician capable of mesmerising millions. But there is one man she fears: Gregori, the Dark One.

With a dark magic all his own, Gregori – the most powerful of Carpathian males – whispers in Savannah's mind that he is her destiny. That she was born to save his immortal soul. And now, here in New Orleans, the hour has finally come to claim her. To make her completely his. In a ritual as old as time . . . and as inescapable as eternity.

978-0-7499-3761-4

DARK CHALLENGE

Carpathian vampire hunter Julian Savage is powerful but tormented. But he has one last duty to fulfill before he gives himself over to the dawn and certain death. He has to warn the famous singer, Desari, that she is being targeted by vicious human vampire hunters who will stop at nothing to hurt those they believe are vampires. But when Julian hears Desari sing he realises she is the woman he has always sought – his lifemate.

Desari is most definitely Julian's match but she has great powers of her own. And she is not happy when a mysterious stranger enters her mind and begins giving her orders!

978-0-7499-3785-0

DARK FIRE

When Darius, the leader of a group of Carpathian musicians, first sees the new mechanic hired to work on the band's touring vehicles, he is astonished to see the red colour of her hair. It has been centuries since he last saw colours or even felt emotions.

Although mechanic Tempest Trine needs the job, she quickly realises that in touring with Darius, she's bitten off more than she can chew. Tempest has always felt different, apart from others. But from the moment his arms close around her, enveloping her in a sorcerer's spell, Darius seems to understand her unique gifts. But does his kiss offer the love and belonging she seeks, or a danger more potent than anything she has ever known?

978-0-7499-3784-3